CHILDREN AT THE GATE

A Novel by

Benjamin Pressley Walker

CHILDREN AT THE GATE

ISBN 978-0-9666145-2-7

Published in the United States by
Jamin Press
Jacksonville, FL

Acknowledgments

Thanks to Barbara Pinkerton for her careful scrutiny of the manuscript and the insightful comments that followed, as well as to her husband Bob, whose internet proficiency often produces instant resource material.

I would also like to thank my long-time friend David Buttrey, who has, in addition to poring over the manuscript of my last two books, assisted me in promotion and book signings.

And thanks to Sony/ATV Music Publishing LLC for permission to use the lyrics to "Eleanor Rigby."

ELEANOR RIGBY
Written by: John Lennon & Paul McCartney
© 1966 Sony/ATV Music Publishing LLC. All rights administered by
Sony/ATV Music Publishing LLC, 424 Church Street, Suite 1200,
Nashville, TN 37219. All rights reserved. Used by permission.

To
Nanos Valaoritis

poet, playwright, and pundit-*provocateur*

CHAPTER 1

Travis Carter made his way up Nob Hill on a cool but sunny afternoon in the summer of 1973. He generally avoided the trek up Taylor Street as the hill was steep at this point, but he felt that he needed the exercise. When he reached the top he turned west and made his way through the usual throng of tourists until he encountered a crowd gathered at the corner of California and Larkin. A cable car had just made its 180 degree turn at Van Ness and disgorged several passengers while others hopped on to take their places.

As the cable car pulled away with its bell clanging, Travis stepped across the street to see what the onlookers were staring at.

A street mime. Not an unfamiliar sight in San Francisco, but this one seemed somehow different. It was, to be sure, a woman. The skintight leotards and black and white T-shirt could not conceal that fact even though she had vainly tried to flatten her breasts with some sort of bandage or strap. The whiteface makeup almost obliterated the feminine features of her face, though not entirely. She had outlined her eyes in black, with vertical lines over and under the lids. The lips were red, or rather purple, and suggested an androgynous creature rather than a human of either gender.

Travis moved closer into the crowd until he was shoulder-to-shoulder between two men, one white and one black. The white man, silver-haired and in his early seventies, seemed annoyed at the jostling and stepped forward and in front of Travis, who was in turn annoyed because the man was now partially blocking his view. The black man, much taller and broad-shouldered, also stepped forward and Travis' view was entirely blocked. So he stepped to his left and settled comfortably behind a man and a woman who were considerably shorter than he was.

The mime, who had been lying prone on the sidewalk for some minutes, now rose from the waist and rubbed her eyes if awaking for the first time that day. She looked around at the crowd, feigning surprise that so many people were taking an interest in her. Then she rose to her feet, yawned, and began a pantomime of performing her toilette. She turned her back to the crowd in keeping with her natural modesty and first removed an imaginary dressing gown and then donned an equally imaginary series of clothing articles; stockings, pants, waistcoat (which she apparently buttoned to the wrong holes, thus eliciting laughter as she fumbled with each button until getting it right), and finally pulled on a pair of white gloves which she was in fact already wearing. Having completed her toilette, she brought her palm to her brow and looked first in one direction and then the other as if getting her bearings. Each supple movement, however minor, elicited laughter or chuckles of recognition.

"What the..." murmured the silver-haired man who had stepped in front of Travis. "Thief!" The man turned around and grabbed Travis by the lapels of his jacket and repeated his accusation. "Thief! Give me back my wallet!"

Travis, startled and uncomprehending, simply shrugged his shoulders.

A policeman, who had also been watching the performance, made his way through the crowd and confronted the two men. "What's going on here?"

"This man," said the elderly gentleman, still clinging to Travis' lapel, "stepped behind me while I was watching the mime and picked my pocket!"

"Let go of his jacket," the policeman said. He was a portly figure, with pepper-and-salt hair and a slightly bored expression on his face. He turned to Travis. "Empty your pockets."

Travis removed his billfold from his jacket and handed it to the policeman. The policeman examined it. "Your name William Travis Carter...the third?"

Travis nodded.

"Check his underwear," the elderly man said. "That's a trick they use."

The policeman looked at the elderly man with disdain, then turned back to Travis. "Raise and extend your arms."

Travis complied. "You won't find anything officer, except some house keys and—"

"Shut up." The policeman frisked him and found nothing but the house keys and a pocket knife, which contained a nail file, a corkscrew, a pair of scissors, and a two-inch blade. "Swiss Army knife. He could have cut your throat with this, mister."

The elderly gentleman gasped as his hand flew to his throat.

The policeman laughed and handed the keys and pocket knife back to Travis. Then he looked around at the crowd, which was beginning to disperse. "Anybody see what happened?"

A few onlookers shook their heads.

"I did."

They all turned in the direction of the mime.

"Watch," she said.

They all complied.

The mime embarked upon a visual reenactment of the crime. First, she described the elderly man by passing her hands over her temples to suggest his long, silvery hair, then cupped both hands beneath an imaginary belly and walked in a circle leaning backward as if struggling to support the weight of it. This elicited loud guffaws from the onlookers and a flush of embarrassment on the face of the elderly man.

Next, she passed her hand over her face to suggest a wholly different appearance of a second man. She puffed out her chest and stood on her toes to indicate that this man was very tall and powerfully built. After a sideways glance, she reverted to the character of the elderly man as he appeared to be enjoying the show and oblivious to all around him. Then she reassumed the persona of the tall man and looked straight ahead as if enjoying the same spectacle while stepping to her left. She wriggled her fingers and extended her hand towards the position of the elderly man and suddenly snatched it back again, tucking some unseen object into the waist band of her pants.

The crowd roared with laughter as she reverted to the persona of the elderly man, suddenly brought her hands to her breast, patted it in great agitation, grabbed an imaginary pair of lapels, and raised the alarm with a silent shout.

The policeman shook his head. "And the tall man—where did he go?"

The mime stood on her toes, placed the edge of her palm over her brow, looked first one way, then the other, and finally pointed up Larkin Street.

"Long gone, eh?" The policeman turned to the elderly man, who still looked somewhat embarrassed. "Sorry, pal. There's nothing I can do. But if you want me to make out a report—"

The elderly man shook his head. "No, no. It's useless. I'll go back to my hotel and call American Express."

"You do that, mister. Cancel your credit cards and cut your losses. And if I were you, I'd invest in a money belt. This happens a hundred times a day in San Francisco, and we can't prevent it unless we catch the perp in the act."

By this time the crowd had completely dispersed and the mime was left looking even more forlorn than ever. She looked at Travis, who looked back. She then reached into an imaginary pair of pockets, appeared to turn them inside out, and then, with palms turned to the sky, contorted the corners of her mouth into an expression of despair.

"No tips, eh?" Travis could barely suppress a smile; she was, after all, a comedienne.

She nodded her head, pouting.

Travis went over to her and put his arm around her shoulders. "Come on. I'll buy you a drink."

Her frown suddenly turned into a broad smile. She made a deep bow from the waist and with a roll of her wrists indicated that he should lead the way.

The mime remained silent as Travis led her up Larkin Street, though he peppered her with questions about her experience and origins. Occasionally she would stop and attempt to answer his questions with the tools of her trade: her body.

He gathered from these exercises that she came from Southern California and had been in San Francisco for only a short time. She was twenty-two and employed as a waitress at an Italian restaurant in the Castro Valley. Where was she staying?

She rented a room in the Haight.

By the time they arrived at Jackson Street, Travis felt that he could find out no more about her through pantomime and wished that she would speak.

And suddenly she did.

"That's him!"

Travis looked to where she was pointing, which was across Jackson at the northeast corner. It was the pickpocket. He spotted the mime—who, after all, was rather conspicuous—apparently recognized Travis, and began running.

Travis ran across the street, dodged a few cars, and continued in hot pursuit. He had always been a fast runner and was gaining ground at the next corner when the man hopped on a cable car heading north. Travis leapt onto the car and pushed his way through the crowd that seemed nonplused at the reason for the chase. Some were annoyed, others seemed to think it was a movie being shot and were delighted to be a part of it.

The man hopped off the cable car at Vallejo and doubled back, weaving in and out of cars as the drivers slammed on their brakes to avoid hitting him.

Travis caught up with him in the next block and tackled him. They both tumbled to the sidewalk.

"Hey, man," the thief said. "What you chasing me for? It wasn't *your* wallet. What's it to you?"

Travis responded by bending his wrist back.

"Ow! What's wrong wid you?" Onlookers stared. "This dude's crazy. Help!"

Travis loosened his grip and got to his feet. "Give up the wallet and—Franklin!"

The thief, slowly rising from the sidewalk and rubbing his wrist, looked hard at his pursuer. "Cap'n Carter? What on God's green earth are you doing in San Francisco? If I'd had known it was you–"

About this time the mime appeared, a little out of breath. "Do as he says. Give up the wallet."

The man Travis called Franklin looked at the mime, then at Travis. "What's this? You an undercover cop, Cap'n?"

Travis smiled. "No, Franklin. I just happened to be in the right place at the right time—or the wrong time for you."

The mime looked at Travis. "You *know* this man?"

Travis nodded. "We were in Vietnam together. Franklin was my first sergeant. He saved my life." He turned to the mime. "Ms..."

"Marcella."

"Marcella, this is Sergeant Ben Franklin. Franklin, Marcella—"

"Just Marcella."

"All right. Just Marcella." Travis turned to Franklin again. The on-lookers, thinking the whole incident had been a stunt, began to drift away. "What gives, Ben? We're not in the army anymore. You don't have to call me Captain. Why are you picking pockets on the streets of San Francisco? If you need money—"

"I got a general discharge, Cap'n. I—"

"Travis."

"Okay. Travis. But it's hard for me to say after—"

"Let's head towards Van Ness." Travis clapped Ben on the back. "I'm late for work and the lady—Marcella—is thirsty after all the exercise she's had today. We all need a drink."

Marcella did not move. "What about the wallet?"

Ben looked around as if considering another run for it.

"She's right, Ben," Travis said. "Better give it up. I'll turn it in at Henry Africa's."

Ben looked puzzled. "Who's Henry Africa?"

"A guy who owns a bar by the same name. It's where I work."

"You a bartender, Cap'n? Why ain't you a banker or something?"

"Long story. I'll tell you about it at Henry's. But first the wallet."

Ben looked around furtively. No one was paying attention to them now aside from a few tourists staring at Marcella. "All right, Cap'n. But I gotta eat."

"We'll take care of that. The wallet."

Ben reluctantly pulled the wallet from beneath his shirt and Travis put it in his pocket. The three of them then walked towards Van Ness Avenue.

CHAPTER 2

Henry Africa, of course, was not the bar owner's real name. He said it was the name of his late mother's boyfriend and it seemed like a good name for a watering hole on the outer edge of the continent.

"It looks like a nursery with fancy colored lamps," Ben said.

"It *is* a kind of nursery," Travis said. "And the children get rowdy at the end of the evening. They need a bouncer, Ben. And I think you're eminently qualified."

"I didn't mean that kind of nursery. I meant—"

" I know what you meant. Come on."

They stepped inside, brushing aside the ferns that nearly overran the place. It was only four o'clock in the afternoon and already it was beginning to fill up with the usual crowd, plus a smattering of tourists.

"I see you've brought your menagerie," a man in jeans and a leather bomber jacket said. He was behind the bar drying glasses and hanging them in the rack above his head.

"That's right, Henry." Travis went behind the bar, removed his jacket, and put on an apron. "They followed me like a pair of lost sheep. The lady in the clown suit is Marcella, and the big guy is Ben Franklin. I told him you need a bouncer."

"True, true." Henry examined Ben from head to toe. "Everyone thinks they're a tough guy after ten o'clock. Never fails. Ten o'clock and suddenly Mr. Milquetoast thinks he's Clint Eastwood and John Wayne rolled into one. You done any bar work, Ben?"

"Some," Ben said.

"Football?"

"Some."

"Boxing?"

"Some."

Henry turned to Travis. "A man of few words. Just what I'm looking for." He turned back to Ben. "If Travis thinks you're okay, then you're all right with me, Ben. Can you start tonight?"

"Sure."

"Set 'em up, Travis. There won't be any need for Ben's services for another three or four hours. On me."

"Thanks," Ben said. "Mr.—"

"Henry. Everybody calls me Henry."

While Marcella and Ben took a seat at the bar, Travis handed the stolen wallet to Henry.

"What's this?"

"Found it on the street near Larkin," Travis said. "Must have fallen out of some tourist's pocket."

Henry examined the contents and emitted a low whistle. "Six one hundred dollar bills...American Express, Diner's Club..."

Ben winced and turned away.

"Guess you better call the cops," Travis said. "They can check with the hotels."

"Illinois driver's license. Chicago. I'd better put this in the safe." Henry lifted the gate to the bar and went into his office.

Travis turned to Marcella. "What'll it be?"

Marcella studied the bar menu. "I'll try the Lemon Drop Martini."

"A beer will do for me," Ben said.

"What kind? We got—"

"Any kind."

Travis served up the drinks and leaned on the bar towards Marcella. "It's nice to hear you speak from time to time, Marcella. Makes communication a little easier."

"Depends on what you mean by communication." Marcella sipped on her martini through a straw.

"Talk. Conversation."

"Conversation doesn't always have much to do with communication."

Travis looked at Ben, who looked back and shrugged his shoulders. "Okay. Let's say body language is a better way to communicate. Then—"

"I didn't say it was a better way. I'm just saying that conversation isn't the only way." She bit off a cherry, chewed it up, and popped the stem into her mouth.

Travis, a little exasperated at this 'conversation,' turned to Ben. "Tell me, Ben—what happened to reduce you to filching wallets in

San Francisco?"

Ben sighed. "It started in the army, Cap'n—I mean Travis. You remember how all the guys smoked a little dope and we bought and sold it among ourselves?"

"Of course not," Travis said with a smile. "I was too busy looking the other way."

"Right," Ben said. "Well, one day the colonel *wasn't* looking the other way. I was on KP duty one night behind the mess tent dealing a couple of lids to my buddies. Nothin' big. Two crummy lids. Well, the colonel just happened to be conducting a surprise inspection and I was up the creek without a paddle."

"Court-martial?"

Ben nodded. "Guilty as charged. But I didn't lie to them, Cap'n. They busted me to corporal on account of my good service and gave me a general discharge."

"A general? That means you can still get benefits."

Ben shrugged and took a sip of his beer. "I guess."

Marcella, who seemed not to be listening to this conversation, suddenly extracted the stem of the cherry from her mouth. "Voilà!" She held the knotted stem between her thumb and forefinger for all to see.

Ben stared at the stem for a moment and picked a fresh cherry out of the container on the bar. "I can do that." He bit the cherry off, popped the stem into his mouth, and within seconds produced the stem again with the requisite knot.

Marcella clapped her palms together in a rapid motion that, like her mime routine, produced no sound.

Travis had seen this trick so many times that he had lost count. A customer called and he went to the other end of the bar.

A patron sitting on the other side of Marcella claimed that he could beat Ben's record, but after several minutes of contorting his face into bizarre and ghoulish expressions, gave it up.

Another patron, sitting at a table nearby, called to her: "Is there a circus in town?"

Marcella turned on her bar stool to face him. Then she hopped off the stool and marched to the bandstand in the corner near the window. Addressing the crowd, which was growing now, she pantomimed a scene that seemed to involve a top hat, a whip and an imaginary lion who was presumed to rest on his haunches on a platform that supported two speakers. She made full use of a three-legged stool at hand, picking it up and using it to punch the air as a defense against the malevolent intentions of the lion. This, combined with the whip she snapped with her wrist, brought peals of laughter from the patrons as she alternately feigned fear and courage in the face of the unruly lion.

By the end of her performance, Henry emerged from his office and stood applauding along with the patrons. She bowed deeply and was showered with tips for her efforts.

Travis and Ben joined in the applause and watched as Marcella collected the money.

At that point, a man dressed from head to toe in black and wearing dark glasses appeared at the entrance to the bar. He was accompanied by two other African-Americans standing slightly behind him. All were wearing leather belts with holsters attached. Each holster contained a pistol. The noise in the bar suddenly diminished and then fell silent.

Henry nodded to Ben and indicated the three men. Ben looked at Henry, then at Travis, slid off his bar stool and walked slowly but deliberately to the front door.

He addressed the shorter man who seemed to be the group's leader. "Hey, Bro, we don't allow weapons in here. You have to leave them outside."

The leader nodded in the direction of the street. "Outside? This ain't the wild west, Brother. Where you think we parked our horses?"

"I don't know, Bro—but you can't bring guns into a nice place like this."

The leader emitted something between a chuckle and a grunt. "Nice? I guess this is a little nicer than what we got in Oakland. A regular fern bar. Lots of nice white folks looking for someone to shack up with. But you're wrong about what I can and can't do. The law in California says I can take my weapon anywhere I want as long as it ain't concealed. You dig?"

Ben stood staring at the leader, who stared back. It wasn't clear what the shorter man would do next, but Henry broke the tense silence by walking over and introducing himself. "I'm Henry Africa, the owner of this establishment." He extended his hand, which was ignored.

"Do tell," the leader said.

Henry withdrew his hand. "You're right, Mister, uh—"

"Bobby."

"Bobby. The law allows you to carry an unconcealed weapon. But we try to maintain a friendly atmosphere here."

The leader broke into a broad grin. "Oh, I'm a friendly fellow, Henry. And so are my friends. You serve black people here, or are they just the hired help?"

"We serve everyone as long as they behave themselves."

The leader looked around the bar, with its fern plants and faux Tiffany lamps and terrified patrons. "Oh, we intend to behave ourselves, Henry. You got Chivas Regal?"

"Of course." Henry said. "Step up to the bar there and Travis will be glad to serve you."

Travis pulled a bottle of Chivas Regal from the shelf and set out three glasses.

"On the rocks with a shot of soda for me," Bobby said.

"Water," one of the other men said.

"Coke," said the third.

Travis scooped some ice into each glass and poured each man his drink. While the three sipped from their glasses, Travis looked around the bar. The patrons were again engaged in conversation and the volume gradually increased until it reached the same level as before. Ben was now at his station at the door.

Marcella was gone.

CHAPTER 3

"Ain't you got a bed?" Ben looked around the studio apartment that Travis had rented a few months earlier. There was a small desk with a flex lamp on it along with some bills and a couple of spiral notebooks. There was also a faux leather office chair opposite the desk and two other chairs, one a comfortable but worn armchair covered in green corduroy. An oriental carpet with a salmon background and multicolored figures of flowers, birds and dragons covered most of the floor.

"Sure I've got a bed." Travis went to the far wall—away from the window in front of the desk, which faced an alley—and slid open a pair of hanging closet doors that revealed a metal framework connected with springs. He pulled on a strap and down came the apparatus with two legs that unfolded and landed squarely on the carpet.

"What the heck is that?" Ben said.

"What does it look like?"

"Well...a bed. But—hey, that's really cool, Cap'n. Where did you get it?"

"It's built in. Came with the apartment." Travis straightened the mattress and tucked in the corners of the sheets. "As you can see, though, it takes up nearly the whole space. You'll have to sleep in it with me."

Ben looked alarmed. "Well...is that gonna be comfortable for you? I mean, I can sleep on the floor."

"There's not much room on the floor. You'll be more comfortable on the bed."

Ben seemed to be perspiring, though it was quite cool in the apartment. "Well, Cap'n—"

"Stop calling me Captain."

"Yeah, okay. Sorry. But look here, Travis, I don't think either one of us will get much sleep with both of us in that bed. I mean, I'm pretty heavy and I toss and turn a lot."

"Relax, Ben. I'm not gay. It's just a practical matter, that's all. But if you'd prefer the floor, you're welcome to it. The carpet's got a little padding to it, but every time you turn over, you're liable to hit something."

"Yeah, well...I guess I'll take my chances on the floor. No offense, Cap—I mean Travis."

Travis smiled and sat down on the edge of the bed. "That armchair's pretty comfortable, too. You might try that."

"Yeah, it looks nice." Ben went over to the armchair and plopped down in it. "Yeah, this is real nice. Like an old glove."

Travis got up and went over to his desk. He emptied his pockets, and deposited a wad of rolled up bills onto the blotter. "A pretty good night for tips. Take whatever you need."

Ben stared at the money on the desk for a few moments. "Why you doing this for me, Travis?"

Travis smiled and looked at Ben. "You saved my life, remember? Besides, you need a place to stay until you get your first paycheck."

"Yeah. Well, you know, I didn't exactly save your life. I mean I didn't really do anything."

"You told me about the grenade. You didn't have to. I would've been blown to bits and nobody would have been the wiser."

Ben reclined in the chair and stared at the ceiling. "Well, yeah. I guess so."

"I *know* so."

Ben rolled his eyes towards the desk. "What are all those notebooks for? You writin' a book?"

Travis laughed. "No. Not yet, anyway. I've signed up for a couple of courses at San Francisco State."

"Oh, yeah? What kind of courses?"

"One's philosophy and the other's a speech class."

"Speech class? You speak real good, Cap'n. Damn! I mean Travis. You don't need no speech class—I'm the one needs some speech trainin'."

"Why don't you sign up, then?"

Ben rolled his eyes back to the ceiling. "Me? I dunno, I may be too dumb. Besides, I ain't got the money right now."

Travis sat down in his desk chair and turned on its swivel towards Ben. "You don't need any money. You can use the G.I. Bill. That's what I'm doing."

Ben looked dubious. "Well, I dunno...you think it might help me get a better job than being a bouncer?"

"Sure. Communication is what it's all about."

Ben fell silent for a few moments. Then he pulled a card out of his pocket and looked at it. "I've already been offered a job—as a coordinator."

Travis looked at the card but was too far away to read it. "Coordinator of what?"

"I dunno. You know that black dude who came into the bar this afternoon? The one with the other two dudes packin' heat?"

"How could I forget? Called himself Bobby something."

"Bobby X. Just 'X' is his last name. Here."

Travis reached over and took the card. "'Bobby X...Recruiter...The Black Puma Party.'"

"He handed it to me on the way out after he and the other dudes finished their drinks. Said I would make a good coordinator...What's a coordinator do?"

Travis turned the card over. There was a phone number. "Depends. For the Black Pumas it might mean coordinating a robbery. Or a jail break."

Ben's eyes opened wide. "They're gangsters?"

"Sort of. They claim to be revolutionaries but they've had a few shootouts with the Oakland police."

Ben closed his eyes. "Maybe I'll pass on the coordinating job. Think I could sign up for that class at San Francisco State? I mean, do you just walk in?"

"Just about. You got a high school diploma?"

"Sure. East Dublin High."

"East Dublin?"

"Georgia."

"Oh. That'll get you in. You can apply for V.A. benefits later."

"Woo-ee! I'm gonna be a college student?"

"You can come with me tomorrow. The speech class is at nine o'clock. You can register at 8:30."

Ben folded his hands behind his head and stared at the ceiling. "I'm gonna have to write my momma about this. Her baby boy's going to college!"

CHAPTER 4

The next morning Travis rose before Ben, who was still asleep in the armchair, and cooked breakfast in the kitchenette crammed into an alcove with a small window that faced the alley.

Ben yawned and opened his eyes. "That smells good, Cap'n. I could eat a horse!"

"You'll have to settle for a couple of scrambled eggs and three strips of bacon," Travis said. "We'll stop at the grocery store on the way home."

Ben rubbed his eyes and looked around the apartment. The bed had been returned to its upright position and once again concealed behind the closet doors. "The place sure looks bigger with the bed folded up."

"That's the idea." Travis transferred the eggs to the plates with a spatula. "Come and get it."

The two sat at a tiny table and looked out the window onto the alley.

"Sleep well?" Travis said.

"Okay...until someone started banging garbage cans together about four a.m. At first I thought it was a mortar attack."

Travis smiled as he cut a strip of bacon in two with his fork. "That's Trader Vic's. You'll get used to it."

"Trader Vic's?"

"A restaurant. Kind of expensive." Travis noted Ben's rumpled appearance. "Where are your clothes?"

"You're lookin' at them."

"That's it?"

"That's it. I had a duffel bag, mostly uniforms. I left it at the bus station in a locker."

"We'll stop there on the way back and find a used clothing store in the Mission. You'll fit right in with a couple of tie-dyed T-shirts and pre-owned jeans.'

They walked the six blocks or so to Market and caught the M-line trolley to San Francisco State.

At the registrar's office Ben was told that he would have to wait until they received his transcripts from East Dublin High before he could matriculate, but that he could audit the speech class in the meantime.

At nine o'clock they entered a large room with raked seating for about 150 students. Travis insisted that they get as close as possible to the podium so they could hear well, and Ben reluctantly followed to about the fifth row where they took their seats.

"I always sat in the back row in high school," Ben said.

"How were your grades?"

"Not so good."

"That may be why." Travis scanned the podium, where two men and an elderly woman were conversing. "Teachers favor students who sit up front. It makes them think they're more motivated."

"How many teaches they got here?"

"Three. The young guy is a professor of international relations. Very sharp. The middle-aged guy is the speech prof. The older woman is a famous writer who once lived in Paris and knew Hemingway and Gertrude Stein."

"I've read Hemingway," Ben said. "We read a story in class about an old guy who hooks a big fish and won't let go even though the fishing line cuts his hands all up like hamburger."

"*The Old Man and the Sea.*"

"That's the one. Hey, look, there's the mime lady."

Travis looked to the front row where Ben was pointing. "Where?"

"Right there. Next to the black girl with the big Afro. She ain't got her makeup on, but it's the same girl."

Travis squinted. "Are you sure?"

"Sure, I'm sure. I can tell by the way she smiles. She got nice teeth."

Travis couldn't even see the girl's teeth and he didn't remember her smiling at all on the street or at Henry Africa's. But he did see a very pretty young woman with long black curly hair and green eyes. "The eyes. Yeah, she had green eyes."

"That, too. Hey, Cap'n, you didn't do perimeter duty like I did in 'Nam. After a while I could tell the difference between a dog and a coyote in the dark at fifty meters. That's the mime lady, all right."

There was suddenly a muffled tapping sound followed by a high-pitched whine over the public address system.

"Can you hear me?" It was the speech professor at the microphone.

Several students nodded in affirmation. "Good. This is Speech 304, which as many of you know by now is a team-taught course. I'm Professor McFarland, and over on my left is Professor Kelso, of the International Relations Department. And of course you all know Ms. Kay Baumgartner of the Creative Writing Department. This is a new concept where we'll be reading and discussing everything from Marx to Marcuse."

Ben looked askance at Travis.

"Of course," Professor McFarland continued, "we'll also be studying conservative thinkers like Fyodor Dostoevsky, Eric Hoffer, and William F. Buckley."

"We in the right class, Cap'n?" Ben shifted his weight in the narrow seat. "I thought we was gonna learn how to talk good."

"There'll be plenty of talking," Travis said. He was hardly paying attention to the professor's introduction, as his eyes were fixed on the girl he now recognized as Marcella. "She looks totally different without the white makeup and her hair tucked under the stocking cap. Totally."

After each of the other two professors spoke about their particular areas of interest and expertise, Professor McFarland passed out a syllabus along with a list of books required for the course. He assigned the first book, which was called *The Revolution Betrayed,* by Leon Trotsky, for the next meeting and dismissed the class.

As the students trickled out of the room, Travis kept his eyes on Marcella until he could make his way to her side. With Ben following, he managed to intercept her just as she stepped out into the hall.

"Oh—" she said, clutching a notebook and two or three text books to her chest. "It's you. Travis, right?"

"Right. You know, I hardly recognized you without your mime outfit. You slipped out of the bar before I could—"

"I didn't want to wait around for the shooting. How are you, Ben?"

Ben smiled and nodded. "Just fine, Marcella. We didn't have no trouble after you left."

Marcella returned the smile. "I'm sure the 'boys' didn't want to tangle with you."

"Nah," Ben said. "They just wanted to strut their stuff. Show that nobody could mess with 'em."

"Still, they made me nervous."

"Say," Travis said, "why don't we all go the student union and have a cup of coffee? We need to pick up some of these books at the book store, anyway."

"Sorry," Marcella said. "I've got another class in five minutes. I'll take a rain check, though."

"Oh," Travis said, feeling that his overture had been rejected. "What class?"

"I'm a theatre major."

"Ah—that figures. But you're already a terrific mime. Why do you need—"

"I can't be a mime all my life. Have you ever seen a help wanted ad for a mime?"

Travis laughed. "Come to think of it, no. I guess you have to branch out a little. But...why don't you come to Henry Africa's tonight for a drink?"

Marcella seemed hesitant. She looked first at Ben and then at Travis. "I've got an audition at the Rose and Thorn at four o'clock. Why don't you come there? We could have a drink afterwards."

"The Rose and Thorn?"

"It's a pub, really. But they have a non-equity theatre upstairs— only 99 seats. Here, I'll write down the address." She pulled out a pen from her purse and wrote the address down on Travis' note- book. "Bye—I'm already late for my class."

Travis watched as Marcella made her way down the hall among a throng of students.

"Hey, Cap'n, I think she likes you."

"Well, at least she didn't blow me off." Travis looked down at the address. "California Street. That's only about four blocks north of my place. I don't have to be at work till six."

"I'll tell Henry you've got business to tend to."

"Don't tell him anything. If I'm late, I'm late. In the meantime, we need to stop by the book store."

"Yeah. Maybe they got *Quotations From Chairman Mao*."

Travis chuckled. "They've also got Eric Hoffer."

"Who's he?"

"A philosopher. In fact, he lives in San Francisco. Come on, we got two more stops after the book store—and all by trolley."

Ben followed Travis down the hall. "You know, I kind of like them things—except when they go too fast around a corner and the boom falls off. Then you got to wait for the driver to get out and hook it up again. Looks like he's fly fishing."

But Travis did not hear this last remark. He was thinking of Marcella's green eyes and black curly hair and how her breasts almost popped out of her tank top when she pressed her books against her chest.

"Hey, Cap'n—you notice how the women around here don't wear bras?"

"Yeah, Ben. I noticed."

CHAPTER 5

Marcella sat anxiously in the third row of the theatre at the Rose and Thorn as a young blond—very pretty, with blue eyes and a girl-next-door quality about her—auditioned for the part of Roxana, Alexander the Great's first wife. She seemed very confident, very professional. And she *was* pretty, even beautiful. What chance would she, Marcella (actually Monica; she adapted the name from Marcel Marceau, the famous mime), have with her black hair and rather odd looks? After all, she had had a severe case of acne as a teenager and there were scars—easily covered by makeup, but still visible—on her cheeks from that humiliating condition. And she had had no time to put on makeup before the audition.

"'Hephaestion! Hephaestion! That name rings in my head like a ship's bell on a dreary, foggy night.'" The blond girl laid the script aside and looked at an elderly man with long white hair, who sat in the front row. "'Why don't you take *me* hunting with you?'"

The elderly man read from his script: "'I would...if you could shoot while riding at a full gallop like the Amazons of the Indus...give me the bow.'"

"'Who says I can't? You've never let me try.'"

"'It takes years of practice...give it to me.'"

The blond girl turned away as if keeping the bow from Alexander and looked again at her script. "'You know I can ride...I rode as a child with my brothers.'"

"'But can you shoot?'"

The blond girl pretended to pull back the string on an imaginary bow. "'Of course I can—hand me an arrow.'"

"All right, that will do," a younger man, the director, said. "Thank you."

The blond girl looked a bit annoyed, as if she were being rudely interrupted just as she was getting into the part.

"I said that will be all for now," the director said. "We'll contact you if we need a call back." He put down the script, picked up a notepad, and read from it: "Ms. Morgan—would you read for us, please?"

Marcella stood and made her way up the aisle. She felt the eyes of the elderly man on her back, as well as those of the director. When she turned around and faced them, she noticed that Travis was just entering the theatre and took a seat in the back row. It crossed her mind that he would make a fine Alexander. Did he intend to audition?

"Now Ms. Morgan," the director said, "Could you read for us from the top of page thirty-four?"

Marcella looked down at her script and turned to page thirty-four, where the blond girl had started. "From 'Hephaestion'?"

"Yes, please."

She began reading and the elderly man again read Alexander's lines. When she finished, she heard clapping. It was Travis. And then the director. A few other onlookers, mostly actors auditioning for various roles, joined in.

"Very nice, Ms Morgan," the director said. "Be sure to leave your contact information with the stage manager." He looked down at his notepad and then stood as Marcella returned to her seat. He faced the actors in the audience. "Now we'll have auditions for the role of Alexander...volunteers?"

A hand went up.

"All right," the director said. He looked again at his notes. "Mr. Sanchez?"

"Alessandro Sanchez," the young man said. He was an imposing figure, about six feet in height with dark hair but a fair complexion. He wore baggy cargo pants and a black T-shirt that fit tightly over his muscular physique.

"Don't assume your name is going to give you an advantage, Mr. Sanchez."

Those in the audience laughed.

"And you're too tall," someone said. "Alexander was only five-foot four."

Sanchez turned to the heckler. "He looked six feet to his enemies."

There was more laughter as he mounted the stage, script in hand.

"All right, Mr. Sanchez," the director said. "Is there any particular passage you'd like to read?"

"Yes." Sanchez turned a few pages. "Act one, scene four. From the top of page sixteen."

The director turned to the page. "Ah...the scene where Alexander rescues Timocleia...we need a Timocleia...let's see...the blond lady who read before Ms. Morgan—"

"Andrea Koslewski."

"Yes, Ms. Koz—"

"Kos*lef*ski.'"

"Right. Ms. Koslefski. Would you care to read the part of Timocleia?"

Ms. Koslewski looked first at Marcella, then at the director. "Sure...why not?"

"We appreciate your enthusiasm, Ms. Koslewski—" Laughter rippled through the audience. "The role of Timocleia is a very good one. But we can always get someone—"

"No, I'll do it. What page did you say?" Ms. Koslewski stood and walked towards the stage.

"Page sixteen. Oh, and we need a soldier. I suppose I could—"

"I'll read the soldier's part."

All turned to the voice from the back of the theatre.

"And you are?"

"Travis Carter. I'm not on your list."

"Well, all right, Mr. Carter. It's not a difficult role. Do you have a script?"

By this time Travis had approached the stage and was standing next to Marcella, who was seated. She handed him her script. "I do now."

"Excellent. Please take your position opposite Ms. Koslewski and a few steps behind Mr. Sanchez."

With all of the actors in position, the director pointed to Sanchez. "Begin."

"'What's the matter there?'" Sanchez said. "'I said—what's the matter? Stop that shrieking!'"

Suddenly Ms. Koslewski began shrieking at the top of her lungs. The audience erupted in laughter, as did the director and the elderly gentleman.

"'Come on, you silly wench!'" Travis said. "'The general knows how to deal with your sort!'"

"'Let me go!'" Ms. Koslewski said, affecting to struggle with Travis.

"'I don't care a fig for your general!'"

"'Tell him yourself—'cause here he is.'"

At this point, Ms. Koslewski bit Travis on the hand, eliciting a genuine cry of pain from him. Again the audience laughed.

Travis raised an imaginary sword over Ms. Koslewski's head as if to strike her. "'Bite me, will you! I'll—'"

Sanchez moved quickly to stop him. "'She's unarmed. There's no need to strike her.'"

"'She don't need to be armed, General. She's already killed a man with no more than her own hands—and her wits. She's a dangerous one!'"

Ms. Koslewski suddenly dropped to the floor of the stage, sobbing.

"'Killed a man,' Sanchez said. 'Who?'"

"'The captain. Of the Thracian regulars.'"

"All right," the director said. "Drop down to line eleven." He pointed to Sanchez. "Alexander."

"'The captain,' Sanchez said. 'What did the captain do?'"

"'He...'" Travis affected a stammer. "'Well, he had his way with her, you might say.'"

Sanchez leaned down to Ms. Koslewski and gently took her hand. "'Stand up, good lady.'" Ms. Koslewski stood. "'I see that you are well born. Now, tell me, what did the captain do then?'"

Ms. Koslewski looked frightened, then angry. "'After he raped me he looked about for jewels, and finding none, he wanted to know if I had any money hidden away.'"

Sanchez smiled. "'And you told him you did—in the well.'"

"'Yes. He gladly followed me to the well—when he looked in, I gave him a push with all my might.'"

"'That she done, General,'" Travis said. "'She's got the strength, I can tell you!'"

"'And now, dear lady,'" Sanchez said, "'with our courageous captain head over heels towards the doorstep of Hades, how did you further assist in his departure from this world?'"

"All right," the director said. "We'll stop there." There was applause from all parts of the theatre. "Thank you, Mr. Sanchez, Ms. Koslewski, and Mr.—"

"Carter," Travis said.

"Right. I don't think we need to look further for our soldier, Mr. Carter. The part is yours if you want it."

"Well..." Travis glanced at Marcella, who gave him an encouraging smile. "Sure. I don't have much experience, but—"

"You don't need much for the role, Mr. Carter. You've got a military bearing and a good speaking voice that can be heard in the back row." The director clapped his hands. "We'll take a ten minute break. Mr. Sanchez, may I speak to you for a moment?"

Travis went and sat down beside Marcella.

"You were wonderful!" she said.

"Oh, come on—it's a bit part."

"Still—you project well, as the director said. And your cry of pain sounded genuine."

"It *was* genuine—she bit the hell out of my hand."

Marcella laughed. "I think she'll get the part of Timocleia—she has that 'high born' look Alexander describes her as having."

Travis looked over at Sanchez, who was in animated conversation with the director. "You think he'll get the part?"

"I'd bet on it. He's very professional. I think I've seen him before—in a movie, maybe."

"But he's Hispanic—he doesn't look like my idea of Alexander."

"He can always dye his hair blond. That's probably what they're talking about now."

Travis looked at the elderly gentleman who was still in his front-row seat, taking notes. "Who's he?"

"That's the playwright—Nearchos Andropoulos. He's a professor of playwriting at State."

"Greek, eh?"

"Very. He made a pass at me the first day of class."

Travis chuckled. "Why wouldn't he? You're a very pretty girl."

Marcella blushed. "Not as pretty as Ms. Koslewski."

Travis looked over at Ms. Koslewski, who was surrounded by several young actors. "She's more the conventional type. Looks like she should be doing soap commercials. I think you'll get the part."

"You mean I look like the typical harebrained Afghan princess?"

Travis laughed. "You want me to say it? I think you're beautiful."

"Why don't I believe you?"

"All right. I say that to all the Afghan princesses. It usually works."

Marcella smiled. "You said you were going to buy me a drink."

"So I did. What about the rest of the auditions?"

"I'm done. So are you. Let's get out of here."

"Okay."

They rose and Marcella gathered up her script and purse. As they started down the stairs to the pub, Sanchez appeared and called to her.

"You were marvelous, Ms. Morgan," Sanchez said. "I'm looking forward to working with you."

"You've got the part? It's the two of us?"

"It seems so." He laughed and rather self-consciously passed his right hand over his hair. "Sam—the director—says I've got to dye my hair blond."

"That's hardly an obstacle. You'll look good as a blond. Just like–"

Sanchez suddenly grasped Marcella's jowls with both hands and kissed her passionately on the mouth.

"We needed to break the ice," he said.

Marcella opened her eyes, looked at Travis, who showed no reaction, and then at Sanchez, who was grinning at her. "Well, I guess that did it. I'll see you soon, Alessandro."

As they descended the stairs, Marcella wondered at what she felt when Alessandro kissed her. She was embarrassed not so much that he did it—actors were always looking for a kiss or a cheap feel on the grounds that it was 'to break the ice'—but that he did it in front of Travis. And Travis seemed not to care.

"Alessandro's rather impetuous, isn't he?" Travis said with a frown as they entered the pub.

Marcella smiled. He *was* jealous, wasn't he? "It's just his Latin temperament." She looked around the pub which was adorned with numerous bottles of English ale on the shelves, a tattered Union Jack on the wall, and a dart board in the corner. "Do you think they know how to make a lemon drop martini here?"

"If they don't, I can show them."

They made their way to the bar.

CHAPTER 6

By the third week of the fall semester, Ben had been admitted as a full-time student at San Francisco State and received both his first pay check from Henry Africa's and his first V.A check, which paid for his tuition. He moved out of Travis's tiny apartment and rented a room in the same house in the Haight where Marcella lived.

Travis, by this time, was spending more of his time at Marcella's than he was at his own apartment. He was annoyed and frustrated, however, by the situation, since the number of people in the old Victorian house at any one time was such that it was difficult to maneuver Marcella into her bedroom. He had invited her to visit him at his place, but she had declined each time, citing her busy schedule with both her classes at SF State and the play.

Travis, however, was even busier since he had the same obligations that she did plus a forty-hour work week at Henry Africa's. Of course, she had a much bigger role in the play than he did, and a heavier load at SF State since he was taking only two courses.

But the main obstacle to the consummation of their relationship seemed to be Alessandro Sanchez.

Alessandro did indeed win the role of Alexander and was quite impressive in rehearsals, both for his stage presence and for his professionalism. He also came often to the house on Haight Street, ostensibly to discuss their respective roles with Marcella. There was a large living room—or 'parlor'—in the house that served as a common room. There was also a large-screen television that tended to serve as the tenants' focus of interest.

One afternoon, Marcella, Travis, Alessandro, and Ben were all watching this television when a special news bulletin interrupted the program with the announcement that Archibald Cox, the special prosecutor for Watergate, had been fired by the Solicitor General.

When the broadcast went back to the regular program, one of Marcella's housemates, a musician, got up from the sofa, went to the television, and turned it off. "Nixon's eighty-sixed."

"Eighty-sixed?" Ben said.

"Done, through, outa here," the musician said. "He lied to us.

About Vietnam, about Watergate, about Cambodia."

"Ford will pardon him," Alessandro said.

Travis said nothing. He was lost in thought about the past five years, wondering what to make of it all.

Alessandro rose from his armchair and addressed Marcella. "Why don't we go to a movie? *The Wild Bunch* is playing at the Castro."

Marcella looked unenthusiastic. "Isn't it pretty violent?"

Alessandro smiled. "Sure. But it's suppose to be very good. Sam Peckinpah directed. And my cousin Jaime is in it."

"I need to write a paper for my set design class," Marcella said. "And we've got a rehearsal tonight at seven."

"I know my lines backwards," Alessandro said. "Anybody?"

"I've got work tonight," Travis said.

"Me, too," Ben said.

"I'll pass," Harvey, the musician, said. "I've got a rehearsal, too."

Alessandro laughed. "What a dull group! All work and no play. Well, I'm going to the movies. I'll see you tonight, Marcella."

"Okay."

They all watched as Alessandro went to the front door, opened it, and looked back at Marcella. "Remember, it's full dress."

"I remember," Marcella said.

Alessandro passed through the door and descended down the steps to the street.

Ben rose from the sofa. "I got to finish that *Rules* book before class tomorrow. I feel dumb when everybody's talking about a book and I ain't read it."

"What *Rules* book?" Marcella said.

"*Rules For Radicals*," Travis said. "By Saul Alinsky."

"Oh, my gosh!" Marcella rose from the sofa, where she had been sitting between Ben and Travis. "I forgot all about it. I'll have to cut class."

"It's not anything you need to know unless you're going to be a community organizer," Travis said. "I can summarize it for you in five minutes."

"Maybe after rehearsal tonight," Marcella said.

"I won't be there. I'm working tonight, remember?" Travis rose and jammed his hands into the pockets of his jeans. "Why don't you come to Henry's afterwards and I'll fill you in."

"All right." Marcella gave him a peck on the cheek. "I've got to finish up that design paper before I go. See you tonight." She then disappeared into the hallway that led to her bedroom.

Travis and Ben were left standing together in the parlor.

"Maybe you can help me with some of the big words," Ben said.

"What's wrong with using a dictionary?"

"It don't always help," Ben said. "Sometimes they got four or five definitions and none of 'em seem to fit."

Travis sighed. "Why don't you get started and I'll duck into your room a little later. Right now I'm going for a walk."

"All right, Cap'n. I'll do what I can."

"And stop calling me Captain—it's embarrassing."

"Okay—Travis. Don't seem right, though."

Travis shook his head and went to the door. As he opened it, he heard the rat-a-tat-tat of Harvey's drums. "Christ," he said to himself, "How does anyone *think* around here?"

He descended to the street and walked west, towards Golden Gate Park.

It was a typical San Francisco day; that is, it was atypical of anywhere else. It was cool enough for a sweater along the Haight, then about ten degrees warmer when he got to the park where the sun was out. Once he passed into a grove of trees, it was cooler again and when he arrived at the tennis courts the players could hardly see each other for the fog. He had a denim jacket on, embroidered with flowers on the breast pockets. A gift from Marcella. He turned the collar up and followed the path to Stow Lake.

What had it all been for? Three years in the army, two in Vietnam. Patrols in the jungle, firefights...he had shot a woman once who seemed to reach for a weapon. Turned out it was a broom. She was pregnant.

He shook this image off and continued to the lake.

All right. It was a mistake. We had no business being there. All wars produce civilian casualties. All soldiers are pawns for politicians. But could it ever be justified somehow? Was there a road to atonement? Was 'atonement' even the right word?

He hadn't thought about the war lately. He spent more time thinking about getting laid. Dating—if that's what they did—Marcella was both fun and frustrating. The house where she lived was always full of people and noise. Drummers, actors, students, drug dealers...it was a zoo. And no privacy. She didn't seem inclined to visit his apartment. Always made some excuse. And what was going on with Alessandro?

When he arrived at the boathouse, he stopped and leaned on a railing overlooking the lake. Young couples were rowing and paddling about, enjoying the romance, the serenity of the calm, sheltered waters. It might be a good idea to ask Marcella to go boating. A few bucks for an hour.

What was the fascination, anyway? He had told her she was beautiful, but she wasn't, really. Her features were somehow a cross between Irish and Japanese. Eyes slanted slightly upwards at the corners, high cheek bones, a fine but slightly crooked nose. Had it been broken? Must have been. How? And the faint pock marks from acne as a kid. And the husky voice. Lord, what did he see in her?

He shoved his hands into his pockets again and circled the lake. An Asian guy—probably Chinese—walked alongside a Caucasian woman pushing a baby carriage. They nodded at him politely as they passed by and he peeked into the baby carriage. The kid looked mostly Chinese, face as round as an apple. This was America. Such things could happen.

By the time he got back to the house, he was in a better mood. He knocked on Ben's door.

"Come in—Oh, Travis. What does 'catalyst' mean?"

Travis stepped into the room. There was a single bed, a small desk like his own, a couple of tattered stuffed chairs, movie posters of black exploitation films, and pinups from *Playboy* and *Penthouse*. "Change. It means change."

Ben looked at him over his shoulder. "Then why don't the man just say that? 'Change' is change."

"It means more than change. It means something that sets change into motion but isn't changed itself."

"Oh." Ben looked down at his text. "You know, this Alinsky guy is beginning to make sense."

"You thinking of becoming a community organizer?"

"I dunno. I'd like to do something to...you know, help my people."

"Your people?"

"Yeah. Black people." Ben suddenly looked uncomfortable. "I don't guess you'd understand that."

"Oh, I think I do. But are 'your' people only black people?"

Ben considered this. "No. You're my people. Marcella's my people. But black people need help. You and Marcella don't need none."

"I'm beginning to think we all need help."

"Well, yeah, if you look at it, like, in the big picture. But speaking of lookin', take a look at this list of words I made up while you was out walking."

"Okay—where's the dictionary?"

After adding at least sixteen words to Ben's vocabulary, Travis excused himself and headed for Henry Africa's.

CHAPTER 7

Andrea Koslewski was a cheerleader at her high school in Indiana and later at Finch College in upper Manhattan. She initially went to Finch thinking she would pursue a career as an artist, but when she was hired by an advertising firm to star in a soap commercial, she changed her major to drama. She dropped out of Finch her junior year and went to Los Angeles, where she was cast in a succession of B movies that flopped at the box office. Disappointed and disgusted with what she called the 'Tinsel Town Sausage Machine,' she moved to San Francisco and enrolled in the American Conservatory Theater. There, she met with even less success and was told by one instructor that she lacked 'empathy.'

One day Andrea saw an ad in the *San Francisco Chronicle* for auditions for a new play called *Alexander in Babylon: The Last Days of a Conqueror*. It called for several female roles, most notable of which was that of Alexander's wife, Roxana. She jumped at the opportunity.

Suffering yet another disappointment when she failed to win the role of Roxana, and livid that the ingenue who did was a student at San Francisco State whose only experience was as a street mime, Andrea set out to get her revenge.

She did this by showing up at Henry Africa's after rehearsal and informing Travis that Marcella had gone off with Alessandro.

"She's not coming?" Travis set a lemon drop martini down on the bar.

Andrea picked up the martini and took a sip. "Yum, delicious. How do you make this?"

"She told you she wasn't coming tonight?" Travis said. "Why would she—"

"She didn't exactly tell me she wasn't coming—I didn't know what her plans were." Andrea took another sip of the martini. "All I know is that she and Alessandro left the theater together."

Travis absently picked up a glass and began drying it with a bar towel. "She can go where she wants—with whom she pleases. But she specifically told me—"

"Marcella's starstruck, Travis. Alessandro has the leading role in the play. And although I don't think it's a very good play, it shows off Alessandro's talents to the max." Andrea drained the rest of her glass and put it down on the bar. "He's got *it*—sex appeal."

Travis picked up the empty glass. "You made short work of that one. You want another?"

"Please."

Travis mixed up another lemon drop martini and shook it vigorously. He glanced at the door where Ben was stationed on his customary stool. He was talking to Bobby X, who had been frequenting the bar lately, unarmed. That was a relief, anyway.

"That doesn't mean you don't, Travis," Andrea said.

Travis turned his attention to her. "Don't what?"

"Don't have sex appeal. You've got that in spades."

Travis blushed slightly and poured out the drink into a fresh glass, the rim covered in sugar.

"Marcella's young," Andrea said. "She doesn't know much about men. She doesn't know, for example, that Alessandro is bi."

"Bi?"

"Bisexual. He's well-known in L.A. Sam Peckinpah is one of his conquests."

"Sam Peckinpah? The director?"

"The same." Andrea picked up her second martini and took a long sip. "And it's rumored that he bedded down Ali MacGraw and Sue Lyon, not to mention a string of starlets you never heard of."

Travis didn't know whether to believe Andrea or not. But why would she lie? Jealousy over Marcella's beating her out of the role for Roxana? Well…possibly. But all this talk of Alessandro's alleged bisexuality. What did she have to gain from that? "You better slow down, Andrea. These lemon drop martinis are sweet but they pack a big punch."

Andrea laughed. "And what about you, Travis? Do you pack a big punch?"

Travis suddenly realized what Andrea had come for. He gazed at her décolletage, which amply displayed her breasts in the white chiffon dress she wore in the play. "My punch is all punched out, Andrea. The army took it out of me."

Andrea's expression suddenly turned grave. "The army? You were in Vietnam?"

"I was."

Andrea took another sip of her drink and seemed to study Travis' face closely. "How could justify that?"

"I've been asking myself that same question lately."

Andrea looked pensive for a moment and then reached out and put her hand on top of his. "I'm sorry if I crossed the line. It must be very personal."

Travis returned her stare for a moment and then withdrew his hand. She was quite beautiful. "Not so personal that I can't talk about it. But it's a real conversation killer. Especially in this town."

Andrea took another swallow of her drink. "Oh, I think some people are so hypocritical about it. They want the military to defend them, but then they condemn our boys in uniform for doing what they've been trained to do. Were you in the thick of the fighting?"

"Sometimes. Towards the end of my tour I just pushed papers in Saigon. I was lucky."

Andrea again put her hand on his. "I think you're being modest. I'll bet you came back with a chest full of medals."

Travis smiled as he withdrew his hand and began washing glasses. "Three. And one was for good conduct."

Andrea laughed. "You're being modest again." She downed the rest of her martini and shoved the empty glass towards him. "I'll have another."

"You driving?"

"I don't own a car. Taxis are cheaper and safer."

Travis prepared another lemon drop martini.

"Hey!" a man at the bar said. "How does a guy get service in this place? You serve only hot chicks here?"

"Shove it, asshole," Andrea said. "You'll get your turn."

The man, rather corpulent and in his late twenties, was taken aback but said nothing.

Travis poured the martini into her glass. "Excuse me, Andrea— I can't neglect the other customers."

"He's a fat prick," Andrea said.

Travis ignored this comment and went to the other end of the bar.

"Sheesh," the corpulent man said to Travis. "What's got into her?"

"Three lemon drop martinis in less than a half hour. What'll you have?"

"Scotch and water. Johnny Walker Black."

Travis poured out the drink. "Run a tab?"

"Sure." The man kept ogling Andrea, who was now turned around towards the bandstand where a solo guitarist had just returned from a break. "She your girlfriend?"

"No—just a friend."

"She's a looker—too bad she's got a dirty mouth."

"She's had a couple of bad breaks lately," Travis said. "I'll have to pour her into a cab after she finishes that one."

"Nice rack on her."

Travis smiled. "I've noticed."

After the guitarist got settled and started singing "Yesterday," Andrea became very quiet and listened with rapt attention. By the end of the song there were tears in her eyes. Travis returned to her end of the bar. "You okay?"

Andrea didn't look at him but only nodded. She then turned around on her stool, picked up her martini and downed the contents of the glass. She looked at Travis. "I'd like to fuck your eyes out."

Travis wasn't entirely surprised at this comment, given the tenor of her remarks to this point. "I think I'd better call you a cab."

Andrea looked at him for a moment and then said in a slurred voice: "I'd rather you called me Andrea." She giggled at her own witticism.

Travis tried to humor her with a comment about her fine performance as Timocleia, then went to Henry's office where he picked up the phone and called a cab. He returned to see Andrea dancing in front of the bandstand. Her long blond hair was in her face and she was swinging it around like Anita Ekberg in *La Dolce Vita*. The men in the bar were clapping and cheering. Even Bobby X was joining in. Finally she fell down, taking out a table along with two guys who were enjoying the show. There was the familiar sound of breaking glass and the sudden cessation of the music, followed by the guitarist and Travis assisting her to her feet. Travis sat her down in one of the armchairs near the window and waited for the cab to arrive.

By the time the cab driver showed up, Andrea was asleep in the chair and snoring. He and Travis helped her into the cab, at which point she seemed to rally. "You're coming with me, aren't you, Travis?" She fell back into the cab, pulling Travis with her.

"I can't," he said. "I've got to close up."

"Then you're coming," Andrea said.

"I don't think so—I've got a class tomorrow."

"Fuck the class." She threw her arms around him. "Fuck me instead."

Travis disentangled himself. "Andrea, you need to get some sleep. You're going to feel rotten in the morning."

"I never get a hangover. Don't you want some free pussy?"

The cab driver was sitting in the front seat at this point, looking at them both in his rearview mirror. His eyes were like saucers.

Travis glanced at the driver's I.D. on the visor. "This man will take you home, Andrea. His name is Bill."

"Well, hi there, Bill," she said. "Do you want some free pussy?"

"I'm married, lady," Bill said.

"Oh, too bad," Andrea said, pouting. "Mrs. Cabby-wabby might not like you diddling your customers."

"You're right about that, lady. She'd bust my balls. What's your address?"

Andrea lay down on the back seat and closed her eyes. "Coit Tower." She giggled. "Coitus Towers."

Bill looked at Travis and threw up his hands. "Nobody lives in Coit Tower. It's a landmark."

"Well, it's near there. I'll show you." She suddenly opened her eyes, sat up, embraced Travis, and kissed him on the mouth. "Come see me tomorrow, sweetie. After your class." Then she closed her eyes again and lay back down on the seat.

Travis didn't answer, but pulled out his wallet and gave Bill twenty dollars. "Make sure she gets inside her place and locks the door."

Bill took the money. "How am I going to make sure she does that?"

"Set it from the inside yourself."

"Right. Thanks, Mac."

Travis returned to the bar and noticed that nearly everyone had cleared out but Bobby X. He was sitting at a corner table talking to Ben. "Last call, fellas."

Bobby X looked in his direction for a moment and then turned back to Ben. As Travis was cleaning up, he got up and left. The fat guy was still at the bar.

"I'll have another Johnny Walker Black," he said.

Travis poured the drink and began wiping down the bar.

"You run this place by yourself?"

"Not usually. The owner's out of town and it's a slow night."

"Oh, I don't know. It was getting pretty lively there with Miss Trash Mouth."

Travis smiled as he soaked some glasses in the sink. "She's a nice person most of the time. Just can't handle alcohol."

"You know her pretty well, then."

"Not that well."

"Say—you don't happen to have her phone number, do you?"

"Afraid not. I'm not even sure she has a phone."

"Shit. What about her address?"

"Don't know that, either. Somewhere in North Beach."

The fat guy downed the rest of his drink. "You know some other chicks around here?"

"A few."

"They always say get to know the bartender when you're in a strange town." He extended his hand. "Chad."

"Travis." After shaking Chad's hand, Travis opened the gate to the bar and began wiping down the cocktail tables. Ben came over to him with a wide grin on his face.

"So what did Bobby X have to say?" Travis said. "You were in deep conversation with him all night."

Ben handed him a card. It said:

BEN FRANKLIN
Free Breakfast Coordinator
San Francisco, CA

Travis turned the card over. It had the logo of a black puma on it with Ben's phone number beneath it. "So that's what a coordinator does."

"Yep." Ben grinned even more broadly and took the card back. "I'm gonna be down in the Mission three days a week."

"Who're the free breakfasts for?"

"Kids. Half of them come to school on an empty stomach."

"Don't the schools already have a program like that?"

"Yeah, but it's junk food, like cheeseburgers and french fries and tacos. The Pumas give 'em soul food."

"Soul food?"

"Yeah. Like collard greens and chicken wings and chittlin's. Much more nutritious."

"You think the white kids are going to like that kind of food?"

"Ain't no white kids. Just blacks and Hispanics."

"See you around, Travis." Chad slipped off his stool and headed for the door.

"Sure," Travis said. "Come back Thursday night. Ladies' Night."

"I'll be here."

"Who's that guy?" Ben said.

"Chad something. Horny dude."

Ben laughed. "Who isn't?"

"Lock the door, will you? I've got to cash out."

Ben went to the front door and locked it. When he came back to the bar, Travis was counting the cash and adding up the credit card receipts.

"One thing bothers me about Bobby," Ben said, as he sat on a bar stool.

"What's that?"

"He wants me to carry a gun."

Travis looked up. "Why would you need a gun?"

"He says the Bay Area cops are all bigots. It's for self-defense, he says."

"Like they're going bust you for feeding six-year-olds?"

Ben didn't laugh. "It's happened, he says."

"Want my advice?"

"Sure."

"Don't carry a gun."
Ben seemed to consider this. "I'll think about it."

CHAPTER 8

The next morning Travis arrived at San Francisco State for his speech class. He spotted Ben and Marcella down near the front of the room and made his way through a throng of students chatting and socializing.

"Hi," he said, addressing Marcella. "What happened to you last night?"

Marcella looked surprised at this question. "Nothing—Oh my gosh! I forgot. Sorry—something came up."

"So I was told by Andrea."

Ben moved away and started to talking to the girl with the big Afro.

"Andrea?"

"She came to the bar and got a little tipsy. Said that you and Alessandro went off somewhere."

Marcella frowned. "Is she your spy or something?"

"No, of course not. She just mentioned that you went off with Alessandro and I...just wondered, that's all. I was afraid something happened to you."

"Nothing happened. Alessandro just wanted to talk about a couple of our scenes together. He's a perfectionist, you know."

"No, I didn't know. Anyway, it doesn't matter. I'm glad to see you're all right."

Marcella was visibly annoyed. "Of course I'm all right. Do I need to report to you every time I—"

"Take your seats, please."

The room fell silent and all turned towards Professor MacFarland, who was at the lectern with Professors Kelso and Baumgartner sitting on either side of him. Ben came back and sat down next to Marcella and Travis sat on the other side of her.

"Today we will have a sort of free-form discussion of all the books you've been reading for the past few weeks," MacFarland said. "Trotsky's *The Revolution Betrayed*, Dostoevsky's *The Possessed*, and Saul Alinsky's *Rules For Radicals*. What do all of these books have in common? How are they different? What are your impressions? I thought we'd start with Professor Kelso giving us a little background on the Russian Revolution. As you know, all three of these writers were either Russians or descended from Russian immigrants, as in the case of Mr. Alinsky." He turned to Professor Kelso. "Professor?"

As Professor Kelso summarized the influence of Marx on Lenin and Trotsky prior to the Revolution, Travis was hardly listening. He regretted his comments to Marcella, which made him seem like a jealous husband. And she certainly bridled at the suggestion that she had in some way to be accountable to him in regard to her whereabouts or who she consorted with.

Still, he couldn't help being jealous of Alessandro. Was he really 'bi,' as Andrea claimed? So far he hadn't shown any interest in the other men involved in the play. And Andrea was hardly a reliable source. Speaking of Andrea, shouldn't he be more concerned about her welfare at this point? He had no idea whether she got home safely or not. And the cab driver—Bill—did he help her into her apartment and then lock the door behind him, or did he lock them both in and take advantage of Andrea's inebriated state? He should have told Ben to lock up the bar and accompanied Andrea in the cab. He should have—"

"No," Professor Kelso said in response to a question. "I do not consider myself a Marxist. Rather, I am a *non*-Marxist."

This comment by the young professor got Travis' attention. What the heck was a non-Marxist?

"I am a student of Marx," the professor said, "but I do not accept all of Marx's ideas, especially as they relate to the modern world. In fact, my new book is entitled *Marx and the Modern World*. Though it is not in the syllabus for this course, I highly recommend that you all go out and buy it." Laughter rippled through the classroom. "You can see that the profit motive is not altogether extinct, even for professors of Marxism." More laughter ensued, and it seemed that Professor Kelso's comments put the class in a more relaxed mood.

Ben raised his hand.

"Yes, sir."

"Professor," Ben said tentatively, "I don't know much about Marx or Lenin, but I do know that the people of South Vietnam don't want Communism. They told me so. And yet the North keeps trying to impose it on them and it looks like they will. What do you say to them people that wants to be free?"

"I would say to them," Professor Kelso said, "that they are hardly free under a capitalist dictatorship now. I would also ask them whether they would be better off under a system that rewards corruption and cronyism, or under a system that distributes the wealth more equitably, even if that system is also a dictatorship."

Ben seemed nonplused. "You mean that they ain't got no choice, except between one kind of dictatorship or another?"

"At this juncture, I'm afraid that's the case. It's a question of economics, not political freedom. For the desperately poor, bread comes before freedom."

Ben fidgeted in his seat. "But they got they own farms. They ain't starvin'. If the government takes their farms, they won't have nothin'."

Professor Kelso seemed to be deep in thought. "If the government takes their farms—and they will—it will distribute the produce of those farms to all the people of Vietnam. Not just to the richest landowners, as is the case now. The poorest people that you're talking about are subsistence farmers; that is, they only grow enough to feed their families. Under a truly Marxist arrangement, they will benefit from the production not only of the largest farms, but from the city factories as well. In the end, they will be better off."

Ben stared at the floor for a moment, then looked up. "But they still won't be free."

Professor Kelso sighed. "They're many different definitions of freedom. But there's no real freedom without economic freedom." He pointed to another questioner. "Let's let someone else into this discussion."

"Professor Kelso," the questioner said, "in light of what you just said about bread coming before freedom, does that mean that you would be willing to give up the political freedoms you have under democratic capitalism for bread?"

"No, I would not," Professor Kelso said.

"But then it's all right for those living under a Communist dictatorship to do so?"

"There's a difference between a post-industrial society like our own and a pre-industrial society like that of Vietnam," the professor said.

"Simply put, we have enough bread for everyone and they do not. Until they do, political freedoms such as we enjoy are meaningless to them."

Professor Kelso continued to parry every challenge to his position of non-Marxist Marxism with skill and authority. Most of the students in the room seemed inclined to agree with him. Travis, however, was more inclined to agree with Ben that freedom was a far more precious commodity than bread. What was the old saying? Ah..."Those who would exchange freedom for bread will receive neither."

While he was trying to remember the name of the author of this aphorism, time ran out and Professor Kelso gave the floor to Ms. Baumgarten.

Catherine, or 'Kitty,' Baumgartner was nearing eighty years of age but appeared to be vigorous both physically and mentally. She had lived in all the major capitals of Europe and seemed to know everyone of note in the literary world during the first half of the twentieth century, including Hemingway, Firzgerald, Joyce, Becket, and of course Gertrude Stein. She was thin, with an angular, weather-beaten face and deep furrows in her cheeks and forehead. Nevertheless, her blue eyes seemed to sparkle and she had a genial, almost infectious, smile that she employed often to disarm her audience.

Ms. Baumgartner eschewed any particular ideology, but was generally supportive of what she termed 'liberation movements.' She was fiercely against the United States' involvement in the Vietnam War, and sympathetic to the civil rights movement, though she had been in Europe during most of the sixties. Since returning to the States, she had applied her considerable influence to the feminist cause.

But to the chagrin of critics who charged her with a 'distant' elitism, she replied that she was a writer, and therefore must write.

Marcella seemed particularly entranced with her, and was on the edge of her seat with her hand up.

"Yes?" Ms. Baumgartner said.

"Ms. Baumgartner, tell us about Paris—what was it like being in the inner circle of Gertrude Stein?"

Ms. Baumgartner smiled. "It seems that that's always the first question anyone asks me. You know, I was very busy writing at the time and only visited Miss Stein once or twice."

"Well," Marcella said tentatively, "what I really wanted to know was, did you know Marcel Marceau?"

"I hate to date myself, but Marcel was only a baby when I was living in Paris in the twenties. I did, however, go to the theater often and became acquainted with Marcel's mentor and teacher, Jean-Louis Barrault."

"Omigosh!" Marcella put her hand to her mouth. "You knew Barrault?"

"Only slightly. He was a charming man, though." Ms. Baumgartner turned the pages of a book on the lectern. "I hope that satisfies our burning desire to know about the private lives of celebrities—at least for now. I'm here today to bring whatever literary insights I have to a discussion of Dostoevsky's *The Possessed*."

Travis was amused at Marcella's awe of Ms. Baumgartner's passing acquaintance with Jean-Louis Barrault, who he had never heard of until now. Her passion for mime was somewhat puzzling to him, though he respected her for devoting so much time and energy to it. Even as the play progressed, in which she had a major speaking role, she continued to perform as a mime on the streets of San Francisco.

Travis had no particular passion at the moment unless it was for Marcella. He had, however, read *The Possessed*, and got into a heated debate with Professor Kelso over whether the radicals in the novel were representative of revolutionaries in general, or whether they were caricatures. Professor Kelso contended that they were, while Travis contended that they were not.

Ms. Baumgartner, to Travis' surprise, supported his view that Stavrogin, the protagonist and a nihilist, was all too real and furthermore, was one of the most intriguing characters in all of literature. As Ms. Baumgartner had the last word before the class broke up, Travis felt vindicated.

"Why don't we go for some coffee?" he said to Marcella. "I didn't get much sleep last night."

Marcella clutched her books to her breast and smiled. "I didn't know you felt so strongly about *The Possessed*. I haven't finished it yet, but Ms. Baumgartner seems to think you have some special insight into the main character."

Travis was flattered by this statement, but troubled as well. "I see a little too much of myself in Stavrogin."

Marcella stared into his eyes as if to uncover some dark secret within his soul. "I'll let you know if you're right when I finish the book."

"Deal. How about some coffee?"

Ben joined them at that point and the three of them headed for the door. When they emerged into the hallway, they saw a young Asian woman standing there. She was staring at Ben.

"Thuy?" Ben said. "God almighty—Thuy!'

"Yes, Ben," the young woman said in heavily accented English. "It's me—Thuy." She pronounced her name 'Twee.'

Ben stepped towards her and lifted her off her feet in a big bear hug. "How did you get here? How did you find me? My God—it's Thuy!"

Thuy broke into a big smile and giggled. "V.A. tell me you a student here. I come, lady at office tell me go here."

Travis and Marcella observed this touching scene with a mix of amusement and emotion.

"Hey," Ben said. "This is my buddy Travis. You remember him, Thuy? He was the captain of our company. And this is his friend, Marcella. She's an actress."

"Oh, actress, eh?" Thuy was obviously impressed. "Movies?"

Marcella laughed. "Not yet. But I'm working on it."

Thuy turned to Travis. "Yes, Captain Carter—Ben tell me all about you."

Travis extended his hand, which Thuy accepted. He didn't remember ever meeting Thuy, or hearing Ben talk about her. "It's a pleasure to meet you, Thuy. Won't you join us for some coffee?"

"Well..." Thuy looked at Ben.

"Oh," Travis said. "I suppose you two have a lot of catching up to do."

"Yeah," Ben said, looking a bit uncomfortable. "Maybe we'll take a rain check on the coffee."

After some awkward leave-taking, Ben and Thuy walked off toward an exit that opened onto a courtyard.

"Well," Travis said to Marcella. "That's extraordinary, isn't it? Ben's girlfriend somehow made it to the States and tracked him down to San Francisco. He's got to be thrilled."

"I'm not so sure about that," Marcella said.

"Why not?"

"She's pregnant."

Travis looked surprised. "Are you sure?"

"Absolutely. Maybe only three months, but it's obvious."

It wasn't obvious to Travis, but he deferred to Marcella's feminine intuition. "I suppose you'll be needing another housemate soon."

"Looks like it—I'm ready for that coffee now."

Marcella and Travis then headed for the north exit, which led to the student union.

CHAPTER 9

Alessandro Prospero Sanchez y Farinacci was the offspring of a Puerto Rican businessman and an Italian actress who appeared in Puerto Rican and Mexican television commercials in the 1950's. She had a bit part in a B movie shot in Mexico and Texas, where the family settled in the early sixties. Alessandro was the third of six children and idolized his mother. His father was a distant figure, often away on business trips and Alessandro dreaded his return because he was a tyrant at home, though he never hit his wife, or his daughters, only his sons.

When Alessandro was a senior drama major at the University of Texas, he came home and announced at the dinner table that he was gay. His mother began crying and his father, though outraged, restrained his usual violent temper and simply told Alessandro that he was no longer welcome in the Sanchez household. Alessandro, having anticipated his banishment, returned to school, graduated with honors, and packed his bags for San Francisco.

On an unusually sunny afternoon in the Castro Valley, Alessandro was doing pushups on the deck of the old Victorian mansion where he shared a top floor apartment with a former classmate at the University of Texas. His roommate, Terry, was at the piano in the living room plunking out a tune at the piano that he was composing for a movie to be shot in San Francisco. The door to the deck was open.

"Seventy-one, seventy-two, seventy..."

"Can't you count to yourself, Alessandro," Terry said. "I can't hear myself think."

"Seventy-three, seventy-four, seventy-five..."

Terry stopped playing. "I *said*—"

"I heard you. Seventy-six, seventy-seven—just twenty-three more."

"Christ!" Terry slammed the lid down onto the keyboard. "Give your muscles a break. They're going to explode one of these days."

"I thought you liked my muscles. Seventy-nine, eighty—"

"I need a drink."

"You'll need a liver transplant by the time you're forty. Eighty-two, eighty-three, eighty-four..."

Terry, who had a very slight build and a rapidly receding hairline, went to the kitchen. "I already *feel* forty." He retrieved a glass from a cabinet, opened the refrigerator, and poured some ice into it. This was followed by a generous shot of vodka and a small amount of tonic.

"Ninety-nine, one hundred. Done!" Alessandro stood on the deck for a few moments catching his breath and admiring the view. Then he came into the living room.

"Put some clothes on," Terry said. "You look absolutely obscene in those bikini panties."

Alessandro grinned. "They're not panties—it's a speedo suit. For swimmers."

"Still, they're obscene." Alessandro walked over to his roommate and wrapped his muscular arms around him.

"Please, Alessandro," Terry said. "I'm working."

Alessandro smiled, took the glass from Terry's hand, and set it down on the kitchen counter. Then he kissed him.

"I'm serious, Alessandro—I've got to get this score done by to-morrow morning. The meeting's at ten o'clock and—"

Alessandro kissed him again and ground his crotch into Terry's.

"No, no, no!" Terry pulled away and went back to the piano, where he sat down and began picking out a new tune.

Alessandro picked up the vodka and tonic and handed it to him. "Here—you'll need this to get the creative juices flowing."

"Thank you." Terry took a sip. "I'm afraid I'll be a nervous wreck until I get this done. Then we can play."

Alessandro sighed. "I'll take a shower and get dressed. I'm going out."

Terry went back to the keyboard, plunked out a melody, and made a notation on a sheet of music. When he heard the shower in the bathroom he put the sheet down and raised his voice. "Where are you going?"

"I told you—out."

"I hope that doesn't mean you're going trolling along Castro Street."

There was no answer from the bedroom and Terry went back to the piano. He was beginning to piece together a song that was a cross between Duke Ellington and a piano concerto by Mozart.

The shower stopped and Alessandro soon reappeared, zipping up his cargo pants and tucking in a fishnet shirt that stretched tightly across his pectoral muscles. "That sounds pretty good. Like Amadeus in Birdland."

"Thank you." Terry turned around and looked at Alessandro's choice of attire. "Oh, my God! You *are* going trolling." He went back to the piano. "Well, just don't bring some bimbo back here. I'm not into a ménage à trois."

"Not even with a woman?"

Terry stopped playing and turned around. "Oh, please. With that girl you brought over here the other night. The clown?"

"She's not a clown. She's a mime. And she's in the play we're doing on California Street. I think she's a very good actress, even though she doesn't know it yet."

Terry turned back to the piano and started from the beginning of his new tune. "Well, she *is* a sweet girl. But rather naive. I hope you won't corrupt her the way you've corrupted me."

"Aw." Alessandro went over to Terry and kissed him behind the ear. "I've brought out the best in you and you know it. Besides, you love to suck my cock."

Terry continued playing. "I only do it because it makes you happy."

"Right. And because it's the biggest cock around. I'm going out."

"Bye."

Terry watched as Alessandro made for the stairs to the ground floor of the house. When he was out of sight, he stopped playing and took a long sip of his vodka and tonic.

"Bitch," he muttered.

CHAPTER 10

Thuy Nguyen was nothing if not resourceful.

After saving up the money she earned as a 'B' girl in Saigon, she managed to purchase a forged I.D. that gave her access to unrestricted areas of most U.S. military bases. This I.D. was very expensive, but was worth more than a first-class ticket to America on a major airline. It enabled her to hitch a ride on a C-130 at Tan Son Nhut Air Base in Saigon to Guam, where she posed as a translator for Army intelligence and spent the night in a comfortable dormitory for WAC nurses. The next day she managed to talk her way onto a flight to Hunter Liggett Army Base in California, about one hundred and fifty miles south of San Francisco, and spent two weeks teaching enlisted soldiers Vietnamese when she stumbled onto a list of recently discharged veterans in the base library. Among the names was Corporal Benjamin Earl Franklin, General Discharge.

Corporal Franklin had listed his intended destination as San Francisco. She bought a bus ticket to San Francisco, put up in a cheap Mission hotel, and went straight to the V.A. center on Polk Street the next morning. There she found the information she needed.

"You always say you want to go to San Francisco," Thuy said. "Why are you corporal now?"

"I'm not anything now, Thuy." Ben sat across from Thuy in the living room of the house on Haight Street with a coffee table between them. "I'm a bouncer in a bar."

"What is 'bouncer'?" Thuy put her tea cup on the table. She always preferred tea to coffee.

"You know, like the guys they had in the bars in Anh Khe. Big guys like me to break up fights."

Thuy smiled. "You always the big guy. No one mess with Ben."

Ben laughed. "Yeah. I don't remember there being any trouble when I was around." He put his bottle of beer down on the table. "But Thuy, what are we gonna do? You can't stay here—it's already too crowded. There's a guy sleeping in the basement and the attic's rented out, too. My room's too small for the two of us."

"We get apartment."

"Apartments are expensive in San Francisco." Ben sighed and leaned back in his chair. "If you get a job, though, maybe we could afford something in Chinatown."

Thuy frowned. "I don't like Chinatown. What about your bar? They need waitress?"

Ben picked up his beer again, took a swallow, and scratched his chin. "Maybe. But it's not like the Red Dragon in Saigon. You'd have to serve drinks and hope for good tips."

"I'm not B girl anymore, Ben. How much tips?"

"I dunno. Travis does pretty good. Maybe he can train you as a bartender."

Thuy smiled. "I can make drinks. We make money. But Ben—" She got up from her chair and sat next to him. "I want to go to school. Can I go to your school?"

Ben put his arm around her and kissed her on the cheek. "Sure. Anybody can go to San Francisco State. But I think you have to have a green card. How the heck did you get here, anyway?"

Thuy snuggled into Ben's shoulder. "Military I.D. I not need passport."

"Whew! You better burn that I.D. It could get you into a heap of trouble."

"It very expensive. Anyway, it come in handy in future."

"Hmm. And something else, Thuy."

"What?"

"You're going to have to start using those little 'the's' and 'a's' if you're gonna be a college student."

Thuy sat up abruptly. "I am translator!"

Ben smiled and took another sip of his beer.

"Oh," Thuy said. "I am *a* translator." She settled back against Ben's shoulder and closed her eyes. Ben seemed contemplative.

After a few moments, the door to Marcella's bedroom, which was just off the living room, opened. Out stepped Alessandro, tucking in his shirt.

Ben looked at him.

"Oh, hi, Ben," Alessandro said. "What's up?"

"Nothing much," Ben said. "I didn't know you was here."

"Just stopped in to say hello to Marcella. Shop talk. Who's your friend?"

"This is Thuy. A friend of mine from Vietnam."

Thuy sat up and looked at Alessandro.

"'Twee'?" Alessandro came over to the coffee table, reached across it, and shook Thuy's hand. "A pleasure to meet you."

"Likewise, Mr., uh—"

"Oh," Ben said. "I'm sorry. This is Alessandro, honey. He's the star of the play Marcella's in."

"Play?"

"About Alexander the Great," Ben said. "It's going to be a big hit."

Alessandro laughed. "We'll see. Opening night's next Thursday. You're coming, aren't you, Ben?"

"Sure," Ben said. His eyes went to the half-open door to Marcella's room.

Alessandro's eyes followed Ben's and back again. "Well, I'd better be going. Got some work to do. Again, it was a pleasure meeting you, Thuy."

"Yes," Thuy said. "Very nice."

Alessandro then proceeded to the front door and disappeared down the steps to the street.

"Nice fella," Thuy said. "A real gentleman."

Before Ben could respond to this statement, Marcella appeared in the door to her bedroom. She was disheveled and buttoning up her denim shirt.

"Oh, Ben—I didn't know you were here. I'm just going to the kitchen for coffee. Do you want some?"

"No thanks, Marcella." Ben held up his bottle. "Having a beer."

"Oh. How about you, uh—"

Thuy stared at her. "No, thank you. I drink tea."

"This is Thuy, Marcella. Friend of mine from—"

At this point the front door opened and Travis appeared. Everyone fell silent as he closed the door behind him. He faced the group. "Is it something I said?" He chuckled at his own joke.

"I thought you were at work," Marcella said.

"I don't go in till six. Henry's hired a new bartender. Hi, Ben, Thuy. What's up?"

"Excuse me," Marcella said, buttoning the last button on her shirt. "I've got to have some coffee—didn't sleep much last night. You want some, Travis?"

Travis looked at the grim expressions on the faces of Ben and Thuy, then at Marcella, whose back was to him as she disappeared into the kitchen. "Sure, why not?" He walked over to the coffee table and sat down. "Did somebody die around here? Cheer up, you two— I just heard about an apartment that'll be available soon in Twin Peaks. Near the school. Cheap."

"Yeah?" Ben said.

"Yeah. A classmate of mine who's graduating at the end of the month. I told him about you two and he said he'd ask the landlord to hold it for you."

"How much?" Ben said.

"I don't know. You'll have to talk to him. But I'm sure it's cheap."

Marcella returned from the kitchen with two cups of coffee. She handed one to Travis, went back to her room, and closed the door.

Travis stared at the door. "What's the matter with her?"

Ben shifted his weight on the sofa and withdrew his arm from around Thuy's shoulder. "She was up late last night at rehearsal. Don't you go to rehearsals anymore?"

"Not anymore. I've only got about twelve lines." He blew across the surface of his coffee. "Is that what Alessandro was doing here? I saw him walk up Castro Street. I guess he was here ironing out some last minute details with Marcella before opening night."

Ben and Thuy said nothing.

Travis stared at them. "Oh." He put down his coffee and stood. "Always the last to know...I think I'll go for a walk." He shoved his hands into the pockets of his jeans, stared at Marcella's door one more time, and left.

CHAPTER 11

Travis walked east along the panhandle brooding over this most recent revelation. What a fool he had been to expect Marcella to be faithful to him, especially as she was working so closely with Alessandro every night at rehearsals. Andrea was right—the man was bisexual and determined to seduce every creature on two legs.

He turned right on Scott Street and continued until he came to Duboce Park, where he sat down on a park bench. A young guy with red hair was throwing a frisbee to his dog, a golden retriever. He always liked golden retrievers—beautiful, tawny animals with a good disposition. Maybe he should get one. Unconditional love and absolute loyalty.

After watching the dog leap into the air and catch the frisbee in his teeth a few times, he got up and continued to Noe Street, where he caught a passing trolley. He wasn't really sure of where he was going. How did Marcella see him? Just a friend? Sexual jealously was completely out of fashion in San Francisco. Most regarded it as a relic of the past, an outmoded, discredited emotion associated with our parents' generation. Still, he was jealous. And even though, say, Andrea, was better-looking, Marcella had a certain intangible quality, more than just sex appeal—though she had plenty of that. He wanted to possess her, and he didn't want to share her with anyone.

He got off the trolley on Market Street and started to walk up Taylor towards his apartment when he remembered that he was suppose to work that night. He turned west on Ellis into the heart of the Tenderloin.

"Hey, Buddy!" came a voice slightly behind him. "Someone stole my wallet and I need bus fare to get home. Can you help me out?"

Travis stopped and looked at the man. He was about thirty-five and had a three-day growth along with a cut over his left eye covered with recently dried blood. He was wearing a dirty moth-eaten cardigan sweater and shoes with the leather tops separating from the soles. He would have been comical except for the look of desperation on his face. "How much do you need?"

The man looked surprised. "I don't know. I think...well, it's a long way to, uh, Milpitas—that's where my sister lives."

"Milpitas? That's near San Jose, isn't it?"

"Uh, yeah. Sort of."

Travis pulled out his wallet, extracted a twenty dollar bill and handed it to him.

The man's eyes bulged as he examined the bill. "Thanks, mister—you're a good man." He then scurried away towards Polk Street where there were several bars. The bus station was in the opposite direction.

Travis knew this. Why did him give him the money?

He turned up Hyde Street with the intention of avoiding the worst part of the Tenderloin. The panhandler had called him a good man. Was he? And was that all he aspired to be? Wasn't that enough?

He caught a cable car at Jackson after having worked up a sweat climbing the hill to California Street. This gave him a respite for about three blocks until he reached Vallejo, where he stepped off the car and headed to Henry Africa's.

The new bartender was a woman named Alice, who said she was a former cocktail waitress at the St. Francis and wanted to move up the ladder of the service industry. She was about twenty-five, blond, and had enormous breasts, which she liked to show off to their best advantage; i.e., she favored low-cut dresses and halter tops. Henry hired her as a day bartender, but she agreed to work a double shift when one of the male bartenders called in sick. The tips poured in at the end of the night, and fortunately, there was an even split for all the bartenders. Alice was easily responsible for two-thirds of the take.

At about ten o'clock, Andrea showed up. She came down to Travis' end of the bar and sat on a stool, which was really a long-legged chair with comfortable upholstered arms and back. "Who's the new broad?"

Travis was cleaning a glass. "That's Alice. Just started today."

Andrea, whose eyesight was poor but refused to wear glasses or contacts, squinted down the bar where Alice was pouring a drink for a customer. "She's about to fall out of that dress. I'll bet they're not even hers."

Travis smiled. "Cantilevered. What'll you have, Andrea?"

"The usual. A lemon drop martini."

"Okay, but I suggest you pace yourself this time. Sip, don't gulp."

Andrea looked at him with a sardonic smile. "What am I—your kid sister?"

"Somebody's got to look out for you. You get home all right the other night?"

"Yeah. The cabbie made a pass at me, but I gave him a hard slap and he folded like a cheap suit."

Travis laughed. "Not your type?"

"Hardly. You gonna mix me a drink or what?"

Travis set about mixing the drink.

Andrea was surprisingly restrained for the next couple of hours, both in her drinking and her behavior. She accepted an offer to dance by one of the patrons and dutifully returned to her stool at the bar. "An insurance salesman from Kansas City. Annuities, whole life. What a bore."

"Maybe you'll get lucky," Travis said.

"I wish. You know, these fern bars seem to attract Middle America— white picket fence, two dogs and a cat, three kids, and wifey stays home to protect the nest while hubby goes hunting for pussy. How about another martini?"

Travis poured some ice into the shaker. "Remember—pace yourself. I don't want to have to pour you into a cab again."

Andrea sat up straight and looked Travis in the eye. "You know the trouble with you, Travis, honey?"

Travis shook the shaker as the band began to play again. "No— what?"

"You're a prig."

"A prig?"

"Yeah. You could have slept with me that night I got sloshed, but you didn't. You could've slept with Marcella by now, but you haven't. You could've—"

"How do you know I haven't slept with Marcella?" Travis poured the martini into a fresh glass.

"Oh, puh-leze! It's obvious. She's frustrated. She wants you to knock her up. But you won't, so she lets Alessandro put his hand up her dress at rehearsals and she doesn't even like him."

Travis stared at Andrea for a moment. "She wants me to knock her up?"

Andrea took a long sip of her drink. "Sure. She wants to have a child and she wants the father to have the right genes. You've got the right genes. Alessandro's genes came out of some Puerto Rican cesspool. Oh, God—why am I telling you this?"

The band was loud enough now that no one could hear their conversation. Travis exchanged glances with Ben at the door as a group of young men filed into the bar. One or two went over to the bandstand and listened. The other three bellied up to the bar. "Excuse me, Andrea. I've got customers."

"Sure." Andrea popped a cherry into her mouth, chewed it up, swallowed, and worked the stem around with her tongue. She pulled the stem out and admired the knot she had just tied. Then she put the stem in her hair behind her ear, as if it were a flower.

"Wanna dance?"

She turned around to see one of the young men who had just come in. He was a kid, twenty-one at the most, and wore tight jeans and a cowboy shirt. "Sure."

As she danced with this kid, who was not bad-looking, with jet black hair and long sideburns like Elvis, she hardly looked at him. Instead, she watched Travis as he poured drinks for the newcomers. When the dance number was over, she declined an invitation from the young man to sit at a table with him and went back to her stool at the bar.

Travis eventually made his way back down to her end. "You okay?"

"Sure."

"Want another martini?"

"No. I'd like a cup of coffee."

Travis was taken aback. "Sugar?"

"And a little lemon. I like lemon in all my drinks. Prevents scurvy, you know."

Travis put a pot of coffee on. When it was ready, he set a cup and saucer down in front of Andrea and poured some coffee into the cup. "You're full of surprises, Andrea."

Andrea suddenly put her hand on his. "Travis, baby—come home with me tonight. I promise I won't drink anymore."

Travis suspended the coffee pot in midair, as Andrea's hand prevented him from putting it back on the burner.

"Please," she said. "I'll be good. And you won't regret it."

"What about Marcella? I can't—"

"Marcella's gone, baby—can't you see that?"

"But you just said that she wants—"

"Your genes? Yes, baby, but she can get your genes in a test tube. It's Alessandro who turns her on. And it's you who turns me on."

Travis continued to stare at Andrea for a few moments, during which time he couldn't prevent his eyes from straying to her breasts.

"Bartender! How about some service here?"

The trance broken, Travis put down the coffee pot and went to serve the customer.

CHAPTER 12

Andrea's apartment in North Beach was near the corner of Lombard and Grant. It was on the top floor of a fifth floor walk-up in a building that survived the 1906 earthquake. And it looked like it had not been painted since then. But on the inside everything looked new: refinished wood floors, oriental carpets, glossy-white three-step moldings, and modern appliances. The view of the bay was spectacular, though leavened with a heavy mist. From the glassed-in sun porch one could see the Golden Gate to the northwest, Tiburon and Sausalito just east of the bridge, and Alcatraz was so close that Travis felt that he could reach out and touch it.

He sat in a wicker chair on the sun porch with his feet up on an ottoman sipping his morning coffee. Andrea hadn't let him sleep much during the night. Just when he felt exhausted and about to fall into a deep slumber, he would feel Andrea's hand rubbing his chest, then his stomach, then manipulating his penis. Each time, he thought he couldn't possibly get it up again, but somehow Andrea prevailed. When he felt that she was satisfied at last and he began to doze off, he was awakened by the sun. Andrea was snoring.

There was nothing to do at that point but to get up and make some coffee.

After about ten minutes he heard Andrea stirring about in the bedroom. First a yawn, then a 'thump'—did she fall out of bed?—followed by an 'Oh, shit,' and finally the sound of the bathroom door closing. Another five minutes and he heard the toilet flush, followed by running water. She was taking a shower.

Travis wondered how he was going to make his exit. It wasn't that he didn't like Andrea—she was very amusing and, he thought, had a good heart. Nor was she lacking in intelligence. She was probably better educated than he was. He couldn't put his finger on it—maybe she was just too, too...promiscuous? No, he didn't know that. She swore like a sailor, but he hadn't known her to go to bed with anyone he knew, at any rate. Not Alessandro, not Sam the director, not Nearchos the playwright, not Bill the cab driver. That is, if he could take her word for it. And what if she was screwing all of them? So what? She was nothing to him—except a friend. He did feel somehow responsible for her, though she would laugh at the idea.

"Hey, Baby, you were wonderful last night." She came up from behind him, kissed him on the cheek and sat on the ottoman, which was covered in a blue and white checkerboard fabric. She had on a white terry cloth bathrobe that barely covered her thighs and exposed about three-quarters of her breasts as she leaned over a glass-topped coffee table and began pouring a white, sugary substance out onto the glass from a plastic bag. She made four neat, parallel lines of it and put the plastic bag in the pocket of her bathrobe. "Want some coke?"

Travis sipped his coffee, put the cup down, and looked at the white lines. In Vietnam, he had participated in a court-martial that sent an enlisted guy to the stockade for snorting cocaine. It wasn't uncommon. Marijuana was so prevalent that he and most junior officers simply ignored it. And of course, he had smoked a little dope himself from time to time. "No, thanks. Caffeine is about all I can handle at the moment."

"Handle? Coke will help you handle anything. You look tired, baby. This will pick you up." She reached for her purse, which was sitting on the chair where she left it the night before, pulled out her wallet, and extracted a ten dollar bill. She rolled it up, inserted it into her right nostril and bent down to the table. After snorting a line into that nostril, she repeated the process with the other. Then she sat up, threw her head back, and closed her eyes.

Travis watched her for a moment.

She lowered her head and opened her eyes. "Oh, that feels good. Come on, baby, those two lines are for you."

Travis looked at the lines of cocaine. "Don't you worry about getting addicted?"

Andrea laughed. "Aren't you addicted to coffee? I'll bet you consumed gallons of it in Vietnam."

Travis smiled. It was true—he must have drunk ten cups a day—sometimes twenty—when he was in the army. And he hadn't entirely broken the habit since. Down to maybe six cups. "Where do you get this stuff?"

"A friend. Don't worry—it's very pure. I don't shell out good money for junk."

Travis stared at the lines again. They could hardly amount to a fraction of an ounce.

"And," Andrea said with a lascivious smile, "it makes for great sex."

Travis smiled back. "I thought you said I was wonderful last night."

"You were, baby, but this will make you more wonderful."

Travis looked at the lines again.

Andrea handed him the rolled up bill. "Here. It won't hurt you—I promise."

Travis looked at the rolled up bill for a moment, took it from her and inserted it into his left nostril. "Like this?"

"It's not complicated."

Travis bent down and snorted one of the lines through the nostril. He sat up and felt a medicinal-like fluid drip down the back of his throat. It was not unpleasant. He bent over and snorted up the other line. Then he leaned his head back like he had just seen Andrea do, and allowed the fluid to run down his throat. Or was it his lungs?

"See, baby?" Andrea stood and untied her robe. She let it drop around her shoulders and held it there for a moment as Travis opened his eyes. She was not wearing anything under the robe, and the sunlight glistened on her public hairs, which he saw clearly for the first time. They were blond, like the hair on her head. Then she dropped the robe to the floor and sat with her legs apart on his lap. He was in his underwear, government-issued boxers. He felt the miraculous resurgence of an erection.

"Oh, baby!" Andrea said, reaching inside his shorts and grabbing his penis, "you've got the most beautiful cock in the world!"

Travis was beginning to feel the effects of the cocaine. It was a kind of rush, but surprisingly mild—he had expected something more dramatic. But Andrea was supplying all the drama. She pulled off his boxers, threw them to the floor, and began sucking his penis. She began stroking it at the same time until he ejaculated and then she threw her head back and closed her eyes as she had done with the cocaine.

She licked her lips. "Your cum is sweet in my mouth. Sweet!"

Travis thought this was the finale, and that he couldn't possibly get another erection, but Andrea began stroking his penis again until it reasserted itself and placed her pelvis over his. Then she inserted it in her vagina and began a slow, rhythmic undulation of her hips. And it *was* slow. It seemed a half an hour before Travis ejaculated again and he fell back into the chair, this time truly exhausted.

Andrea curled up into a ball on his lap and nestled into the crook of his shoulder. "Oh, baby—that was so fine, so fine."

Now it seemed that the effects of the cocaine had worn off. Andrea had fallen asleep. He slowly stood up, cradling her in his arms and carried her back to the bedroom. Once she was comfortable in the bed, he retrieved his boxers from the sun room, gathered up the rest of his clothes, and got dressed. He took one last look at the panoramic scenery, with the fog beginning to lift from Angel Island, went to the front door, and set the lock. After closing the door behind him, he descended the five flights of stairs, and emerged onto Lombard Street.

As he turned south and approached Washington Square, he was still thinking about Andrea. What was he to do with her? He didn't love her and though she claimed that he 'turned her on,' the depth of her feelings hardly matched the intensity of her orgasms, which seemed infinite and frequent.

When he got to the square, he noticed a large number of people gathered at the center of it. There was some kind of performance going on, perhaps a street magician, or perhaps...

He stepped onto a sidewalk that cut through the square and followed it until he could get a better view. On a raised platform, stood a familiar figure dressed in the classic mime's outfit—black spandex pants, candy-striped vest, and a battered stovepipe hat. White makeup and all, it was Marcella.

He stood back a little from the crowd and watched the show, sure that Marcella had not seen him. She took a tumble, righted herself, and continued her escape from an imagined villain. Soon, however, she runs into a 'policeman,' who is, of course, played by herself. The crowd roars with laughter as she tries to explain that she is the

victim, not the criminal, and after momentarily distracting the policeman, hastily makes her escape. Now she is pursued by both the
villain and the policeman, and others join them. The crowd roars
again.

Travis didn't wait until the performance was over. He took another sidewalk that emerged onto Columbus Avenue and crossed
the intersection to Powell.

He realized now that he was in love with Marcella, and only
Marcella, and it brought him to the edge of despair.

CHAPTER 13

Potrero Elementary was a crumbling edifice built in the 1920's and located in what was then a predominately immigrant neighborhood. Irish gangs roamed the streets, to be replaced by Hispanic and African-American gangs in the 50's and 60's. An overpass built for Highway 101 kept a good part of the school in the shadows until around one o'clock in the afternoon. Graffiti adorned almost every surface of the structure, though a couple of Hispanic artists had been brought in lately to paint over much of the graffiti with colorful murals.

On one of these gloomy mornings, Ben and Thuy stood behind a long table set up in the cafeteria some thirty feet opposite the stainless steel counters of the 'pay' line. The line of children at the makeshift tables was long and the food was free.

Ben ladled out blackbean soup into plastic bowls for each child, while Thuy served up dollops of rice with an ice-cream scoop and deposited them onto plastic plates. A third volunteer ladled out a kind of creole gumbo containing everything from shrimp to chitterlings over the rice.

The third volunteer was Bobby X.

"You take all you want, sweetheart," Bobby said to an eager six-year-old girl wearing a ragged calico dress with her hair in braids and red ribbons. "And if you're still hungry, come back for more."

The little girl did come back, as did many of the other children. After forty minutes or so, all of the children in the 'free' line had been served and a bell rang, signifying the start of classes.

Ben, Thuy, and Bobby began cleaning up and breaking down the tables.

"Them kids were sure hungry," Ben said, as he stacked a table in a corner. "You'd think they hadn't eaten for a week."

"Many of them haven't," Bobby said, wiping down the last remaining table. "At least not a proper meal. The white power structure sees to that."

The jargon that Bobby X employed at every opportunity disturbed Ben. "What's the white people got to do with it? Some of them kids are white."

Bobby shook his head. "You need some political education, Brother. I told you about our meeting in Oakland Thursday night, but you didn't show."

"I was working," Ben said. "Besides, I'm getting plenty of political education out at San Francisco State. At least I think that's what it is."

"That's also part of the white power structure."

Ben considered this for a moment. "But the president of the university is a Japanese dude."

"Hayakawa sucked up to the white power structure a long time ago. He identifies with white dudes. And guess who his boss is—Ronald Reagan."

Thuy was listening to this conversation while covering some tupperware containers with saran wrap. She frowned but said nothing.

"I didn't know about that," Ben said. "I just know that there's white dudes, black dudes, yellow dudes, Hispanic dudes—every color and ethnicity you can think of out there. And it seems to me—"

Ben's peroration was interrupted by the appearance of two uniformed policemen at the door to the cafeteria.

"Speaking of your white power structure," Bobby said. "What do you think those dudes are here for?"

"I dunno," Ben said.

"I'll tell you—they don't like black folks like you and me giving out free food to our little brothers and sisters."

"Hello, Bobby," one of the policemen said as he approached. He kept his eyes on Bobby's hands. "I see you're playing the Good Samaritan today."

"Just seeing that little black children get enough nourishment so they can learn. Since when did you start wearing a San Francisco police uniform, Dan? I thought the Oakland force chewed you up and spit you out."

"We had a little disagreement, that's all. My brother-in-law's on the 'Frisco force. Said they needed an officer."

Bobby sneered. "Needed an 'enforcer,' eh? Show these young black dudes in San Francisco who's boss."

The officer named Dan reached out towards Bobby and patted

the breast pocket of his jacket. Then he extracted a chrome-plated .457 magnum revolver. "This to protect yourself from the students who don't care for your choice of cuisine?"

Bobby stood rigidly still. "I got a permit for that."

"Yeah?" Dan said. "Let's see it."

"Ain't got it with me."

"Didn't think so. You know, you could have strapped it to your belt and it would be perfectly legal."

"They don't allow open carry in the school—you know that."

Dan handed the revolver to the other officer. "We'll hold it for you at the Hall of Justice. You know where it is?"

"Yeah. I know where it is."

"And we'll check to see if your permit is up to date. If it is, you'll be on your way." Dan looked at Ben, then Thuy. "I think it's a fine thing you're doing here, Bobby. Who's your friend?"

"Why don't you ask him?"

"Ben Franklin, sir," Ben said. "I'm just helping out."

"Well, with a name like that I'm not surprised. You a Puma?"

Ben looked sideways at Bobby. "Sort of. I guess. I just got back from Vietnam and thought I could help the little kids get some nourishment."

"That's admirable, Ben. Vietnam, eh?" Dan looked at Thuy. "This your girlfriend?"

"Yeah."

"You brought her all the way from Vietnam?"

"Well...she kind of brought herself."

Dan laughed. "I'll bet she did. We appreciate your service there, Ben. You packing heat like Mr. Bobby here?"

"No, sir."

"Mind if I check?"

"Go right ahead."

Dan approached Ben and indicated that he should raise his arms into the air. Ben did so. When he was through patting him down and satisfied that he was unarmed, he turned back to Bobby. "You should follow Ben's example, Bobby. There's no need to arm your-self when you're feeding kids. What were you thinking?" Then he walked away and met the other officer at the door. He turned back for a moment. "See you at the station, Bobby. I'm sure you don't want to donate this piece to the force. Must have cost a bunch." Then he disappeared into the hallway, followed by his partner.

Ben looked at Bobby, who was seething with anger. "I think he's right about bringing a gun in here—"

"Shut up. He ain't got no right to come on these premises. He thinks he can do anything he wants."

Ben said nothing. He looked at Thuy. "You ready, Thuy?"

Thuy nodded.

Bobby looked at Thuy's dour expression, then turned to Ben. "Sorry I was short with you. It's just that that cop is one of the worst. He killed a brother not long ago and got off scot free."

Ben's eyes went to the door. "I ain't heard about that."

"You just got here. You'll learn. You coming to next week's meeting?"

"I...I don't know. Seems to me that I don't need no training to feed school kids."

Bobby sighed and clapped Ben on the shoulder. "You don't want to spend the rest of your life being a bouncer and a house nigger, Ben. I've got big plans for you. And there's money in it."

"Money?"

"Sure. The Pumas got a command structure just like the military. And like the military, the higher you go, the higher the pay grade. What was your rank in the army?"

"Staff sergeant."

"There you go. You got the experience. You have any men under you?"

"Sure. When we went out on patrol, I'd be in charge of six, maybe eight men."

"Patrol. That means combat, doesn't it?"

"Yeah."

Bobby gave Ben another pat on the back. Then he pulled on a pair of black leather gloves. "See you next week at the meeting. Thanks for your help, Thuy. You've got a good man here." He walked to the door and didn't look back.

Thuy's eyes followed him. "Bobby a bad man."

"Thuy..." Ben looked troubled. "Bobby's had some rough treatment from the police. All he's trying to do is help black people gain their rights." He made a sweeping gesture with his hand. "Look at these kids—half of 'em can't afford breakfast, or lunch, neither. Without the Pumas, they'd probably starve to death. And nobody else cares."

Thuy stared at him for a moment, then went to the kitchen and put several containers of food in the refrigerator. A couple of staff members helped her. Then she came back. "Like you said—why you need guns to feed little kids? Bobby just want to make trouble."

Ben sighed and put his arm around her. "You saw that cop—he'd just as soon shoot Bobby as look at him. He's got a right to protect himself."

Thuy caressed his arm. "Ben—you not go to meeting next week."

"I'm not planning on it. I've got to work. Which reminds me—I want to introduce you to Henry at the bar. Come on, let's go."

CHAPTER 14

"What is the relevance of Alexander the Great to contemporary America?"

This was a question posed to the playwright, Nearchos Andropoulos after a sneak preview for the sake of prospective investors.

Andropoulos ran his hand through his long, luxuriant white hair. He sat on the stage in a chair next to that of Sam Thomas, the director. "Alexander was the first to dream of the brotherhood of man. It is still a dream to this day."

"Then he wasn't successful," the man said.

"To a large extent he was," Andropoulos said. "He created an empire that stretched from Greece to China. He united peoples as diverse as the Egyptians, the Afghans, and the Indians. He commanded a ceremony once that married ten thousand of his men to Persian women. He married a Persian princess himself and dressed in Persian clothes."

"Was he gay?" another gentleman asked.

"It is not clear," Andropoulos said, apparently irritated by the question. "He may have been gay, or bisexual, or he may have been strictly heterosexual and the victim of a vicious campaign by his political enemies at home who wished to discredit him as a deviant and a degenerate." He chuckled. "You can see that their efforts were in large part successful—here you are asking that question more than two thousand years later."

There was a rippling of laughter in the audience which consisted of about a dozen potential backers and most of the cast members.

After several more questions, the assembly began to break up. Some left immediately, and some remained with further questions for Nearchos and Sam. Two or three pledged to invest in the production.

Just as the cast members were beginning to leave, Ian, the owner of the pub and the theater, appeared at the entrance. "A round of drinks awaits your pleasure downstairs, my thespian friends. The performance went like a bomb."

The cast members exchanged puzzled looks.

Ian laughed. "Sorry—sometimes I think I'm back in London. I

mean to say that the play looks to be a success. Come, come—be merry." A bit tipsy—as he nearly always was—Ian began herding the cast members through the door like sheep.

Travis found himself walking down the stairs to the pub between Andrea and Marcella. This was not an entirely comfortable position for him. He tried to think of something to say to Marcella without offending Andrea. Or Marcella. "Well, it looks like the play will have some financial backing."

"Did you see the man in the dark pinstripe suit?" Andrea said. "That's Irving Feinstein, the Broadway producer."

"A Broadway producer?" Travis said. "Really?"

"Yeah, baby—" Andrea put her arm through Travis.' "Big time. This thing could really take off."

Travis looked askance at Marcella to see if she noticed Andrea's maneuver. But she was looking over her shoulder.

"Where's Alessandro?" she said.

Travis grimaced. "Talking to Sam. Come on—let's have that drink before Ian changes his mind."

The three of them found an empty booth and ordered their drinks. Andrea nearly dragged Travis into her side of the booth while Marcella sat on the other side. Marcella kept looking to the foot of the stairs as if hoping Alessandro would appear at any moment.

When the waitress brought them their drinks—a Newcastle ale for Travis, a pink gin fizz for Andrea, and a glass of white wine for Marcella—Marcella was still staring at the bottom of the stairs. "What do they have to talk about? The production is ready to go— he's marvelous as Alexander."

"Honey," Andrea said, "I think he and Sam have a little thing going."

Marcella's head whipped around. "What do you mean?"

Andrea took a sip of her drink through a straw. "Where have you been, honey? This is San Francisco—the girls love the boys and the boys do, too. Alessandro didn't come here for the likes of you and me."

Marcella looked stunned. First she looked at Andrea, then at Travis. "Is it true, Travis? Is Alessandro gay?"

Travis shrugged his shoulders.

"Bi, honey." Andrea picked the cherry out of her drink and popped it into her mouth. "He's had a thing going with Sam from day one. And he shacks up with another fairy queen in the Castro."

Marcella again looked at Travis in disbelief. Then she looked to the stairs again and saw Alessandro descending alongside Sam. They both paused for a moment and looked into the pub. Alessandro seemed not to see her and the two of them continued to the street door, which was out of the booth's line of sight.

Marcella returned her eyes to Andrea and Travis, then stared into her wine glass. "I guess I am naive. But he's so masculine!"

Andrea extracted the cherry stem from her mouth and admired the knot she had tied. "A lot of them are, honey. You can't tell by that." She looked at Travis and grinned. "There's natural masculinity like Travis here has, and then there's the phony masculinity like Alessandro has. All that bodybuilding is just a cover-up. A trick to confuse innocent little damsels like you and me." She batted her eyelashes.

Marcella looked at Andrea, then Travis, who tried not to look as if he were saying, "I told you so." She then raised her glass to her lips and turned it up until she had drained the contents. "I think I'll have another."

Andrea sucked on her straw until the glass was empty and the rushing air made a gurgling sound. "Me, too, honey."

Travis ordered another round. While they were waiting, a young man who had been sitting with the investors earlier came over to their booth. He was of an unprepossessing appearance, thin, prematurely balding, a barely noticeable mustache, and oversized horn-rimmed glasses. He wore an expensive, highly-finished leather sports coat that Travis guessed was made in Spain. He held in his hand a snifter full of brandy.

"May I join you?" He directed his question to Travis, but his eyes moved quickly to Andrea and stopped there. He seemed not to notice Marcella.

"Sure," Travis said, indicating the empty space next to Marcella.

Marcella scooted over a little and the man sat down.

"I think your little play looks promising," he said. "Good performances all around." His eyes remained on Andrea, who seemed to

"Have a seat."
enjoy his attention.

"Thanks," Travis said. "But Andrea and I just have bit parts." He gestured towards Marcella. "Marcella has the plum role of Roxana."

The man glanced at Marcella. "Yes, you do a terrific job. You're just right for the role."

Marcella seemed wary. "Thank you."

The young man's eyes quickly returned to Andrea. "But you have a remarkable presence, too, Miss—"

"Andrea."

"Andrea. Even though you're only on stage for a few minutes."

Andrea laughed. "Six minutes to be exact."

The young man smiled. "Seemed longer to me."

There was an awkward silence as the young man continued to stare at Andrea. "Oh," he said. "I forgot to introduce myself. My name is Howard Hill. Let me give you my card." He extracted a card from his wallet and handed it across the table to Andrea.

Andrea took the card. "Hillcrest Productions? Sounds like a movie company."

"It is. Low budget, mostly, but we're growing."

The drinks arrived and Howard insisted on paying for all.

"Thanks." Travis took a sip of his ale. "What kind of movies do you make, Howard?"

Howard smiled. "We're kind of in a niche market. Some people call them 'blue movies.'"

"Oh," Andrea said. "Soft porn."

"You could call them that. Some soft, some a little harder. Depends on the audience you're targeting."

"What brings you here tonight?" Travis said.

"Sam asked me to come. We took a directing class together at USC."

'USC?" Andrea brightened. "The film school?"

"That's right," Howard said. "Sam decided that his forte was the theater and came here. We're shooting in San Rafael, so—"

"San Rafael?" Andrea said. "Isn't that where George Lukas has a studio?"

"Yeah. We're using some of his facilities for editing, but mostly we're shooting at a country inn just north of town."

"How exciting," Andrea said. She sucked on the straw of her gin fizz until the familiar gurgling sound was heard.

"Would you like another?" Howard said.

"Sure," Andrea said. "But I think I'd like to have something less sweet. What are you drinking?"

"Courvoisier."

"I'll have some of that."

It was clear to Travis, as well as Marcella, where Andrea was going to end up at the end of the evening. Or at least who she was going to end up with. Travis was relieved, for until Howard showed up, he wasn't sure how he could disengage himself from Andrea.

"Sam says that Alessandro's having a party at his place in the Castro," Howard said after another round of drinks. "There ought to be some interesting people there. Are you coming?"

Though Howard looked around the table as he said this, it was clear that he was directing his question to Andrea.

"I've got a class tomorrow morning," Marcella said. "But thanks, anyway."

"Me, too." Travis chuckled. "We're still college students."

Howard smiled, then looked at Andrea. "Andrea?"

"Sure. Why not? Do you think you could bring a bottle of this Cour, Cour—"

"Courvoisier? Sure. I'll buy one at the bar." Howard rose and went to the bar.

"Careful," Travis said to Andrea. "Watch what goes into your glass."

Andrea, who was already beginning to slur her words, looked at Travis indignantly. "I can take care of myself, Travis, honey. This could be a big opportunity."

Howard came back with the bottle of Courvoisier. "Ready?"

"Ready," Andrea said.

She rose, as did Travis and Marcella.

"Nice meeting you folks," Howard said. "Good luck with the play."

"Thanks," Travis said. He and Marcella watched as Howard, wielding the bottle in one hand and two brandy snifters in the other, escorted Andrea to the door.

"I hope she'll be safe," Marcella said.

"Sam will keep an eye on her."

"But who will keep an eye on Sam?"

Travis looked at Marcella and shrugged. "I dunno. You want me to call a cab for you?"

"Why don't we walk?"

Travis was a bit taken aback. He didn't expect Marcella to invite him along. "It's a long way to walk."

"I need to burn off some of this alcohol. Besides, we need to talk."

"Okay."

They grabbed their jackets from the booth and headed for the front door. When they stepped out onto California Street, the temperature was dropping and the fog was rolling in from the bay. They put on their jackets and started walking towards Van Ness Avenue.

CHAPTER 15

Travis and Marcella walked about six blocks before either said a word except for Travis' admonition to watch for cars coming over the hill on Van Ness.

They paused for a moment at the corner of Geary and Fillmore to look at the Fillmore Auditorium, which was dark and apparently empty.

"I went to a Jefferson Airplane concert there when I was in high school," Marcella said. "I think everybody was on acid but me."

Travis chuckled. "Why weren't you?"

"I was too naive—I still am, it seems."

Travis thought it best not to comment on this allusion to Andrea's revelation concerning Alessandro. They walked on.

By the time they got to Alamo Square, Marcella was out of breath. Travis had become so accustomed to walking everywhere that he hardly noticed that they had been climbing a rather steep hill. They sat down on the stone steps at the entrance to the square.

"I love these Victorian Houses," Marcella said, gazing at a row of them across the street. "They call them 'painted ladies' since the owners started painting them all of the colors of the rainbow."

Travis noted the 'painted ladies,' but his eyes were drawn to the downtown skyline. "I always thought the Transamerica building looked like the Grand Inquisitor."

"The Grand Inquisitor?"

"Yeah. The priest in *The Brothers Karamazov* who confronts Christ in his prison cell."

Marcella patted his knee. "You're really into Dostoevsky, aren't you?"

Travis smiled. "I guess you could say that. I read most of his books when I was in Vietnam."

"Did you have so much time to read there?"

"Not at first, but by the end of my second tour, Nixon decided to give up 'pacifying' the villages and I was base-bound. Spent most of my time in an office without much to do."

Marcella put her head against his shoulder. "So what did this Grand Inquisitor do?"

"He didn't do much of anything. It was what he said that left an indelible impression on me."

"Which was..."

Travis laced his fingers between hers. "The whole thing was a fantasy, a dream. The Grand Inquisitor was at the top of the food chain during the Spanish Inquisition. That part was real. But Dostoevsky's dream—actually, it was Ivan Karamazov's—was that Christ returned to earth during the Middle Ages and walked about Spain preaching and healing. But this threatened the power of the Catholic church. So the Grand Inquisitor has him thrown into prison and just before he orders his execution, he explains why he must do it."

"And why did he feel he had to?"

"Because, he says, there would be no need for the church if Christ were to reveal himself. And that without the church, men would have no authority to surrender their will to. And that the last thing that men wanted was to be free."

Marcella sat up. "But that's crazy—everyone wants to be free."

"Are you so sure?" Travis nodded in the direction of a procession coming up the street. It was a group of twenty or thirty young people dressed in saffron gowns, the men with their heads shaved, the women with their heads covered with silk scarves. All were carrying candles that they cupped with their hands to keep the flames from blowing out in the strengthening breeze. An older man led the procession chanting something unintelligible every few seconds, and the followers answered with an equally unintelligible response. When the procession reached them, it turned up the steps and passed into the park without noting their presence.

Marcella looked over her shoulder until the last 'pilgrim' had disappeared. Then she turned to Travis. "They're hardly typical."

"Aren't they? They're just more demonstrative than most. And they've abandoned everything that they were taught was of value. Their guru, or whatever he calls himself, will create a new set of values for them, and they will not question those values until it's too late."

Marcella stared at him in silence for a moment, then put her head on his shoulder again. "You're too cynical. Or maybe too philosophical. What do you intend to do when you graduate from State?"

"I don't know. Still searching, I guess."

As they sat without speaking for a moment, the chanting in the park grew louder. They turned and looked over their shoulders. The pilgrims had built a large bonfire and set it alight. The smoke from it was blowing east, towards them.

"Come on," Travis said. "I think we'd better get out of here before they set the whole park on fire."

They rose from the steps and started walking down Steiner towards Haight. After a few blocks, they heard sirens.

They stopped for a moment and looked back. Smoke and flames were billowing up from the park and could be seen for miles around. A police car, siren blaring, raced by them.

"And did they kill him?" Marcella said.

"Kill who?"

"Christ."

"No."

"Why not?"

"Because once the Grand Inquisitor was finished with his spiel, Christ said nothing. He merely kissed him. The Grand Inquisitor was so stunned that he opened the cell door and let him go."

Marcella seemed contemplative as they continued to Haight Street.

When they arrived at the house, they entered the parlor and were surprised to find no one there. Then they heard the rat-a-tat-tat of Harvey's drums, which was muffled since Harvey's room was on the third floor.

"Coffee?" Marcella said. "Or some beer? I think there's some Coors in the fridge."

"Coffee," Travis said. He looked around the parlor as Marcella went into the kitchen to prepare the coffee. He noticed for the first time that there were some old photographs on the wall behind the sofa. He stepped closer to examine them.

They were black and white photos of the 1906 earthquake. The one on the left looked like Union Street in Cow Hollow, only several buildings were crumbling and seemed about to topple over. Firemen were furiously scurrying about, some manning an old-fashioned pump on a water wagon, others carrying buckets up into the buildings. Various bystanders stood around, looking confused, some guarding whatever belongings they could salvage from the wreckage.

Another photograph showed what appeared to be Fisherman's Wharf, or maybe the piers farther south, near the business district. Ships were sunk at their moorings, some with only their masts visible above the water line. Men in overalls and visored caps stood around, staring at the ships, seemingly not knowing what to do. A lone policeman paced along the Embarcadero, as if to guard against looting of the waterlogged cargos.

Marcella came out into the parlor with the coffee on a tray and set it down on the table in front of the sofa. "Aren't those great photos?"

Travis continued to study them. "Where did you get them?"

Marcella went to the wall and stood beside him. "They came with the house. An old woman owns it. When her husband died she rented the house out and moved into an apartment on Russian Hill. Left everything pretty much as it has been for the last fifty years."

"I wonder where all these people went."

"Hotels, churches, the YMCA. Some had to live in tents for months."

"You seem to know a lot about it."

"My grandparents were among the survivors. One uncle died fighting the fires."

"Your grandparents lived here in San Francisco?"

"On my mother's side. We all moved up here from L.A. when my dad got a job on the docks. This is where he got interested in acting. Then we moved back to L.A. so he could break into the movies."

"And did he?"

"Not exactly. He got a couple of bit roles, but it wasn't enough to pay the bills, so he opened a barber shop. Mom became a seamstress. She actually did more movie work than he did. What did your folks do?"

"Dad was killed in Korea. Mom remarried when I was twelve and my stepfather shipped me off to boarding school. Why don't we have some of that coffee before it gets cold?"

"Oh—All right."

They sat down on the sofa and sipped their coffee.

Travis looked up at the ceiling. "Harvey must be worn out—the drumming has stopped."

"Maybe he's just taking a break. Sometimes he practices until two or three in the morning. I've gotten used to it."

"Is he in a band?"

"Sure. Two or three. The latest one is called something like…The Flying Tomatoes."

Travis laughed. "It's silly enough to be a huge success."

"That's the music business for you—ninety percent hype, ten percent talent. Harvey's very good, though."

Travis put his cup down. "Mime work is just the opposite, I would think. Total silence. No backup. No amplifiers. You have to rely one hundred percent on your talent."

Marcella sighed. "Sad, but true. And there're aren't many gigs." She seemed contemplative for a moment, then brightened with a smile. "Have you ever seen *Children of Paradise*?"

"No. What's that—a play?"

"No, a movie. Come on, I want to show you something." She rose and headed for her bedroom. Travis followed.

Marcella's bedroom was one of the larger ones in the house, converted from a dining room designed to entertain twenty or more guests. A side door led to a butler's pantry and the kitchen. There was oak wainscotting all around and a four-poster bed against the far wall in the center of the room. Above the wainscotting were a number of posters, some of them framed, nearly all yellowed with age.

"This is quite a collection," Travis said. "Where did you get them?"

"Some from curio and memorabilia shops, but most I got from my mom, who worked at MGM for several years in the costume department. This is my favorite." She pointed to a faded poster that featured several actors ranging from a woman in a red dress sitting on a divan in the upper left corner, to several men in 19th century dress to the right of her, with a young woman in the center, all admiring the woman in red. Behind them was a balcony in a crowded theater with a rowdy-looking group of young men dangling their legs over the railing. In the shadows behind the woman in red was the face of a mime in white makeup staring with a kind of melancholy longing into the distance. Below this image were the words 'Un film de Marcel Carné' followed by the names of the actors and in large print the title, *Les Enfants du Paradis*.

"Ah," Travis said. "And that must be Jean-Louis Barrault, the famous mime."

"Correct. And you see, there are two images of him. One in the shadows in his mime makeup, and one to Arletty's left in a hat and formal dress as a member of the audience."

"Arletty?"

"That's the name of the actress in red. She was a bit older then, but she was still a beauty and a fabulous actress."

"Why did you want to be like the mime? Why not the beautiful temptress in red?"

Marcella looked pensive. "Because my father beat me so badly once that I couldn't speak for a month. During that time I saw the film, and I saw myself in that mime. He was sad. He never smiled. But he expressed his feelings through the language of his body—and his face."

Travis put his arms around her. "But you smile a lot. And you're beautiful when you do."

Marcella looked up at him for a moment with a sad expression on her face as if to belie this statement. But then she smiled. And he kissed her.

It was a long kiss, but he felt her moving away from him. He dropped his hands and watched as she went to the door. "I'm sorry, Marcella. I didn't mean to—"

Marcella closed the door. "Don't be sorry, Travis. That's the nicest kiss I've ever had." She came back to him and put her arms around him. "I think I'd like another."

Travis kissed her again, this time a bit longer, but then she pulled away from him and went to a closet. She opened the door and pulled off the sequined vest that she wore for the role of Roxana. Beneath that she wore a silk blouse. She removed the blouse and turned around to face him. "You'll make me self-conscious if you keep staring at me with your all clothes on."

Travis began unbuttoning his shirt as Marcella turned away again to hang her blouse in the closet. There were several long scars across her back. Though a bit startled at this sight, he said nothing and continued to undress.

Marcella removed the pantaloons she wore for the part, and then a pair of bikini panties. She turned to face him again with a smile, but observing the somber look on his face, the smile disappeared. "If you're concerned about the scars—"

"No, no," Travis said. "I've got a couple myself." He removed his shirt and turned his back to her. "See? They're not as pretty as yours, though."

"How did you get those?"

"Shrapnel. I was standing too close to a hooch when a mortar hit."

"What's a hooch?"

"A hut."

Marcella, now stark naked, came to him and examined the scars. "We make a pair, don't we?"

"I was hoping we would," Travis said.

Marcella smiled and led him over to the bed, where she turned out the light on the nightstand. She pulled back the sheet and settled in the middle of the bed. Travis removed his pants and followed. He began kissing her on the neck.

"Travis," she said.

"Hmm?"

"We'll have to do something about those boxers."

He lifted his head. "What's wrong with boxers?"

"Too old-fashioned. I'll get you some red bikini ones."

"Like Superman?"

"Like guys under forty."

Travis laughed. "Okay. But no red ones."

CHAPTER 16

Andrea was drunk. She knew she was drunk. She was happy to be drunk.

Howard had consumed nearly half of the contents of the brandy bottle, but seemed unaffected by it. He was talking to Alessandro's roommate, Terry. Terry was very slightly built, more than a little effeminate, but a sweet guy.

Sam, the director, was nursing a glass of red wine and talking to Nearchos, the playwright. A fiftyish woman with streaks of gray in her otherwise jet black hair stood alongside Nearchos. Andrea supposed that she was his wife.

Why wasn't anyone talking to her? She suddenly felt naked and alone. Well, she just might get naked. That would liven things up.

On the other hand, it felt stuffy in here. Some people were smoking. She hated cigarette smoke, pipe smoke, and ugh! Cigar smoke. She noticed the door to the balcony was open. A breeze was coming through, but it was blowing the wrong way. She needed to get upwind.

She weaved her way through the crowd, somewhat wobbly, and noticed that people were making a wide berth to let her pass through. What was wrong with them? Did they think she was going to throw up on them?

There was some soft jazz on the stereo, Miles Davis, or Thelonius Monk, or somebody like that.

She made her way to the balcony and went to the railing. What a fabulous view! The whole city seemed to be at her feet, like a jeweled robe. Mostly white lights, but a few spots of red and green and...what? Pink? Pink lights? Who would have pink lights on their—Oh, this was the Castro Valley, wasn't it? Fags—oops!—sorry. Gays all over the place. Well, let them have their pink lights and pink tights and pink earrings and—speaking of gays, where was Alessandro? It was his apartment after all—"

"Andrea? Are you all right?"

She turned around—a little too quickly, she almost lost her balance—and saw...Alessandro. "Hi, Alessandro...I'm fine. Great party. Can't you crank up the music a little? I mean something not so morbid—like the Grateful Dead, or Jefferson Airplane, or the Stones, or—"

"You feel like dancing?"

"Sure."

"Come on." Alessandro grabbed her by the hand and led her into the living room, where people made way for her again. He went over to the stereo and cut off the volume for a moment while he looked for another LP in the tall book shelf next to the equipment. Suddenly, everybody seemed to be staring at her. She liked that.

Alessandro put on a Stones song—"Under My Thumb"—and turned up the volume. A couple of men started dancing together. In fact it was Sam and Terry. Nearchos and his wife started bobbing their heads and shuffling their feet in a small circle like older people do when they're trying to be hip.

Alessandro took her hand and twirled her around until she again became a little dizzy. But she kept her balance and followed his lead. He was a terrific dancer!

The others stopped dancing and made room for them. Alessandro would spin her like a top, let go, then catch her before she could fall. It was thrilling!

She began to work up a sweat, even though the white chiffon dress she wore for the role of Timocleia in the play was light and silky. She was hot. Why not take it off?

She reached down to the hem and pulled it over her head. Poof! It was gone.

Everyone clapped.

Alessandro grinned at her and made some suggestive moves with his hips. She started to move towards him when she nearly lost her balance. Heels! She reached down and pulled off her shoes. Now she was barefoot and thus more stable. She realized she was bare breasted, too, but Alessandro seemed not to notice. He kept his eyes locked on hers and put both hands on her waist. Well, she still had her panties on—some discretion was in order, after all.

When the song was over, she and Alessandro were left standing together in the middle of the room, she naked but for her panties and he but for his jeans. He had stripped off his shirt during the dance and his muscles glistened with perspiration. What a beautiful man he was! She felt a little dizzy again, stumbled, and he suddenly picked her up in his arms. Her eyes half-open, she stroked his shoulders and felt the bulge of his biceps.

Someone put on another record and Alessandro carried her across the room to a door. Someone else—she thought it was Howard, the film maker—opened the door for them and they passed through into a bedroom with a king-sized bed in the middle of the room. It was on a sort of pedestal, and had a huge red quilt on it, along with a dozen assorted pillows. Well, what was he going to do with her? He was gay, wasn't he? Maybe just put her down and let her sleep a little. Too bad—she wasn't really that sleepy and the dancing had gotten her, well, excited. Dancing was like foreplay.

"You into multiple partners, Andrea?"

She opened her eyes and saw Alessandro at the foot of the bed taking his jeans off.

"Multiple? Multiple, like—with who?"

"Me, Howard—maybe Terry if you like."

"Terry?" Andrea looked at Alessandro's now erect penis. It was huge! "Terry's gay."

"Of course he is. But he likes a little variety—like me."

"What about—" She looked at Howard, who was fiddling with some device he had pulled out of his leather jacket.

"Howard?" Alessandro said. "He's a film maker, remember? This is like an audition."

"She looked at Howard again, who was now peering at her through the lens of the smallest movie camera she had ever seen. "Audition? I don't know."

"It'll be strictly confidential, Andrea," Howard said. "If you don't like it, I'll destroy the negative."

By this time, Alessandro was on the bed and pulling off her panties. She didn't resist. "All right, but I don't know about Terry. Where is he?"

"Just outside," Howard said. "I'll get him." He opened the door and stepped outside for a moment.

Alessandro began kissing her thighs, then moved up to her abdomen.

"You've got a big cock, Alessandro."

"I know. Back door or front?"

"I'm not that much into anal sex."

"Okay—we'll do it missionary style."

At this point the door opened again and Terry stepped in, followed by Howard.

"Omigod!" Terry said. "Are you sure you want to do this, Andrea, sweetheart? Alessandro will split you open with that big cock of his. He's already put me on a liquid diet."

This made Andrea laugh. "You can be the donkey, sweetie. I'll be the mare."

As Terry began removing his clothes, Howard began filming. The music in the living room had stopped and Andrea heard doors opening and closing. The guests were leaving.

She spread her legs as Alessandro, now on his knees, clasped her hips.

"Damn," Alessandro said.

"What's the matter, honey?" Andrea looked at Alessandro's penis and knew immediately what the matter was. "Can I help?"

"Well..." Alessandro turned to Terry, who was now standing at the foot of the bed. "Come on, Terry—come give me some head."

Terry climbed onto the bed and approached Alessandro, who turned on his side. He began sucking Alessandro's penis.

"Ah," Alessandro said. "Yeah, baby—oh, yeah."

"Hello!" Andrea said. "I'm still here."

Alessandro pulled away from Terry and started to approach Andrea again, now with a full erection.

"Wait a minute," Andrea said. "Terry, honey, would you mind?" She turned over on her stomach and patted her rear end.

Alessandro was nonplused. "I thought you weren't into anal sex."

"I'm not. A penis is too big, baby. Especially yours. But a tongue is just right."

Alessandro sighed and glanced at Terry, who looked hesitant. He nodded and Terry put his hands on Andrea's buttocks and spread her cheeks. He applied his tongue.

"Oh, Terry, baby," she said. "That's divine!"

Alessandro remained on his knees with his arms crossed over his chest. He looked at Howard, who was still filming and trying to get closer.

"All right, all right—that's enough." Alessandro grabbed Terry by the shoulders and nearly threw him off the bed. "I can't wait forever." He turned Andrea over on her back and she obligingly spread her legs.

"Come on, baby," she said. "I want to see what a deep fuck is like."

Alessandro said nothing but proceeded to insert his penis. After some rhythmic hip action, he was indeed deep inside her.

Andrea locked her ankles behind his back and hung on for the ride. "Omigod!"

At this point, Howard was on his knees at the side of the bed with his camera focused on the action about eighteen inches from their bodies.

"Great!" he said. "Great!"

Andrea paid no attention to Howard. She was on her way to a second, third, and fourth orgasm. A high-pitched scream accompanied each one.

At last, Alessandro withdrew and fell on his back, panting. His penis seemed to wilt to a fraction of its previous size.

"Oh, baby," Andrea said. "That was heaven." She opened her eyes and looked at Alessandro lying on his back. "Don't give up on me now, honey." She stroked his penis. "We're just getting started."

Alessandro's eyes were closed, his muscular torso motionless. "I'm done, Andrea. Wasted. Maybe Howard would like to play."

Howard stopped filming. He looked alarmed.

Andrea saw the look on his face and laughed. "Strictly a spectator, huh, Howard?" She looked at Terry who had snuggled up beside Alessandro. "Terry?"

Terry opened his eyes and looked at her. "Sorry, Andrea. The whole idea sort of...well, it disgusts me. I can't help it. Now that Alessandro's had his fun, can't you leave us alone?"

Howard looked at Terry, then Andrea. "Maybe you'd better get your clothes on, Andrea. I've got enough footage."

Andrea sighed. "What a bunch of party poopers!" She rolled over and sat up on the side of the bed. "Where're my panties?"

Howard retrieved her panties from the foot of the bed and handed them to her.

"Thanks," she said. "Now my dress ought to be around here some-where. Oh, it's in the living room. Will you get it for me, Howard, honey? I need to visit the little girls' room while you're doing that."

Howard went into the living room to find her dress.

CHAPTER 17

Ben Franklin sat pensively on the fiberglass seat molded, it seemed, to fit his rear end. The BART train was slick and shiny, everything brand new. He had never been on a train like this—no smoke, no vibration, no noise from the wheels perfectly fitted to the tracks they glided over like skates on the smoothest ice. He gazed out the window, but there was nothing to see except when they came into a station and then there were lights and the name of the station set in tile, and the weirdly metallic voice over the intercom that warned to 'watch your step' when exiting the car.

He didn't tell Thuy he was going to the Puma meeting. She didn't seem to understand. He didn't see himself as a revolutionary, he just wanted to help out all those black kids who arrived at school every day on an empty stomach. It wasn't right. Bobby X had the right idea, but he wasn't sure that he agreed with his tactics. There was no use in arming black people so they could protect themselves from the police. They would always be outgunned and besides, it just caused a backlash with whites and made things worse.

Still, it made him angry that a cop like the one that showed up at the school—Bobby called him 'Dan'—could get away with murdering a black man. Bobby didn't go into the details, but the circumstances didn't matter. It happened all the time. And it wasn't right.

The train eased into the 12th Street City Center station and stopped at the platform. The doors slid open, the metallic voice warned everyone to watch their step, and Ben mounted the escalator. He pulled the card out that Bobby had given him and chuckled as he read the address. Franklin Street. That seemed like a good omen.

He walked down 12th Street until he reached Franklin and, checking to see which way the numbers ran, turned north. Oakland was nothing like San Francisco. Everything was flat and the buildings all looked rundown. Many of them were vacant, with graffiti scrawled over every available surface. It reminded him of Columbus, Georgia, where he had done his basic training. He remembered taunts and racial slurs from white teenagers in passing cars when he and his buddies were on a weekend pass.

He arrived at the Franklin Street address and looked at the sign. It was the logo of the Black Pumas, like on the card, but no lettering. Just the logo. In the windows were posters, one of the 1968 Olympics with the medalists standing on the podium, their arms raised in a black power salute. Another was of Che Guevara with his familiar red beret and scraggly beard. Still another was of a helmeted white policeman, his face obscured by sun glasses and a crudely drawn circle superimposed on it with crosshairs.

He went to open the door, when the door seemed to open by itself. A stocky black man, wearing a black beret and a bandolier across his chest, stood just inside. He had a 9mm pistol stuffed in his belt.

"You a brother?"

Ben handed him the card Bobby had given him.

The stocky black man looked briefly at the card and smiled. "Come on in, Brother. The meeting's about to start."

Ben stepped inside. There were about fifteen to twenty people there standing around in small groups talking to each other. Most were men, but there were a few women. One was the black woman that he had been chatting up in the speech class at SF State. He had been thinking of asking her out until Thuy showed up.

There wasn't much furniture in the place. Just two tables, one set back a few feet from the entrance with several stacks of flyers on it, the other at the far end of the room where he presumed Bobby or some other member would address the group. There were maybe forty or fifty folding chairs facing the front.

He picked up a flyer that was entitled "The White Man's Plan: Genocide." He put this one down and picked up another: "The Black Puma Revolutionary Army Free Breakfast Program—Open to All Races." These two contradictory messages troubled him. He folded the second flyer lengthwise and put it in his coat pocket.

"Brother Ben!"

He felt a hand clap him on the shoulder and turned to see who it was. Bobby.

"I was afraid you weren't coming," he said.

"I was able to get off tonight," Ben said. He noticed that the girl from San Francisco State was coming up behind him.

Bobby turned to her. "Tanya, this is Ben Franklin. Ben—"

"We've met," Tanya said. "How are you, Ben?"

"Fine." Ben wasn't sure what her relationship was to Bobby, and was at a loss as to what to say.

"How do you like that, Tanya?" Bobby said with a grin. "I've recruited one of the Founding Fathers of America. Only now he's black. That's a sign that we're turning this country around." He laughed loudly at this little joke, though Tanya only smiled politely.

Ben smiled back.

"Close the door, Brother Gillis." This baritone voice came from a tall, lanky man near the front of the room who Bobby had been talking to when Ben came in.

"That's Brother Erskine. Lonnie Erskine, the writer. He's our Minister of Education. That's why I invited you here tonight, Brother Ben. I'll introduce you after the meeting. Come on, let's take a seat up front."

Bobby led them to the front row of chairs and they took their seats opposite the table. Lonnie Erskine was an imposing man, over six feet in height, and like most of the Pumas, sported a full Afro. Ben felt a little out of place in this regard, since he still kept his hair close-cropped like he did in the army.

Erskine picked up a .45 automatic pistol that had been lying on the table and used it as a gavel. "This meeting will come to order!" He banged the butt of the pistol on the table two or three times. "As Minister of Education, I will be standing in for Brother Newsome, who, as you all know, is a guest of our friend Fidel in Havana. Sister Braun is out organizing a new group in Richmond."

After quoting every revolutionary leader from Robespierre to Mao Tse-tung, Erskine launched into a diatribe against the white-dominated public school system.

"They teach white history," he said. "And as we all know, white history is to history as military music is to music.'

This elicited laughs and ejaculations of "You know it, Brother!" and "You tell it!"

"The pigs," Erskine continued, "want your children to look white, think white, and be white. They say nothing about the genocide that has murdered fifty million African-Americans over the past three hundred years. They say nothing about the lynchings in the South and the police brutality in our cities like Oakland and Los Angeles. They say nothing about the political prisoners in our prisons who are guilty of nothing more than being black!"

Cries of "Hear, hear!" and "Ain't it the truth!" reverberated throughout the room.

Erskine tapped the butt of the pistol on the table for silence. "And I'm here tonight to tell you all that is about to change."

Clapping all around.

"We have new school programs in Bay Area cities like Hayward, Fremont, Milpitas, San Jose and even that citadel of capitalist hegemony, San Francisco."

More clapping and whistling.

"Now some of our L.A. chapters have closed down because of the violence of the pigs against our brothers and sisters there. But we're about to change that, too. Now this is a new tactic that the pigs don't know how to deal with. We're pulling our children out of the schools and educating them in the proper way at our homes, our rec centers, our churches, and our businesses. The pigs don't know how to deal with it. They can say that the kids must be, by law, in school. Well, they *are* in school. Our schools, where they are taught that black is beautiful, that we have built this country by the sweat of our brows, that we are entitled to free medical care, free housing, free food and most importantly, trial by a jury of our peers."

Clapping and cheers.

"Now you may say that this last item I mentioned is embedded in the pigs' constitution. That is so—but it only applies to white people! We want a jury system of *our* peers. Black juries for black defendants!"

This elicited even more enthusiastic cheers and shouts of "Tell it, Brother!" and "Death to the pigs!"

Erskine tapped the butt of the pistol on the table. "Now we have to make a distinction between the pigs and well-meaning white people."

There were groans and mutterings among the audience.

Erskine raised his hand for silence. "Now, now, I know you don't trust white people. But there are some that are sympathetic to our cause. And we need them. They have money and power. They have influence in the legislatures, in the mayor's office. Sister Braun almost made it into the mayor's mansion here in Oakland only recently. And it was because she has white friends there. No, all whites aren't pigs. The real pigs are the cops!"

Cheers and whistles.

"But that's another issue. We'll leave that for the next meeting. Tonight's meeting is about education."

Though he vowed to restrict his address to education, Erskine continued to digress into numerous subtopics, covering Marxist ideology, Maoism, the North Atlantic slave trade, the Algerian war of independence, American and European colonialism, conspiracies against leftist leaders like Fidel Castro and Salvador Allende, as well as Protestantism, Catholicism, and Mormonism. Judaism was singled out as a particularly pernicious religion.

At the end of his address, Erskine asked for questions, but there were none, possibly because the audience was worn out from his hour and twenty minute harangue, and possibly because he was wielding a .45 caliber pistol.

The meeting was thus adjourned, and various members of the party coalesced into groups to discuss their particular concerns.

Ben felt somewhat numb from Erskine's long-winded oratory, and was about to leave when Tanya came up to him.

"Well," she said. "What do you think of Brother Erskine's ideas?"

Ben was reluctant to offer an opinion, for he wasn't sure of Tanya's positions and didn't want to alienate her. Besides, she seemed more attractive than ever, with her light, cocoa butter skin, her large brown eyes, and her perfectly formed teeth. "I don't know, exactly. It's a lot to take in."

Tanya smiled. "It is a lot to take in, and he tends to ramble on too much. But he's a dynamic speaker."

"I guess so."

"He motivates people. I think he'll go a long way in helping us to gain our rights. Don't you?"

"Yeah. He gets you going, all right."

Tanya frowned. "You seem unsure."

"Well, yeah, I guess I am a little. After fighting the 'Cong, I'm a little uncomfortable with all this talk about Marx and Mao. Seems like they don't respect people's rights once they get into power."

"Don't you know that you were being used in Vietnam? You were just a pawn of the white man."

Ben knew she was right, but he couldn't help but think of his white buddies who died in his arms, or the officers like Travis who slept in the mud with him in the rice paddies. "When you're under fire all you think about is protecting your buddies. Nobody talked about Marx or capitalism, or black and white."

Tanya studied his face for a moment. "But this isn't Vietnam. This is America. And nothing has changed."

"Well..." Ben tried to gather his thoughts and was prevented from responding by Bobby, who stepped between them and put his arm around Tanya.

"You hittin' on my girl, Bro?" Bobby said this with a smile, only half-jokingly. Tanya glanced sideways at him as if to say, "I'm not your girl."

"We was just talking about Brother Erskine," Ben said. "He's sure some speaker."

"That he is, that he is. And as Minister of Education he's your boss. El Supremo." He stood on his toes and looked around the room. "I wanted to introduce you, but hell, he's already gone."

Ben and Tanya also looked around and didn't see Brother Erskine.

"We'll do it at the next meeting," Bobby said. He reached into his leather jacket and extracted a .38 revolver, the kind that officers carried in Vietnam and that police officers used to carry until they started using the more powerful .357 magnums. "I promised you this. For self-defense."

"I don't think I really need it," Ben said, staring at the pistol.

Bobby shoved it into his hand. "Believe me—you need it. That pig who came to the school last week will be back. And he'll be watching you—he knows you're our rep in San Francisco. He'll be looking for an excuse to bust you, and if you so much as look sideways at him, he'll shoot you in the back and claim you were resisting arrest."

Ben looked at the gun, then at Tanya. "I can't carry this around at

San Francisco State."

"Sure you can. It's legal."

"But it ain't legal at the kids' school."

"Universities are different. It's legal. Just keep it in your belt. Better yet, buy a holster for it. At State, you can wear a jacket over it so it don't freak out your professors. I know. I've done it."

"You went to college?"

"Sure. Merritt College right here in Oakland."

Ben looked again at Tanya, who seemed to be affirming what Bobby said, and put the pistol in his jacket.

"No," Bobby said. He extracted the pistol from Ben's pocket and jammed it into his belt. "Display it here in Oakland. The pigs will see it, but they can't do anything about it. They're watching us right now. You hide it in your pocket and they'll bust you before you get two blocks up the street."

On the way back to San Francisco, Ben reflected on the events at the meeting. He sat almost alone at the rear of the car—the rear! It was a habit—and stared out into the darkness as the train passed under the bay.

What had he gotten himself into? Yes, he wanted to do something to help these kids. He was going to be a father soon himself. But he didn't like the Puma's love affair with guns. Sure, the cops could get out of control—but brandishing guns in public only put them on edge, made them *want* to shoot a brother. And in any case, they would always be outgunned. He liked Martin Luther King's strategy better. Some say he was an Uncle Tom...but he was effective. Look at the civil rights acts of the past few years...Then again, it might be window dressing. Kids were still living in substandard housing, not getting enough to eat, dropping out of high school, hitting the streets and finding that there were no jobs for them. Maybe Tanya was right—nothing had changed...

By the time he stepped off the platform at Balboa Park, it was dark. He caught a trolley, got off at Portola Drive, and walked the rest of the way. He had thought that Twin Peaks would be a pretty fancy neighborhood, and maybe it was, but the house that Travis' friend vacated was rundown and infested with fleas. The guy must have had a kennel in there. He and Thuy were always scratching and killing the things. It was hard to sleep at night. They called the landlord and he said he'd send an exterminator but it had been two weeks and the exterminator hadn't showed.

When he walked in the front door he smelled the unmistakable aroma of coriander. Coriander and ginger. He loved Vietnamese food. Thuy was in the kitchen with her back to him and an apron tied around her waist. She was beginning to show a little.

When he closed the door, she turned around briefly. "You like Bánh cuôn?"

"If you cook it, I like it," Ben sat down in a dilapidated armchair bequeathed to them by the former tenant. In fact, all of the furniture, if you could call it that, had been left by the guy and his girlfriend. Travis said they were moving up to Oregon, where they planned to build a house in the woods.

"Bánh cuôn very good for you," Thuy had turned back to her cooking and was stir frying some vegetables. "It just an appetizer."

"Sounds good." Ben started to pick up the latest issue of the *San Francisco Chronicle*, but as he leaned over he felt the gun jab into his midsection. He had forgotten about it. He didn't want Thuy to see it, so he carefully removed it from his waistband and slid it under the cushion of the chair. Thuy never sat in that chair anyway.

"We have mám cá thu for main course. Fish. You like that?"

"I told you—I like anything you cook. It smells great."

Thuy continued with her cooking as Ben read the paper. As the aromas filled the room—the kitchen and living room were not separated by a wall—Thuy let the main dish simmer in a pot and brought out a plate of hors d'oeuvres.

"What's this?" Ben said.

"I told you—báhn cuôn. Also chá lua—sausage."

Ben stabbed the chá lua with a small fork she had provided and put it into his mouth.

"You like?"

"Mmm. I love it! This is a meal in itself."

"Not to eat too much. More to come. Oh—I forgot. You want beer?"

"Sure."

Thuy went to the kitchen and came back with a bottle of Anchor Steam beer.

"Thanks. I ain't seen this kind before."

"The man in market say it San Francisco's best."

Ben took a swallow. "Yeah, it's good." He gave her a kiss on the cheek. "You're too good to me."

Thuy smiled, started to say something, and went back to the kitchen. Ben went back to reading the paper.

"Ben?"

"Yeah?"

"Did you see Bobby today?"

Ben put the paper down. Thuy was again at the stove with her back to him. "Bobby? No, why?"

"Then where did you get that gun?"

Ben looked down at the seat cushion. The chair was so dilapidated that his body weight had pushed the arm out so that the handle of the .38 stuck out in plain view. He sighed. "Okay—I went to the meeting. Bobby stuck the gun in my waistband and I didn't want to argue with him."

"Why you go to meeting?"

"I just thought I ought to. I'm the Free Breakfast Coordinator for San Francisco. Lonnie Erskine, the Minister of Education, was there. I thought I ought to hear what he had to say."

Thuy came back from the kitchen, drying her hands with her apron. "He say you need a gun to protect little kids from police?"

Ben smiled. "No. He didn't say anything about guns. Mostly about feeding the kids and making sure they get a good education."

"So you don't need gun."

"No, not really."

"Excuse me." Thuy bent down and picked the gun up from beneath the cushion. "Maybe gun good for killing fleas."

Ben laughed. "Maybe so."

"I put gun in cupboard. High up, where fleas live. Maybe it scare them away. Okay?"

Ben considered this proposal for a moment. "Okay."

CHAPTER 18

There is a tension on opening night that suffuses the air. If one were to stumble unwittingly into the performance—as many did at the Rose and Thorn—one would immediately know that this was something akin to the birth of a child.

A few of the gentlemen who attended the backers' performance were in the audience, though none had as yet committed to the venture. Nearchos Andropoulos sat in the very back row to observe the audience's reaction. With him sat Sam Thomas. The prospective backers sat just in front of them.

The rest of the seats were filled by an assortment of friends and family members, devotees of the theater who scoured the entertainment pages of the *Chronicle* each week for new plays, and those patrons of the Rose and Thorn who had had a bit too much to drink and thought the stairs led to the restrooms.

The most watched member of the audience, however, was Clarence McGill, the drama critic of the *Chronicle.* Not everyone recognized Mr. McGill, or even knew who he was, but Sam and Nearchos knew him by sight and read the columns he wrote with scrupulous attention to every phrase, every word. Nearchos, especially, did not often agree with Mr. McGill's opinions, but he nevertheless was aware that a mere nod of approbation from McGill's pen could launch a play into the national media spotlight, or conversely, a dismissive remark could consign it to oblivion. The gentlemen sitting just in front of him were aware of this phenomenon as well.

The real tension in the air, however, was generated backstage by the performers. Even Alessandro got the jitters on opening night, and Marcella, though experienced as a street performer, had never had the leading female role in a play. Travis was less worried, as he had only a few lines, but even he was nervous, thinking that if he bobbled a single one of his lines that it would bring down the whole production. Only Andrea was calm and unperturbed. In fact, she was somewhat contemptuous of the whole endeavor, especially since the principals had lacked the foresight and acumen to cast her as Roxana.

If one had stood by the door and watched the face of Nearchos rather than the actors on the stage, one might have observed more drama and nuances of feeling there than were visible before the footlights. There was agony, joy, disappointment, laughter, terror, devastation, and a host of other emotions that the good professor rarely evinced at home or in the classroom. And all these feelings were expressed within the space of one hour and thirty-two minutes.

"Good show," Clarence McGill said to Nearchos after the lights came up and the actors were taking their bows. He extended his hand almost as an afterthought and without enthusiasm. "I was expecting something more...lofty in thought, perhaps, from a professor of drama, but...it works quite well as a crowd pleaser."

'Crowd pleaser!' Nearchos was crestfallen. He withdrew his hand and nodded politely. McGill turned and made his way to the door, stopping only once to say something to Marcella.

"Well," Sam said to Nearchos. "I think he liked it. We'll have to wait for the morning papers, though."

Nearchos nodded again, his leonine head seemingly about to topple to the floor from the weight of it. "Yes. We'll have to wait." He passed his hand through his shoulder-length white hair and picked up his script and began marking it with a blue pencil.

Sam went to the front of the stage once most of the patrons had dispersed and clapped his hands. "Notes, people! Notes! It'll only be a few minutes. You were all marvelous!"

After the notes were delivered, during which Sam admonished Alessandro for 'strutting like a peacock,' the cast retired for the usual libations in the bar. Travis, Marcella and Andrea somehow ended up in the same booth they had occupied on the evening of the backers' preview.

"Did you hear what Sam said to Alessandro?" Andrea said.

"How could we miss it?" Marcella said. "He dressed him down in front of the whole cast. I think he should have taken him aside and talked to him privately."

"The cocksucker deserved it," Andrea said, stirring her pink lady with a swizzle stick. "He *is* a strutting peacock. Someone needed to put him in his place."

"But wasn't Alexander a kind of strutting peacock himself?" Travis said. "Great King of Persia, Lord of Asia—"

"He was no shrinking violet, honey." Andrea sucked up a good third of her drink through a straw. "But Alexander was a self-effacing gentleman compared to Alessandro."

"That may be," Marcella said, "but I think Alessandro thinks that the role calls for that sort of preening and strutting. You know, he can show tenderness, too, like the scene where—"

Andrea laughed so loudly that several other patrons turned to look at her. She looked around sheepishly and covered her mouth with her hand. "Oops! Sorry. But I couldn't help it. I know the man a little better than you do, sweetie. He's an egomaniac."

"Well..." Marcella started to say something but checked herself. She glanced sideways at Travis, who looked away and caught sight of Alessandro regaling a group of actors at the bar. "I suppose you do know him better."

"Oh-h-h, yes," Andrea said. "I know him *very* well." She made a gurgling sound with her straw as she sucked up the remainder of her drink. "All done. Travis, honey, can you get the attention of that bartender? I'd like another drink."

"I'm afraid you'll have to do it yourself, Andrea. If I were working here, I'd have to cut you off."

Andrea stared wildly at Travis. "What are you, my keeper?" She stood up. "Maybe Alessandro will help me. Like I said, he's a real gentleman." She then made her way to the bar.

"That was mean, Travis," Marcella said.

"Somebody needs to slow her down occasionally. When she drinks, she drinks so fast she becomes a kamikaze. She's headed for total destruction one of these days if she doesn't impose some sort of discipline on herself."

Marcella smiled and sipped on her drink. "You sound like you're her father."

Travis bristled. "She needs a father. I wonder if she has one."

"She does. He's a Wall Street banker."

"How do you know that?"

"She told me. He once ran his family's farm equipment business in Indiana, sold it for ten million dollars and moved to New York City where he became an investment banker."

"Ten million?"

"That's what she said."

"And probably worth more than that now. Did she say anything else about him?"

"Only that she hasn't seen him in five years."

"Why?"

"He disapproves of her lifestyle."

"I can understand that. I think I'll have another beer."

"Careful, Travis, dear. You don't want to turn into a kamikaze."

Travis smiled. "I won't as long as you're around. You want another?"

"I'm fine."

Travis rose and went to the bar where Alessandro was still telling a story and Andrea was sitting on a stool listening with rapt attention, as were the others.

"Brando's a great actor," Alessandro said. "But Pacino's more interesting. Like Brando, he's difficult to work with, but you can learn so much from him."

"What about De Niro?" the actor who played Hephaestion said.

"A consummate professional." Alessandro downed the remaining contents of his glass and put it on the counter with a bang, indicating to the bartender that he wanted another. "He stays in character throughout the production. Like Pacino."

"You were in *Godfather*?"

"I had a bit part. Unfortunately, my scenes were left on the cutting room floor."

"Still," another actor said. "What an opportunity!"

Travis paid for his beer and made his way back to the booth, where he found Sam sitting across from Marcella. He slid into the booth next to her.

Sam Thomas was a good-looking man in his early thirties, with a full beard and soft brown eyes. He had trained as a director at the University of North Carolina at Chapel Hill, where he earned an MFA degree in theater. He was a bit of an intellectual, it seemed to Travis, with his tastes running from the avant-garde to the classics. He could quote Jean-Paul Sartre and Shakespeare in nearly the same breath.

He nodded towards Travis as he sat down, then turned back to Marcella. "You've got a great future, Marcella. Regardless of how this play turns out, I'd like to work with you."

Marcella beamed. "I don't really know what I'm doing, Sam. I just try to do what you tell me to."

"You'd be surprised how many actors can't do that," Sam said. "All I have to do with you is give you a hint, a suggestion, and you run with it."

"I suppose it's my mime training," she said. "You learn to do a lot with a little."

"I'm sure it helps," Sam said with a smile. He glanced at Travis. "Well, I'd better move on. I want to try to get some sleep before the papers hit the newsstands tomorrow morning."

After Sam had gone, Travis said to Marcella: "You're going to stay up for the papers?"

"I don't think so. There's a lot more at stake for Sam and Nearchos. Are you hungry?"

"I was just thinking the same thing. Why don't we go to that new Italian restaurant on Divisadero?"

"Okay."

This time they hailed a cab in front of the Rose and Thorn. The restaurant was only a few blocks from Haight Street and after a satisfying meal of pasta with a hearty red wine, they walked the rest of the way to Marcella's house.

When they entered the parlor, they were almost overwhelmed with the aroma of cannabis. The lights were low and there was a good deal of smoke in the room, but they could make out Harvey sitting on the sofa rolling a joint. There were five of his friends, three male and two female, sitting in various attitudes of repose on the sofa, on chairs, and in the case of one of the young men, lying on the floor. All were dressed in the unofficial uniform of Haight-Ashbury; i.e., jeans, tie-dyed T-shirts, and colorfully embroidered, hand-stitched vests.

"Greetings, man," Harvey said to them without distinction as to sex. "Want some weed?"

Marcella looked at Travis, who shook his head. "Thanks anyway, Harvey. We're pretty tired. Think we'll turn in."

Harvey exhaled a cloud of smoke. "Suit yourself, man. This is really good weed. Acapulco Gold. Straight off the boat."

"Hey, man," the one lying on the floor said. "Put on some music."

"Right."

As Harvey got up—slowly—to put on the music, Marcella and Travis went into her bedroom and closed the door.

Travis stood just inside the door for a moment and listened. "Procol Harum. I guess we can live with that."

Marcella yawned. "I didn't realize how tired I was. You don't mind if we just sleep, do you, Travis?"

"Mind? I'll be out like a light as soon as my head hits the pillow." He pulled off his jacket while Marcella went to the closet.

When she had stripped to her panties and came back to the bed, Travis was sound asleep.

CHAPTER 19

Travis wasn't sure whether he was dreaming or awake. It seemed at first that he was in Bangkok at the Good Luck G.I. Joe Bar...then the Dreamland Hotel with that Thai girl...what was her name?...Arinya...she said it meant 'beautiful woman who is knowledgeable'...well, she was knowledgeable, all right..and beautiful...he could feel her lips against his chest, moving down to his stomach, his crotch...she took his penis in her mouth and rolled her tongue over the head of it like it was a lollipop...

He opened his eyes. Light was streaming through the curtains. Was he still dreaming? He looked around the familiar room, then down at an even more familiar head of auburn hair. Marcella was licking his penis, just like Arinya had done in Bangkok. Not just rolling her tongue over the head of it, but doing it with relish.

She looked up, sensing that he was now awake. "Good morning."

"Good morning. I didn't mean to interrupt you."

Marcella laughed. She still had his penis firmly in her grasp. It was growing more erect. "I'm glad you did. I was beginning to wonder if there was any way to revive you."

"This way worked."

She laughed again and moved up a little to kiss him on the lips, her hand still on his penis.

"Can I ask you something?" he said.

"Sure."

"Have you always liked sucking cocks?"

Marcella laughed. "Not always. Not with just anyone, either."

"I always thought women did it just because they thought they were supposed to. To please their man. But you seem to really enjoy it."

She touched the tip of his nose with her forefinger. "I told you—only with the right man."

"Okay. I'm glad I'm that guy. But what's so enjoyable about it? I mean, for me it feels great. But for you—you can't have an orgasm doing it. It can't turn you on that much."

"Oh, but it does."

"Why?"

"The texture, the feel of it in my mouth—the knowledge that it's turning *you* on."

"Oh."

She bent down to run her tongue around the tip. "Now let me ask you a question."

"Shoot."

"That's just it. Why haven't you ejaculated?"

"Because I'm holding it for something better."

She smiled. "Like what?"

"Want me to talk dirty?"

"Sure."

"For making whoopee."

Marcella fell onto her back, laughing. "Oh, please! You call that talking dirty?"

"We did back in Michigan. Sitting around the camp fire on the Upper Peninsular telling stories. 'Tell us about the time you made whoopee with Mary Beth, Travis.' It got pretty raunchy."

Marcella smiled. "You're too funny. Don't they ever call a thing by its real name in Michigan?"

"Like 'fucking'?"

"No—like making love."

Travis leaned over and kissed her. "Well, that, too."

She returned his kiss, but with more passion. "Let's not talk anymore."

An hour later Marcella was asleep again. Travis extricated himself from her embrace, put on his jeans, and stumbled out into the parlor. There were four or five bodies on the floor, the sofa, one guy asleep in a chair. Harvey had apparently retired to his room in the attic.

He put on some coffee and went out to the front porch looking for the paper. It was a sunny day and he saw people out walking their dogs. Kids playing frisbee in the park, and the usual panhandlers staking out their territory. He picked up the paper, which was lodged between two potted plants, and went back inside.

By this time, Harvey's friends had begun to stir and Marcella was in the kitchen taking the pot off the stove. Travis made his way through the wreckage in the parlor and sat down at the kitchen table, where Marcella was now pouring the coffee.

"Is there a review?" she said.

"Don't know." Travis turned several pages. "Ah! Here it is: 'Is this Alexander's Ragtime Band?'"

"Uh, oh. Doesn't sound good." She sat down opposite Travis and blew across the surface of her coffee.

Travis read the article out loud:

"'Professor Nearchos Andropoulos' new play about Alexander the Great opened last night at the tiny Rose and Thorn Theatre on California Street. As one would expect, much of the language is rather academic, even poetic, but the characters never quite come to life with the exception of Roxana, played with fine sensitivity and nuance of emotion by a newcomer, Marcella Morgan. Ms. Morgan is a delight.'"

Travis looked up at Marcella, who was beaming. He smiled at her, took a sip of his coffee, and continued:

"'Alessandro Sanchez, however, who plays Alexander, though more experienced than Ms. Morgan, nearly drove this reviewer out of the theater with his histrionic portrayal of Alexander. Mr. Sanchez never lets an opportunity go by to flex his muscles or expose his well-developed chest to the audience, or to upstage the other actors, including Ms. Morgan.

"'Hepahestion, as Alexander's best friend and possible lover, is well played by Jonathan Stockardt, and Ms. Andrea Koslewski does a creditable job as Timocleia, an aristocratic Theban who has been ravished by one of Alexander's men.

"'On the whole, however, Professor Andropoulos' play falls short. It is more of a pastiche of well-known episodes in Alexander's life without the dynamism that is often attributed to the man himself.'"

Travis looked up. "There's more."

"That's enough." Marcella poured some sugar into her coffee and stirred it. "It doesn't sound good, does it?"

"Except for your performance. It looks like you've got a bright future ahead of you."

"But the play isn't going anywhere. Not after people read that review."

Travis put down the paper. "Reviews don't guarantee anything. If people like it, they'll tell their friends."

"We'll see."

One of the denizens of the parlor drifted into the kitchen. "Mind if I take a look at the entertainment section?"

"Not at all." Travis handed the section to him.

"Want some coffee?" Marcella said.

"Yeah. That'd be nice." The young man, who didn't bother to introduce himself, was tall and lanky with a beard down to his collarbone and frizzy brown hair pulled back in a pony tail. "There should be an ad for the concert in here somewhere."

"What concert?" Travis said.

"Our concert. The Flying Enchiladas. Ah—here it is." He read over the ad, then handed it to Travis.

Travis looked at the ad. It was a quarter of a page, full-color. "The Fillmore. Friday night. How did you get booked at the Fillmore?"

"Our agent's friends with Bill Graham. It was a slam dunk."

"Your agent?"

"Yeah. The asshole takes ten percent of everything we make. But he hustles."

Travis looked at the ad again. "Sixty dollars for a ticket? How many people can afford that?"

"You'd be surprised. They scrape it up somehow. We should gross 180 G's." Barry, as he was known to his friends, then drank his coffee in nearly one gulp and walked back into the parlor.

Travis and Marcella were left staring at each other.

"I think we're in the wrong business," Travis said.

"Looks like it," Marcella said. "I guess I'd better dust off my mime outfit. I can make more in an hour on the streets than I can
in a week with this play. Assuming it lasts another week."

"We'll see," Travis said.

CHAPTER 20

Despite the poor review by Mr. McGill, the play continued to attract at least enough customers to fill the small theater for the next few weeks. This may have been in part due to the subject matter; i.e., Alexander the Androgynous, and partly due to the fact that Alessandro was beginning to build up an almost cult following, mostly from the Castro.

Sam did not like this situation and was increasingly irritated by Alessandro's refusal to tone down his performance and employ the 'real' acting that he knew Alessandro was capable of. The whole production was becoming a camp event that undermined Sam's ambition to establish himself as a serious director.

Nearchos had nearly washed his hands of the production. He had some of the same concerns that Sam did, and they discussed the possibility of firing Alessandro, but there seemed no one able or willing to take his place for the miserably low compensation. The 'investors' had dispersed as quickly as they had appeared. No, there was nothing to do but to let the play run long enough to pay the rent and the salaries and then shut it down. Nearchos went back to his teaching at San Francisco State and thought little more about it.

Travis, who had been juggling his schedule at Henry Africa's to allow him to continue, often left the theater after his scene with Andrea and went to work.

He had just started his shift on a Friday night when Bobby X showed up with Tanya on his arm. Bobby wore a cape over his shoulders and over the cape was draped a white silk scarf, the ends dangling nearly down to his knees. Tanya was equally well-dressed, wearing an orange taffeta dress with a low-cut bodice and spaghetti straps at the shoulders. It seemed that they had just come from some gala event.

Travis did not see a gun on Bobby's hip, but it was possible that the cape covered it.

They both seemed in good spirits and were apparently enjoying the attention they were getting from the mostly white patrons of the bar. Bobby stopped at the door and spoke briefly to Ben before ordering a couple of drinks. Thuy, who was now a part-time waitress, happened to be on duty and offered to seat them at a table, but Bobby declined and insisted on mingling with the crowd. A jazz trio that Henry had recently hired was on break, and Bobby seemed to know one of the musicians.

Travis served up the drinks and glanced at Ben, who was grinning at him. He wondered if Ben had ever armed himself, as Bobby had urged him to. Many bouncers in the city carried guns, but Henry didn't like the idea, and Ben's physical presence was so intimidating that it didn't really seem necessary.

Thuy returned to her station at the end of the bar after serving a couple sitting near the bandstand. "That Bobby—he no good."

"Well," Travis said as he soaked some dirty glasses, "he seems well-behaved tonight. Out on the town with his lady friend."

Thuy frowned. "Trouble has way of finding men like Bobby."

"I hope you're wrong, Thuy. Besides, he doesn't have his goons with him tonight. Only his date—say, I think she's in one of my classes at State. Yeah, that's her. Tanya's her name."

"Tanya?"

"Yeah, Ben—" Travis checked himself. "Ben knows her better than I do."

Thuy looked at him, then cast her eyes on Tanya, who was now talking to a black man near the window, which was nearly obscured by ferns. "So she a friend of Ben's?"

"She's just a classmate, Thuy. That's all."

Thuy was not convinced that Ben's relationship with Tanya was entirely platonic and kept her eyes on her as she went about serving customers.

Travis, for his part, kept his eyes on Bobby, who in turn seemed to monitor Tanya's conversation with the man near the window. Travis recognized this man as a running back with the San Francisco 49ers. He was dressed in jeans and an expensive leather jacket, and wore a gold chain around his neck.

When the jazz trio began to play again, Bobby moved toward the window. Tanya seemed to be enjoying the conversation and didn't notice that Bobby had come up behind her. Suddenly he grabbed her by the arm and pulled her away from the window. She resisted and the football player, whose name was DeShawn Washington, stepped between them. There were words exchanged that Travis couldn't hear followed by a roundhouse swing from Bobby that Washington managed to duck. Washington came back with a swing of his own that put Bobby on the floor.

The trio stopped playing. Ben started to move towards the bandstand from the door. Everyone in the bar was now staring at them.

Before Ben could get to the bandstand, Bobby sprang up from the floor wielding the .457 magnum that he had retrieved from the police station a few weeks earlier. He used it as a club and proceeded to beat Washington with it.

Meanwhile, Henry had called the police and a cruiser came screeching to a halt, lights flashing, just in front of the bar. Ben managed to pull Bobby off of Washington, who was now bleeding profusely from his nose and temple.

Travis came around from the bar and assisted Ben in restraining Bobby, who had uttered a couple of 'mother fuckers' during the attack, but who was now venting his fury on Tanya, who he called a 'slut' and a 'no good cunt.'

Two policemen came through the front door, one with a truncheon in his hand, the other with his hand on the leather strap over his pistol. This second policeman was none other than Dan, the one who had taken Bobby's gun away from him at the elementary school.

When Dan saw the magnum, which was pointed down at the floor as Travis restrained Bobby's arm, he drew his gun. "Drop it, Bobby—don't make things worse."

Bobby stared wildly at Dan, then at Washington, who sat in a chair now with his hand covering his face, blood pouring through his fingers. He dropped the gun.

Dan's partner went over and kicked the gun away towards the center of the floor, while Dan holstered his own weapon and pulled out a pair of handcuffs, which he snapped around Bobby's wrists.

"This ain't any business of yours," Bobby said, ejecting spittle through his teeth.

"Oh, but it is," Dan said. "Disturbing the peace, assault and battery, and carrying a concealed weapon. You've been warned."

"He was messin' with my woman."

Dan glanced over at Washington, who was now being assisted by Thuy with a towel, then at Tanya who was standing in a corner, trembling. "Mr. Washington here is a respectable citizen. Never had trouble with the police. On the other hand, Bobby, you've got a rap sheet as long as my arm. Let's go."

Bobby resisted, but between Travis, Ben and the second cop, he had little chance of breaking free.

Dan looked at Ben, as if noticing him for the first time. "You the bouncer?"

"Yes, sir."

"Okay, you can let go now. Armed?"

"No, sir."

Dan nodded to his partner. The partner let go of Bobby and patted down Ben.

"He's clean."

"I think we've met," Dan said. "Your name is—"

"Ben."

"Right. Thanks for your help, Ben. We'll take it from here." Dan turned to Travis. "You, too, bartender. Let go."

Travis, who was still looking at the gun in the middle of the floor, reluctantly released his grip on Bobby's arm.

Dan looked at the gun on the floor and nodded to his partner again, who went over and picked it up. Then he turned to Washington. "You need an ambulance?"

Washington shook his head.

"You intend to press charges?"

Washington looked up at Dan, then at Bobby. One eye was nearly swollen shut, his nose was broken, but the bleeding had mostly stopped. He nodded in the affirmative.

"Come on down to the station when you're ready," Dan said. "The Hall of Justice on Bryant Street. Come on, Bobby."

Bobby now appeared to be subdued and went along willingly, though not before glaring at Ben. "You're nothing but a damn Uncle Tom."

Ben said nothing and only watched as Bobby was led to the front door.

Once out on the sidewalk, Dan opened the rear door of the cruiser while his partner turned Bobby around and started to back him into the seat, his hand on Bobby's head to make sure it cleared the opening. But as he did this, and Dan circled around the front of the car to the driver's side, Bobby snatched the second cop's pistol from its holster and fired point-blank into his midsection. As the cop clutched his stomach in pain, Bobby pushed him to the pavement and started running up Van Ness Avenue.

Dan used the cruiser as a shield and aimed his pistol with both hands directly at Bobby's back. He fired once and Bobby dropped to the pavement.

Ben emerged from the bar just in time to see Dan fire the fatal shot.

"No!" he screamed.

Dan looked at Ben. "Stay where you are."

Ben was livid, but complied. Travis, who did not see the shooting, came out the door and stood behind him. Henry came out behind Travis.

"Go back inside," Dan said. He reached into the cruiser, picked up his microphone, and called the dispatcher.

Travis and Henry had to pull Ben back into the bar, where some of the patrons were craning their necks at the window to see what had happened.

"He shot him in the back!" Ben said. "He murdered him!"

Travis had not witnessed the shooting, but saw Dan's partner lying in a pool of blood on the sidewalk, clutching his stomach. He was still moving, writhing in pain. "He shot a cop, Ben."

"But Dan shot Bobby in the back. He didn't give him a chance."

"There'll be an inquiry. Don't assume anything."

"Inquiry?" Ben turned to look at Travis with contempt. "Police inquiry? What do you think they're gonna say? Nigger tried to escape. Case closed."

Travis looked at Ben uncertainly. "You don't know that, Ben. We'll have to wait and see."

Ben stared back at Travis for a moment, then at Henry, who showed no reaction. He went to the bar, sat on a stool, and folded his arms across his chest.

Sirens pierced the night air and soon Van Ness Avenue was filled with police cruisers, their lights flashing, some parked in the middle of the street, some up on the curb. Officers redirected traffic. An ambulance arrived and white-coated emergency personnel hovered over the fallen policeman in front of the bar, while others tended to Bobby a half a block up the street.

Travis went over to the bandstand where Tanya was sitting at a table, still trembling. "You all right?"

Tanya shook her head. She looked over at Washington, who was sitting only a few feet away from her, clutching the bloody towel to his face. She looked back at Travis. "They killed him, didn't they?"

Travis shrugged. "I don't know. Apparently, Bobby grabbed the other cop's gun and shot him."

Tanya stared at him for a moment and buried her head in her hands. "I want to go home."

"I'll call a cab for you. The street should be clear by the time it gets here."

"All right, folks," Henry announced. "Sorry for the disturbance. It's all over now. Drinks on the house." He signaled for the trio to start playing again.

CHAPTER 21

The San Francisco Chronicle reported the incident the next morning on page one—of the metro section. It was treated as a routine crime story with the interesting aside that Bobby Summers, aka Bobby X, was also a member of the Black Puma organization.

The Oakland Tribune, on the other hand, printed the story on the front page of its first edition, with the headline:

BLACK PUMA SHOT DEAD BY SF COP

and went on to mention that Bobby had shot and seriously wounded another policeman while resisting arrest for assault and battery in a San Francisco bar.

The San Francisco Examiner, an evening paper, announced in seventy-two point type:

SAN FRANCISCO COP GUNS DOWN PUMA IN SHOOT OUT

An internal investigation of the shooting was launched in accordance with the San Francisco Police Department's standard procedure.

In the meantime, the black community in Oakland was incensed, with many vocal protests calling for an independent investigation by the Justice Department, though the Justice Department declined to comment. The Black Pumas, under the leadership of Minister of Education Lonnie Erskine, staged a rally in Jack London Square in which Erskine declared that the San Francisco police had now joined forces with the Oakland police to destroy the Black Puma Party. This rally was played down by the major metropolitan papers of the Bay Area, but several black-owned weeklies put it on page one.

Nor did it fail to gain air time with local news stations which in turn brought the incident to the national media.

By the end of the week, Bobby X, Lonnie Erskine, and Sergeant Dan Watt were all on the cover of *Time Magazine*. The cover featured Bobby and Erskine in sunglasses and black berets holding

AK-47s across their chests and Sergeant Watt in the background with his hand on his holstered pistol. The caption read:

PUMAS vs. POLICE: IS THIS WAR?

This cover, in addition to the other local reports, prompted Professor Theodore Kelso to invite Lonnie Erskine to address his class at San Francisco State on 'Marx and Racism.'

Minister Erskine promptly accepted.

Marcella, Travis, and Ben all attended the class that day, though Tanya did not appear.

Professor Kelso introduced Mr. Erskine as 'a noted writer of talent and a leader of the Black Puma Party.'

Erskine took the podium as Kelso sat down in a chair behind him. Professors McFarland and Baumgarten sat in their usual chairs on either side of Kelso.

Erskine, to the disappointment of some, was dressed not in bandoliers and a black beret, but a dark brown business suit with white dress shirt and a striped regimental tie. He could have been a lawyer or a banker if judged by his appearance. His rhetoric, however, quickly dispelled any such illusion.

"The pigs have gotten the upper hand since Karl Marx's day," he said. "There was no military-fascist-industrial state in the 19th Century. But in the past fifty years or so the FBI, the CIA, and metropolitan police forces have all combined their efforts and considerable resources to infiltrate and destroy any individual or group that dares to challenge their authority."

This opening statement was met with thunderous applause. Only Travis, Marcella, and a few others refrained from joining in. Even the three professors on the dais applauded politely.

"You see what has happened recently in San Francisco," Erskine said. "A policeman who was kicked off the Oakland police force for shooting a black man in the back—and that was his *only* punishment—was immediately hired by the San Francisco police department and—surprise, surprise—he does exactly the same thing again to another brother. They say the brother—Bobby Summers, also known as Bobby X—resisted arrest and shot one of the pigs who had arrested him in doing so. But I ask you—"

Erskine pointed his finger towards the assembled crowd, which included many nonstudents, some of whom stood at the back wall dressed in the fashion depicted by the *Time Magazine* cover.

"I ask you—the students and citizens of San Francisco—which of you would not have fought back with whatever means available to you if the police arrested you, or trumped up charges of 'disturbing the peace,' so that they could take you to some stinking cage in the bowels of the so-called 'Hall of Justice' where they could beat you—even kill you—without fear of retribution or accountability? What kind of man would allow himself to be treated like that? Well, I say that that man would be no man at all. A real man would fight back with everything he had—and that's what Brother Bobby did. But alas, for all of his courage, all of his wits, all of his bravery, it was not enough. They shot him down. They killed him. And someone's going to pay. And that someone is Sergeant Dan Watt. I'm calling him out!"

There was loud applause from the rear of the auditorium, along with shouts of 'You said it, Brother!' and 'That's right!' and at least one demand to 'Kill the pigs!'

Erskine continued in this vein for some twenty minutes and as the applause tended to be less frequent and less enthusiastic except for the black-bereted contingent at the rear, he became less animated, awkwardly thanked his hosts, and abruptly sat down.

Professor Kelso then rose and went to the lectern. "Thank you, Mr. Erskine, for such a passionate and heartfelt address. I would have to take issue with you, however, on several points. First, I think it is unfair to characterize all policemen as 'pigs.' Many are conscientious and only trying to do their duty. Second, though I would agree with you that the 'military-fascist-industrial complex' exists—that is a variation, of course, on Dwight. D. Eisenhower's original term—nevertheless, there is little evidence that this complex is so pervasive and monolithic in its power that it orchestrates the systematic arrest and abuse of every dissident at every level. The fact that I stand before you as a free man—as you do, sir—is testament enough to that."

Laughter rippled through the seated portion of the audience.

Erskine stared straight ahead, betraying no emotion.

"Also," Professor Kelso said, "I would take issue with the notion that the state was any less oppressive in Marx's day than our own. The capitalists of the latter 19th century hired their own police forces to break strikes and even to infiltrate worker's organizations with their spies. All of this—including murder—was done with impunity and the tacit, if not explicit, approval of judges, politicians, and the bourgeois class."

There was little reaction to this statement and Kelso continued.

"Finally," he said, "I think that it is premature to judge whether or not Sergeant Watt was justified in shooting—"

There was an eruption of shouting from the back of the room. "He shot him!" "Everybody knows he murdered Bobby!" and "Watt did it and he's gonna pay for it!"

Kelso remained calm until the shouts died down. "We don't know all the facts yet. There will be an inquiry—"

"A police inquiry! It'll be a whitewash!"

"Again," Kelso said, "we don't know that. If the inquiry *is* a whitewash, there are other avenues of appeal and—"

At this moment, Kelso was interrupted by a disturbance in the back. A half a dozen or so young men dressed in Neo-Nazi uniforms suddenly rushed in through the side door from the hallway and attacked the Pumas with ax handles. The Pumas, though suited up in paramilitary garb and bandoliers, were unarmed due to a campus rule against open-carry weapons. There were more of them, however, than there were of the attackers, and the Pumas seemed to be getting the better of them when campus police officers rushed in to break it up. The police, unfortunately, were now caught in the middle of the fracas, and they were suffering greater injuries.

Meanwhile, Professor Kelso urged professors McFarland and Baumgartner to leave by another door just off the dais, which led into the same hallway. Mr. Erskine, for his part, left the dais and made his way to the rear of the auditorium, where he started punching one of the Neo-Nazis. At last a contingent of San Francisco police arrived, and swinging billy clubs, succeeded in subduing members of both organizations, including Mr. Erskine, who was handcuffed. The whole troop of combatants was then led out into the hallway, and into the quadrangle outside the building, where they were hustled into waiting police vans.

Marcella, Travis and Ben were all left standing and staring at each other.

"I think that means class is over," Travis said.

"It was insane," Marcella said. "Why can't people discuss their differences without violence?"

"Try telling that to the police," Ben said.

Travis looked at Ben. "Kelso's right, Ben. We don't know exactly what happened yet."

"I know what happened. I saw Dan Watt shoot Bobby in the back."

"But you didn't see what happened before that."

"I didn't need to. Murder is murder."

Travis shoved his hands into his pockets. "The cops ask you to testify yet?"

Ben picked up some books and a notebook he had been writing in before the fight broke out. "Yeah. I got to go down to the Hall of Justice on Tuesday. It won't do no good, though."

Travis started to say something and thought better of it. He turned to Marcella. "Coffee?"

"I need something to calm my nerves."

"How about that restaurant in Stonestown? A glass of wine, maybe."

"Okay."

"Ben?"

Ben shook his head. "I've got to go shopping with Thuy."

"Shopping? For what?"

"Baby clothes. She thinks we ought to do it together. I'll see you around."

Ben then left by the same door as the professors used earlier.

Marcella and Travis followed Ben with their eyes and then looked at each other.

"He's pretty upset about this," Marcella said.

"Yeah. It's a good thing he didn't have a gun with him that night or he'd be lying on a slab in the morgue right beside Bobby."

Marcella shivered. "I don't want to think about it. Can we go and get that glass of wine now?"

Travis nodded and escorted her out of the classroom by the same door that Ben and the professors had used. By this time, the other students had dispersed through both exits and soon the classroom was empty.

CHAPTER 22

"Soft porn or hard porn—the choice is yours."

Andrea looked across the white linen tablecloth at Howard, who lifted a glass of scotch to his lips as he said this. She didn't answer immediately, but lowered her eyes to the gleaming white plate in front of her with the stylized image of a blue fox at its center. This was one of the most expensive restaurants in San Francisco, known for its celebrity clientele. She looked up. "What's the difference?"

Howard put his glass down. "Soft porn involves nudity—full nudity—but no intercourse. Hard porn is the full Monty—you actually engage in sexual intercourse with another actor and it's filmed from every angle."

"What's the difference in pay?"

"Soft porn conforms to SAG pay scales. As the female star, you'd receive compensation somewhere near the top of the scale. But remember, this is a low-budget film. We can't pay you what a bankable star in Hollywood gets—SAG allows for that."

"And hard porn?"

"You would either get the SAG scale with a bonus if the film makes a profit, or you could take a chance and forgo any salary at all and take a percentage."

"Of the gross?"

Howard shifted his weight in his chair. "Of the net profits."

Andrea smiled. She knew this game. After all, her father was an investment banker. "I'll do it for ten percent of the gross."

Howard looked uncomfortable. He glanced sideways at their neighbors, who seemed not to be listening, but he knew better. "That's not doable, Andrea. Even big stars don't get ten percent of the gross."

"But it's my body, my body exposed to the world. It could end my career before it gets started." Andrea looked down at her martini, which she hadn't touched. This was business and she wanted to be perfectly alert. "I'll do it for five."

Howard looked around again. The place was packed, but relatively quiet. A waiter was rolling a tray of hot hors d'oeuvres their way. "Two and a half."

"Five." Andrea smiled at the waiter, who was standing beside their table now with the silver cover in his left hand and a dainty fork in the other.

"Madam?" he said.

"Oh, that looks delicious," she said. "I'll have a couple of whatever that thing is wrapped in bacon."

"Truffles," the waiter said. "Baked with goat cheese and marinated with brandy."

"Wonderful."

The waiter doled out two or three of these tantalizing morsels to each of them and moved on to the next table.

"All right," Howard said. "Five. But remember—if the film makes nothing, you make nothing."

"I understand the concept, Howard." She popped a bacon-wrapped truffle into her mouth. "Oh, these are divine! Try one, sweetie."

Just as the negotiations were concluded, Andrea spotted Alessandro with a tall, balding man trailing behind him. She waved and Alessandro and the man came over to the table.

Alessandro gave her a kiss on the cheek. "You look gorgeous tonight, Andrea, as always." He nodded to Howard. "Are you two an item?"

Howard blushed. "Partly social and partly business."

"Ah, well...I'd like you to meet my friend David Willingham. He's just landed a role in a new movie with Robert Duval."

"Robert Duval?" Andrea brightened. "Really?"

"Not a major role," Willingham said. "But a good opportunity to work with one of the best."

"You started shooting yet, Howard?" Alessandro failed to suppress a smirk on his face as he glanced at Andrea.

"Not yet," Howard said. "I'm lining up the financing."

"Well, good luck with it—Oh, our table's ready. See you later, folks."

"Charmed," Willingham said, as he followed Alessandro to their table.

Andrea took a sip of her martini. "Asshole. I'll bet he's fucking that dickhead every night while poor Terry sits weeping at his piano in the living room. Did you see that, Howard? His head looks like a dick. I mean, look at his ears, the way they flare out beneath his bald head. Just like a dick. It's called the glans. I learned that in college."

Howard smiled and lifted his glass. "Shall we drink to your future?"

Andrea smiled back and lifted her glass. "Why not? I don't suppose you could recruit Robert Duval for my stud muffin, could you, Howard? Not that he's that attractive, but think of the box office!"

Howard clinked his glass against hers. "I'm afraid he would be too expensive, Andrea. But I think I can find a *real* stud muffin for you."

Andrea winked. "I hope so, sweetie. Just as long as he's cute and has lots of stamina."

"I'll make a note of it," Howard said.

CHAPTER 23

The play closed after a six week run.

Travis no longer had to juggle his schedule to accommodate his studies at San Francisco State while dashing between the theater and the other two venues. All this dashing, however, had been facilitated lately by his purchase of a vehicle: a 1964 Volkswagen van with a sunroof. Though more than ten years old, it was in very good condition. The only negatives were the fact that the sunroof leaked and the paint job, though fairly recent, included a large peace sign on each of the sliding door panels. The blue doves and yellow sunflowers that covered every remaining inch of space on the vehicle announced that the owner was a 'flower child,' though Travis felt this misrepresented his sentiments and allegiances.

"I love it." Marcella examined the vehicle from every angle as it rested against the curb. "You're now an official ambassador of The Haight."

"I'm afraid that it makes me a little conspicuous," Travis said. "But the price was right and it runs like a top."

"Do you know anything about cars?"

"I know how to turn the key and operate the windshield wipers. Oh, and I can change the oil."

Marcella put her arms around him. "That's so reassuring—especially if we breakdown somewhere in the desert."

"What desert? There's a desert around here?"

"I'm thinking of Southern California."

"What do we need to go down there for?"

Marcella dropped her arms and suddenly looked pensive. "Sam's been asked to direct a play at the Mark Taper. He wants me to go with him."

"The Mark Taper?"

"It's the main theatrical venue there. The play's *The Glass Menagerie* by Tennessee Williams. He wants me to play Laura, the super-sensitive younger sister of Tom, Williams' alter ego."

Travis put his arms around her and lifted her off the ground. "That's great! It's the break you've been looking for, isn't it?"

"It is, I guess. But I'll have to move back to L.A."

Travis put her down. "Well...I'm not wedded to this bartending job."

"What about school?"

"I'll transfer. What is it down there? California State at Los Angeles?"

"There're several branches of Cal State there, actually, but it may not be worth it. The play will only run a few weeks, maybe a month or two."

Travis sat down on the curb and Marcella joined him. "I'd hate to be without you for two whole months. Besides, what if you get another job there?"

"Sam says that if the production is successful, it might go to New York."

"New York?" Travis picked up a pebble and tossed it into the street. "I suppose I could follow you there, too."

Marcella leaned against his shoulder. "You'll never get your degree that way. I don't want you to ruin your career because of me."

"Career? What career? I don't even know what I want to do. My major is philosophy. And the more I study philosophy, the more I want to lie in a field of daisies and make love to you."

Marcella smiled. "I guess the van suits you after all."

They sat in silence for a while, or at least as much silence as could be found on Haight Street as traffic began to increase and musicians began their afternoon jam sessions.

"Why don't we go for a drive?" Travis said.

"Okay. Where?"

"I don't know. North. Marin County. Napa. The wine country. Anywhere they have daisy fields."

Marcella laughed. "Let me get my purse."

"You don't need your purse. I've got money—gobs of it. The tips were better than usual last night."

"All right."

They got up from the curb and climbed into the van. As they did so, it began to rain.

"Don't worry," Travis said. "I'm prepared for inclement weather." He turned the wiper knob and nothing happened.

Marcella laughed.

"I think you have to be going at least forty miles per hour for them to work. Besides, this is a microclimate. As soon as we get to the Golden Gate we'll be above the clouds and it'll be sunshine all the way into Marin."

"Forever the optimist," she said.

"Have to be. Here we go."

By the time they got to Golden Gate Park, the sunroof began to leak.

"I'll stop at a hardware store and get some caulking," Travis said.

"I like it like this," Marcella said. "It gets us closer to the elements."

"The last time I was close to the elements I was in a foxhole and my teeth were chattering. See what's on the radio."

Before they emerged from the park, the rain stopped, the sunroof was opened, and "Peace Train" was playing on the radio.

"Does this make us hippies?" Travis said.

"I don't know," Marcella said, "but it makes me feel that I'm in the right place at the right time with the right guy."

Travis glanced at her and smiled. "Then why go to L.A.?"

Marcella frowned. "Don't spoil it."

She turned up the music.

CHAPTER 24

The internal investigation of the San Francisco Police Department concluded that Sergeant Dan Watt was justified in shooting Bobby X, even though Bobby was running away from him at the time. The rationale was that Bobby had just shot a policeman—who had since recovered—and though handcuffed, was wielding the policeman's service revolver and might have shot an innocent by-stander or even have turned around and shot Watt.

This explanation did not sit well with the Pumas, of course, nor was it accepted by the black community of San Francisco at large. The local chapter of the NAACP also voiced its outrage, and vowed to bring a civil suit against both Watt and the City of San Francisco.

In the meantime, Lonnie Erskine was released from jail after put-ting up bail and agreeing to appear in court. When he appeared before the judge at the appointed time accompanied by his lawyer and a dozen news reporters, his 'victims,' i.e.; members of the White People's Resistance Party, failed to appear and the charges were dropped.

Lonnie Erskine, however, was not satisfied with this state of af-fairs.

One morning while Ben and Thuy were serving free breakfasts to the disadvantaged children at Potrero Elementary, Erskine appeared at the door to the cafeteria. It was a rather cold, overcast day, and Erskine was wearing a plaid mackintosh that might have been mod-eled in *Gentlemen's Quarterly*.

"Good morning, Ben," Erskine said as he approached the serving table. His hands were deep within his pockets.

"Morning, Mr. Erskine," Ben said.

Erskine smiled and glanced at Thuy, who seemed to study him closely. "Call me Lonnie. Who's your lady friend here?"

"That's Thuy—my fiancée."

Erskine glanced down at Thuy's belly, which was quite prominent at this point. "How are you, Twee? Don't let me interrupt your good work. These children need their nourishment."

Thuy nodded and managed a smile. She went back to serving a young boy who stared wide-eyed at Erskine.

Ben stirred a pot of red beans.

"You heard the verdict of the pigs' internal investigation, I suppose," Erskine said.

Ben nodded without looking at Erskine. "Yeah, I heard."

"Well...what do you think we ought to do about it?"

Ben looked up. "Do? I don't know. What can we do?"

"There are a number of options," Erskine said. "I'd like to discuss them with you when you're free. That is, if you care about justice for one our fallen brothers."

"Sure, I care. But I don't see what—"

"I'll explain it to you when we have a little more privacy. Where do you go from here?"

"Well, I've got a class at San Francisco State at ten. Another one at eleven. After that, I'm free till I go to work at six."

"How about that Italian restaurant at Stonestown? I forget the name."

"Giorgio's, I think. Or Giovanni's. Anyway, I know the one you're talking about."

"Let's say twelve-thirty. Give you time to collect your books and whatnot."

"Okay."

"See you then." Erskine turned to Thuy. "A pleasure to meet you, Twee. Keep up the good work." He then made his way through a group of children, stopping briefly to say something to them that made them laugh.

"He's much nicer than Bobby," Thuy said. "He has good manners."

"Yeah, I guess."

"What does he want to talk to you about?" Thuy's English was improving rapidly.

"About Bobby. He's still pretty angry—like me."

Thuy served the last child and began cleaning up. "Anger is no good. Better to forget about it."

"I can't forget, Thuy. I saw a man murdered and his killer has gone scot free."

"Bobby shot a policeman."

Ben made a clatter with the stainless steel serving trays as he began stacking them. "What else could he do? They might have beat him to death at the police station. He had a right to defend himself."

"We have a saying in Vietnam," Thuy said. "'Ai lam nay chiu.'"

"What's that mean?"

"'Whoever sows wind shall harvest storm.'"

Ben finished stacking the trays and began wiping down the table. "It was Dan Watt who sowed the wind. And he'll be the one who harvests the storm. Come on—we've got two transfers and I've got to stop at the apartment so I can get my books."

* * *

Ben made his first class just in time but hardly paid attention as he was preoccupied with his appointment with Erskine. What could Erskine have in mind? It occurred to him that he was planning on assassinating Dan Watt on some street corner. If that was his plan, he—Ben—would have nothing to do with it. Not that he would be sorry to see Watt gunned down, but they would never get away with it. And even if they did, what would it accomplish? The cops would get their revenge by stopping every black male on the street and finding some excuse to put him in jail. The cycle of violence would be endless. He saw that in Vietnam. After a while, ideology and even patriotism had nothing to do with it. When your buddies got killed, you wanted your revenge.

He sat through the second class, which was the so-called speech class. Professor McFarland, the speech teacher, led this one, spouting off Marxist rhetoric that could have been uttered by Ho Chi Minh himself. There were some things about it, though, that made sense. The oppression of the proletariat—in America, that meant black people—and the corruption of the industrial elite. They seemed to control everything: the economy, the courts, even Congress.

By the time he got to the restaurant, Erskine was already there, waiting for him in a booth at the rear. He stood as Ben approached.

"What are you having, brother?" He clapped Ben on the back and indicated the seat on the other side of the table.

Ben sat down. "I don't know—pizza, I guess."

"The works?"

"Sure."

A waiter came over and Erskine ordered the pizza along with a pitcher of beer. While they waited for the beer, Erskine seemed to study Ben closely.

"Where are you from?" Erskine said.

"Georgia."

"Georgia, huh? What part?"

"Dublin."

"Where's that?"

"Kinda east of Macon."

The waiter arrived with the pitcher of beer and two glasses. He poured out the beer and disappeared again.

"How were you treated down there?" Erskine took a sip of his beer. "I mean by the whites?"

"Okay, I guess."

"Okay? No run-ins with the KKK?"

Ben took a long swallow of his beer. "My daddy was a sharecropper—and a preacher, too. One time, after he delivered a sermon at the church about black folks needing to get out and vote, the Klan burned a cross in our front yard."

"And your daddy? What did they do to him?"

"They dragged him out of the house and beat him with their shotguns and rifles."

"They kill him?"

"No."

"And your daddy—what did he do about it?"

Ben looked around the restaurant. He and Erskine seemed to be the only black people in the place. "He went to the sheriff, but since they all had hoods on, he couldn't identify them."

"And that was that."

"Pretty much." Ben took another swallow of his beer. "But later, after the Voting Rights Act passed Congress in '65, federal marshals came down and stood guard at the polling station while my dad voted." Ben smiled for the first time during the interview. "He said that was the happiest day of his life."

Erskine leaned back. The waiter arrived with their pizza and set it down in the middle of the table. "Well, that's some progress, at least. But it's not enough. You go to school there?"

Ben picked up a slice of pizza and took a bite. "Yeah."

"Integrated?"

"Not at the time. Later, when I was in the army, I heard that they were."

Erskine picked up a slice of the pizza and put it on his plate. Then, to Ben's surprise, he picked up a knife and fork and cut off a piece before putting it into his mouth. He chased it down with a swallow of beer. "The white man will give you a little morsel now and then, but only after you beg long enough. He'll never regard you as his equal, and therefore he'll deny you equal justice. And that's what we've just seen in the case of Dan Watt. White man's justice at work."

Ben said nothing and continued eating.

"What we need in this country," Erskine said, "is justice of, by, and for the black man."

Ben swallowed and reached for his beer. "How you going to do that? You can't just set up a whole separate system of justice for blacks."

"Oh, but we can. It's already set up. And that's where Dan Watt is going to receive the justice he truly deserves."

Ben was now staring at Erskine in wonderment. "You mean vigilante justice?"

"No. Vigilantes are disorganized hoodlums. The Pumas have their own system of justice which, ironically, is modeled on the United States Constitution. We recognize that those white crackers back in 1789 did something right. They just forgot to include black people. And for all the civil rights movements and all the George Washington Carvers, and all the Ralph Abernathys and all the Martin Luther Kings, we still don't have justice!" Erskine pounded his fist on the table to emphasize his point.

Ben glanced around the restaurant and noticed that the other patrons were staring at them. Erskine noticed, too, but seemed not to be concerned.

"How're you gonna get Watt to this court?" Ben said. "And where is it, anyway?"

"The court will be held at our headquarters in Oakland. And getting Watt there is where you come in."

"Me?"

"You drive a car?"

"Sure. Don't have a California driver's license, though."

"Don't worry about that. I'll get you one."

Ben swallowed some more beer and put his glass down. "You saying you want me to help you kidnap Dan Watt and drive him over to Oakland?"

Erskine smiled. "Something like that. Only we call it 'unilateral extradition,' since the city of San Francisco doesn't recognize our status as an independent government."

Ben wiped his mouth with the back of his hand. "Kidnapping. I don't know, Mr. Erskine. I feel bad—real bad—about what happened to Bobby, but kidnapping—ain't that a federal crime?"

"Not when you're dealing with a war criminal like Dan Watt." Another smile came to Erskine's lips as he pushed his plate away. He had hardly touched his pizza. "You let me worry about the legalities, Ben. When the Pumas have adjudicated Mr. Watt, we'll invite the press in and the verdict will overshadow whatever means we used to get him there. Are you with us?"

Ben looked down at the remaining pizza, but was no longer hungry. "I don't know. I'll have to talk it over with my fiancée."

Erskine's eyes grew large. "Your fiancée? That little Vietnamese girl? What can she know about a man's duties and responsibilities? Are you pussy-whipped, Ben?"

Suddenly, Ben was on the defensive. "No. No way. I just trust her advice, that's all."

Erskine leaned forward. "Look, Ben, if you can't make an important decision like this on your own, we'll find somebody else. This has got to be top secret until the court has rendered its verdict. You understand? Then the whole world will know about it and you can discuss it with Two—"

"Thuy."

"All right. You can discuss it with 'Twee' all you want. And she'll be proud of you, Ben. I can guarantee you that. And you know why? Because you will have been a part of history, Ben. That's right—you will have made history as one of the select few bold enough to demand—and receive—justice for the black man. Now...I'll ask you one more time—are you with us?"

Ben stared at Erskine for a moment, looked around the restaurant full of white people who were no longer paying any attention to them, and then back at Erskine. "All I got to do is drive the car?"

"That's all."

"There be guns?"

"No guns. They won't be necessary."

"Then how you gonna get him into the car?"

"Chloroform. It won't hurt him, and by the time we get to Oakland, he'll be conscious. Only he'll be handcuffed."

Ben considered this for a moment. "When?"

"In a few days. I'll let you know in advance. You got a phone?"

"Sure."

"Then write down the number on this napkin." Erskine shoved a napkin across the table, pulled a ballpoint pen out of his jacket and handed it to him. Ben wrote down the number.

"What if Thuy answers?" Ben said. "And I'm not there?"

"I'll leave a message: 'Brother Erskine's train leaves at such and such a time.' Get on the BART and get off at the Montgomery Street station. We'll pick you up there and you'll take over the driving. Simple. Okay?"

Ben laced his fingers together, then pulled them apart. "Okay."

"Good man." Erskine got up and reached over the table with his hand raised for a solidarity handshake. Ben took his hand and squeezed it firmly. "I know I can count on you, Ben. Don't worry about the tab." He then threw a few bills on the table. "You might as well finish that pitcher. Too much beer makes me feel sleepy, and I've still got work to do. See you again soon."

Ben watched as Erskine made his way to the front door. When he was gone, he poured himself another glass of beer, took a swallow, and sighed. "I wish I could tell Thuy."

CHAPTER 25

Travis' optimism about the weather was not unfounded. After they crossed the Golden Gate with its spectacular views of San Francisco and the East Bay, they descended down the winding road to Sausalito, where they stopped at the marina and watched the sailboats come and go for a while. Then they got back into the van and headed for Mt. Tamalpais, where they climbed to the top and surveyed the surrounding area.

"Where's San Francisco?" Travis asked.

"That way." Marcella pointed in a southerly direction where there seemed to be an indistinct line between water, fog, and clouds.

"Oh. Well, then, we've seen everything. Let's go."

Marcella shook her head. "Men."

Once in the van again, they took the Panoramic Highway through the park and about twenty minutes later emerged from the west entrance and headed towards Stinson Beach. By this time it was nearing nightfall and they stopped to watch the sunset.

"Isn't it spectacular?" Marcella said.

"Yes, it is," Travis said. "Or was. Now the sun's sinking out of sight and it'll be dark before we get to Bolinas. Let's go." He stood and brushed the sand from his jeans and headed for the parking lot.

"Men," Marcella said.

When they rolled into Bolinas, the last rays of the sun shot fingers of light into the cirrus clouds suspended several thousand feet above the horizon. The orange, gold and crimson colors struck even Travis with something approaching awe, and they lingered at a railing overlooking the beach for a while before entering a B&B called simply Nirvana. They had no intention of staying overnight, but there were few people in the restaurant and the proprietors, a middle-aged couple, urged them to make a romantic weekend of it.

"There's a path down to the beach just behind the inn," the husband said. He was in his late fifties, Travis guessed, and balding, but thin and fit-looking. "I use it myself every morning when I go out to run. The sunrise is spectacular."

"The sunrise?" Travis said. "But the sun rises in the east."

"Yeah, over Mt. Tam. But it's still spectacular. Of course, it's really spectacular in the evening when it sets. You just missed it."

"No, we didn't," Travis said. "We just watched it from the road."

"Then you know what I mean."

"I guess so."

"Travis has a high tolerance for natural beauty," Marcella said. "It seems to have no effect on him."

"That's not true," Travis said. "It's just that when you've seen the sunset in Bali, it spoils you for everything else."

"Actually," the innkeeper said, "the sunset in Sri Lanka is more beautiful than the one in Bali, and the sunrise over Annapurna surpasses them both."

Travis was stymied. "You've done some traveling, I see."

"We've lived in Hong Kong, Tahiti, and Colombo," the innkeeper's wife said, "where we had B&B's. This is our last stop."

Marcella looked at Travis. "Maybe we should stay—it'll be so educational."

Travis stared at Marcella for a moment, then turned to the innkeeper. "Okay. Put us down for a room. But we don't have any luggage."

"There're terry cloth robes in all the rooms," the wife said. "And there might be a nightgown in one of the drawers. I'll—"

"I don't think it will be necessary," Marcella said. "But thanks anyway."

"Okay," Travis said. "Now that that's settled, can we get something to eat?"

Once settled at their table, they discovered that they had a good view of the beach and watched as the waves crashed over it. It was still light, and the colors that had been confined to the clouds earlier now streaked across the water.

"I wonder if they need a bartender," Travis said. "I could get used to this."

"Your tolerance level is receding." Marcella smiled and picked up her menu.

As they studied their menus, another couple entered the dining room. Travis seemed not to notice, but Marcella tugged on his sleeve.

"Look who just walked in," she said.

Travis looked up from his menu and saw Andrea standing at the reception desk with a man he had never seen before. "What luck. Our old friend and fellow thespian. Who's that guy?"

"I don't know. He's kind of cute, though."

"Hmm. I'd have to say he's not bad-looking. A new flame?"

At that point, Andrea spotted them. She suddenly became animated and waved at them.

"Oh, well," Travis said, "there goes our romantic weekend."

"Maybe they're just here for dinner. Here she comes."

"I can't believe it!" Andrea said. "What a coincidence!" She bent over—her low cut dress displaying her ample bosom—kissed Marcella on the cheek, then Travis.

"It is quite a coincidence, Andrea," Travis said. "We didn't even know we were coming until late this afternoon. How did you—"

"We're shooting in San Rafael. Oh, how rude of me—" She indicated her escort. "This is Blaine Pedersen, my co-star."

"How do you do, Blaine." Travis extended his hand. "I'm Travis Carter, and this is Marcella Morgan."

Smiles all around, but Blaine said nothing. He simply nodded his head.

Andrea seemed embarrassed. "Say something, Blaine. They're not going to bite."

"Hi," Blaine said.

There was an awkward silence that Travis tried to bridge. "Well—won't you join us for dinner? We haven't ordered yet."

"Oh, that would be wonderful," Andrea said. "Are you sure there's room? What a lovely view!"

The proprietor brought a couple of extra place mats and utensils. Andrea and Blaine sat down and ordered drinks.

Travis tried to make conversation with Blaine while Marcella and Andrea shared some gossip as if they were old friends.

"Where are you from, Blaine?"

"L.A."

"L.A.'s a pretty big place. What part?"

"Long Beach."

"This your first movie?"

"No."

"Well...how did you get this role? What's it about, anyway?"

"I've been in a couple of Howard's movies. It's not about anything, really."

"It's got to be about something."

"Not really. Just suck and fuck."

Travis suddenly remembered who Howard was and what kind of movies he made. "Oh. I guess it doesn't take much acting."

"Nope."

Andrea stopped talking to Marcella when she heard Blaine's comments. "Blaine, honey—you don't have to tell people about the details. There *is* a story to it."

For the first time since they sat down, Blaine smiled. "Sure."

Andrea grimaced, turned back to Marcella, and continued their conversation. Marcella glanced at Blaine and pretended to be absorbed in Andrea's film-industry name-dropping.

By the time they were finished with dinner, Andrea and Marcella seemed like sisters who hadn't seen each other for years. Travis marveled at Marcella's patience, for it was Andrea who was doing most of the talking. What they were talking about, he wasn't quite sure, but he picked up certain phrases like 'net profits,' 'front end,' and 'back end.' He assumed Andrea was preparing Marcella for her own contract negotiations.

While he was searching for topics of conversation with Blaine, Andrea suddenly turned to them.

"Marcella and I need to go to the powder room," she said. "You boys hold down the fort."

Then the two girls got up and disappeared into the lobby.

"How are the rehearsals going?" Travis said to Blaine, thinking that showing an interest in his work would animate him.

"Rehearsals?"

"Yeah. Don't you rehearse scenes like in a play?"

"Not really. We have a few lines to memorize and then Howard tells us where to stand, or sit, or lie down and in what position."

"Oh." Travis noted that this was the longest answer Blaine had offered since they had met. "Well...how do you, uh, maintain an erection while all this is going on? I mean with the lights, and cameras, and—"

"I never have problems with an erection."

"Oh. Just wondered."
Blaine smiled.

* * *

No sooner than she had closed the door of the powder room behind her, Andrea burst into tears.

"Andrea!" Marcella said. "What's the matter?"

"I feel like a whore!"

Marcella was tempted to point out that having sexual intercourse in front of cameras with an all male crew standing around watching was bound to generate some epithets of that kind. Instead, she tried to be as sympathetic as possible. "I thought you were looking at this as simply a business venture. A launching pad for your career, you said."

Andrea wiped her tears away and pressed her back against the door. "I do look at it that way. But then Howard suggested that Blaine and I come to Bolinas before our big scene together and get to know each other a little better. All the way over here from San Rafael, Blaine didn't say two words to me."

"Well, he seems very shy." Marcella indicated a settee against the wall. "Why don't we sit down?"

They sat.

"He's not shy," Marcella said, beginning to cry again. "He just doesn't care. I'm an animal to him. I could just as well be a sheep."

Marcella offered her a tissue from a dispenser on the console next to them. "He just sees it as a business venture, that's all. Like you said you do. Is it necessary that you feel affection for each other?"

"Yes." Andrea blew her nose. "I can't open my legs to a man, I can't even get wet, unless I like him. Blaine is a robot, a monster."

"Oh, Andrea. I don't think you've given him a chance. Why don't you go for a stroll on the beach with him, ask him about his childhood, his family, his—"

"I tried that. He had a horrible childhood, he said, and doesn't want to talk about it."

"Well, then...why don't you just go up to your room, order a bottle of champagne and put on some soft music?"

Andrea wiped her nose and sniffed. "The champagne sounds good, but...say, why don't you and Travis join us? I'd feel so much better and more comfortable."

"Join you? In your bedroom?"

"Sure. We could swap partners. I think you'd like Blaine better than I do, and you might even get him to talk. Travis and I get along and I've always thought he was cute."

Marcella recoiled as if bitten by a snake. "Andrea...you can't be serious."

"Sure I am. Travis has a way with women. He doesn't have the biggest cock in the world, but—" Andrea stopped short.

Marcella was stunned. "You've been to bed with Travis?"

"Only once. It was kind of a friendly encounter. I was down in the dumps and he cheered me up."

"I'll bet he did."

"Oh, Marcella, I'm sorry. It just slipped out. It wasn't anything, really. Two ships in the night."

Marcella stood. "I think we'd better go back now. They'll start wondering what we're doing for so long."

Andrea stood. "Please, honey, don't take what I just told you seriously. Travis was at loose ends at the time and now he's found you. I'm so happy for both of you."

Marcella managed a smile and gave Andrea a kiss on the cheek. "I'm not jealous in the least, Andrea. And think about that walk on the beach with Blaine. I think it'll do wonders for your relationship."

"Well...I'll try."

Marcella waited while Andrea fixed her mascara and they returned to the dining room.

After dinner, Andrea and Blaine went for a walk on the beach and Travis and Marcella went up to their room. Light from a full moon streamed in through the curtains and its reflection on the ocean could be seen from the fourposter bed. There were antique chests, tables, and even a Windsor rocking chair resting on a hooked rug in the center of the room.

Marcella, however, seemed unmoved by the romantic atmosphere. She stripped down to her panties as usual before they turned in, climbed into bed, pulled the quilt over her and faced away from

Travis towards the window.

"You feel all right?" Travis said. He pulled the quilt back to expose her shoulder and kissed it.

"The crab I had didn't sit well on my stomach," Marcella said. "I think somebody left it out too long."

"Can I get you some Alka-Seltzer? There must be some around here somewhere. I could go downstairs and ask at the desk."

"No, no. I'll be all right. I just need some rest."

This sudden change of mood, Travis thought, couldn't be due solely to an upset stomach. Marcella looked fine when she came back from the powder room, but she was cool towards him from that point on. "What did you and Andrea talk about in the powder room?"

"Just girl talk."

Travis ruminated over this for a few moments. "She told you about us."

"Us?"

"Me and her. She invited me over to her place that night after I walked in on you and Alessandro."

Marcella sat up. "Walked in on me and Alessandro? What are you talking about?"

Travis noted that it was the first time their eyes had met since dinner. "Well, I was spared the graphic details, but it was that day that I dropped in to see you, and Ben and Thuy were there. I had seen Alessandro leaving just as I was coming in. You were disheveled when you came out of the bedroom. I put two and two together."

"You're trying to tell me we're even?"

"I don't look at it that way."

Marcella fluffed up a pillow and propped herself up against the headboard. She crossed her arms over her chest. "Well, how *do* you look at it?"

Travis sighed. "I look at it like I was jilted and had probably lost you forever."

Marcella looked skeptical. "It's not the same."

"I didn't say it was."

"I thought I was in love with Alessandro until I found out he was gay. You just tumbled into bed with Andrea when she batted her eyes at you."

Travis fluffed up his pillow and leaned against the headboard. "So what was the harm? She was there, offering me her love and affection and you weren't."

"Love and affection? Andrea? She was offering you her body."

Travis smiled. "That, too."

They sat in silence for fully two minutes. Then Travis leaned over and kissed her. "Can't we make up?"

"I don't know. I'll have to think about it. Good night." Marcella slipped back down into a prone position, turned away from him, and pulled the quilt over her.

Travis sat staring at her for several moments, then turned out the light. "Good night, Marcella."

CHAPTER 26

Ben came home from San Francisco State one afternoon and found Thuy folding laundry. Her belly was big now and she had some trouble keeping it away from the furniture as she moved around the apartment. Ben was glad to see her sitting comfortably in an armchair as she folded underwear and T-shirts in her lap and stacked them on the arm of the chair. Behind her stood an ironing board with an iron resting upright and one of his shirts stretched out on the narrow end of it.

He put his books down on the kitchen table.

"I can iron my own shirts," he said.

"It's okay. I'll iron them."

"Better you stay off your feet whenever you can."

"It's all right. I like the exercise."

Ben marveled at Thuy's improved grammar. It was better than his own. "Maybe you'd better tell Henry you need a leave of absence for a while. I'm sure he'll understand."

Thuy smiled. "You worry too much. I've still got three months. You want a sandwich?"

"I'll get it." Ben went to the refrigerator and started pulling jars and meats and a half gallon of milk out. He put it all on the kitchen table and began spreading mayonnaise on a couple of slices of bread.

"Mr. Erskine called," Thuy said.

Ben stopped what he was doing. "Erskine? What did he want?"

"He just said to give you a message. I wrote it down by the telephone."

Ben put down the knife he was using and went to the end table next to the sofa where the phone was. There was a pad there for messages. He peeled the note off and read it to himself:

Brother Erskine's train leaves at 2:45 today

"Where is he going?" Thuy said. She finished folding the underwear and stood slowly and a little unsteadily. "Is he making a speech?"

Ben folded the note in half and put it in his pocket. "I think it's a book signing. He's a writer, you know."

"Oh." Thuy approached the ironing board, wet her finger, and tested the iron to see if it was hot. "I like him. He's very polite. The kids at Potrero like him, too. Maybe he could come and talk to them. They probably never see a real writer before."

"Yeah. Good idea. I'll ask him." Ben went back to making his sandwich. He looked up at the clock over the stove. One-thirty. "You want a sandwich?"

"No. I'll have some of that cha lua from last night. You want some?"

"Yeah. I'll have that as a side dish."

After lunch, Thuy said she was tired and needed a nap. Ben put away the laundry and cleaned up the kitchen. When he was through and sure that Thuy was asleep, he stood on his toes and reached to the top shelf of one of the cabinets.

It was still there: the .38 revolver. He opened the cylinder and checked to see that all six chambers contained bullets. Bobby didn't given him any extra cartridges and he didn't need them. Not then, not now. It would just be a precaution in case something went wrong.

He put on his jacket and slipped the revolver into a side pocket. He checked one last time to see that Thuy was still asleep and left by the front door, quietly closing it until he heard a click. Thuy would be safe while he was gone.

He walked to the corner where he caught the Muni to the Balboa Park station and sat next to a young white kid with a rainbow-colored Mohawk and an array of tattoos on his arms and neck. One of the tattoos on his forearm was of a swastika.

"I know what you're thinking, dude."

Ben looked at him. "You do?"

"Yeah. Skinhead with a swastika tattoo. Must be a Neo-Nazi. That's not me, bro."

Ben turned away and looked straight ahead.

"Most people don't know that a swastika is a very ancient symbol. Out of India. It means 'fertility and fulfillment.' Or in some places, 'good luck.'"

Ben continued to stare straight ahead.

"You know, some of my best friends are black dudes."

Ben said nothing. The kid stared at him for a moment, then turned towards the window. Two stops later, he got off.

Ben got off at the Montgomery Street station as he was instructed. He stood at the corner on Market and Montgomery and checked his watch. It was precisely 2:45pm.

Suddenly a late model Lincoln Continental pulled up to the curb and the passenger window slid noiselessly down. It was Erskine, wearing a pair of sunglasses. He opened the door and got out.

"Slide across. I'll get in the back."

The driver, also wearing sunglasses, opened his door and got into the back with Erskine.

Ben slid across to the driver's seat and adjusted the rearview mirror. He now recognized the other man from the meeting in Oakland. His name was Emmett something.

"Turn left at Sansome and go up to Washington," Erskine said.

Ben put the car into gear and drove to the next block where he turned left. When they got to Washington, Erskine instructed him to turn right on Kearney.

"Chinatown."

Ben glanced in the rearview mirror and saw Erskine grinning.

"Like in the movie," he said. "Stop in the middle of the next block. See—there's his cruiser."

Ben looked up Kearney and saw the cruiser parked at the curb.

"Ease up right behind him," Erskine said. "He should be coming out of the restaurant at any moment."

Ben pulled up behind the cruiser and stopped. He could see a cop in the driver's seat, apparently waiting. "What about the driver?"

"Don't worry about him," Erskine said. "Just be ready to go when I tell you to."

Ben was getting nervous. He glanced in his rearview mirror and saw a delivery truck behind him. The driver honked his horn and gestured for him to move on.

"Ignore him," Erskine said.

Ben turned his attention again to the cop in the driver's seat of the cruiser. Were they going to chloroform him, too? His window, as far as Ben could tell, was closed. They would have to open the door—what if it was locked?

"There he is," Erskine said. He rolled down his window.

Ben looked to his right and saw Dan Watt emerge from the restaurant. He was carrying a brown paper bag—a takeout order.

Ben looked in the rearview mirror just as Emmett opened his door and stepped out into the street. Then he saw the shotgun in Erskine's hands. "No!"

But Erskine pulled the trigger almost at the same time as Ben's shout. There were two blasts in quick succession. The expression on Watts' face was one of surprise then shock as the blasts knocked him down onto the pavement. The brown paper bag exploded and spread Moo shu pork all over the sidewalk and the window of the restaurant. Moo shu pork mixed with Watt's blood.

Ben looked to the cruiser in front of him. Emmett had a pistol in his hand and fired one shot through the window. The cop in the driver's seat slumped over.

Emmett jumped back into the car.

"Go!" Erskine shouted.

Ben put his foot to the accelerator and pulled around the corner. Bystanders were frozen, staring at the body lying in a pool of blood on the sidewalk.

"Take a left on Broadway," Erskine said. "Slow down and merge with the traffic."

Ben did as he was told and suddenly it seemed as though they were part of the afternoon traffic and that nothing unusual had happened.

"Go to Van Ness Avenue and turn right," Erskine said. "You know, you almost blew the whole thing up, Ben."

"I didn't know you were going to kill him," Ben said.

"I didn't either," Erskine said. "Didn't you see him go for his gun? He brought it on himself."

Ben turned right on Van Ness. "Where we going?"

"North. Over the Golden Gate. We'll go up 101 to San Rafael, then over the bridge at Richmond. We'll ditch the car at a chop shop there."

"How will I get home?"

"Same way we will. BART." Erskine chuckled. "The white man's marvel of technology."

Ben drove over the Golden Gate and looked east. A beautiful panorama of the East Bay. And of Alcatraz.

"Mr. Erskine."

"What is it, Ben?"

"Why did you pick me to drive the car?"

"Because you have no criminal record. If the cops stop us, you're clean. Any more questions?"

"No, sir."

"Good. But I want you to remember something, Ben."

Ben didn't respond but looked in the rearview mirror where his eyes met only Erskine's sunglasses.

"If you have any thoughts about turning us in, you're an accessory. They'll call it murder. We call it justifiable homicide. And the Pumas have a way of dealing with turncoats. You understand?"

"Yes, sir."

"Good." Erskine leaned back in his seat, looking very satisfied. He gazed out over the Bay. "Looks like we'll go by my alma mater— San Quentin. We'll be sure to wave at the boys, won't we Emmett?"

Ben looked at Emmett, who hadn't said a word through the entire ordeal. He still said nothing. There was only a faint smile that came to his lips.

* * *

When Ben arrived home, it was dark. He tested the front door and saw that it was unlocked. He pushed the door open. "Thuy?"

He heard the TV going.

"Ben?"

He sighed with relief and closed the door behind him. "Did you go out while I was gone?"

"Yes, to the grocery store. Where have you been?"

"I went to Henry's but he said it was slow so I could go home. What's on?"

Thuy hadn't moved from the sofa. "News. There was a gun fight in Chinatown."

"Oh, yeah?" Ben took off his jacket and went around the sofa to the kitchen. "What happened?"

"Some gangsters shot two policemen in front of a restaurant and drove off. They're looking for a Lincoln car, I think."

Ben extracted the revolver from his jacket and replaced it on the top shelf of the cabinet. "What happened to the policemen?"

"One was killed—Oh, Ben! It was that Sergeant Watt who shot Bobby. And the other was his partner. They say he's at the hospital in critical condition."

"Critical?" Ben went to the sofa and sat down next to Thuy. He put his arm around her. "Did he say anything?"

"Not yet. He's unconscious. Ben—you don't think it was the Pumas, do you?"

Ben avoided Thuy's earnest gaze. "I don't know. That would be a dumb thing for them to do. Everybody would suspect them.'

"Ben—"

"What?"

That note that Mr. Erskine left you. About leaving on the train at 2:45. Why would he want you to know that?"

"I don't know. I guess he just wanted to let me know he was going out of town in case I needed him for anything. We got any beer?"

"Sure."

Ben got up and went to the refrigerator. He was aware that Thuy's eyes were on him all the way. "Want something?"

"No. Ben—"

"What? Thuy—I'd just like to relax, okay?"

"You know something about this, don't you?"

Ben opened his beer on the counter and came back to the sofa. He sat down and stared at the TV. "Yeah. I know something about it."

"You didn't go to Henry Africa's, did you?"

"No." He took a swallow of beer and put it down on the coffee table. "I drove the car."

"Ben! Why? Why did you—"

"I didn't know they were going to kill him. Erskine told me they were going to kidnap him and put him on trial in Oakland. By the time I realized what was going down, it was too late."

"Ben—you've got to call the police."

"I can't. The Pumas will kill me."

Thuy folded her arms over her belly and looked down at the floor. Ben reached over the coffee table and cut the TV off.

Thuy started crying.

Ben put his arms around her. "I'm sorry, Thuy. I screwed up. I should have told you about it—you'd have had the sense to figure it out. But I can't call the cops. Even if I get a light sentence for driving the car, the Pumas will come after me."

Thuy wiped her tears away. "Did you take your gun?"

"Yes."

"Did you shoot, too?"

"No. I never touched it."

"Then you can tell the police the truth. Erskine tricked you."

Ben sighed and leaned back in the sofa. "Yeah. He tricked me, all right. I was a goddamned idiot."

Thuy picked up the phone from the end table and put it in Ben's lap. "Call them, Ben. Call them now."

Ben looked at her, then her belly. He picked up the phone, but hesitated. "Shouldn't I call a lawyer first?"

"Okay. Call a lawyer."

"I don't know any."

"Call Travis. He'll know."

Ben stared at her for a moment, then started dialing Travis' number.

CHAPTER 27

Travis returned from the airport in time to hear his phone ringing. He had dropped Marcella off for her flight to L.A. and was in a bad mood. He wasn't sure he would ever see her again.

"Hello?" At first he heard nothing but heavy breathing. He thought it was a crank call and started to hang up.

"Travis?"

"Ben? What's up?"

"I got a problem."

Travis slipped off his jacket and sat at his desk. "What problem?"

"You heard about Dan Watt?"

"Watt? No. Was I supposed to?"

"He was gunned down this afternoon."

Travis looked around his sparsely furnished apartment. He should get a television. "It was on the news?"

"Yeah."

"You know who did it?"

"The Pumas."

"Erskine?"

"Yeah."

Travis knew the answer to his next question. "You were with him?"

"Yeah."

Travis sighed. "You've got a problem, all right. Tell me this, Ben. Did you shoot him?"

"No. Just Erskine and another guy. I was the driver."

"You knew it was going down?"

"No."

Travis sighed again, but with relief this time. He leaned back in his chair and stared out the window at the brick wall across the alley. "You're going to need legal help."

"I know. That's why I called you. You know any lawyers?"

Travis thought for a moment. "Only one."

"Who's that?"

"Professor Kelso."

"Kelso?"

"Yeah. He's got a law degree. I don't know if he's ever practiced, though."

"Well...maybe he knows someone who does practice."

"I'll call him."

"Okay. I'm not going anywhere."

Travis hung up and pulled a phone book out of his desk drawer. He found the number and noted that Kelso lived in Pacific Heights. It was now about diner time, but Travis figured this was an emergency.

"Sorry to bother you this time of night, Professor, but—"

"You're not bothering me. And call me Ted."

"All right. Ted. You know Ben Franklin? He's one of your students."

"Sure. He's making a lot of progress, considering his lack of preparation for college work."

"Well, he's gotten into a little trouble."

"What kind of trouble?"

"You heard about that shooting this afternoon?"

"Uh, oh." There was a pause. "Was he the shooter?"

"No. He assures me he wasn't. He only drove the car and didn't know it was going to happen."

"And you believe him?"

"I do."

Kelso sighed. "Why are you calling me?"

"I understand that you're a lawyer. I don't know any others."

"I was a prosecutor in Manhattan before I decided to go into teaching. Mostly securities fraud. What's Ben's number?"

Travis gave him the number. Kelso thanked him and hung up.

He rose from his desk, put on his jacket and went out to look for a copy of the *Examiner*. It was San Francisco's only afternoon paper, and maybe the shooting was early enough to make the deadline.

He only had to walk to the corner to find a newsstand. The headline screamed:

COP GUNNED DOWN IN CHINATOWN!

This was a special edition. Travis put a quarter in the machine and took it back to his apartment.

He sat down at his desk again and spread the paper out on it. Lurid, sensational photos of Watt's blood-spattered body on the sidewalk, blood on the pavement, blood on the shattered window of the restaurant, even blood on the doors of the police cruiser.

BLACK PUMAS SUSPECTED!

The article suggested that it was an assassination as retribution for Watt's shooting of Bobby X a month earlier. Witnesses said the shooters were in a black Lincoln Continental with a dirty California license tag that obscured the numbers. The shooters, at least two of them, were both African-Americans. The driver was a big, husky man, also African-American. The second cop, Watt's partner, died at the hospital.

Travis folded up the newspaper and tossed it onto the armchair near his desk. What could he do to help Ben?

After all they had been through together, and just when Ben seemed to have his life together, the first in his family to go to college, volunteering to help feed hungry school children, Thuy expecting—this happens. Sure, he was torn up about the shooting of Bobby X. But he wasn't the type to seek revenge. How did Erskine con him into driving the car?

Restless, he decided to go for a walk.

He walked up Taylor Street towards Nob Hill. He smiled at the irony of his living only a couple of blocks from the wealthiest neighborhood in San Francisco. A few blocks in the other direction and he would be in the Tenderloin—the poorest neighborhood.

At the top of the hill, he waited for traffic and crossed California Street. A few blocks to the west was the Rose and Thorn. Amazing how compact this city was.

At the corner, taking up nearly the whole block between California and Sacramento, was Grace Cathedral. He had walked by it many times, but had taken little notice of it. It was well-known as a rallying point for social causes.

He stopped at the entrance as he noticed a number of people, mostly black, hurrying into the church. A calendar of events was posted near the entrance. In large letters opposite the day's date it read:

EMERGENCY MEETING
White Backlash to Killing of
Sergeant Dan Watt?
7pm

He decided to go inside.

It was a very traditional Gothic cathedral with vaulted ceilings and stained glass windows high above the nave. It must have had a capacity of over a thousand people.

He sat down in one of the back pews and observed the proceedings, with a black man in a dark suit and a clerical collar smiling as he greeted many who were apparently old friends. After the exchange of pleasantries, everyone but the clergyman took their seats.

"The citizens of San Francisco have received a shock today, as you all know," he said. "The purpose of this meeting is to discuss the possibility of a backlash from the white community and if there is, what we, as concerned citizens, can—or should—do about it."

Travis was impressed by this minister's demeanor and calm articulation. The members of the congregation, if that's what they were, were similarly composed and restrained. He had never witnessed a large assembly of black people quite like this.

"Is there a representative of the Pumas here tonight?" The minister looked around the church, alert to any raised hands, but seeing none, he continued.

"Naturally, the Pumas are going to be the first to be accused of this crime, and many of us, though we may not support the tactics and strategy of that organization, are known to be sympathetic to its ideals and goals. This, in turn, will place all African-Americans—however law-abiding—under suspicion. Now—are there any suggestions as to how we might deal with this potentially explosive situation?"

Several hands went up. The minister pointed to a woman in her forties wearing a tweed jacket and a grey fedora with a red feather in it. She stood.

"I think we should call a press conference and make it clear to the media that this heinous crime is in no way condoned by the African-American community of San Francisco."

There was applause all around and the woman sat down.

A young man in an oversized newsboy's cap and a colorful vest over a green shirt stood. "The man got what he deserved. If a Puma did it, more power to him."

There was a weak applause from scattered areas of the church and he sat down.

"Anyone else?" the minister said. He recognized an elderly man dressed in a houndstooth jacket and a bow tie.

"Whether this Watt fellow deserved it or not is immaterial," he said. "The fact is, it was vigilante justice and it's no different than hanging horse thieves or sending the KKK out to lynch a black man accused of raping a white woman. Let the courts decide who's guilty and let God judge the judges."

There was a more enthusiastic applause for this sentiment and the elderly man sat down.

Another man stood. He was short and stocky, wearing a longshoreman's jacket and work boots. "The white man's justice is no justice at all. You look at the statistics: African-Americans are fifteen percent of the population, but they're forty percent of the prison population. These Pumas ain't the answer, but at least they have the guts to fight back."

There was loud applause from the young man in the newsboy's cap, but from no others, and the longshoreman, a bit unsettled, sat down.

After several more people expressed their views, the clergyman announced that, as the lady in the gray fedora with the red feather suggested, there would be a press conference at ten o'clock the next morning in Gresham Hall, adjacent to the main building. He invited all present to attend, and said that the dean of the cathedral would make a statement.

As the meeting broke up, Travis rose and lingered about the cathedral, curious about the architecture, and especially the labyrinthine design in the floor. He walked about in it, trying to stay within the lines to see if he could emerge from the other side without coming to a dead end.

"It's meant to produce a state of meditation."

Travis looked up and saw the clergyman standing a few feet away from him on the other side of the labyrinth, with his hands clasped behind his back. "Oh—I thought it was like a puzzle, or a game."

"It is, in a way. But it's said to focus and sharpen the mind in the presence of God."

Travis looked skeptical.

"I can see that you are struggling with belief," the priest said. "You want to believe, but you find it difficult to make the leap from your rational mind to the suprarational."

"The suprarational?"

"Well, there are many names for it—the suprarational, the supernatural, the spiritual, the 'other' reality, or, as I like to think of it, the Dimension of the Divine."

Travis had never heard of this last term before, but it appealed to him. "Do you mean that there's another dimension in the universe that operates under a different set of physical laws?"

"Something like that. Scientists these days are always proposing that there may be not one, but perhaps dozens of universes, all with their own physical laws. But I think there's one that envelopes them all, and that one is the Kingdom of God."

Travis stared at the priest for a few moments. The priest simply smiled at him. "I'll have to think about that."

"I hope you do. I'd be happy to have further discussions with you in the future, if you like. My office is just across the courtyard.

"Well...maybe I will."

The priest extended his hand. "My name is Father Lattimore."

"Travis Carter." After shaking Father Lattimore's hand, Travis stood awkwardly for a moment, simply looking at him. He seemed to have a serenity about him, a kind of peace, that Travis envied. Suddenly, apropos of nothing, he said, "Are you married?"

Father Lattimore seemed not to be surprised by the question. "I am. My wife and I have three children."

"That's...that's nice. Well, I'd better go now."

"It was a pleasure to meet you, Travis. By the way, I noticed that you were one of the few white people to attend the meeting. Do you have a special interest in the tragic event that occurred this afternoon?"

"You might say so. A friend of mine—well, you might say he was involved."

"A black friend?"

"Yes."

"I see. Has your black friend notified the police of his involvement?"

"He will, I think. He may have already."

"Good." Father Lattimore looked up towards the ceiling. Travis followed his line of sight, but could not determine the object of his interest, unless it was one of the images in the stained glass windows.

Father Lattimore lowered his eyes again. "I would hope that you would stand by your friend in this difficult time, whatever his culpability."

"I intend to."

"Tell him...tell him that I will be available to counsel him, should he desire it."

"I will do that, Father Lattimore."

Father Lattimore simply nodded with a smile and walked off to a side passage that Travis supposed led to his office.

He lingered for a while longer, surveying the cathedral. It *was* a beautiful, serene place. The light was dim at this time in the evening, but there were spotlights that illuminated the stained glass windows and he noticed that in addition to the usual saints, there were images of more contemporary figures, including John Glenn, the astronaut, and Albert Einstein. Einstein...a Jew and a scientist reputed to be an atheist.

Travis looked down at the floor. He was still standing in the middle of the labyrinth. Suddenly he saw the way out. He kept his feet carefully between the lines and emerged on the other side. Then he went to the entrance and passed through the ornate gilded bronze doors, which he stopped for a moment to examine.

When he emerged onto the steps, the fog was rolling in, the ships in the bay were sounding their horns, and the temperature had dropped several degrees.

He buttoned up his jacket and headed back down Taylor Street towards his apartment.

CHAPTER 28

The next morning at the Hall of Justice Ben was booked and put into a special holding cell for his own protection. Two hours later, after Kelso posted his bail, he walked out of a side door only to be met by a phalanx of reporters.

"Are you a Black Puma, Mr. Franklin?"

"Is Ben Franklin your real name?"

"Did you shoot Dan Watt?"

"If not, who did?"

Ben, on the advice of Professor Kelso, answered none of these questions. Kelso addressed the reporters himself:

"Gentlemen, my client, Mr. Franklin, will be happy to answer your questions in due time. At the moment, however, his life may be in danger and he will proceed to a secure location with around-the-clock security. Make way, Gentlemen."

As Ben, Travis, and two police detectives ducked into a waiting car, Kelso remained for a few minutes and took questions.

"Aren't you Theodore Kelso, Professor of International Relations at San Francisco State?"

"I am."

"And you're a lawyer?"

"I am that, too."

"Why did you take Mr. Franklin's case?"

"He's a student of mine."

This last answer seemed to silence the reporters for a moment and they began furiously writing in their notebooks.

By the time they looked up, Kelso was in his car and driving up Sixth Street.

Later that day, the Oakland Police arrested Emmett Smalls, aka Abdul-Jalil, at an Oakland limousine service where he worked. He was charged with resisting arrest with violence and first degree murder.

Lonnie Erskine was more elusive. A man who matched his description was taken off a plane at Oakland International Airport, but it was discovered that the man was not, in fact, Erskine, but a medical device salesman returning to his company's headquarters in Omaha, Nebraska. The real Lonnie Erskine departed fifteen minutes earlier on a plane to Mexico City under an assumed name. By the time the police realized their mistake and notified Mexican authorities, Erskine was on his way to Havana, Cuba.

This did not mean, however, that Ben was out of danger. There were elements in the Black Puma organization that wanted to see him dead. Thus, the San Francisco police contacted the commander of the Presidio and got his permission to allow Ben to be temporarily housed at a barracks that was slated to be torn down. He would be guarded by two San Francisco detectives around the clock and, of course, MP's guarded the perimeter gates. Kelso was given a pass to come and go as he pleased.

Travis was the only other visitor allowed in the compound, at Ben's request. Not even Thuy was allowed in, as she was a Vietnamese national and the commander of the base considered her a security risk.

Ben, Travis, and Kelso sat at a table in the NCO's office, where Kelso explained to Ben his options.

"Under California law" he said, "if you were a participant in the planning of the murder of Watt and his partner, Cirelli, you would be as culpable as if you had pulled the trigger yourself."

"But I didn't know they was going to kill'em," Ben said.

"I believe you," Kelso said, "but the prosecutor may not. I'm just laying out the options—both his and yours."

Ben glanced at Travis, who was sipping his coffee. "All right."

"In some states they call that an 'accessory before the fact,' but in California it is the same as a principal, that is, the perpetrator." Kelso, who almost never wore a tie, but was dressed in a blue blazer and blue oxford shirt with an open collar, leaned back in his chair. "We only have your word for it that you didn't know that Erskine was planning to murder Watt. Is there anyone who might have overheard your conversation with Erskine in the restaurant in Stonestown?"

"I don't know. I don't think so."

"Did you tell anyone about it afterward? Like, say, Travis here?"

"No."

"Or maybe Thuy? Since you're not married to her, she could testify on your behalf."

"No. I wanted to, but Erskine said not to."

Kelso leaned forward again. He hadn't touched his coffee. "That makes it more difficult. On the other hand, the prosecutor probably won't even charge you as an accessory before the fact. He wants to nail Erskine and Smalls."

"But Erskine's out of the country," Travis said.

"And unextraditable," Kelso said. "The prosecutor will have to deal with him later. He'll probably have to bring in the State Department. Maybe even the FBI and CIA."

"You mean they'll kidnap him?" Ben said.

Kelso smiled. "That's a sweet irony, isn't it? You planned to kidnap Watt, which is a serious offense in itself, and the CIA routinely kidnaps fugitives abroad who have fled to countries with whom we have no extradition treaty. But the prosecutor—his name is Stanley Feinberg—is not likely to charge you with accessory to kidnapping since there *was* no kidnapping. In fact, the whole kidnapping plot was a ruse to get you to drive the car. Correct?"

"Correct," Ben said.

"Now—the real difficulty is that whether you were aware of Erskine's intention or not, you drove the getaway car. And that makes you an accessory *after* the fact."

"What's the difference?" Ben said.

"The difference is that you cannot be charged as a principal in the murders, assuming they believe your story that Erskine tricked you into thinking it was only going to be a kidnapping. That means you will be subject to a lesser sentence."

Ben stared at Kelso for a moment. "How much lesser?"

"No more than three years."

"In prison?"

"Of course."

Ben banged his fist on the table. "But you said if I turned myself in, they would drop the charges of 'aiding and abetting.'"

"Calm down, Ben. No charges have been made yet. They're after the killers, not you. And your testimony is critical to their getting a conviction. They're likely to give you every break they can, but I'd be surprised if they let you off altogether. More likely, you'll have to serve a year or two. But I'll do the best I can."

Ben glanced again at Travis, who nodded towards Kelso as if to say, 'trust him.' "Doesn't it count for something that I turned myself in and named Erskine and Smalls?"

"Sure it does. They may not charge you at all, but I want you to be prepared for the worst." Kelso stood. "And the worst isn't bad, considering the mess you've gotten yourself into. I've got to go now, Ben." He looked around the barracks office, which was decorated with company flags, citations, a rifle on the wall, and a photograph of Richard Nixon. "You'll be safe here. The Pumas are in disarray at the moment, and in any case, they're not going to attack a military base. Do you need anything else?"

Ben looked up at Kelso, glanced at Travis, then at the door where he knew a detective was standing on the other side. "I'm worried about Thuy. She doesn't know where I am."

"I'll tell her. And I'll have the SFPD put another guard at your apartment." Kelso reached across the table and extended his hand. "Buck up, Ben. You're an honest man with no criminal record. It's going to be all right."

Ben shook his hand. "Yeah. I guess."

Kelso started to say something, looked at Travis, and left.

Travis, the inveterate coffee drinker, got up and went to the coffee maker. "You want a cup?"

"No, thanks. I'll have enough trouble sleeping tonight as it is." He looked around the office. "What am I going to do around here, anyway?"

Travis sat back down at the table. "You could study for Kelso's exam. I'll go by the apartment, let Thuy know you're all right, and bring you your books."

"The exam? What good is that going to do me if I have to go to jail?"

"I don't think you're going to jail. Kelso knows what he's doing. Besides, the judge will be impressed that you're furthering your education."

Ben smiled. "Jailbird earns college degree. Yeah—has a nice ring to it. What's the exam about? I can't even remember."

"All the books we read this semester. You have read them, haven't you?"

Ben looked up at the ceiling and rubbed his chin. "Let's see...all except that one by the Russian dude—what's his name?"

"Dostoevsky?"

"Yeah. What's it called?"

"*The Possessed.*"

"Yeah. That's it."

"I'll bring it to you."

"Okay. I hope it's a long one. I got nothing else to do."

"It'll definitely keep you occupied. In fact, you might want some coffee to keep you awake."

Ben looked up at the wall displays. "I feel like I'm in the army again. Think they'd mind if I turned Nixon's picture around?"

Travis smiled and glanced at the photograph. "It's your pad for the next few days." He finished his second cup of coffee and stood. "I'll be back in forty-five minutes."

"Yeah. Okay." Ben continued to stare at the photograph. "Travis..."

Travis stopped at the door and turned around. "Something else?"

"Yeah. You remember that hand grenade you discovered in your desk that day in Saigon? The one with the trip wire?"

"How could I ever forget?"

"I put it there."

"I know." Travis opened the door and left.

Ben stared at the closed door for several moments, then at the photo of Nixon. He got up and turned the photo around.

"Asshole."

CHAPTER 29

Stanley Feinberg, the prosecutor, offered to charge Ben as an accessory after the fact for driving the getaway car, and to recommend a sentence of one to three years in exchange for Ben's testimony against Emmett Smalls. But Kelso, in his negotiations with Feinberg, convinced him that not only was Ben duped into participating in the ambush, but feared for his life if he refused to continue to drive the car afterwards. Kelso also reiterated the fact that Ben turned himself in as soon as he felt safe. Feinberg agreed not to charge him as long as he continued to cooperate.

Smalls was arraigned and charged with the first-degree murder of Cirelli and as a principal in the murder of Watt.

Erskine was traced to Algeria by the FBI, with the help of the CIA.

Marcella called Travis when she heard the news. "Is he all right?"

"He's fine," Travis said. "He aced his final exam."

"The exam? He's had time to take an exam?"

Travis laughed. "He's had plenty of time at the Presidio. Kelso gave him an oral exam in the barracks."

"So he doesn't have to go to jail?"

"Apparently not. But he's still a target of the Pumas. Smalls' trial isn't for another two months."

"He's like a prisoner, then."

"Sort of. But he can come and go as he pleases. Shops at the PX. With a detective in tow."

"And Thuy?"

"She's got her own detective. A woman. Marcella—"

"What?"

Travis wanted to tell her he loved her, but the words wouldn't come out. "How's the play going?"

"Okay. We're still in rehearsals. I'm thinking of flying up and taking my own exams so I don't have to withdraw."

"Have you got time for that? I mean with all the—"

"I already know the stuff. And the play here will get me an 'A' in my theater class. Can you pick me up at the airport?"

"Sure."

"Three-thirty-five. Tomorrow afternoon. Air California."

"I'll be there."

"Bye...and oh, Travis—do you think we could book a room at that B&B in Bolinas? I need lots of peace and quiet."

"Sure. I'll call them now."

"Great. Gotta go."

Marcella hung up and Travis was left staring into the mouthpiece of the receiver as if not believing the conversation he'd just had. Did she want to make up? Or did she want this to be some sort of study date?

He called Nirvana in Bolinas and booked the same room for the weekend. Then, since he didn't want to lose his parking place near the apartment, he decided to walk to work.

As he crested the hill at California Street, he started to turn left, as usual, and stay on the south side of the street until he reached Larkin. But something told him that he should cross to the other side of the street and stick his head inside the cathedral. Some tourists were leaving as he mounted the steps to the great doors and one stopped to ask directions to Ghiradelli Square. Then he went in.

Though late in the afternoon, it was a sunny day and the stained glass windows were brightly illuminated. He stood looking up for a few moments.

"A beautiful sight, isn't?"

He looked to the sound of the familiar voice. "Father Lattimore."

Lattimore was standing off to one side of the nave with his hands folded in front of him. "It does me good just to stand here for a few moments at the end of the day, bathed in the light of the saints, so to speak. How are you, Travis?"

"Fine. Just fine. I don't know what drew me in. I'm on my way to work."

"And where is work?"

Travis was almost embarrassed to say. "At Henry Africa's. A bar."

"Oh, yes. I'm familiar with it. One of the more popular watering holes in San Francisco."

Travis started to explain that he was also a student, but Father Lattimore spoke first:

"I see that your friend has had the charges dropped against him."

"Actually, they never charged him at all. He's going to testify against the real killers."

"I'm happy to hear that. Unfortunately, the real killer appears to be Mr. Erskine, and he is unlikely to be punished."

"He's safe for now it seems."

Lattimore looked up for a moment, then leveled his gaze at Travis again. "Do you believe in capital punishment, Travis?"

"No."

"And why not?"

"Because studies have shown it's not a deterrent."

"So your objection is a purely pragmatic one?"

"Not entirely. I also think that killing another human being when he or she is helpless is simply murder."

"What about war?"

"Again, when the victim is helpless or unarmed, murder."

"Well, most victims in war *are* helpless. Isn't that so?"

"I suppose so."

"Then war is murder?"

"In most cases."

"What about your case?"

Travis was taken aback. "What do you mean?"

Lattimore smiled. "Your jacket. I noticed the patch on the shoulder."

Travis looked down at the shoulder patch. He hadn't worn this field jacket for a while and generally avoided wearing it simply because San Francisco wasn't the place to advertise one's military service. He had been in a hurry to get out the door. "You were there?"

"Yes. Up in the mountains, with the Montagnards."

"You asked about my case."

"Yes. I'm sorry if I overstepped my bounds."

"No. You have a right to know. I shot an unarmed woman once. She was pregnant."

"And how do you feel about that?"

"Awful."

Lattimore sighed. "I was a chaplain. I'm in no position to judge you. But I'm a great listener. Would you like to step into my office? For a cup of coffee, perhaps?"

"I would like that, Father. But I'm already late for work. Goodbye."
Travis then turned and left without shaking Lattimore's hand.

He was angry, partly with Father Lattimore for peeling back his layers of self-defense, but mostly at himself for having allowed a nearly perfect stranger to do it.

CHAPTER 30

The next afternoon Travis drove out to the airport and met Marcella at the gate. She was dressed like he'd never seen her before, in a gray pant suit and carrying an expensive-looking handbag. Her black curly hair was straight and much shorter than before, pulled back in a bun. She reminded him somewhat of Audrey Hepburn. He gave her a quick kiss, which she returned just as quickly, almost automatically, as if they were a couple that had been married for years.

"How was the trip?"

"Okay. Not much to it."

Travis took her overnight bag, which had little wheels attached, and trailed it behind them. "The play going well?"

"Very well. Sam's a terrific director."

They walked without speaking for a minute or two amidst the hubbub of the terminal, with the usual public address announcements of arriving and departing flights.

"You look great," Travis said.

"Thanks. The makeup artists down there can do wonders—even for an acne-scarred teenybopper from San Pedro."

"You exaggerate that temporary affliction of your adolescence. It's hardly noticeable without the makeup."

Marcella smiled ironically, as if he were patronizing her. "Oh—let's stop at that newsstand. I want to get a copy of *Variety*."

"*Variety*?"

"The Hollywood Bible." She picked up a copy of the newspaper, paid the cashier, and began walking again while turning the pages.

"You looking for something?"

"Nothing in particular. Just catching up."

With Marcella's head buried in *Variety*, they continued to the parking lot. Travis had to jerk her back from the curb to prevent her from stepping in front of a slow-moving cab. "Careful! You'll have plenty of time to read it in Bolinas."

Once they arrived at the van, Marcella paused for a moment to look at it. "I think you ought to paint it. Flower power is on the way out."

Travis put the overnight bag in the back and opened the front door for her. "Then I guess I'll have to give this to someone else." He brought his left hand from around his back.

"Oh, Travis! Roses!"

"Maybe the lady at the toll booth will like them."

"Don't you dare!" Marcella took the flowers and brought them to her nose. "They're lovely. You're so thoughtful." She gave him a kiss, this one a little more enthusiastic and prolonged than the one at the gate.

"I didn't know whether to get red or yellow, so I got a combination of both. What color would you call that?"

"Apricot. We'll have to put them in water as soon as we get to the inn."

Once on the Bayshore Freeway to San Francisco, Marcella put the flowers aside and picked up her copy of *Variety* again.

"What's so fascinating about *Variety*?" Travis said.

"Not fascinating, really. Just all the new movies in production, box office figures, gossip, etcetera.'

"Okay—what's new?"

"Alessandro has landed a role in a movie with Robert Duval."

"Robert Duval? Really?"

"His new boyfriend—David something—is in it. I think he used his influence to get him a bit part."

"You've seen Alessandro since you've been down there?"

"He came by a rehearsal one afternoon." Marcella looked sideways at him and smiled. "You jealous?"

"I don't know."

"Don't be. Alessandro says he's bi, but his behavior says otherwise. Oh, look!"

"I can't. I'm driving."

"Andrea's movie just premiered in San Rafael."

"Really? What's it called?"

"*The Vicar's Secret Chamber.*"

"Sounds cheesy. You want to go see it?"

"I don't know. It may not be—oh, here it is. At the San Rafael Art House. Two, four, six—"

"Nonstop till midnight, eh?"

"And beyond." Marcella put down the paper and looked out at the San Francisco skyline. "It's not the movie—it's the other patrons I'm worried about."

"They won't be the violent type."

"Hmm. I guess you're right. But the sleaze factor will be off the charts. I'd better change into jeans at the inn."

"You could wear your mime makeup."

Marcella shot him a disdainful glance. "Please."

"That's history?"

"No. It's just that 'mime' and 'porn' should not be mentioned in the same breath. It's like playing Mozart on a kazoo."

"I understand that Mozart had his sexual peculiarities."

"Oh? Well, that's beside the point. His music is sublime."

"So that means that we're not going?'

"Of course we'll go. It's just a matter of keeping our perspective. Besides, we owe it to Andrea."

Once settled at the inn, Marcella changed into her jeans and Travis got directions from the proprietors to San Rafael. They arrived just in time for the six o'clock show.

The plot consisted of Polly, played by Andrea, entering a small country church in seek of guidance concerning her troubled marriage. It seems that her husband traveled most of the time, and when home, had little or no interest in sex. Brought up in a conservative Catholic household, Polly naturally turned to the parish priest for advice. After a private interview with the vicar, played by Blaine Pedersen, Polly is led through a secret door by Mary Ann, his assistant. Mary Ann asks Polly to remove her clothes and lie down on a divan with only a towel over her strategic parts. Mary Ann gives her a massage while repeating verses from the Bible that emphasize service, humility, and obedience.

Just as Polly is about to fall asleep, the vicar comes into the room wearing a magnificent white robe embroidered with a gold border and carrying a seven-foot staff. He is wearing a mitred hat, like the pope. He raps the staff on the stone floor sharply three times and Polly opens her eyes.

"Do you know who I am, my child?"

Polly shakes her head.

"I am the Vicar of Christ."

Polly stares at the Vicar of Christ in awe and reverence.

"I have come to relieve you of your pain and give salve to your wounds."

Polly continues to stare at him as he removes his magnificent robe, which reveals that he is naked underneath.

"Take the member of Christ in your hand, my child."

Polly reaches out to the Vicar's penis, which is now swelling into an erection.

"Now, Mary Ann, prepare Polly for the Holy Spirit to enter the precious vessel of her womanhood."

At this point Mary Ann removes the towel from Polly and pushes her legs apart. She then picks up a brass ewer and 'anoints' her vagina with sacramental wine. The vicar then enters her and the audience is treated to a series of moans and screams of delight from Polly. After twenty minutes or so of this, Mary Ann gets into the act by removing her clothes and smothering Polly with kisses, while the vicar enters her from behind. At the end of this stirring drama, Mary Ann returns Polly's clothes to her, and she and the vicar, who is now dressed again in his day-to-day priest's garb, stand on the steps of the church and wave goodbye to a happy and fulfilled Polly—who vows to return.

"Good grief," Travis said as they exited the theater. "That was even raunchier than I expected."

"Not to mention boring," Marcella said. "Or at least I thought so." She smiled at him as they approached the van. "I noticed that it held your rapt attention."

"Well...it was hard not to look. Kind of like watching a train wreck."

Marcella got into the passenger's side, while Travis settled into the driver's seat. "Do you normally get an erection while watching a train wreck?"

Travis looked down at his pants. They were stained with semen.

Marcella laughed. "Somehow your critical faculties and your libido are not communicating."

Travis blushed.

Marcella leaned over and kissed him on the cheek. "Come on—let's go back to the inn and have dinner. I'm starving."

After dinner, they went for a walk on the beach and though it was well after dark, there was a full moon that illuminated the ocean and the beach. There had been little conversation at dinner, and it seemed that it was Travis, not Marcella, who was holding something back.

"Why so quiet?" Marcella said.

"Quiet? I don't know. Thinking about Ben and his problems, I guess."

"I thought you said Kelso made a deal with the prosecutor. He's not going to jail, you said."

"No, but he's still in danger. And he can't stay at the Presidio forever."

"I suppose not."

They continued walking for a while in silence.

"Travis—"

"Yes?"

"Do you have any interest in acting? I mean as a career."

Travis shoved his hands into his jeans. "Not really. Why?"

"Because I do."

"Of course you do. You're very talented."

"And I may be going to New York."

"You told me that."

Marcella stopped walking and faced him. "Travis—you don't understand. How can we continue this relationship if I'm off in New York and you're here in San Francisco tending bar?"

"I'm not going to be a bartender forever."

"Then what *are* you going to do?"

Travis started walking again. "Get my degree and then—I don't know."

Marcella caught up with him. "You must have some purpose, some plan. You can't just drift through life aimlessly."

Travis stopped and looked at her. "What if I became a priest?"

Marcella seemed stunned. "A priest? Like the vicar in Andrea's film?"

"Of course not. Like a real priest. It would be a way to contribute something, help people."

Marcella stared at him for a moment, then put her arm through his and they continued walking. "I think that's wonderful that you want to help people. But aren't there other ways to do that? An actor helps people, for example, to escape from their humdrum lives, or better yet, to see themselves as they are, as others see them. Or you could become a lawyer, like Kelso, and defend the indigent or the unjustly accused, or even teach—I think you would be a terrific teacher."

"Lawyers, they say, abandon their idealism the day they graduate from law school. And teachers—they spend half their time grading papers and the other half wondering whether their students have learned anything or not. I'd rather reach people on a deeper level and really help them."

Marcella sighed. "I didn't know you were so religious."

"I'm not, really. I'm not even sure I believe in God."

"Then how can you become a priest?"

"That *is* a problem...Hey, we're running out of beach."

"Let's go back to the inn. I've got to study for my theater final, remember? What about you?"

"I'm done. I got an 'A' in Kelso's class."

"The best I can hope for is a 'B.' You see, you're smarter than I am. You can do anything you want."

"You've got talent. That's better."

They walked back to the inn and went up to their room, where Marcella pulled a copy of Stanislavsky's *An Actor Prepares* out of her overnight bag and sat on the bed with her back to the headboard. Travis sat in the Windsor rocker that faced the window and the moonlit beach.

Marcella saw that he was reading something. "What are you reading?"

"*Either/Or.*"

"Was that in the curriculum?"

"No. I just thought I'd see what it was all about."

"Oh."

Marcella went back to her book and Travis continued reading his. After a half hour or so he glanced over at her.

"Would you like to be married to a priest?" he said.

She looked up. "I didn't know priests could marry."

"Episcopal priests can. Would you?"

Marcella put her book down. "Are you proposing?"

"It's a hypothetical question. I'm not a priest yet."

"Then I'll have to give you a hypothetical answer. I don't know. I might be a different person by then, and you might be, too."

Travis stared at her for a moment, sighed, and went back to his reading.

CHAPTER 31

As seemed to be her habit, Marcella was not interested in sex until the sun peeked through the curtains, as if fumbling around in the dark beneath the covers was a remnant of Victorian times. Travis awoke to her tickling his nose. He opened his eyes, she smiled, kissed him, and ran her fingers down the middle of his chest and inside the waistband of the bikini underwear she had bought him after their first night together in the Haight.

This was the routine for the next two or three days, during which time Marcella prepared for her exams and then had Travis drive her to San Francisco State where she passed all of them with flying colors. Her course work done, she had only to apply for her degree and wait for it to be delivered in the mail. She and Travis spent her last night in San Francisco in his tiny apartment, and the next morning he drove her out to the airport.

They parted on good terms, but there was no further mention of marriage.

When Travis got back to his apartment, his phone was ringing. It was Ben.

"They've got Thuy."

"What? Who's got Thuy?"

"The Pumas. They kidnapped her."

Travis threw his jacket across the armchair and sat down at his desk. "When?"

"This afternoon, about 3pm. She came back from the grocery store with Phyllis, the detective. Phyllis was carrying the groceries since Thuy is nearly due. As Thuy stepped onto the curb, two guys jumped out of a truck and forced her into it."

"What did Phyllis do?"

"She dropped the groceries and pulled out her service revolver, but it was too late. They were gone."

Travis sighed. "Does Kelso know?"

"He's the one who called me."

"What about the cops?"

"They've sent out an APB, but it won't do no good. I'm afraid they'll kill her. And the baby, too."

Travis tried to gather his thoughts. He knew Ben was frantic, though it didn't show in his voice. And he didn't want him to do anything stupid, like going over to Oakland and shooting up the Puma head-quarters. "What did Kelso tell you? I mean about staying put?"

"That's exactly what he told me. But Travis, I don't know if I can do that. I'm going stir crazy out here as it is, and if those motherfuckers so much as touch a hair on Thuy's head, I'll kill everyone of 'em."

"Calm down, Ben. This isn't a firefight. You've got to trust the cops to do their job."

"Yeah. Like Watt did when Bobby X ran up Van Nuys Avenue."

"Knock it off, Ben. It's an entirely different situation. And Watt was one bad apple. Those two detectives still there?"

"Just one now. And he's a moron."

"Look, Ben—have I ever given you bad advice?"

"No."

"Okay. Then trust me one more time. STAY PUT."

There was a sigh at the other end. "Okay. For now. Wait a minute, there's something about it coming on the TV."

Travis could hear some voices emanating from the television as Ben turned up the volume. But he couldn't make out all of it. "What are they saying?"

"Shh!"

Travis could distinguish the voices a little better now.

"Police say that the kidnappers abducted an Asian woman believed to be the fiancée of Ben Franklin, the star witness in the murders of San Francisco police officers Dan Watt and Salvator Cirelli last month in Chinatown. A police detective guarding the woman—whose name is Thigh Ing-yen—said that the suspects were two black males in their late twenties or early thirties wearing all black and full Afros. The vehicle is described as a late 60's white panel Ford truck with California plates, but no tag number is available...We'll have an update at six o'clock as more information comes in..."

Ben clicked off the TV. "You hear that?"

"Yeah," Travis said. "I'll call Kelso and see what he knows."

"He don't know nothin.' Just that it happened."

"The police must have called him and told him what they know. I might be able to help."

There was a silence again at Ben's end.

"Ben?"

"Yeah. I'm still here."

"Tell me what you're thinking. Be honest, now."

"I'm thinking…'Thigh Ing-yen'…' Are they all idiots at that TV station?"

Travis chuckled. "Why don't you call them up? I'm sure they'd appreciate it and maybe they'll get it right next time."

"Yeah. Okay."

"I'll keep you posted."

"Okay."

Travis hung up and looked in his desk for Kelso's number. Kelso answered in one ring.

"Kelso."

"Ted?"

"Travis? You've heard?"

"Ben called me. I tried to calm him down. I think he'll be okay."

"Good. You know him better that I do. I was afraid he'd grab a gun at the Presidio and go on a rampage."

"He's going to stay put. Is there anything I can do to help?"

"Maybe. The police detective who was guarding Thuy—what's her name?"

"Phyllis."

"Right. Phyllis says she could only memorize three or four numbers and letters of the license plate, but that was enough to narrow it down to the owner of a florist shop in Palo Alto. The guy reported it stolen this morning."

"My old stomping grounds."

"What?"

"I went to Stanford before I dropped out and went into the army."

"Stanford? You know the area then."

"Pretty much."

"Ever heard of Bernard's Bouquets?"

"Sure. French guy. We used to buy flowers for our girlfriends from him."

"Hmm. The cops are down there questioning him now. I don't

think they're likely to get any farther than that, though. Obviously the Pumas stole the truck and dumped it off somewhere. You got a car?"

"Sure."

"Maybe you could drive down there and talk to Bernard."

"What's he going to tell me that he wouldn't tell the cops?"

"I don't know. Cops make people nervous. You think he remembers you?"

Travis laughed. "I was his best customer. I fell in love about once a week in those days."

"Good. Maybe he'll feel more relaxed with you. It's worth a try, anyway."

"I'm on my way."

"Travis?"

"Yes?"

"I know you and Ben are both Vietnam vets. You don't carry a gun, do you?"

"Never touch the things."

"Good. We're just fishing for information. Don't approach these guys if you learn of their whereabouts. Call me."

"Will do."

Travis hung up the phone and considered what Kelso was asking him to do. What was it, exactly? Pump Bernard for information about a couple of black guys who stole his truck? What else could he know? And if he does know more, why would he hold it back from the cops?

Bernard...Bernard Blériot. Like the aviator who was the first to fly across the English Channel. Bernard claimed to be a second cousin or nephew or something.

Travis grabbed his jacket and headed out the door.

CHAPTER 32

Driving down the Bayshore Freeway, memories of his days at Stanford began to flood back into Travis' mind. He decided to turn off on Woodside Drive so he could drive through Menlo Park. He and several buddies had rented an old ramshackle house near the corner of Oak Grove and El Camino. This stretch had always been very commercial, but now it seemed that every other shop was some sort of computer store. Handheld calculators were the thing now, devices that would have taken up a whole room a decade ago. He wondered if some of his former Stanford classmates were now computer millionaires.

At the corner of Oak Grove, he saw the familiar Seven Eleven where he and his housemates used to get snacks and beer. But the house just behind it was gone. Demolished. There was some construction equipment sitting idle where the front yard had been. So much for nostalgia.

He continued into Palo Alto and was reassured to see the sign for Bernard's Bouquets just off El Camino. After an interminable wait at the light, he turned left onto University and found an empty parking space right in front of the shop.

He wasn't sure that Bernard would recognize him, and he didn't—at first.

"Hello, Bernard."

"Yes. Hello. May I—Travis?"

"None other. How've you've been?"

Bernard, who was rather short and had gained weight, threw his arms up as he came around from behind the counter. "Bon ami! Where have you been?"

Travis returned his embrace. "Lately, San Francisco. How's business?"

"Oh, so-so." Bernard stepped away to examine him. "What happened to the beard?"

"It was hot in Vietnam. Shaved it off to keep cool."

"Vietnam?" Bernard shook his head. "A troubled place. No good. We French were there for thirty years and when we finally extricated ourselves, poof! The Americans rush in. You are all right?"

"Yeah. I was lucky. You seen any of the guys lately? Pete, Tommy?"

Bernard sat down in a chair between two huge pots bursting with purple, pink and white hydrangeas. There were no customers in the store. "Pete, I think he graduated and went to medical school. Tommy, I heard that he started a computer software company. These boys are prospering. And you?"

"Well—"

"Sit down, sit down. You must catch me up."

Travis sat in another chair near the window. "I'm back in school. At San Francisco State."

Bernard nodded without comment, as if he considered this a step down in Travis' life.

"How's Emile?"

"Oh, he's off at school, too. Berkeley."

"Good for him. And Emma?"

A broad smile came to Bernard's lips. "She's a senior at Palo Alto High. Homecoming queen."

"Good for her! She always was a beauty, even as a little girl. And your wife, Jeanne?"

"The same. But Travis, you must come to dinner. You need a place to stay?"

"No, no. I have to get back to the city. Thanks anyway."

Bernard stared at him for a moment. "You want something? I don't have much money. In fact—"

"No, nothing like that, Bernard. I heard about your truck being stolen."

"The truck? Who told you about that?"

"Well...it's in the papers by now in San Francisco. Didn't the police tell you?"

"The police? Oh, yes. They think the black boys who took it have something to do with a kidnapping."

"A friend of mine's fiancée is the kidnapee."

Bernard sat forward in his chair. "A friend of yours?"

"I'm afraid so. She's Vietnamese. And about nine months pregnant."

"Ai, ai, ai! We really must do something!"

"That's really why I'm here, Bernard. Did you know those black guys?"

Bernard started to say something when Emma appeared from a back room. She was stunning. Blond hair cascading over her shoulders, sparkling blue eyes, and a figure that Travis found hard to reconcile with the little flat-chested girl he knew when he was at Stanford. He stood.

"Daddy, I—Oh. You have a customer. Sorry."

Bernard got up. "Emma—don't you remember your dreamboat?"

"Dreamboat?" She squinted at Travis. "Travis! Oh, you've come back!" She came around from behind the counter and gave him a big hug. "What happened to your beard?"

"The army didn't like it."

"The army? Oh, you didn't go to that horrible war, did you?"

"I'm afraid so. But I'm okay."

Emma put her hand to her mouth. "Oh, I'm sorry. I don't know how you feel about it. I—"

"About the same as you do. You've grown up, Emma."

"Well, I'm still in high school."

"You could be a coed at Stanford."

Emma glanced at her father, who was beaming with pride. "I *will* be a coed at Stanford. Next fall."

"Scholarship," Bernard said. "She's a smart girl."

"Oh, Daddy—it's not a full scholarship."

"Three-quarters, maybe. And you'll live at home."

"Just freshman year."

"We'll see. In the meantime, we need to sell lots of flowers."

After a few more pleasantries Emma asked her father about a floral arrangement, took her leave of Travis, and disappeared into the back room.

Bernard sat back down in his chair. "You wanted to know something about the boys who stole my truck."

"You know who they are?"

Bernard looked from one side of the shop to the other, then to the window. "That your VW?"

"Yeah. My girlfriend thinks I should paint it."

"Good idea. The hippies are passé."

"Bernard—"

"Yes?"

"Do you know who those boys are?"

Bernard rubbed his chin. He seemed to be sweating. "I want to help."

"You didn't tell the police, did you?"

Bernard shook his head.

"Bernard, this Vietnamese woman—her life may be in danger."

Bernard looked down at the floor for a moment, seeming to struggle within himself. "One of them used to date Emma."

"Was it serious?"

"I don't think so. He came around to the shop a few times and seemed like a nice boy. I'm not prejudiced, you know, so I wasn't really worried. Well...a little worried. I didn't think he was right for her."

"And did you tell her that?"

Bernard sighed. "Not in so many words. But she sensed it."

"And?"

"She broke it off. That was all."

Travis wondered how he would feel if he had a daughter who dated a black boy. "Are you sure he was one of the ones who stole your truck?"

"Oh, yes. No question. I left the engine running when I remembered I had a delivery I had forgotten about. I came back into the shop, picked up the arrangement, and suddenly heard the door of the truck slam shut. I saw him through the window. It was Kenny, all right."

"Kenny?"

"He looked a little different." Bernard raised his arms and made a gesture with his hands as if his head were exploding. "A big Afro. He was always neat and clean-cut when he came around to see Emma."

"He's her age?"

"No. A couple of years older. I heard he went to prison for dealing drugs."

"You say his name was Kenny. Kenny what?"

Bernard rubbed his chin and began sweating again. "He may be quite dangerous now."

"No doubt. Especially to Thuy, my friend's fiancée."

Bernard seemed to think it over. "His name was Kenny Morris. But Emma told me he changed it while in prison to some Muslim name. Mohammed, I think."

"You know where he lives?"

"Somewhere in East Palo Alto. That's all I can tell you, Travis. I'm afraid he—or his friends—might try to do something to Emma."

"I think it's more likely they might try to burn your store down. But the police will be watching it 24-7."

Bernard wiped the perspiration from his brow with a handkerchief. "It only takes a few seconds to throw a bomb through a window."

"These guys are pretty conspicuous. They'll be spotted before they get anywhere near the shop." Travis rose from his chair and shook Bernard's hand with both of his. "Thanks, Bernard. You may have just saved my friend's fiancée's life."

Bernard didn't get up. "But who's going to save mine?"

"Your name won't be mentioned. They'll never know."

"Are you so sure?

Travis glanced out the window and saw a police car parked across the street. "You've already got an armed guard watching the place."

"Oui?" Bernard rose from his chair and looked out the window. "That's Jerry. A good cop. He buys flowers from time to time for his wife."

Travis patted Bernard on the back. "See? They're taking a personal interest in you. But I won't be reporting to the Palo Alto cops. The SFPD's handling it. I'm just a runner."

Bernard nodded, not really convinced.

"Relax, Bernard. I think this is going to be wrapped up pretty soon. I'll keep in touch."

Travis climbed into his van and drove to the Palo Alto library, where he got out a phone book and discovered that there were several Morris' listed, but only one in East Palo Alto: Adele Morris, on Euclid Avenue.

CHAPTER 33

East Palo Alto had always been somewhat of an embarrassment to the mostly white, affluent residents of Palo Alto, who saw themselves as politically progressive and committed to civil rights. Poverty in East Palo Alto, however, was persistent and the fact that the Bayshore Freeway separated the two vastly different communities seemed a conscious design to shut out black residents from the American Dream.

Euclid Avenue was just east of the freeway and the roar of traffic was a constant noise. The houses were nearly all alike, small two and three bedroom frame structures with white stucco exteriors. It seemed that every third window was broken out, no shutters or decorative molding. Some lawns had old tires on them serving as planters. Others had old tires serving only as old tires. Toys in the driveways shared space with rusted-out Chevys, Fords and Cadillacs. Bondo seemed to be a popular solution to the rust. It reminded Travis of some of the suburbs of Saigon except for the cars. A couple of boys, maybe five or six, were racing their tricycles in and out of the driveway.

"Your mother here?"

The boys stopped suddenly and looked up as if they hadn't noticed him before. "She in the house."

"Thanks. That's some machine you've got there. Is it fast?"

"It a Rocket Starship," the oldest boy said. He seemed to be cultivating his own Afro.

"Then it must be fast," Travis said. He walked up the path to the front porch, careful to step over the toys, and saw a woman staring at him through a screen door. She was very heavy and her features were hard to distinguish through the screen.

"What you want?" she said.

"My name is Travis Carter. I was hoping you could help me locate your son, Kenny."

"Kenny don't live here no more. I don't know where he is."

"He must come to visit occasionally."

"Not no more. He act like he don't know me. What you want with him?"

"A friend of mine wants to see him. A black friend."

Mrs. Morris squinted through the screen to examine him more carefully. "You a drug dealer?"

"No, ma'am. Neither is my friend."

"What's your friend's name?"

"Ben. Ben Franklin."

"Ben Franklin? Like the man who stand out in a thunderstorm flying a kite?"

"The same. Mind if I come in for a minute?"

"You got a warrant?"

"I'm not a policeman, Mrs. Morris. I can't come in unless you ask me to."

Mrs. Morris stood in the shadow of the screen for a few moments, then opened the door. "Come on in, then. But only for a minute. I ain't got a lot of time, what with the laundry and the cookin' and the—Hey! You boys stay out of the street! You like to get kilt."

The boys stopped peddling and stared at their mother—grandmother?—for a moment, then turned their three-wheelers into the drive.

The house was dark and stuffy and smelled of collard greens and fried chicken. There was a portrait of Jesus in a gaudy frame over the sofa, a dimly lit floor lamp, two armchairs with the stuffing poking out at the seams, and a scuffed coffee table between them. A few more toys and some children's clothing were strewn around the living room and Mrs. Morris bent over, somewhat laboriously, to pick them up. "I cain't keep up with these chillun at my age, and what with my rheumatism and diabetes, I ain't gettin' any faster. Sit down anywhere you like."

Travis looked around and decided the sofa was the sturdiest and safest. Mrs. Morris went into a hallway with some of the clothes and toys, threw them into a bedroom and slammed the door. She came back into the living room, wiping her hands on her apron, which looked as if it needed washing.

"You want some iced tea? Or lemonade?"

"Iced tea would be fine."

"Got plenty of that. The boys drink all the lemonade before I can get some new cans at the store. You just wait a minute while I get some glasses."

She went into the kitchen and Travis examined the room a little more carefully. There was a large console with a television built into it against the wall opposite the sofa. A little alcove just to the left of that served as a dining room, with a small oval table covered with a white linen cloth. One of the family photos on the wall adjacent to the alcove caught his eye. It was of a handsome young man with neatly trimmed hair wearing a silvery blue gown and a graduation cap. He had an engaging smile.

Mrs. Morris came back into the living room carrying a silver-plated tray that was nearly black with oxidation. On it were a pitcher— also oxidized silver—and two rather elegant-looking glasses cut or stamped with a diamond-shaped pattern. "They ain't got no sugar in 'em. Got to watch my diabetes, you know. But you can put some in yours with that little spoon there."

Travis took one of the glasses and used the tiny, delicate spoon to add a fraction of an ounce of sugar to it.

Mrs. Morris put the tray down on the coffee table and sat in one of the armchairs. She took a long sip of the tea. "Ah! That shore hits the spot. Yours okay?"

"Yes, ma'am."

"Now you was sayin' about your friend Ben Franklin. What's he want with Kenny?"

Travis didn't really know how to broach the subject. Here she was so kind and trusting and he couldn't quite bring himself to tell her that her son was wanted for kidnapping and possibly murder. He glanced at the television. "You've been watching the news?"

"The news?" She glanced at the set. "That thing's been broke for a month. Just too much to fix it. It looks nice in that cabinet, though. Is Kenny got into some kind of drug trouble again? I thought he learned his lesson sittin' in that prison for two years. Came out talkin' about Mohammed and the Koran and how he wasn't gonna ever take another drink of hard liquor or smoke no dope, neither. He done fall back into the wrong crowd again?"

"Well, he apparently fell in with another crowd—the Black Pumas."

Mrs. Morris seemed unperturbed by this news. "He told me that.

He said they was good Muslims. I don't care what crowd he run with as long as they don't drink and carouse and get high on dope."

"Well, they do other things sometimes that gets them in trouble with the law."

"The law? Like what?"

Travis put his glass down on the tray and leaned on his knees with his elbows. "I don't know how to tell you this, Mrs. Morris, but I think Kenny and one of his Muslim friends has kidnapped my friend Ben's fiancée."

Mrs. Morris' glass, which she had just brought to her lips, stopped in midair. "Kidnapped?" She put the glass down on the table. "Lawdy—why would he do that? He askin' for money?"

"Not yet. And I don't think he intends to."

"Then what *do* he want? Lawd, that child has been a mystery to me ever since he graduated from Paly High and turned down a job at Hewlett-Packard."

"He turned down a job at Hewlett-Packard?"

"Good job, too. Something with computers. Fact is, he took the job at first, had some argument with his boss man, and walked out. Next thing I know, he's running around with gangsters selling dope. But I thought he turned hisself around."

"He's made a 180 degree turn all right—but now instead of drugs, it's ideology."

"Ideology?"

"A peculiar brand of Islam that seeks to overthrow the government, starting with local police departments. And by any means possible, including kidnapping and murder."

"Murder! Oh, Lawd..." Mrs. Morris clutched her throat and seemed to have trouble breathing.

Travis stood up and went to her side. "Are you all right, Mrs. Morris? I'm sorry, I shouldn't have put it so bluntly."

"No, no. I'm all right. Just let me have another swaller of that tea."

Travis handed her the glass and she took a long swallow.

"I'm all right," she said. "I should a knowed all this talk about Mohammed and Black Power and all that would lead to no good. Where do you think they got this girl? And what do they want with her?"

"I don't know where they've got her. That's what I'm trying to find out. But they took her, it seems, to prevent Ben from testifying against one of their members who shot a policeman in San Francisco."

"Oh, Lawd, Lawd. Just when I think we was out of the troubles and on the path of righteousness. If only Earl was still here."

"Earl?"

"My husband. Died of a heart attack when Kenny was only seven. If only he'd been around—"

"Mrs. Morris, I'm sorry to have upset you, but I've got to find out where they're keeping Thuy."

"Twee?"

"Ben's fiancée."

"Oh, yeah, that's right. Well, I don't know no more than you do."

"Has Kenny been around here lately?"

"Well…yeah, he was here just a couple of days ago. With some boy I didn't know. Seemed polite, though."

"Did he say anything about what he planned to do?"

"No. Nothin.' Just something about going back up to San Francisco to help feed poor little black chillun. At the elementary school there. Portrayo, I think the name of it was. I thought that was a good thing."

"What did he want from you?"

"The usual. Some money. Didn't have none, though. I run through Earl's Social Security check by the middle of the month. And food stamps ain't much. He didn't want those. So he and his friend left. Didn't even say goodbye to his nephews out there in the driveway."

"His nephews?"

"His sister's chillun. She left them with me when her husband done left her to go to Vegas with his girlfriend. Now Sheila's got four kids and no job. She's tryin,' though."

"Mrs. Morris—if I can find Kenny I might be able to convince him to release Thuy and maybe the judge won't be so hard on him. He's not asking for money."

"What is he asking for?"

"We don't know yet. At least I don't. But it's likely that he's been duped into this by some men higher up in the Puma organization who want to see one of their own—a cop-killer—set free."

"Kenny's done some bad things, but he ain't never hurt nobody."

"And I'm sure he doesn't want to start now. If he lets the girl go free, he's still got a chance of getting on the right path."

Mrs. Morris sighed. "I shore hope you're right. But how you gonna find him?"

"I think I know where to look now."

"That elementary school in San Francisco?"

"It's a start."

She got to her feet with a good deal of effort. "You won't let the poh-lice hurt him, will you?"

"They won't hurt him if he gives up the girl. And we'll get him a good lawyer."

"Lawd, Lawd. I hope he's better than the last one he had. Well, I got to go back to my cookin'. I got two more chillun coming home from school any minute now."

"Thank you, Mrs. Morris. I'll do everything I can."

CHAPTER 34

Travis could see Potrero Elementary from the freeway. He was tempted to get off at Potrero Avenue and see if he could locate Kenny's hideout, but he had no more information than that it was in a twenty-square-block area.

When he got back to his apartment, he phoned Kelso.

"What did you find out?" Kelso said.

"That one of the kidnappers is named Kenny Morris, but now goes by Mohammed."

"Mohammed? Mohammed what?"

"I don't know. But I talked to his mom and she says that he joined the Pumas recently and the last time she saw him he was on his way to San Francisco to help with the breakfast program at Potrero Elementary."

"Hmm. So you think they're holding Thuy in that area?"

"Just a guess."

"Good work, Travis. I'll notify the detective in charge. You can relax now."

"What about the truck?"

"They found it abandoned in the Glen Park BART station. The tag had been switched shortly after they stole the vehicle. That's why it took so long to locate it. Apparently, they hustled Thuy onto a train and got off somewhere between there and Richmond or Fremont. She could be anywhere. But it's interesting that they got on at Glen Park. The next stop would have been the Mission."

"A few blocks from Potrero."

"Right. This is a good lead. I'll keep you posted."

"How's Ben?"

"He's at my place now."

"Your place?"

"Yeah. The cops say they can't spare even one detective now, and the commander of the base was getting pressure from his boss. He's probably safer here. Word was leaking out that he was at the Presidio and for a military base, they're as porous as Swiss cheese. You throw a stick there and you hit a tourist."

"Can I come see him?"

"Sure. Call first. Gotta go."

Travis hung up the phone and wondered what to do next. The new semester wouldn't begin for another week and he hadn't even signed up for classes. He wondered how Kelso had time to teach.

He still had to go to work, however. Henry was a little miffed that his bouncer had been taken out of circulation, but he was supportive of Ben. He had no love for the Pumas, especially after the shooting that night that Watt killed Bobby X. He always maintained that Watt was justified in what he did.

After a snack and a short nap, he headed for Henry Africa's.

It was a relatively slow night and Henry had not hired a new bouncer. Alice, the day bartender, stayed over to fill in for Rob, who called in sick.

About seven o'clock Andrea walked in arm-in-arm with Blaine Pedersen. She was wearing a very low-cut dress—the neckline almost to her navel—and a blue-sequined jacket draped over her shoulders.

"I told you he'd be here," Andrea said to Blaine. "He never sleeps." They both took a seat at the bar.

"How are you, Andrea, Blaine." Travis was surprised to see them together after their first 'date' at Nirvana.

"Things couldn't be better," Andrea said. "Blaine and I are heading for Amsterdam, via New York."

"Amsterdam? What's in Amsterdam?"

"The European premiere of *The Vicar's Secret Chamber*."

"The European premiere? That's great. What'll you have?"

Andrea ordered her usual lemon drop martini and Blaine ordered a beer. Once served, Andrea elaborated. "The film has been a huge success in California. Howard says we've already recouped the production costs."

"So it's all profit from now on, eh?"

"Well, there're still some costs associated with marketing. The major venues in the U.S. are hard to break into, except for New York and California. Howard says the real money is in Europe, where the audiences aren't so puritanical." Andrea took a sip of her drink. "Oh, sweetie, this is so good. Nobody makes a lemon drop martini the way you do."

"Thanks. This one's on me."

"You're such a doll. Isn't he a doll, Blaine?"

Blaine shrugged. "Sure."

"You stopping in New York?" Travis said.

"Yeah. The New York premiere's in Times Square in one of those art houses on 42nd Street. I'm going to see my dad."

"Your dad? He approves?"

Andrea giggled and took another sip of her martini. "Not exactly. He was angry when he first found out about it—my brother saw it in L.A.—but when I told him what the first weekend's gross was he did the math and now he thinks it's terrific."

Travis glanced at Blaine, who seemed to be interested in Alice's bartending skills. "Just you, your dad, and Blaine, eh?"

Andrea laughed. "Blaine doesn't watch his own films, do you Blaine, honey?" She patted Blaine on the thigh and noticed him watching Alice. "Blaine, you dirt bag! I'm talking to you!"

"What?" Blaine turned toward her. "I was just watching how they make those drinks."

"Right," Andrea said. "And you didn't even notice her boobs falling out of her halter top." She turned back to Travis. "I have to keep him on a short leash."

Travis managed a smile.

"Blaine's staying with a friend while we're in New York," she said. "No sense in tempting dear old dad to deck him when he sees us *in flagrante delicto*."

Travis wondered at Andrea's audacity. She was even undaunted at the prospect of her father seeing her have sexual intercourse on the big screen. "When do you leave?"

"At 8:15 tomorrow morning. In the meantime, Blaine and I are going to have one last fling in San Francisco. Come on, Blaine—drink up! We'll be late for dinner."

"Where's dinner?" Travis said.

"The Blue Fox. Then on to North Beach to hear Oscar Peterson."

"I didn't know you were a jazz fan."

Andrea finished her drink, leaned over the bar, and gave Travis a kiss on the lips. "There're a lot of things you don't know about me, sweetie. I'm not your average porn star." She looked at Blaine, who again had his eyes on Alice. "Come on, Blaine, there's something in this world besides tits and ass. I'm going to broaden your horizons with a little culture. Ta, ta, Travis."

"'Bye, Andrea. Have a good trip."

"Oh, we will." She pulled a hundred dollar bill out of her purse, folded it with the fingers of one hand, and slid it across the bar. "Treat Marcella to a night out."

"Thanks." Travis watched as Andrea nearly dragged Blaine off of his bar stool and they disappeared through the front door.

Henry came up to the end of the bar and watched the couple get into a cab. "Some broad, huh?"

"Yeah. She's about as predictable as an earthquake."

Henry put his forefinger to his lips. "Don't say that word in here. Half our clientele are tourists, remember?"

"Sorry."

Henry nodded towards the door where a group of four middle-aged men in business suits appeared. As Alice was on break, Travis went to that end of the bar and put down four cocktail napkins.

"What'll you have, gentlemen?"

CHAPTER 35

The next morning after a workout at the YMCA on Turk Street, Travis returned to his apartment and called Kelso.

"We've got a problem," Kelso said. "Though not an unexpected one."

"You've heard from Kenny?"

"Mohammed Al-Rashid. Via Algeria."

"Algeria?"

"I'll fill you in later. Ben's about to explode. Can you get here in a half an hour?"

"Fifteen minutes."

Travis hung up the phone, took a quick shower, dressed, and tried to remember where he had parked his van the night before. He found it around the corner on Sutter Street and headed for Pacific Heights.

Only minutes from the Tenderloin, Pacific Heights was probably the second wealthiest neighborhood in San Francisco after Nob Hill. Kelso's house was on Jackson about a block east of Alta Plaza. Like so many houses in San Francisco, whatever the neighborhood, it was a Victorian style, two-story affair built after the 1906 earthquake. It looked much like Marcella's old digs on Haight Street, but the location—and the view—made it much pricier.

He parked his van in front of the house and turned around to take in the view. It directly overlooked the Marina, with the red tiles of the roof of the St. Francis Yacht Club visible and the masts of dozens of sail boats dotting the little harbor. Beyond that to the north was Alcatraz, and beyond that Tiburon. To the northwest was the Golden Gate, which always seemed to be illuminated with some artificial light source designed by the Chamber of Commerce.

He turned around and faced the house. At the street level was a two car garage with a steep set of stairs up the left side that made a ninety-degree turn to a little deck over the garage. From there, the stairs ascended to the entry. He now saw that it was a duplex. It was painted a blue-gray with red and white trim around the windows. An elaborately decorated cornice crowned the roof.

He climbed the stairs and pressed the bell on the side that contained a mailbox labeled 'T.E. Kelso.' After a few moments, the door opened and an attractive young blond appeared.

"Travis?"

"That's me. Is, uh, Ted home?"

"Of course." She opened the door wider and Travis stepped inside.

"I'm Vera—a friend of Ted's. He's in the parlor with Ben."

As Vera led the way from the foyer to the parlor, Travis noted that she had a vaguely European accent, but he couldn't quite place it. German? Swedish?

He stepped into the parlor and saw Kelso and Ben huddling over a piece of paper on the coffee table. The room, like the foyer, was elegantly furnished with an eclectic mix of Victoriana, oriental, and continental European furniture and artwork. The hardwood floors looked to be recently refinished.

Kelso looked up. "Travis! Come in—we're just trying to make sense of this message Vera brought from the Consulate. Don't go, Vera— we still need your help." He stood as Travis approached the coffee table, as did Ben.

"Ain't seen you for a while, man," Ben said. "Not that I missed you much—Professor Kelso and Vera been treatin' me like a king."

Kelso laughed. "We try to make our guests comfortable. Sit down, Travis, and tell me what you think of this."

Travis took a seat on the sofa and looked at the paper on the coffee table. It looked like an official communiqué of some kind, like the ones he often got from battalion headquarters when he was in Saigon. He read it aloud:

"From: The People's Democratic Republic of Algeria
   To: The Consul General of the Union of Soviet Socialist
         Republics, San Francisco, California, USA
         Attention: Vera Mandlikova"

Travis looked up at Kelso, then at Vera.

"Vera translated it into English for us," Kelso said. "Go on."

Travis continued reading:

"Greetings, your Excellency. Comrade Erskine wishes you to convey this message to Comrade Benjamin Franklin vis-a-vis his attorney, Professor Theodore Kelso, San Francisco State University, to wit:

"Our comrades, fighting to destroy the capitalist engine of black genocide, have taken precautionary measures to rescue one of our bravest and most dedicated servants to the cause, Abdul-Aseez. These measures include, but may not be limited to, the detention of Miss Thuy Nguyen for a period not to exceed ten days in the event of your cooperation; the unavoidable martyrdom of Miss Nguyen if you do not; and the deposit of 100,000 dollars, U.S., in a Swiss bank account in your name if you and Miss Nguyen agree to flee the U.S.A. to Algiers and take up residence there at the Algerian government's expense. Please reply promptly, as time is of the essence.

> Cordially yours,
> Lawrence Erskine, Esq.
> Minister of Education
> TBPP wire: Emb/CCCP, Algiers"

Travis put the message down on the coffee table. "This is bizarre. Why did he send it to the Soviet Consulate? Why not a simple note directly to Ben?"

"Because he doesn't know where Ben is. And he wants an answer, right? He's opened a line of communication that can't be intercepted by the FBI or the SFPD."

Travis looked at Ben.

Ben looked back. "I ain't going to Algeria—not even for a hundred thousand dollars."

"I doubt you'd ever see the hundred thousand," Kelso said. "He wants to lure you to Algeria not only to prevent you from testifying against Smalls, but against himself should he decide to return to the U.S. and take over the leadership of the Pumas."

Travis looked at the message again. "How did Erskine know that Vera would pass this on to you?"

"Erskine met Vera at San Francisco State prior to that Neo-Nazi debacle in my classroom. We had coffee together. He was fascinated with Vera—for obvious reasons—but also because she works at the Soviet Consulate as a cryptologist."

"A cryptologist?"

"She's an expert at deciphering codes. Officially, she's an administrative assistant to the Consul General, but mainly she decodes cabled messages and then takes them to her boss. Erskine knew she wouldn't take this one to the Consul General."

Travis stared at Kelso for a moment, then at Vera, who only smiled. "This is beginning to sound like a spy novel."

Kelso laughed. "The Russians want nothing to do with Erskine or the Pumas. They're an embarrassment to them. Not to mention a potential threat to détente."

Travis looked at the note again. "How did Erskine get into contact with Kenny Morris? Or did Kenny and his pal do this on their own?"

"Who knows? Maybe they did it to prove that they're worthy of the Pumas and Erskine simply read about it in the papers. Or maybe he's directing the whole show from Algiers with help from their intelligence service. Obviously, he has access to the highest levels of authority there."

"Okay. Now I get it. I think. But the question is, what do we do now?"

"Not much we can do." Kelso got up from his chair. "I've notified the FBI agent in charge and he says he thinks Morris and his accomplice are holed up with Thuy somewhere in that twenty-block area around Potrero Elementary."

"What about the school itself?"

"That's a possibility. They could use the kids as a shield. Or even take more hostages. But they've searched the school and come up empty-handed."

"How does he know that they're in that area?"

"He doesn't, but several witnesses called in and said they saw two young black men with large Afros escorting an Asian woman off the BART train at 24th and Mission. They said the Asian woman appeared to be drugged."

Travis glanced at Ben, who leaned forward in his chair and put his head in his hands. "What if I go down there and look around? They won't be expecting a hippie in a VW bus to be snooping around the neighborhood like they would guys in dark suits and unmarked cars."

Kelso smiled. "Maybe not." He walked over to the window and looked out. "It's worth a try, I suppose. I'll let Becker—that's the FBI agent—know you'll be in the area. Make some casual inquiries. Maybe you could pretend to be looking for a bartending job."

"Good idea. Plenty of bars in the area. And they're likely to know everything that's going on in the neighborhood."

"Be careful."

"I intend to." Travis rose and gave Ben a pat on the shoulder. "Don't worry so much, Ben. Thuy's no good to them dead. And she's a tough cookie."

Ben looked up. "Yeah. She's tough, all right."

Travis looked at Vera, who seemed to never stop smiling. "A pleasure to meet you, Vera."

"The pleasure is mine," Vera said. "Ben is fortunate to have such a good friend."

Travis nodded, glanced at Ben, who again had his head buried in his hands, and allowed Vera to escort him to the door. Before he reached the van, however, Kelso came running down the steps with something in his hand. It was a wad of bills.

"Seed money," he said. "Distribute it liberally—but evenly—like planting a garden."

Travis took the wad of bills and stuffed it into his pocket. He climbed into his van.

CHAPTER 36

Travis drove down Divisadero Street, into the Castro, until he hit 24th Street. It was only a dozen blocks or so to Potrero Avenue.

He thought about Kenny Morris—or Mohammed al-Rashid, as he now called himself—and wondered at his transformation from a bright young man with a future, to drug dealer, and finally, to black militant on the road to self-destruction. For however this kidnapping caper turned out, Kenny seemed destined to spend most of his adult life in prison—if the FBI and cops didn't kill him. Even Emma found something attractive and worthy about him, and she was a very conscientious, almost pious, girl. He remembered that when he had been attending Stanford, Bernard was concerned because she was always volunteering to work in soup kitchens or homes for the elderly. "That girl," Bernard used to say, "I'm afraid she's going to become a nun. And to think I left France to get away from the Catholic church!"

Travis smiled at this thought. Bernard had named her Emma, after Emma Bovary, not because of the latter's promiscuity, but because of her rejection of the narrow parochial environment that she grew up in.

He traveled about six or eight blocks down 24th Street, and must have passed as many bars. He didn't know where to start. At the next one, at Guerrero Street, he decided to pull over and park the van. It was still early, about ten o'clock. A fairly sunny day, at least in this part of the Mission.

He reached into his pocket and pulled out the wad of bills Kelso had given him. He counted it. Five hundred dollars, mostly in twenties. Two one hundred dollar bills. The latter two, he supposed, would be for especially rich sources of information.

Once out of the van, he noticed a man sitting on the sidewalk with his back up against the wall of a vacant storefront. He was sitting on three sides of a flattened cardboard box, the fourth as a kind of back rest. Sneakers with holes in the toes, a dirty pair of jeans, and an equally dirty parka with the hood over his head. Grizzled beard.

"Hey, buddy—can you help me out?"

Travis was reminded of the panhandler he gave twenty dollars to not long ago in the Tenderloin. He glanced up at the sign over the bar only two doors down. "Sorry friend—I'm on a mission."

The panhandler laughed. "On a mission? This *is* the Mission. Can't go no further down than this. Come on, help a fellow creature out."

Travis took a few steps towards the bar and stopped. He turned around and looked at the man, who looked back expectantly. Then he pulled out his wallet and extracted a ten dollar bill. He handed it to the man. "Buy yourself a new pair of sneakers. Your feet are bleeding."

The man looked down at his feet. The toes were sticking out from both shoes, one with a popped blister. The sock around it was soaked with dried blood.

"Yeah. Sure," the man said. "I'll get a new pair down at the thrift store. Thanks."

Travis continued to the bar, admonishing himself for being such a soft touch. He'd never make it as an undercover agent.

It was a corner bar, with wood-latticed swinging doors just like in the Old West. He pushed through the doors and saw pretty much what he expected: a vinyl floor of some indeterminate color, a scuffed and scratched oak bar with an iron—not brass—rail at the bottom, a big mirror behind the bar with patches of its silver backing missing, and a couple of neon signs: Budweiser, the King of Beers, and Crown Royal Special Reserve Canadian Whisky. There was an aging jukebox in the corner and a single pool table in front of it. Two or three patrons sat at the bar, while two young Hispanic men seemed intent on their pool game.

"What'll you have?" the bartender said.

"I don't know. It's early. How about a bloody mary?"

"Coming up."

The bartender looked to be about fifty, heavy jowls, and a balding head with a comb-over. Caucasian, he looked as if he had been that age all his life, and had spent most of it behind this very bar.

Travis sat down on a torn naugahyde stool and looked to the patron on his right. He was about the same age as the bartender, stout, but with a full head of hair pulled back in a ponytail, streaked with gray. He looked vaguely Hispanic.

This was already looking unproductive. What would any of these people know about the kidnapping? Did they even read the newspapers?

"That your van?" the guy with the ponytail said.

Travis looked to the window at the front of the bar. The van was clearly visible. "Yeah."

"Had one just like it a few years ago. Sold it for a bike. Sometimes I wish I had the van back. You get tired on the road, you just pull over and take a nap."

Travis chuckled. "I've never slept in it."

"Oh, yeah? What'd you buy it for—to get laid?"

"Haven't used it for that, either. I just liked the paint job."

The bartender set a bloody mary down on the bar. "Buck and a quarter."

Travis put two dollars on the bar.

"Where you from?" the man with the pony tail said.

"Here."

"Born and raised?"

"No. Michigan. How about you?"

"San Jose. Up here looking for work."

"Me, too." Travis took a sip of his bloody mary. Out of the corner of his left eye, he noticed someone sitting on the bar stool next to his.

"Jack!"

Travis looked at the newcomer. It was the man he had encountered on the street.

"Jack! A Crown Royal." The man slapped the ten dollar bill down on the bar that Travis had given him. "On the rocks."

Jack reached into the well and pulled out a bottle of Crown Royal. He scooped up some ice in a glass, set it down in front of the man and poured the whisky into it. Then he took the ten dollar bill to the register.

"I thought you were going to buy some new sneakers," Travis said.

The man looked at Travis as if he hadn't noticed him before. "Oh—they was out. I'll try 'em again next week when they get some more in."

"You won't have much money left by then."

"Them's cheap shoes. Four, five bucks." He lifted the Crown Royal to his lips, sniffed at it, took a tiny sip and put the glass down. He seemed to savor the whisky as if it were a fine wine.

Travis sighed. Same result as the time he gave a twenty to the guy in the Tenderloin. He turned and looked at the man with the ponytail, who was grinning at him.

"Wayne probably makes more money than I do," the guy with the ponytail said. He looked over Travis' shoulder at Wayne. "What do you take in in a day, Wayne? Fifty, sixty bucks?"

"Sometimes a hunnert," Wayne said, without the slightest embarrassment, in spite of the proximity of Travis.

Travis was beginning to feel like his mission in the Mission was useless. He wasn't cut out for this kind of thing. What was he going to do with all the money that Kelso had given him? He took another sip of his bloody mary, put the glass down, and left the change on the bar.

Out on the sidewalk, the sun was bright and he stood motionless for a few moments, waiting for his eyes to adjust. What next? Maybe a bar patronized by blacks rather than Hispanics. That made more sense.

He got into his van and drove another six blocks or so past the BART station, past a number of vacant storefronts, past a Chinese restaurant, past a soul food grocery store. He turned right on South Van Ness. At the next corner, he saw a bar with a colorful mural on its side wall depicting black musicians wailing away on saxophones and trumpets. The sign in front was of purple neon with a martini glass containing an olive speared through with a toothpick. The name on the sign read 'Ella's Place.'

He parked the van on a side street and walked back to the bar.

Once inside, he paused for a moment to let his eyes adjust to the darkness, and stepped up to the bar. This one was also made of oak, but clean and highly polished. The floor consisted of black and white ceramic tile, with a hardwood dance floor in front of a bandstand. There were a couple of black musicians on the bandstand, tuning their instruments.

"I'm Ella. What'll you have, Mister?"

Travis, who had been watching the musicians, turned to the sound of the voice. It belonged to a black woman perhaps in her late thirties, with heavily braided hair wrapped around her head and pulled into a knot at the back. The knot sparkled with red, white and green beads.

"Um, a bloody mary," he said.

Ella smiled. "Most popular drink this time of day. Make yourself comfortable."

Travis sat on a bar stool while Ella made his drink. He looked around the place. No pool table or juke box. Several tables around the dance floor. It really was a jazz nightclub.

A couple of black women, well-dressed, sat at one of the tables, sipping on some sort of tall, sweet-looking drinks, through straws. They occasionally exchanged comments with the musicians. At the other end of the bar sat two or three men, two deep in conversation, one staring at him.

"Want to run a tab?" Ella put the bloody mary on the bar.

"Sure." Travis noticed there was a little umbrella sticking out of the glass, along with a straw. He took a sip. "Good drink. A little spicy."

"Too spicy?"

"No, no. I like it this way. The band play this early?"

"No. They don't start till three. Louis and Red like to make sure everything's right before they go on. Sometimes they jam a little."

"Must be a popular place."

"We do a good business. You like jazz?"

"Sure."

"Then stick around. Oops! Another customer. I'll be back."

Travis watched as Ella walked to the end of the bar closest to the street. A couple of black men, maybe in their forties, bellied up to the bar. One was dressed in a white suit, black shirt, white tie, and a white fedora. He made a conspicuous display of two or three diamond rings. The other looked a little younger, dressed in a similar way, though less ostentatious. A dark suit, gray tie, no hat. Ella served them without asking what they wanted.

The man in the white suit kept staring at him. Finally he came over to Travis. "You a musician?"

"No. I'm a bartender."

"Bartender? Can you make a White Russian?"

"Sure."

"What's in it?"

"Vodka, Kalua, and cream."

The man in the white suit laughed. "You got the job." He extended his hand. "Jimmy. Jimmy Hart."

Travis shook his hand. "Travis Carter."

"Glad to meet you, Travis Carter. What you doing down in the Mission. Slumming?"

"No, not at all. I'm looking for a job."

Jimmy seemed to study him for a moment. "Why here? Why not the Haight, or Upper Van Ness? Maybe North Beach."

Travis was beginning to feel uncomfortable. Was Jimmy a gangster? Was this his territory? "I'm new in town. Just got off 101. Seemed as good a place to start as any."

Jimmy looked skeptical. The other man came over to join him. "You know this place has been crawling with cops lately?"

"No, I didn't know that. Why?"

"The Pumas—you heard of the Black Pumas?"

"Sure."

"The cops think they kidnapped some Vietnamese woman. You heard that?"

"I think so. On the radio."

"Well, they've been asking a lot of questions. But nobody seems to know anything. Maybe it was the Pumas, maybe not. Seems like black people always get blamed for these things. You know what I mean?"

"I guess it happens a lot."

"You bet it does. You like another drink?"

"Haven't finished this one."

Jimmy nodded to Ella, who was standing nearby, listening. "You just tell Ella if you need anything else."

"Thanks."

Jimmy and his friend went back to their end of the bar.

Now Travis wondered what he had gotten himself into. Jimmy obviously thought he was a cop. And whether he knew anything about the whereabouts of Kenny Morris and Thuy, he wasn't about to reveal it to him. On the other hand, he seemed to make it his business to know everything that happened on his turf. How could Kenny and his pal hide out in the Mission, with an Asian woman no less, without his knowing about it? And if he could be bought, would even five hundred dollars be enough?

It was approaching noon and more people began to trickle into the bar. Mostly young black people, but some Hispanics, too. He seemed to be the only white person there. But he didn't feel uncomfortable, except for the presence of Jimmy.

Jimmy, by this time, had moved around the bar, greeting most of the customers by name, buying them drinks. Then he and his friend sat down at a table near the dance floor and ordered some food from the kitchen, which Travis noticed for the first time when a tall black man in a white toque and apron emerged from it to shake hands with Jimmy.

"Play something, Louis," Jimmy said.

Louis looked at Jimmy, then at Red. "Kind of early, Jimmy. We was gonna get a bite to eat."

"Play something." Jimmy said. "This place is like a morgue. You can eat on your break."

Red picked up his saxophone. Louis looked again at Jimmy. "Bud won't be here till three. Need a bass man for a proper trio."

"Play."

Louis picked up his trumpet and began to play a Charlie Parker tune. Red came in with his sax after a few bars and the two began to improvise.

"You're a friggin' genius, Louis," Jimmy shouted. "You don't need a bass."

From this point on, Ella's Place became a beehive of activity. More and more people came in from the street. Bud, the bass man, came in early and joined the other two. Finally, one of the women that Travis had seen sipping her drink when he first came in got up on the bandstand and started singing a song straight out of an Ella Fitzgerald song book.

By this time, Travis was on his third bloody mary—fourth, counting the one at the first bar. He was having such a good time, he had forgotten why he came into the place. Then he remembered. He pushed his glass away and put a twenty dollar bill on the bar. Then he got up to leave. This wasn't the way to find out where Thuy was being held. He needed to sober up, get some coffee somewhere, and figure out a better strategy.

Just as he was about to reach the door, the 'friend' that was with Jimmy came up behind him and gently grabbed him by the elbow. "Jimmy wants to see you."

"Jimmy?"

"In the back. Follow me."

Travis followed the man into a long hallway that ended in a cul-de-sac with a heavy oaken door displaying a sign that said 'private.' The man opened the door and stood aside, indicating that Travis should go first.

Inside sat Jimmy behind a heavy partner's desk with fluted pilasters at each corner crowned with carved lions' heads. Photographs of mostly black musicians and athletes adorned the walls, many autographed and addressed 'to Jimmy.'

"Sit down, Travis Carter," Jimmy said. "Make yourself comfortable."

Travis didn't think he was going to be very comfortable, but he sat down in a red leather armchair anyway.

"I'll be upfront with you, Travis," He said. "I know you're a cop, or at least you've been sent by the cops. Probably 'sent,' because you seem to be an amateur. Smart. Because I can spot a real cop a mile away. Cigar?" He reached into a humidor.

"No, thanks. Don't smoke."

"You mind if I do?"

"Not at all."

Jimmy took out one of the cigars, lit it with a sliver lighter, and leaned back in his chair. He took a few drags. "Havana. Best in the world. Too bad the U.S. government doesn't want to do business with Castro. Big mistake." He leaned forward again. "The Pumas, on the other hand, *do* do business with Castro, but not in the right way. Instead of cigars, or marijuana, all they want from him is guns, and Castro ain't sellin.' At least not to them."

Travis said nothing.

"Needless to say," Jimmy continued, "I don't care much for the

Pumas. They're a pain in the ass. Shoot cops for no good reason. Bring the SFPD down on our necks, not to mention the FBI. I don't like this Mexican standoff. Bad for business. You dig?"

"I think so."

"Good. So I'm prepared to go against my better instincts and co-operate with you and your friends down at the Hall of Justice. But, of course, there's a price."

"Of course."

"I happen to have some information as to the whereabouts of this Asian girl. What's her name?"

"Thuy."

"Right. Twee. Now—down to business. I have an address here. What's it worth to you?"

Travis shifted his weight in his chair and tried to look as if he were considering some number. But he really had only one number in mind. "Five hundred dollars."

Jimmy leaned back in his chair and took another drag on his cigar. He smiled. "I would consider that a down payment. Word gets out that I've given you this information, it could mean war between me and the Pumas. I'd win, of course, but it would turn the Mission into a battlefield with lots of casualties. I'd like to avoid that."

"How much do you want?"

"Five thousand."

"What if it turns out to be the wrong address? Or they're gone by then?"

Jimmy leaned forward. "A, it *is* the right address. B, if they move the girl, I'll know about it. You got the five hundred on you?"

"I do."

"Let's see it."

Travis considered this for a moment. If he didn't produce the five hundred, the goon standing behind him would probably take it from him anyway. He reached into his jacket pocket and pulled out the wad of bills that Kelso had given him and tossed it onto Jimmy's desk.

Jimmy picked up the wad of bills, removed the rubber band, and counted it. He held up a couple of the bills to the light. "Looks okay. When can you get the other forty-five hundred?"

"When can I get that address? There may not be much time. They could kill her while we're here talking."

Jimmy frowned. "They ain't gonna kill her. But I'll tell you what I'll do. I'll give you the address. You take it back to your handlers. If the information turns out to be wrong, I'll keep the five hundred for my trouble. If I'm right, then you come back to Ella's and make a deposit with her. Forty-five one hundred dollar bills."

"What if I don't come back?"

Jimmy rolled his eyes to the ceiling and took another pull on the cigar. "You'd be a very foolish person. And you don't look like a fool to me."

"How about the address?"

Jimmy stared at him for a moment and then took a pen from its holder on the desk. He wrote something down on a note pad, tore off the note, and shoved it across the desk.

Travis leaned forward and took the note. '550 20th Street.'

"Put the forty-five hundred in an envelope," Jimmy said. "Address it to Ella. Have a drink on the house before you leave. And don't forget to leave Ella a tip."

Travis stood. "I won't forget. Mind if I find my own way out?"

"Be my guest." Jimmy stood and extended his hand. "It's a pleasure doing business with you, Travis Carter."

Travis shook his hand. "Likewise." He turned to see Jimmy's 'friend' go to the door and open it for him.

He shoved the note into his jacket and made his way down the hall and into the bar. Ella was pouring a customer a drink and smiled at him.

"Come see us again, Mr. Carter," she said.

"I will, Ella. Thanks." He stepped out into the bright sunlight, waited for his eyes to adjust, and tried to remember where he parked his van.

CHAPTER 37

Travis located his van and drove up South Van Ness with the intention of going directly to Kelso's house in Pacific Heights. But when he got to 20th Street and stopped at the light, he pulled out the note Jimmy had given him and looked at the address again.

He turned right on 20th and saw that the numbers descended towards the bay. Twenty, thirty blocks. The closer he got to the bay, the more rundown everything looked. He passed under the Bayshore Freeway, and realized the address was probably on the waterfront. At Third Street he stopped and had second thoughts. This van stuck out like a sore thumb. What if Kenny and his pals knew it was his? Mrs. Morris, who mostly played dumb while he was at her house in East Palo Alto, might have alerted them.

He continued on Third, and when he got home he called Kelso.

"I know where they are."

"Good work!" Kelso said. "You've got the address?"

"Yeah, there's one hitch, though."

"What's that?"

"I gave the whole five hundred to a gangster named Jimmy Hart. It's his turf. He knows everyone, everything that moves there."

"So what's the hitch?"

"He considers the five hundred only a down payment. He wants another forty-five hundred."

"Hmm. But you've got the address."

"Yeah, but I don't think it would be a good idea to cross him."

"Okay—I'll get the other forty-five hundred. What's he want—to see it before the FBI moves in?"

"No. Says he'll just keep the five hundred if the address proves wrong, or the chickens fly the coop. But if he doesn't get the forty-five hundred by the end of the show, he'll have his goons hang me up by my toenails."

Kelso laughed. "You're beginning to sound like Humphrey Bogart. Okay, what's the address?"

"Five-fifty 20th Street. I drove down that way. I think it's one of those abandoned factories or warehouses on the docks."

"Could be. I'll call Becker. You sit tight while I go to the bank."

"You're going to take it out of your own account?"

"Where else is it going to come from? I'll just add it to my fee."

"Fee? Ben doesn't have any money."

"He will when this is all over. I may even waive it for a share of the royalties of the book."

"What book?"

"Don't worry about it. Gotta go."

After Kelso hung up, Travis wondered at Kelso's magnanimity. What was he going to get out of it? A new career as a criminal defense attorney? Maybe he was going to write his own book.

When he was in Jimmy Hart's office at Ella's, his adrenaline shot up and he didn't feel any effect from the alcohol. Now that he was safe at home, he could feel all those bloody marys lulling him to sleep. He got up from his desk, went to the opposite wall, and pulled down the Murphy bed. As he sat on the bed and pulled off his shoes, he thought of Marcella. What was she doing right now?

He looked at his watch. Two p.m. She was probably at a rehearsal for *Glass Menagerie*. Or maybe having lunch with some Hollywood mogul who wanted to put her in a movie. She was right. This relationship could never work, not with her acting career taking off and him remaining in San Francisco tending bar and going to school. He still had two more semesters to get his degree. And then what?

He lay down on the bed, stretched out his legs, and curled and uncurled his toes a couple of times. He would take a short nap, get up, make a sandwich, then give Kelso a call for an update.

As he slipped into unconsciousness, he began to see a variety of bizarre images. But then what other kind were there in a dream state? At first there was Marcella in her white mime makeup, performing on a street corner. He tried to identify the neighborhood. A street sign said Broadway. North Beach. But then there was another Broadway: New York. Now Marcella was performing on a stage. Another actor appeared. This seemed to be Alessandro. Marcella shrank away from him. Alessandro, in leotards but without the whiteface, danced around her in a kind of ballet. Marcella turned and watched him as he did so. Suddenly, Alessandro pounced on her like a tiger on a fawn. Marcella's mouth opened as if she were screaming, but no sound came out.

Now, just as suddenly as Alessandro had appeared, he, Travis, materialized. But he was dressed in his army jungle fatigues with grease to camouflage his face. He leveled his M-16 at Alessandro and ordered him to get off of Marcella. Alessandro did so, but reached for some kind of weapon. Travis pulled the trigger on the M-16, but suddenly Alessandro was transformed into a woman. A Vietnamese woman. The woman crumpled to what was now a dirt floor and Travis went over to investigate. He turned the body over and saw that it was Thuy. Her belly had been ripped open by the bullets, and a baby spilled out onto the dirt floor. The baby's face was horribly disfigured.

He woke up, sweating. He looked at his watch. Three o'clock. A whole hour. It seemed like he was asleep for only a few minutes. He got up to make some coffee. Before he finished the first cup, the phone rang. It was Kelso.

"I need a babysitter."

"What?"

"It's Ben. He's about to jump out of his shorts watching the SWAT team surround the ironworks."

Travis drained the cup. "What's a SWAT team?"

"The cops. Aren't you watching it on TV?"

"I don't own a TV."

Kelso sighed. "Well, you can watch mine. The cops and the FBI have surrounded the old shipyard ironworks on 20th Street and there's a standoff. Your gangster friend's information was absolutely correct. I've got to get down there. But somebody's got to watch Ben. Vera's at the consulate and she can't restrain him, anyway. Can you be here in fifteen minutes?"

"Ten."

"I'll wait for you."

Travis hung up the phone. He was starving. But food would have to wait.

Good as his word, he arrived at Kelso's Pacific Heights digs inside of ten minutes. Vera greeted him at the door. Apparently, she had been watching the standoff on TV, too, and rushed home to see if she could help.

Ben was pacing back and forth in the living room in front of the

TV set with his hands in his pockets. Kelso rose from the sofa.

"Ben needs some TLC," Kelso said. "See that he gets it."

"I don't need no TLC, Ted," Ben said. "I need to get my hands on those assholes down at the ironworks."

"That's exactly what we don't need," Kelso said. "Don't let him out of your sight, Travis. If cooler heads prevail, Thuy will be home in time for dinner tonight." He then gave Vera a quick kiss, rushed to a stairway that led to the garage, and ran down the steps.

"The FBI and SFPD SWAT Team have surrounded the hideout of the alleged kidnappers of Thuy Nguyen, the fiancée of Ben Franklin, a star witness in the upcoming Black Puma murder trial."

Ben went back to the TV to watch and listen, as did Travis.

On the screen a female reporter was holding a microphone, facing the camera. "We have just gotten an update from Eric Becker, the FBI agent in charge here, who says the kidnappers have demanded a chartered jet to fly themselves, Ms. Nguyen and her fiancé, out of the country. Otherwise, they say, they will kill Ms. Nguyen, who is said to be nearly nine months pregnant."

"The bastards," Ben said.

"It is now thought," the reporter continued, "that the mastermind of this scheme, which has obviously gone awry, is Lonnie Erskine, the alleged trigger man who gunned down San Francisco police officer Dan Watt in Chinatown last month as he emerged from a restaurant. A bestselling author and high-ranking member of the Black Puma Party, Mr. Erskine is thought to be living somewhere in Algeria, which has no extradition treaty with the United States."

Travis sat down on the sofa, as did Vera, but Ben remained standing. The camera panned across the waterfront, taking in a couple of police boats, an abandoned-looking factory with several windows broken out, and a ring of squad cars with lights flashing in front of the factory. SWAT Team members, bulked up with body armor and helmets, stood or crouched behind what looked like an armored troop carrier, ready with shotguns and assault rifles.

The camera panned back to the reporter. "I have agent Becker here, David, who has some important news that may facilitate a peaceful resolution to the standoff."

Agent Becker suddenly appeared on the screen next to the reporter.

He was a tall, imposing-looking man in his early forties, wearing a dark suit and sunglasses.

"Agent Becker," the reporter said, holding the microphone to Becker's face, "what can you tell us about this new development?"

"Only that we have been able to locate the mother of one of the suspects and that she will be here shortly to help with the negotiations."

"Can you give us her name?"

"I'd prefer not to at the moment. Things are at a very delicate stage."

"Well, then, can you tell us if there has been any communication with Mr. Erskine, or other ranking members of the Black Puma Party?"

"None at all at the moment."

As Becker moved away, the reporter, an attractive Asian-American woman, turned back to the camera. "That's all we have for now, David. We will alert you and our viewers to any new developments. This is Trudy Yamamoto, KRON-TV News."

Ben walked over to the TV and turned it off. "What do we do now? Play canasta?"

Vera looked puzzled. "What's canasta?"

"Card game," Travis said. "Like gin rummy."

"I know that one," Vera said. "I'll get the cards."

"Get two decks," Ben said.

While Vera went to find the cards, Travis watched Ben as he paced around the living room.

"They're gonna kill her," Ben said.

"Not with Mrs. Morris there."

"Who's Mrs. Morris?"

"Kenny Morris' mother," Travis said. "I had a long talk with her the other day in Palo Alto. He's not going to kill a pregnant woman with his mother standing fifty feet away."

Ben, who was at the window staring out at Alcatraz, turned and looked at Travis. "You think she'll get inside?"

"That appears to be the plan. They let her in and she'll probably walk out with Thuy."

"Think so?"

"There's a good chance."

Vera returned with the cards, a notepad and pencil, and sat at the dining room table. She began to shuffle the cards. "Are you boys hungry?"

"Starved." Travis got up and went to the table.

Ben followed. "I ain't had nothin' to eat all day."

"How about some borscht?" Vera said. "My own recipe."

"Sure." Travis pulled out a chair and sat down. "That's soup, isn't it? Maybe a sandwich to go with it."

"Piroshki. Better than sandwiches, and just as filling."

"Sounds good."

While Vera went off to the kitchen, Ben took his seat at the table and watched Travis deal out the cards. "Last time we played this game we got interrupted."

"Yeah," Travis said. "Mortar attack. Charlie had no respect for our leisure time."

"I was up 118 points."

Travis smiled as he dealt the last card and picked up his hand. "You've got a memory like an elephant."

"Keeps guys like you honest."

"Guys like me?"

"Officers." Ben grinned. "Can't trust 'em."

"If I had been cheating, would I be down 118 points?"

Ben picked up his hand. "It's possible to cheat like crazy and still lose."

"So if I don't cheat, I'll win?"

"Makes no difference. I'll kick your ass, anyway."

CHAPTER 38

The reviews for *The Glass Menagerie* were very good, with both Marcella and Sam mentioned as emerging talents to be watched. There was little money, however, and the hoped for move to Broadway in New York was a distant prospect at best. Revivals, the reviewer for *The Los Angeles Times* said, were successful in New York when there was a dearth of new plays, which was not the case at the moment. Young, new playwrights of the babyboom generation were emerging, and they were angry: angry about the Vietnam War, angry about the slow progress of the civil rights movement, and angry about the inequalities between men and women, particularly in the market place.

Marcella was interested in this latter group, especially the feminist writers. She was tired of playing demure, passive Laura in *The Glass Menagerie*, however much she was praised for her subtle and sensitive interpretation of the role. And now that the play was about to come to an end, she wasn't sure what would come next.

There was a ray of hope, however. And this came in the form of one Ray Weismann, a film producer who had seen her performance in *Menagerie* and said he wanted to cast her in the title role of his next film, about a young woman caught in an abusive relationship who kills her husband in self-defense but is charged with murder. The title, Ray said, was *A Woman Down*, but he was open to suggestions. First, however, he needed a studio position, without which he could not get funding.

"Why don't you like anal sex?" Ray settled into the leather sofa at the foot of his bed next to Marcella. Both were wearing terry cloth robes that Ray provided for all of his lady friends after inviting them for a dip in the pool. And both were sipping on cups of espresso Ray had made for them with his new espresso machine that he kept in a little kitchenette off the master bedroom.

"Because it hurts," Marcella said. "Besides, I think it's unhealthy."

"Matter of opinion." Ray, a man of about fifty with rust-colored hair and a slight paunch, put his espresso down on a lucite table in front of the sofa and went to a bookshelf, where he retrieved a manuscript. "How did you get those scars on your back?"

"My father is a violent man." Marcella sipped her espresso while watching the television, from which no sound emanated.

"Hmm," Ray said. "No problem. I know the best makeup artists in the business. What are you watching?"

"Some standoff with the police in San Francisco. Can you turn up the sound?"

"Turn it up yourself. There's the remote on the coffee table."

Marcella looked and saw a silver gadget next to a stack of art books. "That thing?"

Ray laughed. "Don't they have high tech TVs in San Francisco? I thought that's where they were invented."

"Too expensive for starving artists. How do you work this thing?"

"Push the 'up' arrow on the volume button."

"Oh." Marcella pressed the button several times and a familiar voice filled the room.

"This is Trudy Yamamoto of KRON-TV, San Francisco."

"Looks like a scene from *On the Waterfront*," Ray said.

"Shh!"

"Police and FBI," Ms. Yamamoto said, "have cut off all avenues of escape for the kidnappers. They have threatened to kill Ms. Nguyen if their demands are not met, but a new element has been introduced into this standoff and that is the presence of one of the kidnappers' mother, who is with Agent Becker now. I'll try to get him to give us an update—wait. The kidnappers' mother is now approaching the factory door alone."

"What the hell is this all about?" Weismann said.

"The Black Pumas have kidnapped the fiancée of a man who intends to testify against one of their members in an upcoming murder trial," Marcella said. "They're threatening to kill her unless they get safe passage out of the country."

"How do you know all that?"

"Her fiancé's name is Ben Franklin. He's a friend of mine."

"A friend of yours? How—"

"Shh!"

"Agent Becker," Trudy Yamamoto said, "can you tell us what this, this—Mrs. Morris, isn't it?"

"That's right. She's the mother of one of the suspects. He's asked for her help."

"What kind of help?"

"Apparently Ms. Nguyen has gone into labor. The kidnappers won't let anyone else into the factory."

"Labor? Can't one of the emergency personnel go to assist her?"

"They won't allow anyone in but her. We'll just have to hope that she knows what to do."

Ms. Yamamoto turned back to face the camera. "You can see, David, that the situation is very, very tense here." She was handed a note and took a moment to read it. "We've just learned that the mother's full name is Adel Morris, and her son's name is Kenneth Morris, also know as Mohammed al-Rashid. She's been admitted to the factory through a side door now, and out of our sight. This could take some time. Back to you, David."

Weismann picked up the remote and pressed the mute button. "This could make a great movie!" He turned to Marcella. "You say the woman's fiancé is a friend of yours. Do you think he'd sell the rights to the story?"

"For Pete's sake, Ray." Marcella brushed her hair back and pulled her legs up underneath her on the sofa. "The woman—she's a friend of mine, too—and her baby are about to die. And all you can think of is whether you can get the rights to the story?"

Weismann took a sip of his espresso and leaned back in the sofa. "I can't help it. It's my business. What's this woman like?"

"Her name is Thuy Nguyen. She's Vietnamese. She and Ben met in Vietnam."

Weismann sat bolt upright, nearly spilling his espresso. "God! That's perfect. American G.I. falls in love with Vietnamese B-girl—was she a B-girl?"

"I think she was."

"Great! All the pieces are falling into place. G.I. falls in love with Vietnamese girl, girl follows him to America—wait! Is he a Black Puma?"

"He was...sort of."

"Black then."

"Sure."

"Hmm. The mixed race thing. Of course there was *Guess Who's*

Coming to Dinner a few years ago. I wonder if we could get Poitier? Expensive...you sure he's black?"

"Very."

"Okay. We'll work around that. He could be white, but he witnesses a murder that gets him in trouble with the Pumas. Or maybe some Neo-Nazis. I like that better."

"Christ." Marcella stood up from the sofa. "I'm getting dressed."

"If you want to shower, remember that the lever starts out cold and all the way to the left it's scalding hot.'

"I'll remember."

CHAPTER 39

"I've got to get down there!" Ben paced around the living room of Kelso's house like a caged tiger. "She's having the baby!"

"Calm down, Ben." Travis went to the TV set and turned it off. "There's nothing you can do at this point. It would only complicate the negotiations. Besides, you would be a sitting duck for any Puma who decided to take you out."

"I don't care! Thuy's having my baby!" Ben headed for the door, pulled on it, and finding it locked, fumbled with the mechanism. "If you don't take me, I'll get a cab. What the fuck is wrong with this door? I ain't a prisoner. You can't keep me here!"

"All right," Travis said. "I'll take you down there. But you've got to promise not to do anything rash once we get there. Remember, there're cops everywhere and they're armed."

"Okay. How the fuck do you open this door?"

Vera, who had been watching and listening from the kitchen, went over to the front door. She turned the lock. "It's the old-fashioned kind. You turn it in the opposite direction."

Ben stared at her for a moment. "Oh. Sorry about my French, Vera. That was good persorski."

"Piroshki."

"Whatever. Come on, Travis. Let's get a move on!"

Travis followed Ben to the door, but by the time he got there Ben was already halfway down the steps.

"I'm afraid I've let Ted down," Vera said.

"It'll be okay. The main thing is to not let Ben charge into the factory like a bull in a china shop. The cops will handcuff him if necessary. Thanks Vera—you've done your part."

"I'm not so sure. Be careful." Vera watched as Travis bounded down the steps after Ben.

By the time Travis and Ben arrived at the 20th Street pier, there were at least a dozen police cars parked in a phalanx pointing towards the factory door with their lights flashing. Trudy Yamamoto stood just behind them and in front of a camera, while Kelso stood to one side talking to Becker, the FBI agent.

Kelso glanced at them as they approached and then did a double take. "Ben! Travis! What are you doing here? I told you to—"

"I couldn't stop him," Travis said. "I thought it better to bring him down here myself to make sure he doesn't hurt himself—or someone else."

"This the fiancé?" Becker said.

"Yes," Kelso said. "Ben, this is agent Becker; Eric, Ben Franklin."

Ben shook Becker's hand while staring at the factory door. "She okay?"

"As far as we know," Becker said. "Morris' mother has been in there for nearly an hour now. Not a peep out of any of them."

"Can't we do something?"

"Nothing," Becker said. "The best thing to do is wait."

Ben sighed. "Can't you throw tear gas in there or something?"

"It's a possibility," Becker said. "But it'll be a last resort if negotiations break down. Besides, there's a chance they may start shooting wildly if they're blinded and confused. Better to wait and see what Mrs. Morris can do. After all—"

Suddenly someone appeared at the factory door. It was Mrs. Morris carrying something in her arms. The crowd, which had been noisy and animated until now, fell silent.

"That the guy's mother?" Ben said.

"That's her," Becker said. "Looks like she's got a baby." He moved away and spoke to the police captain.

Ben stood on his toes to get a better look. "Do you see Thuy?"

"Not yet," Travis said. "It looks like they closed the door behind them."

They all waited patiently—except for Ben, who jockeyed for a closer look—as Mrs. Morris walked towards the phalanx of police cars. A policeman and an emergency medical worker met her just as she passed into the phalanx. Ben rushed forward.

"Ben!" Kelso said. "Stay back!"

Ben ignored him and approached Mrs. Morris. She looked up from the bundle in her arms and stared at him for a moment. "You the daddy?"

"Yes, ma'am," Ben said. "Is the baby okay?"

Mrs. Morris smiled and looked down at the child. "Shore. A

healthy, bouncing boy. You want to hold him?"

A wide grin came to Ben's face. "Yes, ma'am."

Mrs. Morris carefully handed the baby to Ben. It was quite bloody and wrapped in oily rags. "Wasn't nothing but rags in that old factory. Had to borrow Kenny's penknife to cut the umbilical cord."

Ben held the baby up in the air and the crowd clapped and cheered. It started crying and he let it settle in his arms and rocked it back and forth.

Mrs. Morris smiled at the baby, then looked at Ben. "I saved your baby—now you can save mine."

Ben looked at her, startled. "Your baby?"

Mrs. Morris jerked her head in the direction of the factory. "He in there with his buddy and your fiancée. He say he no baby-killer, but he ain't guaranteein' the life of the girl. He say he ain't goin' back to prison nohow."

Ben looked around and saw Becker on one side of him and Kelso on the other. The police and several hundred onlookers were all staring at him. He looked again at Mrs. Morris. "He a Muslim?"

"That what he say."

Ben handed the baby back to her, looked one last time at Becker, and started walking towards the factory.

"Ben!" Kelso lunged forward, but Becker restrained him.

Ben kept walking slowly, deliberately towards the door. When he arrived, he raised his fist and knocked loudly against the rusted metal. "As-salamu alaikum!"

"What's that mean?" Kelso said.

"Peace be with you," Becker said. "Standard Muslim greeting."

Ben knocked again and again repeated the phrase. After a few moments, the door opened by a few inches.

"Wa-Alaikum salam," came the belated response, and the door opened wider.

Ben stepped inside and the door closed.

"What if they kill them both?" Kelso said.

"Not likely," Becker said. "They started out with one card to play—now they've got two. Why would they want to throw away a good hand?"

"Good point," Kelso said. "What if they ask for safe passage again?"

"They're not getting it. But they know that they *can* get a lighter sentence if they surrender and give up the girl. Especially since they've already proven they're not craven monsters by allowing Mrs. Morris to deliver the baby."

Kelso smiled. "I gather you've done this kind of thing before."

"A few times."

"Anything I can do?" Travis said.

Becker looked at Travis as if noticing him for the first time. "Who are you?"

"This is Travis Carter," Kelso said. "Ben's best friend."

"Then you should know something about Mr. Franklin's character," Becker said. "Can he persuade these thugs to drop their guns and walk out peacefully?"

"I don't know," Travis said. "But I do know that he's fearless."

Becker smiled and looked again towards the factory door. "That's encouraging."

Another half hour passed. The sun was going down, throwing shafts of light through the broken windows of the factory. The brick façade began to glow a soft orange.

"How much longer can we wait?" Kelso said. "When it gets dark, they might be able to slip out somehow."

"Another fifteen minutes and we'll go in with the gas," Becker said. "It's risky, but you're right—the darkness will give them an advantage we can't afford to give them."

A moment later the factory door opened. A moment after that, Thuy appeared, supported by Ben. Her clothes were soaked with blood.

Becker nodded to the police captain, who nodded to an EMT worker. Three white-suited medical personnel rushed a gurney to Thuy and Ben helped them put her onto it. Then Ben followed the gurney as it was wheeled to a waiting ambulance.

Once Thuy was in the ambulance and the noise from the cheering crowd died down, Becker picked up a bull horn. "You've done the right thing. Now don't mess it up by staying in there. Come out one at a time with your hands on your head. You won't be hurt."

Becker put down the bull horn and waited. Another minute went by. Two minutes.

Suddenly, a young black man with a large Afro appeared in the doorway. He put his hands on his head and walked slowly towards the police cars. A second young man appeared, also with an Afro, but cut a bit shorter. Both were wearing jeans and dashiki-style shirts.

Mrs. Morris handed the baby to Travis and started to rush forward but the police captain held her back. Four helmeted SWAT Team members, automatic weapons across their chest, met the two young men at the halfway point between the factory and the phalanx. They forced them facedown on the pavement and handcuffed their hands behind their back.

"Don't hurt him!" Mrs. Morris cried. "He done what you say!"

Becker nodded again to the police captain. The police captain released Mrs. Moore, who rushed to embrace her son, now standing with a SWAT officer guiding him and his partner to a police van.

"Oh, baby, baby!" Mrs. Morris exclaimed. "It's gonna be all right! You done the right thing. You done the right thing."

Kenny Morris, aka Mohammed al-Rashid, looked at her almost as if he were embarrassed for her, then stared at Ben, who was standing next to the ambulance. Ben stared back for a moment, then nodded, as if there were some silent agreement between them.

The door to the police van opened and the two young men were pushed inside. The doors closed and the van moved slowly through the crowd.

Travis stood nearby looking down at the baby, which was smiling at him. Strands of wet, straight black hair stuck to his forehead. His skin was a golden brown and his eyes decidedly Asian. "Welcome to a troubled world, Ben Franklin, Jr."

Ben came over and took the child in his arms. "What are you saying to him?"

"Just that I'm glad he's here."

"That's good, because you're his godfather."

"What's a godfather do?" Travis said.

"I dunno. Say a prayer for the kid and take him to ball games, I guess."

"Doesn't sound too difficult. I accept the responsibility."

"I didn't say you had a choice."

"Ben!"

"Gotta go. The Dragon Lady wants to see her son." Ben kissed the child on the forehead and returned to the ambulance where Thuy was waiting.

CHAPTER 40

Marcella was apprehensive about seeing Travis for the first time in five years. She had been amazed to discover that he had the same phone number as he did in their days together in the '70s. At first she assumed that he must still be living in that tiny apartment on Taylor Street with the Murphy bed. He laughed at that and said that he now had more spacious 'accommodations,' but in the same neighborhood.

She was flying in from New York where she had just won a Tony award for best actress in a new play. The invitation from the San Francisco State Theater Department chairman to speak to the undergraduates was both flattering and appealing for the opportunity to present herself as one who had 'made it,' despite the fact that she didn't feel that she had 'made' anything yet. Ray Weismann had proved to be both an abusive lover—if you could call him that—and a third-rate producer. *A Woman Down* was shot in fifteen days and flopped at the box office. She would love to work with someone like Robert Altman or, better yet, Francois Truffaut.

Travis was waiting at the baggage claim when she stepped off the escalator. He was easy to spot, though he was dressed more conservatively than in the days they were together at San Francisco State. And in the play—oh, yes, *that* play. She had already forgotten the name of it, only that she played Alexander the Great's wife and Travis a mere soldier.

He still looked fit and as good-looking as ever. His sandy blond hair was a bit shorter, but the fine nose, firm jaw, and bright blue eyes were the same. He wore a burgundy turtleneck sweater, and a pair of navy blue slacks and penny loafers. In the old days it was always a collarless shirt, jeans, and cowboy boots.

"Travis!" She dropped her carryon bag and threw her arms around him.

"So good to see you, Marcella," he said. "Which one is yours? I'm afraid I'll get a ticket with my van idling at the curb."

"Your van? You still have that hippie van?"

Travis laughed. "I sold it. This is a new one."

"That one's mine," she said.

Travis picked the bag up from the carrousel and they headed for the curb.

"Oh," she said. "It's like a soccer mom's van. I expect to see kids pouring out of it at any moment."

Travis threw the bag into the back. "As a matter of fact, I do haul a bunch of kids around from time to time."

"Kids? Are you married?"

"Not yet. Are you?"

"No time for it. Where are we going?"

"My place." Travis opened the door for her and he went around the other side. A cop waved him on and they pulled out into the traffic.

She wondered what he expected when they got to 'his place.' She had told him on the phone that she was planning on staying at her sister's house in San Mateo, but that her sister was having marital problems and she was afraid of making things worse by staying there. Travis offered to put her up and said besides, San Mateo was too far from the city. He wanted to take her out to dinner at a new restaurant, and show her a few other things that had changed since she left.

As they pulled out onto the Bayshore Freeway, she tried to make conversation. "How are Ben and Thuy getting along?"

"They're doing fine. Shortly after the murder trial they got married in a Buddhist ceremony and three years later, Ben graduated from San Francisco State with a degree in Speech Therapy. He's teaching now in the Mission."

"That's wonderful. What about Thuy?"

"She had another child, a girl named Anh."

"Un?"

"Spelled A-n-h. But Thuy pronounces it like 'Un.' Everybody else calls her Ann, including Ben."

Marcella laughed. "So they've settled down now and Thuy's kids are Americans. Whatever happened to that other Black Puma? The writer who fled to Algeria?"

"Erskine? He's still abroad, apparently. Last I heard, they booted him out of Algeria and he went to France. The Feds are trying to extradite him."

"And Kelso?"

"He's still teaching at San Francisco State. But he found time to defend Kenny Morris and got him a fairly light sentence—three years, plus two on probation."

"Kenny Morris?"

"Also known as Mohammed al-Rashid. Thuy's kidnapper. I heard that he got his old job back at Hewlett-Packard."

Marcella sighed and closed her eyes as she leaned against her headrest. "I guess I've got a lot of catching up to do."

She must have dozed off, because when she opened her eyes Travis was parallel parking the van next to a large building. She peered out the window at it. "You live next door to a church?"

"I live *in* the church."

"*In* the church? Travis—you haven't become a priest, have you?"

Travis set the hand brake and smiled. "I'm afraid so. You don't mind shacking up with a priest, do you?"

Marcella was stunned. "What—why didn't you tell me? And why don't you wear a—you know—a reverse collar?"

"Today's my day off. Those starched collars can be uncomfortable." He opened the door and got out, but ducked his head back into the van. "I was just kidding about shacking up. You'll stay in a guest apartment. I've got my own across the hall."

She remained in her seat for a moment. "You finally did it, didn't you? I thought it was just a passing thought. What church is this?"

"Grace Cathedral. It's where I had an epiphany, you might say. And a little encouragement from Father Lattimore. Slide out this way—you'll get run over if you go out the passenger side."

Travis took the carryon bag and offered his free hand to help her out of the van. Then he went around to the back and retrieved her suitcase.

They entered by a side door and emerged into a long hallway that took them past several offices. Travis nodded to the staff people through the windows and was greeted by a couple of passing priests wearing the customary collars. They then passed through some double doors into an area that contained the apartments.

"This one's yours," Travis said. He put down the suitcase and opened the door. It wasn't locked.

She stepped inside. It wasn't large, but tastefully furnished. There was a sitting room with a chintz-covered sofa, a couple of Queen Anne-style armchairs, an attractive coffee table with a pierced railing around the top, and a little kitchenette. She assumed that the door to the right of the sitting room was a bedroom.

Travis put down the suitcase and the overnight bag and went to the curtains against the far wall of the sitting room. He pulled it back to reveal a large window. "You've even got a view of the courtyard. I'm just a rookie, so I only get a view of the street. I'll have to work my way up to one of these."

She approached him and gave him a kiss. "You're the most thoughtful man I've ever known."

"And you're the most beautiful and talented woman I've ever known. Tell me about New York. And about the Tony award. I'm afraid I haven't kept up much with the theater lately."

"I need to take a nap first. I'll tell you about it at dinner. By the way, where are we going?"

"A little place down on the Embarcadero. Vietnamese. Ben and Thuy turned me on to it."

"Oh. Umm..."

"You don't like Vietnamese food?"

"Sure. But..."

"Someplace else you'd like to go? Name it."

"I've always wanted to eat at Ernie's."

"Ernie's? That's the most expensive restaurant in San Francisco. I don't even know if we can get a reservation this late."

"I can afford it now. It'll be my treat."

"We'll go Dutch."

"Whatever. Give them a call."

While Marcella unpacked her suitcase in the bedroom, Travis called Ernie's. As luck would have it, there was a cancellation and he secured a reservation for seven-forty-five. He went into the bedroom to tell her but found her on the bed asleep. He went over to her, kissed her on the cheek and closed the door behind him.

CHAPTER 41

Ernie's Restaurant had been a fixture on the social as well as dining scene in San Francisco for over a half a century. Originally an Italian trattoria, the sons of the founder completely refurbished it in the 1950's and transformed it into an elegant, albeit somewhat gaudy, dining establishment. Long mahogany bar with stained glass set into the wood panelling behind it, Victorian crystal chandeliers, burgundy carpets, walls covered with red silk brocade.

"It looks like a 19th century bordello," Travis said as they stepped up to the maitre d's stand.

"Shh!" Marcella said. "They'll hear you."

"I doubt it—it's pretty noisy. When the hostess comes back—well, look who's here."

Marcella looked in the direction of Travis' gaze and saw Ted Kelso sitting at the bar with a strikingly attractive blond. "Professor Kelso. And who is that with him?"

"That's Vera Mandlikova, Ted's girlfriend. Or maybe his wife by now, though I don't think either one of them would stoop to something so bourgeois as marriage."

"He sees us."

After the hostess came back and told them that they would have to wait a few more minutes for their table to be cleared, they went over to the bar.

Travis shook Kelso's hand. "Hi, Ted—you remember Marcella Morgan?"

"Of course I do," Kelso said. "One of my better students. Congratulations, by the way, Marcella, on your Tony award."

"Thanks, Professor—"

"Please—call me Ted. This is my significant other, Vera Mandlikova."

Vera extended her hand. "So pleased to meet you. You are an actress?"

Marcella still blushed when she was treated as a celebrity. "I'm working on it."

All laughed and Ted signaled the bartender for a round of drinks. "Why don't you join us? Maybe they could push two tables together. Or better yet, a banquette."

"Good idea," Travis said.

Kelso went over to the maitre d' and spoke to him. After a moment or two he came back to the bar. "It's all set."

The maitre d' waited patiently while they picked up their drinks and led them to another room containing the banquettes.

Once settled, Ted looked over the top of his menu at Travis. "I didn't know you could dine at Ernie's on a priest's salary. This a special occasion?"

Travis smiled. "Indeed it is—Marcella's return to San Francisco. And I didn't know you could dine here on a professor's salary. Is this a special occasion?"

"Indeed it is," Kelso said. "This is our first anniversary."

Marcella nudged Travis with her foot.

"Congratulations," Travis said. "You never told me you were getting married." He raised his glass and all followed suit, clinking their glasses together.

"It became a legal necessity," Kelso said. "Vera was about to be recalled to Moscow and now that Gorbachev is determined to dismantle the Soviet Union, we thought it might be prudent to give her legal status in the United States."

"Very romantic, no?" Vera said.

All laughed and a waiter arrived to take their orders. This being done, the conversation resumed.

"Speaking of Moscow," Travis said, "have you heard any more about Lonnie Erskine?"

"Yes," Kelso said. "He's back."

"In the U.S.?"

"In Oakland as a matter of fact."

"Oakland?"

"He's surrendered to the police there."

Travis was stunned. He looked at Marcella, who also expressed surprise. "He's in jail?"

"Out on bail. I've decided to defend him."

Travis could hardly take this in. "Why? What's to defend? And why did he come back? Was he extradited from France?"

"No, he came of his own free will. He says he's now a born-again

Christian."

Travis glanced at Marcella, who also looked dubious. "Well, I suppose even the worst of us can be redeemed. Though I never would have guessed it in Erskine's case."

Kelso settled back in his seat. "You're jumping to conclusions, Padre. He says he's innocent."

"Innocent? How could he be innocent? Ben saw him pull out a shotgun and murder Watt in cold blood."

Kelso toyed with the swizzle stick in his drink, pushing the ice cubes around. "He has a different version of the events of that day. He says that he meant only to 'persuade,' was his word, Watt to get in the car and come with him to the Puma headquarters in Oakland to stand trial for the murder of Bobby X."

"That's ridiculous."

"On the surface of it, I would agree. But Erskine says that though he took along the shotgun to 'persuade' Watt to come with him, he never intended to kill him. Instead, he says, Watt saw him in the car and immediately pulled out his service revolver and aimed it at him. Erskine beat him to the punch and fired the shotgun, killing him instantly."

"And you believe him?"

Kelso shrugged. "I don't know. But it's plausible."

Travis stared into his glass for a moment. "Watt was carrying a bag of takeout Chinese food at the time. How could he have had time to pull out his revolver?"

"Easy. One hand to carry the bag, the other free to extract the revolver from its holster."

"Wasn't it strapped down?"

"It's not clear. According to Erskine, Watt often kept it loose. Says a lot of Oakland cops had the same habit. And he spent most of his career with Oakland."

"Ben know about this?"

"I called him right after Erskine called me. He says he's prepared to testify against him."

Travis leaned back in the booth and sighed. "Poor Ben. He's back in the frying pan. And maybe the fire."

"It will make it more difficult for the defense. But Erskine came back willingly. The judge—and jury—will take that into account."

"Anything I can do?"

"I'd like you to talk to Erskine. You're a man of God now. Erskine might be more forthcoming with you than with me. I don't want any surprises when we go before the judge."

"Sure. I'll talk to him. And Ben, too. I might even enlist the services of Father Lattimore."

"Father Lattimore?" Kelso said.

"He's my superior and mentor. And like Erskine and Ben, he's black."

Kelso smiled and lifted his glass to his lips. "Good point."

The two couples spent the rest of the evening discussing everything from movies and Marcella's acting career to the likelihood that Gorbachev could reform the Soviet Union, a prospect that both Kelso and Vera supported but were not optimistic about. Vera even suggested that she might apply for U.S. citizenship.

When they returned to Grace Cathedral, Marcella asked to see the interior of the cathedral itself.

"This is so beautiful!" She looked around at the images in the windows. "Why do they have a portrait of Einstein? He was Jewish, wasn't he?"

Travis chuckled. "This is a very progressive church. Not only are Jews welcome, but even atheists."

She looked at him curiously. "You told me once that you weren't sure you believed in God. You do now?"

"I'm still not sure."

"And you're a priest? How can you be a priest and not be sure you believe in God?"

"Like I said, this is a progressive church. They're very tolerant. And I don't think it's necessary to believe in an anthropomorphic god to also believe that there is a higher power, a supreme being, even if it's no more than an abstract collection of molecules."

Marcella laughed. "You sound like Luke Skywalker in *Star Wars*. 'May the Force be with you.'"

"That makes more sense than the notion that Jesus was born of a virgin and spent a great deal of his time performing miracles."

"Does Father Lattimore know you feel this way?"

"Actually, I haven't put it to him in just that way. But he knows I have a philosophical cast of mind. And he encourages that."

She looked up at the stained glass windows again. "Well, that explains what Einstein is doing here."

They walked down the center aisle towards the altar.

"What's this pattern on the floor?" she said. "I think it's lovely, but does it have some special meaning?"

"It's a labyrinth. It's supposed to be a metaphor for life's many twists and turns, but always with the hope and possibility of a way out to a better world, perhaps even a divine existence."

"Perhaps?"

"Perhaps."

They approached the altar. Marcella stared at the cross for a moment. "This is all so familiar and yet so strange. I was raised a Catholic."

"The Episcopal and Catholic churches have a lot in common," Travis said. "The rituals and imagery are much the same, but the doctrines are different. Are you still a Catholic?"

"I haven't been to mass in years. Since I was fifteen, maybe."

"You still haven't answered my question. Are you still a Catholic?"

Marcella continued to stare at the cross for a moment. "I don't think so. When you told me a few years ago that you weren't sure you believed in God, that was the first time I really began to think about it."

"And what was your conclusion?"

She smiled. "Same as yours, I guess. I can't really be sure. But somehow I feel a spiritual connection to...to something. Especially when I'm acting."

Travis' eyes were drawn to the vast spaces over the chancel and the stained glass images above and behind it. "I never felt it while acting, but I do when I'm in here. I suppose there are different ways to make that connection."

They stood for several moments, lost in thought. Then, almost unconsciously, Travis reached for Marcella's hand, and without looking, she reached for his.

CHAPTER 42

Travis dropped Marcella off at San Francisco State and then he and Father Lattimore headed for Pacific Heights.

When they arrived, Vera opened the door and ushered them into the living room where Kelso and Lonnie Erskine sat on the sofa poring over some documents. They both stood as Travis and Father Lattimore entered the room.

Travis had never met Erskine before and though he had seen him at San Francisco State years ago when he attacked the Neo-Nazis, he was surprised at how composed and well-mannered he seemed to be. Tall, athletic-looking, conservatively dressed in a dark suit, but no tie, he smiled and reached out to shake first Travis,' then Father Lattimore's hand as Kelso introduced them.

"Travis was a student of mine back in the day before he became a priest," Kelso said. "And this is Father Lattimore, I presume."

"A pleasure," Lattimore said.

"Father," Erskine said.

After an awkward silence, Vera asked if anyone wanted coffee and all accepted.

"Sit down, gentlemen," Kelso said. "Make yourselves at home." He sat down in the sofa as did Erskine, while Travis and Father Lattimore sat in the armchairs opposite. "You may be wondering why I've invited you all here today."

Father Lattimore looked at Erskine and Erskine locked eyes with him.

"Mr. Erskine," Kelso said, "has recently returned from France and turned himself into the SFPD to face charges that he conspired to murder a police officer several years ago. Though he denies the charges, he has gone through a transformative experience during his sojourn abroad. That transformative experience has involved a spiritual crisis, which he says has completely changed him. He is now a born-again Christian. He has therefore requested an interview, particularly with you, Father Lattimore, to discuss this transformation and what it may mean in the upcoming trial." He turned to Erskine. "Is that a fair assessment of your position, Lonnie?"

Erskine nodded. "Yes. You see, Father Lattimore, I was never baptized in any church. My early years consisted of growing up in L.A. without a father and no role models like yourself. I fell into the wrong crowd, sold and used drugs, raped women, was convicted of armed robbery when I was nineteen and sent to Soledad, later San Quentin. When I came out of San Quentin, I was very, very angry and the newly-formed Black Puma Party greatly appealed to me. I joined and quickly assumed a leadership position."

Lattimore listened intently. "Did you murder Sergeant Dan Watt?"

Erskine seemed surprised at the directness of this question. "No, Father, I did not. I only planned to talk to him. And, I confess, kidnap him and take him to the Puma headquarters in Oakland for what I then considered the only justice possible given the political power structure at the time."

Vera arrived with the coffee and set the tray down on the table. Erskine's eyes followed her as she returned to the kitchen.

"I am delighted," Father Lattimore said, "that you seem to have found solace and perhaps even redemption in Jesus Christ. But I am still troubled by the circumstances, as far as I know them, of that tragic incident on the streets of San Francisco five years ago. It seems that Sergeant Watt was killed by a shotgun blast at close range while walking out of a restaurant carrying a takeout dinner. I'm not a lawyer like Mr. Kelso here, but it's hard to imagine that you fired in self-defense."

"I was afraid," Erskine said, "that without the shotgun, Watt would not agree to get in the car. But I didn't touch it until after I called out to him and he immediately pulled out his service revolver. At that point I had no choice. It was kill or be killed."

Father Lattimore seemed to digest this. "That is the truth of the matter? The full truth?"

Erskine put his hand over his heart. "As my heart belongs to my Savior, Jesus Christ, Father, that is the whole truth."

Lattimore expressed skepticism. "I want to believe you, Mr. Erskine. But I warn you, if you are in the smallest particle of your soul insincere, your punishment, if not on earth then in the after life, will be most severe."

"I understand that, Father."

"I hope so." Lattimore looked to Kelso, then back to Erskine. "Just what is it that you expect of me, Mr. Erskine?"

"Well, Father..." Now Erskine looked at Kelso, as if for assistance. "I thought, and Mr. Kelso thought, that if you would be willing to testify on my behalf at the trial as my, uh, spiritual adviser, it might help my case."

Father Lattimore sighed. "I don't know you well enough, Mr. Erskine. Not at this point. When is the trial?"

"In about three weeks," Kelso said. "That should be sufficient time for you to get to know Mr. Erskine better."

Lattimore suddenly stood up. "I don't like being used, gentlemen. And though I am a man of God and pledged to succor the sick and the afflicted, and yes, even murderers, I cannot lend myself to a scheme to miscarry justice."

"Miscarry justice?" Erskine stood, flushed with anger. "What kind of justice is it that allows the black man to be herded into ghettos and beaten by the police with impunity? What kind of justice allows black people to be made into slaves to white people and rewards only those who bow and scrape to them with a few crumbs from their table and some petty position as a head waiter or a porter on the white man's train? Where were you, Father, when the police were cracking black heads and shooting black brothers in the sixties?"

Kelso stood. "Easy, Erskine, this is not—"

"I was in Selma and Montgomery in the sixties, Mr. Erskine," Lattimore said. "And yes, I had my own head cracked open a couple of times. I went to jail. But we won those battles, Mr. Erskine. We won in the courts, we won in Congress, and we're still winning every day. And all without violence or anger in our hearts, but with love and patience."

"Patience," Erskine said contemptuously.

"Yes, patience. Or forbearance, if you will. I'm afraid that any long-lasting change for the better requires it. And in spite of your professed conversion to Christianity, I can see that that is one quality that is still missing in your character. However, if you are really sincere in this conversion, I trust that you will do your best to cultivate that all-important quality, a quality most exemplified by our Savior Jesus Christ."

Travis and Kelso exchanged glances.

Lattimore turned to go. "Thank you for the opportunity to meet with you and Mr. Erskine, Mr. Kelso. And thank you for the coffee. But I have a busy schedule today and must go." He looked at Travis, who started to follow him. "Don't bother, Travis. I know you have duties to tend to in the Mission. I'll catch a cab."

"Father..." Erskine said in a barely audible tone, "I'm sorry I lost my temper."

Lattimore paused for a moment. "I apologize, too, Mr. Erskine, if I lost mine or appeared rude. After you've had time to think this little meeting over, I would look forward to having further discussions with you. My door at Grace Cathedral is always open."

With that invitation, Lattimore continued to the door, where Vera was poised to open it for him. He complimented her on the quality of the coffee and left.

Kelso stood at the window and watched as Lattimore descended to the street.

"I'm sorry, Ted," Erskine said. "I messed everything up."

"Well...it's not critical, though his testimony as a character witness would be helpful." Kelso turned around and faced Erskine, who was standing near the coffee table. "What *is* critical is that the jury believes you when you tell them that you saw Watt pull out his service revolver. If that was the case, then it should have been lying on the sidewalk when the cops arrived, which was minutes after the incident. In Emmett Smalls' trial, there was no testimony at all as to the location or position of the weapon."

Erskine shrugged. "I don't know what happened to it. I just know that I saw him go for it."

"Go for it? Then you didn't see whether he got it out of the holster or not?"

Erskine seemed to reach back into his memory. "I saw the light reflect off of the chrome plating of the gun. Watt liked flashy weapons. Whether he got it out of the holster or not, I don't know. I didn't wait for him to point it at me."

Kelso paced in front of the window for a moment. "You saw the light reflecting off of the chrome plating. Then he must have gotten the gun at least part way out of the holster. But that would mean that either it wasn't strapped down, or he somehow loosened the strap with his one free hand and almost simultaneously withdrew the weapon from the holster—and the jury's not likely to buy that."

Erskine shrugged again. "I don't know. All I know is what I saw."

"Hmm," Kelso said. "We need a witness who either saw Watts' pistol lying on the sidewalk—and maybe put it back in its holster—or who saw the whole incident and can testify that Watt went for the weapon as you claim. It's been five years—memories blur, witnesses die or disappear. But if you're telling me the truth, Lonnie, we'll find a way."

"As God is my witness," Erskine said.

Kelso looked at him as if to peer into his soul, then at Travis. "Thanks, Travis. You've been a great help. I think with another meeting or two, Father Lattimore might come over to our side. In the meantime, I've got to track down some of those witnesses."

Travis glanced at Erskine, who stared back at him with limpid brown eyes, then at Vera, who had returned to the parlor. He was tempted to ask her what she thought of Erskine's story, but it was hardly the time to do so. "Thanks, Vera. I'll let myself out."

He descended the steps to the street and was surprised to find Father Lattimore still standing at the curb.

"I can't seem to get a cab," Lattimore said. He looked sheepishly at Travis. "Maybe Mr. Erskine was right—we haven't made that much progress when a black man—even in a clerical collar—can't get a cab in San Francisco in broad daylight."

Travis smiled at Lattimore's good nature, even sense of humor, at such an outrageous state of affairs. "Let me try." He stepped out into the street just as a cab crested the hill and turned onto Jackson. He whistled and waved at the driver, who pulled over to the curb. He opened the rear door and Lattimore got in, shaking his head.

The cab driver looked first at Lattimore, then at Travis. "What's this?"

"You know how to get to Grace Cathedral?"

"Sure."

"That's where Father Lattimore would like to go."

The cab driver looked at Travis for a moment, then at a smiling

Father Lattimore sitting in the back of the cab. "Sure thing."

The cab drove off and Travis, after watching it for a moment or two, climbed into his van and headed west to Park Presidio and then south through Golden Gate Park. From there it was a straight shot to San Francisco State, where he hoped to catch at least some of Marcella's address to the theater students.

CHAPTER 43

After lunch at a Stonestown deli, Marcella accompanied Travis to the Mission. He explained that he had volunteered his services as a soccer coach at Potrero Elementary at the behest of Ben, who was now on the faculty there.

"I didn't know you were a soccer player," she said as they drove past Mission Dolores.

"I had a scholarship at Stanford my freshman year," Travis said. "Unfortunately, I lost it when my grades plummeted."

"Stanford? You never told me you went to Stanford."

"Long story. Or rather, short one. I was only there for two years before I went into the army."

Marcella smiled. "Soccer player, army officer, priest. Not your usual progression."

"Don't forget actor and bartender."

She laughed. "You *could* have been a fine actor, you know. You just didn't have the desire. And I'm glad."

"Glad? Why?"

"Because you'll do a lot more good in this world as a priest. Actors are merely entertainers."

Travis glanced at her as he pulled into the parking lot at Potrero Elementary. "I seem to remember you telling me just last night that you felt a spiritual connection to the audience when you were acting."

"I do. But it's just a feeling. Oh, look! There's Ben."

Travis parked the van and Ben came over to the passenger door.

Marcella got out of the van and embraced him. "Ben! It's so good to see you."

Ben gave her a bear hug and lifted her off her feet. "Marcella! I saw you on TV at the Tony Awards. Congratulations!"

"Thanks, Ben." She stood for a moment looking at him. "You look just the same."

Ben grabbed his belly. "Gained a little weight. Thuy's cooking is too good to resist."

"And you're a father now."

"Ben and Ahn. Ben's trying out for the soccer team."

"And how's Thuy?"

"Fine. She went back to school after Anh was born. Majoring in Oriental languages. Studying Chinese now."

"Where can I suit up, Ben?" Travis said.

"I'll show you where the locker room is." Ben looked at his watch. "The kids will be out in fifteen minutes. Marcella, you can wait in the bleachers if you like." He looked towards the field. "Emma's already there. She'll keep you company."

"Emma?"

"A new teacher. Just introduce yourself. Come on, Travis."

Travis followed Ben to the locker room, while Marcella made her way through a maze of parked cars to the soccer field. As she passed through an open gate, she gazed up into the bleachers and saw the woman Ben was talking about. A pretty blond, probably not yet twenty-five, wearing a stylish car coat. It was a bit chilly, with some wind coming off the bay.

She climbed the stairs to about the fifth row and introduced herself. "Hi, I'm Marcella Morgan."

The young woman looked at her for a moment, stunned. "Marcella Morgan? The actress? Oh, it *is* you!" She stood up and offered her hand.

"Don't get up. Ben told me that you're a new teacher here." Marcella shook her hand and they both sat down. "Emma, isn't it?"

"That's right," Emma said. "How do you know Ben?"

"We went to San Francisco State together years ago. And we were housemates in the Haight."

"The Haight? Then you were hippies?"

Marcella laughed. "If we were, we didn't know it. How did you come to teach here?"

"I majored in Education at Stanford. When I couldn't find a job after graduation, I went for a master's degree and by that time the market was a little better."

"So this is your first job?"

"It is. And I was lucky to get it. I want to help underprivileged kids and here I am in San Francisco!"

"Where are you from?"

"Well—oh, here comes Ben with the new soccer coach. I understand he's a priest."

"He is."

"You know him?" Emma stood to get a better look as Ben and Travis approached. "Omigod! It's Travis!"

Marcella, surprised that Emma knew Travis' name, stood as well.

"Emma!" Travis ran up the steps in his cleats and shorts and jersey and embraced her. "Ben told me your name was Emma, but I didn't dream that—"

"Oh, Travis!" Emma held him tight. "I thought I'd never see you again. And here you are!"

Marcella found this reunion somewhat disturbing. Travis had never mentioned a girl named Emma when they were dating. But she must have been a child then.

Travis turned to Marcella. "You two have gotten acquainted, I presume."

"Yes," Marcella said. "I didn't know—"

"Emma is the daughter of an old friend in Palo Alto," Travis said. "Bernard Blériot. She used to help out in his florist shop."

"I'm afraid I wasn't much help," Emma said. "I mostly just got in the way."

"Don't be so modest, Emma," Travis said. "Your dad said that— oh, here come the kids. You'll have to introduce me, Ben."

Ben went to the field and gathered the kids together. Most were Hispanic, but there were a number of African-Americans as well as Asians. They regarded Ben as a lovable giant, but obeyed him without question. Travis, with his slightly outdated soccer gear and pale skin, seemed a curiosity.

But once Travis explained the principles of the game and demonstrated his skill with the ball, they clamored over each other demanding a position on the first team.

"Whoa," Travis said. "First, we'll do some drills. Three lines—no, four."

After some twenty minutes of drills, Travis divided them into two teams and engaged them in a scrimmage.

Marcella, Emma, and Ben sat in the bleachers and watched.

"Heck," Ben said. "I didn't know Travis was such a jock."

"I used to watch him play when he was at Stanford," Emma said.

"He was the star of the team."

Marcella watched Emma out of the corner of her eye as the scrimmage progressed. It was obvious that she was infatuated with Travis. And he didn't even seem to notice.

At one point, Travis, dribbling the ball down the field, passed it to one of the Hispanic kids, who caught it with his hands.

"No, Miguel!" Travis shouted. "Empleada sus pies, no los manos!"

Ben chuckled. "I didn't know Travis spoke Spanish. He's going to be a hit with these kids."

Marcella saw that Emma was beaming with pride at this comment, as if Travis were her lover. Obviously, she hoped to be.

After the practice Travis and Marcella drove back to Grace Cathedral where Travis had a series of appointments with parishioners. Marcella went to her apartment and tried to take a nap, but couldn't sleep. She got up, went to her carryon bag, and extracted a script for a new play that Sam Thomas asked her to read. This was a play that Sam had written himself, and though he was an excellent director, she found his play to be rather tedious. Still, she promised him she would read it.

She had fallen asleep in one of the armchairs when she was awakened by a knock at the door. It was Travis.

He came in smiling from ear to ear.

"You must have had a successful meeting with your parishioners," she said.

"Yes, it went well."

He seemed strangely taciturn.

"Is anything the matter?"

"No," he said. "On the contrary, everything's fine."

"Well," she said, noting the contrast between his relaxed manner at the soccer practice and his rather formal demeanor now that he was dressed for his clerical duties. "Why don't you sit down?"

"Thanks. I will." He sat down in one of the chairs and she went back to hers. He picked up the script lying on the coffee table and turned a few pages. "New play?"

Yes. It's one Sam wrote. He wants me to play the lead female role, but I'm afraid it's not for me."

"Oh. Well—I guess you'll be going back to New York in any case."

"I have a flight out tomorrow. What is it, Travis? I have a feeling you're trying to tell me something."

Travis grinned. "You're right. And I guess I'm not doing a very good job of it. I don't want you to go back to New York. At least not for a while."

"You don't? Then what do you want me to do?"

Travis extracted something from his coat pocket and handed it to her.

"What's this?" She looked into the palm of her hand at a small velvet bag with a gold-colored drawstring securing it.

"Open it," Travis said.

She loosened the drawstring and turned the bag upside down. Out fell a diamond ring. "Oh, Travis! It's beautiful! Whose is it? How did you get it?"

Travis laughed and suddenly seemed like his old affable self again. "It's yours. And I got it from my mother, who got it from her mother. It was their wedding ring."

"Travis!" She clutched the ring in her hand and brought it to her chest. "Oh, Travis—you can't be asking to marry me!"

"That's the usual implication when a man presents a diamond ring to the woman he loves."

She started to speak, choked on the words, then rose from her chair, as he did. She embraced him and started crying. "Travis, Travis—I'm so flattered, I don't know what to say."

Travis chuckled. "Just say yes."

She loosened her embrace and wiped the tears from her eyes, then looked into his. "I can't."

Travis' face fell. "You can't? Why not?"

"There're...there're just too many reasons. My career, my—"

Travis put his hands on her shoulders. "I've thought of that. I wouldn't interfere with your career for anything in the world. I want you to succeed. And I don't mind you being in New York or L.A. for long periods. I've got my work here, which overwhelms me at times. The commute is nothing these days. And I'm sure you'll want to take a break from acting when you have children."

Tears started streaming down her cheeks again and she wiped them away. "That's the other thing. I can't have children."

Travis was stunned. "Can't have children? Why not?"

"I once told you about my father. How he used to beat me."

"Yes, of course. I don't care about that. At least it doesn't—"

"Once, when I was in high school, I got pregnant. By a Mexican boy."

Travis remained silent.

"My father detests Mexicans, among other ethnic groups. But especially Mexicans. He punched me in the stomach—and the abdomen—until I miscarried."

Travis sighed and embraced her again. "I'm so sorry, Marcella. I should have inquired more about your relationship with your father. I always thought it was best not to talk about it. But a miscarriage doesn't mean—"

"In my case, it does. The doctor at the hospital said that there was permanent damage and that I could never have children."

"Did you get a second opinion?"

"No."

"Then he could've been wrong. You could go to another doctor."

"I'm afraid it's hopeless, Travis."

"Well...we could adopt a child. Two, three, four children. There're thousands of orphans out there and they all need a home."

"You're such a good man, Travis. But it would never work."

"I don't see why it wouldn't." He put his forefinger beneath her chin and tilted her head up. "You're in love with another man. In New York."

"No, no. I live alone—like you do. I hardly have time for romance, and besides, half the leading men I work with are gay."

"Well—then I only have to worry about the other half."

Marcella laughed. "You're incorrigible. But Travis, I'm serious. Marriage simply isn't for me. I'll always love you, but—"

"But what?"

"If you're determined to marry, I think you should marry someone else."

"Like who?"

"Like—Emma."

"Emma?" Travis laughed and sat down in the armchair. "Emma's a child."

"She's grown up now. Don't tell me you didn't notice that she has a great figure when she hugged you."

Travis rubbed his chin. "I did notice. She's got boobs now."

Marcella sat in his lap and put her arms around his neck. "See? And she's not that much younger than you—seven or eight years. And it will seem even less when you're older." She kissed him.

Travis looked at her curiously. "You've got an odd way of making love. Encouraging me to marry someone else and seducing me at the same time."

"I'm not trying to seduce you. I just love you and want what's best for you."

He sighed. "And what's best for me is to marry Emma. What if she doesn't see it that way?"

"She does. Trust me."

"She does? She told you she's in love with me?"

"Yes. With her eyes."

Travis leaned back in the chair and stared at the ceiling. "I still can't help seeing Emma as a little girl. And she probably sees me as her big brother."

"Not anymore. She's madly in love with you."

He sat up. "Keep the ring."

"I can't do that—it's your mother's. And someday—"

"Maybe it will be Emma's. But in the meantime, I want you to have it. Even if you keep it in a drawer. At least then I'll have some connection with you."

Tears came to her eyes again. "Oh, Travis—I love you so much."

"Then—"

"Shh!" She put her forefinger to his lips. "No more talk of marriage." And she kissed him passionately, as if for the last time.

CHAPTER 44

The next morning, Travis took Marcella to the airport. She declined to keep the ring but promised to keep in touch. Travis was skeptical, but decided that there was still a chance that she would change her mind. She kissed him at the gate with all of the fervor of the night before, which drew stares from the other passengers.

His next stop was the Tenderloin, not far from his old apartment. Specifically, he was to meet with the director of the YMCA on Turk Street to set up a program for dealing with the homeless population of the neighborhood, San Francisco's poorest and most crime-ridden.

He parked on Leavenworth and walked to the Y, noticing the same half a dozen men sitting on the sidewalk, their clothes tattered and dirty, their shoes without laces and their faces unshaven. Wary of panhandling in the presence of a priest, they simply stared at him as he smiled and stopped to speak to a couple of the men that he knew.

Just as he approached the Y, however, he noticed a man lying on what appeared to be a fairly expensive sleeping bag, and unlike the soiled and frayed bedding of the others, was relatively clean and intact. The man, perhaps in his early thirties, seemed to be asleep, with a nearly empty bottle of cheap wine close to his head. He was using a backpack for a pillow.

As Travis paused for a moment to reflect on this scene, the man opened his eyes and looked up.

"Alessandro?"

The man blinked and seemed to focus his eyes on Travis. Then he closed them again and laid his head down on the backpack.

Travis went to his side and knelt down. "Alessandro—can it be you?"

Alessandro opened his eyes and raised his head. "Travis?" He rubbed his eyes, as if to make sure he wasn't hallucinating, and tried again to focus on the figure before him. "Why are you dressed like a priest? You in a play?"

"I *am* a priest. Alessandro, what's happened to you?"

Alessandro rubbed the stubble on his chin and sat up with his back against the wall of the building. He picked up the bottle, ascertained that there was still some wine in it, and took a swallow. "It's a long story. Why did you become a priest?"

"Also a long story. Alessandro—we need to get you off the street."

Alessandro took another swallow of the wine and saw that there was no more. "Damn! You can't lend me a couple of bucks, can you?"

"Alessandro—this is not solving any problems. Let me help you to get back on your feet."

"That's nice of you Padre. But I don't really give a damn anymore."

"Why? What's happened?"

"Terry."

"What about Terry?"

"He died."

Travis sighed. "I'm sorry, Alessandro. I truly am. How did he die?"

"AIDS. And if he had it, I've got it. You sure you can't lend me a couple of bucks?"

"Have you been tested?"

"What's the point?" Alessandro's eyes suddenly welled up with tears. "It was horrible, Travis. You should have seen him—emaciated, his organs shutting down one by one. And...it was my fault!" He dropped the empty bottle on the sidewalk, which immediately shattered, and burst into tears.

Travis put his arm around his shoulder, which he noticed had lost much of its former muscle. "It couldn't have been your fault, Alessandro. It's an epidemic now. You may not have it, but even if you do, they have drugs now that can suppress the symptoms."

"No, they don't. None of them work. They tried them on Terry, but they only made him sicker. Oh, God, if only I had been faithful to him!" Alessandro began sobbing again and Travis, not sure of what to do, looked around. The other men on the sidewalk were watching them, as if it were an entertainment.

"Come on," Travis said, attempting to lift Alessandro up by the armpits. "We'll go inside the Y and get you cleaned up. I think I can arrange for you to get a room."

Alessandro fell back against the wall. In spite of his loss of weight, he was still a heavy man. "Forget it—they'll only lecture me and try to get me to join AA. And no offense, Travis, but I'm fed up with Catholicism—I left the church a long time ago."

"I'm not a Catholic, Alessandro—I'm an Episcopalian."

"What's the difference?"

"Well—it doesn't matter. Come on, you can at least get a hot shower and some food in you."

Alessandro sat like a sack of potatoes for a moment, then started moving his legs and rubbing his thighs with his palms. "Do you suppose they'd let me work out for a while? I haven't done that in years."

"Sure. Sure they will. It will help you get your health back." Travis again placed his hands beneath Alessandro's armpits and lifted. This time, with Alessandro pushing up from his thighs, he succeeded in getting him to his feet.

Alessandro waggled his forefinger at him. "Remember—no preaching. And I'd still like a couple of bucks so I can get a cold beer after my workout."

"Don't worry—no preaching. And we'll see about that beer later."

Travis helped Alessandro into the main lobby of the Y and told the receptionist he had an appointment with Eddie Chang, the director. Eddie came out, shook Travis' hand and looked at Alessandro. "Who's your friend?"

"This is Alessandro Sanchez," Travis said. "We were in a play together once. A fine actor, but he's had a run of bad luck."

Eddie extended his hand to Alessandro, who reciprocated. "Nice to meet you, Alessandro. Let's go into the conference room."

Once inside the conference room, they sat down at a table.

"You been in any movies?" Eddie said.

"Sure," Alessandro said. "Lots. You see *Gringo Heaven?*"

"I missed that one. Anything else?"

"I had a supporting role in *Cruising.*"

"Missed that one, too. I've seen you out on the sidewalk. What do you say we give you a hot shower and something to eat. Then we can have a talk about your future."

"I don't have a future."

"Everybody's got a future, Alessandro. You just need to let us help you get on the right road so you can find it."

"I've got AIDS."

Eddie looked at Travis.

"He needs to be tested," Travis said.

"We can arrange that," Eddie said. "I'll show you to your room, Alessandro. We have strict rules here for our residents. No smoking, no alcohol, and we lock the doors at ten o'clock. Think you can live with that?"

Alessandro stared at Eddie for a moment. "Can I use the gym?"

"Sure. The gym's open to everyone. We encourage it."

"What if I go out for a beer afterwards?"

Eddie glanced at Travis again. "I wouldn't recommend it, but I can't stop you as long as you're back here before ten o'clock and you don't bring it in with you. And if you're drunk, we have to turn you away and you'll be back on the street again."

"I'll just have one."

Eddie sighed. "That usually doesn't work, Alessandro. But it's up to you if you want to risk it."

"I'll make sure he's back before ten and sober," Travis said.

"Okay," Eddie said. He stood and went to the door. "Come on, Alessandro. Accommodations are Spartan here, but the sheets are clean and the beds are soft. I'll have one of the maids bring you a toothbrush and a safety razor."

Alessandro stood. "What about my sleeping bag?"

"You won't need it. But bring it if you want."

Eddie then escorted Alessandro and Travis to the fourth floor, where Alessandro tested the mattress and promptly fell asleep. Eddie then closed the door gently and followed Travis out into the hall. "I don't like this idea of him going out for a beer, Travis. You're asking for disaster."

"I won't let him out of my sight," Travis said. "Besides, where we're going, they only serve one beer to a customer."

"Oh, yeah? Where's that?"

"Grace Cathedral."

Eddie laughed and slapped Travis on the back. "You Episcopalians. At my church they only have sacramental wine."

"We have that, too. But I think a twelve ounce can of Coors will be harmless. And even that won't be necessary if he sleeps past ten."

"That's a possibility," Eddie said. "He looks like he hasn't slept in a week. Now let's get to work on that homeless project you're proposing. But I warn you—every single one so far has failed."

"I've got a new idea. We'll need funding, though."

"Ah," Eddie said, as they got on the elevator. "That's the key. Know any rich benefactors?"

"Maybe," Travis said, as he watched the elevator doors close.

CHAPTER 45

Kelso gazed out of the plate glass window of his 42nd floor office in the Transamerica building. There was a magnificent view of the Bay Area, with the Golden Gate to the northwest, Alcatraz and Tiburon to the north, and Berkeley and the Bay Bridge to the east. It was a far cry from his cramped, windowless office at San Francisco State.

He had tendered his resignation to the International Relations Department the day after he accepted Lonnie Erskine as his client. It also happened to be the day that he was offered, and accepted, a partnership in the law firm of Dunn, McCracken and Glickstein. The notoriety of Erskine and the fact that he, Kelso, had succeeded in getting the charges against Ben Franklin dropped in exchange for his testimony against Emmett Smalls five years earlier made him a very desirable addition to the firm. Once again, he was a full-time lawyer, this time defending the very man who Ben Franklin testified had murdered Sergeant Dan Watt in cold blood.

It was a difficult situation. But one that Kelso relished. Should he call Ben to testify for the *defense* of Erskine? Ben had never claimed to know whether Erskine intended to kill Watt. Only that he had seen the shotgun in his hands seconds before Erskine fired. He was in the driver's seat away from the curb, so he couldn't see Watt clearly—in fact, Ben was so tall that the top of the passenger window cut off his view of anything but Watts' legs as he was exiting the restaurant. He had no idea whether Watt pulled his service revolver out of its holster before—or after—Erskine produced the shotgun.

A buzzer went off on the intercom. He went over to his desk and pushed a button. "Yes?"

"A Mr. Pollard is here to see you."

"Pollard? I don't know a Mr. Pollard."

"He says he was with the SFPD at the time of the Watt incident."

"The Watt *incident?*"

"That's what he calls it."

Kelso tried to remember if that name had come up at the Emmett Smalls trial. "Send him in."

A few seconds later, Angela, his secretary, opened the door and a man in his early thirties, with a boyish face and a stocky build, stepped into the office. Angela closed the door behind her.

"Come in, Mr. Pollard," Kelso said. He met Pollard halfway and shook his hand. "What can I do for you?"

"Well, I was thinking I could do something for you. For both of us, actually."

Kelso, rather than going behind his massive partner's desk, indicated one of two armchairs in front of the desk. "Have a seat, Mr. Pollard." Pollard complied, and Kelso sat in the other chair. "Now, what is this mutually beneficial proposal that you have in mind?"

Pollard's eyes darted around the room as if he were looking for something. "Is this completely confidential?"

Kelso smiled. Just like a cop. "There are no listening devices in this room, Mr. Pollard. This isn't a foreign embassy."

Pollard didn't see the humor in this. "I was a rookie on the force back in the late seventies when the Watt incident took place."

"Why do you call it the Watt 'incident'?"

"Because...because I don't know what else to call it. All the papers screamed that it was murder, but I know better."

"You do? What do you think it was?"

"Self-defense."

Kelso thought this was too good to be true. "How do you know it was self-defense?"

"Because me and my partner at the time were the first to answer the call. We were parked at Washington Square right around the corner, watching a crowd form around a street entertainer, a mime, I think. We arrived on the scene in front of the Chinese restaurant in three, four minutes."

"And what did you see when you arrived?"

"First, Watt lying in a pool of blood on the sidewalk. Second, chow mein, or whatever, all over the place. Third, shattered glass where the restaurant's window had been."

"Anything else?"

"Yeah." Pollard seemed hesitant. "You know, I'm not asking for any money for this."

"I would hope not," Kelso said. "It would undermine your credibility.”

"Right. Just so you understand.”

"Go on.”

"Okay. I bent down over Watt to see if he was still alive. He wasn't. Then I noticed that his service revolver—a chrome-plated .357 magnum—was sticking halfway out of his holster.”

"What about the strap?”

"The strap was loose.”

"How do you think it got loose?”

"Only one way it could have got loose. Watt had to do it himself.”

"The blast from the shotgun couldn't have knocked it loose?”

"Maybe. But not likely. The strap, the holster, the revolver—it was all intact. No pellets or nothin' hit it.”

"So then what did you do?”

Pollard looked nervous for the first time during the interview. He swallowed hard. "Maybe I shouldn't have done this, but I put the gun back in the holster and secured the strap.”

"Why did you do that?”

"I dunno. I guess I thought that it might look bad.”

"Did your partner see what you did?”

"No. He was talking to the owner of the restaurant and a couple of bystanders.”

"I don't remember you at the Emmett Smalls trial. Did you testify there?”

"No. My partner did, though. He was the vet and he was driving the cruiser. I guess the D.A. thought he was more important than me.”

"What about the EMT guys? Did they see you do this?”

"No. They arrived about two minutes later. By that time, I was directing traffic around both cruisers and the sidewalk.”

Kelso got up and paced around in front of the desk. "You want something to drink? Coffee? Tea?”

"No, thanks. Maybe some water. My throat's kind of dry.”

Kelso punched a button on the intercom. "Angela—could you bring us a couple of glasses and a pitcher of water?” Then he sat down in the chair again. "What did you do after that? Did you tell anyone?”

"Yeah. I told the desk sergeant back at headquarters."

"And what did he say?"

"He said, 'Keep your mouth shut. That nigger shot a cop. He's gonna fry for it.'"

"Do you remember the desk sergeant's name?"

"I'm afraid not. I was new to the force. I didn't know many of the other cops and I didn't want to get into trouble."

The door opened and Angela appeared with a tray and put it down on the table between the two chairs. She poured them each a glass of water, Kelso thanked her, and she left. Pollard immediately drained about half of his glass.

"Better?"

"Much. Thanks."

Kelso didn't touch his glass. "Now maybe you can clarify something for me, Mr. Pollard."

"Shoot."

"When Angela—my secretary—announced that you were here to see me, she said you *were* with the SFPD at the time of the Watt 'incident.' Am I to understand that you are no longer with the force?"

"That is correct."

"Why not?"

"I was fired."

"On what grounds?"

Pollard took another long swallow of water. "Accepting free drinks at a bar in the Tenderloin."

"And that's all?"

"That was enough. Me and my partner at the time—same guy— were on the night shift and got off about midnight. We stopped to get a drink in this sleazy Polk Street bar where a lot of wineheads hang out. But it's right down the street from the Northern Station, so it was convenient. We're still in uniform, but officially off-duty. So the bartender knows my partner real good and pours a couple of drinks for us. We hang around for a couple more and then get ready to leave. I reach into my pocket for my billfold and my partner laughs. So does the bartender. I get the picture and put my billfold back in my pocket and we leave. The next morning the desk sergeant—a different one—calls me on the carpet about 'extorting' free drinks from a barkeep. Next thing I know, they take my badge and gun and I'm out on the street."

"Who turned you in?"

"I dunno. Some bar patron, I guess. Or maybe my partner. He's still on the force."

"Why didn't you appeal?"

"I did. I was told not to make trouble. That was it."

"You said that there was something I could do for you."

"Yeah. Not money or anything like that."

"What, then?"

"I'd like to get my old job back. I thought maybe you could help me do that."

"Maybe. Can't promise anything. You working now?"

"Yeah. Downstairs."

"Downstairs?"

"Security guard. They move us around some, but I've been here for the last six months."

Kelso smiled. "I thought you looked familiar."

"People look right through security guards. Policemen get respect."

"You're willing to be deposed?"

"Deposed?"

"Have your deposition taken. The D.A. has a right to see it before we go to trial."

"Sure."

Kelso stood, as did Pollard. "Stop at the reception desk on the way out. Angela will make the appointment for you." Kelso shook Pollard's hand and escorted him to the door. When he was gone, he went to the window and stared out at Alcatraz. "Cops. And to think I wanted to be one like my dad." He sighed. "Well, Karl Marx put an end to that. Sorry Dad—and sorry, Karl Marx. Now I'm part of the bourgeois capitalist power structure." He turned around and surveyed the spacious room, with its antique Persian carpet, abstract paintings, mahogany paneling, and objets d'art. "Shocking, isn't it?"

CHAPTER 46

Travis was awakened from a nap at his apartment at Grace Cathedral by the telephone ringing. He opened his eyes, yawned, and looked at his watch: 4:15pm. He picked up the receiver.

"Travis?"

"Yes?"

"Don't you recognize my voice? It's Andrea."

Travis sat up and turned on the light. "Andrea? Where are you?"

"At the Top of the Mark. The view's gorgeous here. Why don't you join me for a drink?"

Travis put his feet on the floor and rubbed his eyes. "I must have fallen asleep. Where did you say you were?"

"The Top of the Mark. At the Mark Hopkins. I just flew in from Amsterdam. I can't believe you're still living in that tiny apartment on Taylor Street."

"I'm not. But I'm just up the street. About two blocks away, actually."

"Well, get over here then. I'd love to see you. We've got a lot of catching up to do."

Travis hung up the phone and slipped on his shoes. He went to the mirror over his dresser, combed his hair and straightened his collar. He wondered how Andrea would react when she saw that he was a priest.

In ten minutes he found himself in the lobby of the Mark Hopkins, facing the elevators. He pushed the button labeled 'Top of the Mark' and after stopping at several floors to pick up passengers, he stepped out into the bar with its famous view of the city and the bay. He scanned the tables for some sign of Andrea. Suddenly, a hand went up and waved. It was attached to a plump blond woman dressed in a pants suit.

When he approached the table, she stood up and gave him a hug and a kiss.

"Travis! You rascal. What have you been up to? Why are you dressed like a priest? You in a play?"

Travis chuckled. "That's the second time this week someone's asked me that. No, Andrea—I'm dressed like this because it's my job."

Andrea looked at him blankly for a moment. "You're kidding."

"No. I'm not. Why don't we sit down and I'll fill you in."

They sat down and Andrea, her mouth still agape, awaited an explanation.

"I don't know where to start," Travis said. "After I graduated from San Francisco State, I applied to the Church Divinity School of the Pacific in Berkeley—some people call it 'Holy Hill'—and after that applied for a job as an assistant rector at Grace Cathedral and that's where I am today."

Andrea still seemed speechless until a waitress arrived. "A double vodka martini, honey—two cherries, no olives. What'll you have, Travis?"

"A glass of white wine will be fine."

"Give him a glass of that Freemark Abbey Chardonnay, honey. He can relate to that."

Travis chuckled. "I don't think Freemark Abbey is run by monks, Andrea."

"Whatever. It's good stuff—I had some last night for dinner."

As the waitress went to place their order, Andrea continued to stare at Travis. He stared back, seeing that she had gained some twenty pounds since he last saw her, and was dressed far more conservatively than in those days, with a silk blouse buttoned to her neck and a suit jacket barely able to conceal her expanding breasts.

"You're the only priest I ever fucked," she said. "I mean in real life."

Travis laughed. "I wasn't a priest then."

"Yeah, but you must have been thinking about it. Were you thinking about it when we fucked like rabbits in my apartment in North Beach?"

The waitress returned with their drinks. She was a cute blond wearing a frilly-collared low-cut blouse, the kind that Andrea used to favor. Travis glanced at her décolletage, which wasn't missed by Andrea.

"It didn't cross my mind at the time," Travis said.

Andrea took a sip of her martini. "Good. And I see that you haven't lost your eye for the ladies."

"A clerical collar doesn't necessarily suppress a man's libido."

"Obviously. But speaking of which, whatever happened to Marcella?"

"Haven't you heard? She won a Tony award."

"I've been in Europe for the past five years. Haven't kept up with the New York theater scene. But that's terrific. You still seeing each other?"

Travis sipped his wine. "That's a very good Chardonnay."

"I thought you'd like it. You didn't answer my question. You still seeing each other?"

"Some. She was just here for a visit."

"And now she's back in New York?"

"Yes."

Andrea seemed to consider this. "Why don't you two get married?"

"I've been asking myself that same question lately."

"Is it because you're a priest?"

"No. She says it's because of her career."

"Her career? What's that got to do with it?"

"San Francisco, New York, L.A. She thinks the travel would be too much of a strain on the marriage. That and the fact that she can't have children."

"Can't have children?" Andrea finished off her martini and signaled the waitress for another. "Why's that?"

"Just a fact, that's all. Andrea—what about you? Are you still making, uh, those films?"

"You mean porno films? I sure am, honey. Only I'm in the business end, now. Blaine does the casting and directing."

"Really? You're still together?"

"Strictly a professional relationship now. But it's very profitable."

Travis took another sip of his wine and noted the diamond bracelet on Andrea's arm. "It seems to be. What are you doing in San Francisco?"

"Distribution deal. Those dirt bags in L.A. won't even talk to me. But here they're open to anything."

"That's San Francisco."

"You seen any of the old crowd? Alessandro, Terry?"

Travis looked into his wine glass. "Terry's dead."

"Oh, that's so sad. He was such a nice kid. What happened?"

"AIDS."

Andrea let out a low whistle. "That's an epidemic here, isn't it? I mean among the gays."

"I'm afraid so. And now Alessandro has it. Or at least he's tested positive for it."

"Maybe he won't get it. Some people carry the virus for years and don't get it."

"That's what the doctors say, but they're keeping him under observation for a while."

"Where?"

"UC Medical Center."

"Has he got insurance?"

Travis sighed. "I'm afraid not. He had some with the Screen Actor's Guild, but he let it lapse. I'm trying to see if they'll reinstate it, but in the meantime he's running up a huge bill at the hospital."

"Can I see him?"

"Sure."

"When?"

"Anytime you want. He doesn't have many visitors."

Andrea downed the last of her martini. "Let's go."

"Now?"

"Yeah, now. I'm only going to be here a couple of days. And I'm all tied up tomorrow."

Travis heard the muffled sound of a phone ringing.

Andrea reached into her purse and pulled out what looked to Travis like a field telephone. "Hello? Howard? Yeah, yeah. I'm all settled. Tomorrow at nine o'clock? Right. See you then." She pushed a button and put the phone back into her purse.

Travis was mystified. "Does it work on batteries or what?"

Andrea laughed. "Batteries, radar. Who knows? It works, that's all that's important."

"Are they expensive?"

"This one was four grand. But they say the price will come down."

"Maybe we could call Alessandro at the hospital and let him know we're coming."

"Sure. You know the number?"

Travis gave her the number and she called the hospital. After a brief conversation with a nurse, she put the phone back into her purse. They both rose and started for the elevator.

"What about the bill?" Travis said. "I'll—"

"It's on me, Travis, honey. They've got my room number. Let's get out of this dump. They don't even have lemon drop martinis. Can you still make one?"

Travis chuckled as they stepped into the elevator. "It's like riding a bicycle—once you know how..."

They took a cab to UC Medical Center on Parnassus Avenue near Golden Gate Park. After signing in with the receptionist, they went up to the fourth floor and knocked on Alessandro's door.

"Come in."

Andrea pushed the door open. "Baby, it's me. Andrea."

Alessandro was sitting up with his back against a pillow watching a television mounted on the wall opposite his bed. "Andrea?"

"None other." She went over to the bed and kissed Alessandro on the forehead. "You don't look bad for a guy with AIDS."

"I don't have AIDS," Alessandro said. He lifted his arm to emphasize the IV tube attached to it. "But they're pumping me full of antibiotics just in case."

Travis stood near the foot of the bed and glanced at the TV. He had been there only hours before and Alessandro seemed to have taken his presence for granted. "What are you watching, Alessandro?"

"M.A.S.H. They're already into reruns. David's got a plum role."

"David?" Andrea pulled up a chair and sat down next to the bed.

"David Willingham," Alessandro said. "You met him once at the Blue Fox."

"Oh, yeah." Andrea looked up at the screen. "I remember. He was your boyfriend at the time. Doesn't look like he's got the virus, does he?"

"No," Alessandro said. "I think he's immune somehow."

Andrea turned her gaze back to Alessandro. He had lost weight, maybe thirty pounds since she had last seen him. His face was drawn and thin. "Alessandro, baby, are they treating you right here? You getting enough to eat?"

"Sure. They're great. But I don't have the appetite I used to. Some things I can't keep down."

"Poor baby." Andrea leaned over and kissed him again, this time on the cheek. "What if I bring you some chicken soup?"

Alessandro laughed, though with some difficulty. "They've got plenty of that here. I'm sick of chicken soup. A juicy ribeye would be nice."

"I'll have them send one up."

"I don't think they'll let you."

"Then I'll call the Blue Fox and have them deliver it."

Alessandro chuckled. "Same old can-do Andrea. What are you up to these days?"

"Film company. Based in Amsterdam. When you get well come and see me. We could use an actor with your, um, attributes."

Alessandro smiled, but suddenly seemed tired. "I just might do that."

A nurse came in and checked his vitals on a monitor. Then she went over to Alessandro, who had his eyes closed now, and fluffed up his pillow. "He needs to rest. Gets exhausted sometimes just talking to people."

Andrea and Travis thanked the nurse and left the room. As they were walking down the hall, Andrea stopped at a window and gazed out at Golden Gate Park. She wiped a tear from her eye. "He's going to die, isn't he?"

"Looks like it," Travis said.

Andrea reached into her purse and pulled out a handkerchief. She wiped another tear away. "What's the tariff around here?"

"I think it's about a thousand dollars a day. Plus the medications. I don't know how long they'll keep him."

"A thousand a day? How long has he been here?"

"Let's see. Four days, I think."

"And counting." Andrea reached into her purse again and pulled out a check book. "What do you say I make it out for ten thousand? Call it a down payment. Can I make it to you?"

Travis was taken aback. "Maybe you'd better make it out to UCSF Medical Center."

"I'd rather make it out to you. Then you can pay whoever he owes it to." She finished writing the check, tore it off, and handed it to him. "Let me know if he needs more. I'll give you my phone number and address when we get back to the hotel."

Travis took the check and put it in his coat pocket. "You're a kind soul, Andrea."

She wiped another tear away with her handkerchief and started down the hall. "It's so sad. He was such a beautiful man."

CHAPTER 47

Ben didn't know what to think of Ted Kelso. First Kelso defends him and gets the charges dropped so he can testify against Emmett Smalls, and now he defends Lonnie Erskine, the real trigger man in the murder of Dan Watt. And he didn't like the way Kelso was cross-examining him.

"Just tell us what you saw, Mr. Franklin." Kelso was standing only a few feet away, looking not at him, but at the jury. He was dressed in a fancy pinstriped suit and wingtips, a far cry from the jeans and sandals he used to wear at San Francisco State.

Ben looked at the jury—which was made up of two black men, three black women, four white men, two Hispanic women and one Asian male—then at the gallery, which was even more diverse. "I saw the shotgun in Mr. Erskine's hands, then he stuck the barrel out the window, then there was a blast that took down Watt."

"You saw Sergeant Watt go down?"

"Yes."

"Did you see Sergeant Watt go for his service revolver before the shotgun blast?"

"No."

"Did you see Sergeant Watt *at all* as he came out of the restaurant?"

"Sure. I saw him come out."

"And what was he doing? I mean, what was he carrying, if anything?"

"He was carrying a package, like takeout food, I guess."

Kelso again looked at the jury. "You guess?"

"Well...I saw him carrying a package. I don't know what was in it."

"Then what?"

"I just told you."

"You told me you saw a shotgun in Mr. Erskine's hands followed by a blast and that followed by Sergeant Watt falling to the pavement. What did you see in between?"

"In between? Nothing."

"Your witness, Mr. Feinberg."

Kelso went back to his table and sat down next to his client, Lonnie Erskine. Ben stared at Erskine, who stared back.

Feinberg, the prosecutor, stood but did not move from his table. "Did you have a clear view of the area in front of the restaurant prior to the shooting, Mr. Franklin?"

"Objection!" Kelso stood and addressed the judge. "We've established, your honor, that Mr. Franklin, at six-foot six inches in height, had only a limited view of the sidewalk from the driver's side of the car. He has testified that he only saw Sergeant Watts' legs, not his waist or torso."

"I only asked the witness if he had a clear view of the area in front of the restaurant, Your Honor," Feinberg said. "I didn't ask him which of Sergeant Watts' body parts he saw."

There was a tittering of laughter among the spectators.

"Objection overruled," the judge said. "You may answer the question, Mr. Franklin."

"Um, I could see the area in front of the restaurant," Ben said. "Sometimes I scrunch down a little when I'm in a car so I can see better."

"And do you think you could have seen Sergeant Watt go for his pistol from where you were sitting?"

"Objection!" Kelso said.

"Overruled. You may answer the question."

"I'm sure I could have."

"And *did* you see Sergeant Watt go for his pistol prior to your hearing the shotgun blast?"

Ben thought for a moment, careful to choose his words. "I didn't see Sergeant Watt do anything but walk out of the restaurant with a package in his hand."

"Which hand?" Feinberg said.

"The left."

"You're sure of that?"

"Yes."

"And which hip was his holster on?"

Ben thought for a moment. "The left."

"You know that Sergeant Watt was left handed, don't you?"

"No, I didn't know that."

"Thank you, Mr. Franklin," Feinberg said. "That's all I have for this witness, Your Honor."

The judge then excused Ben and he stepped down from the witness stand. He buttoned his jacket as he passed the defendant's table without looking at either Erskine or Kelso.

After a recess, Kelso called several witnesses on behalf of Erskine, who continued to sit with his hands folded together almost in an attitude of prayer.

Finally, Kelso called Mike Pollard, the former SFPD patrolman. Pollard recounted his story of being first on the scene and replacing Watts' revolver in his holster and securing the strap. Kelso then sat down and Mr. Feinberg was allowed to cross-examine.

"Can you tell us, Mr. Pollard," Feinberg said, "why you were fired from your job with the SFPD?"

Pollard looked uncomfortable and shifted his weight in the chair. "Yes, sir. I was fired for accepting free drinks in a Tenderloin bar."

Feinberg looked gravely at the jury. "Fired for 'accepting' free drinks. You knew at the time that that was an offense punishable by immediate termination?"

"Well...I guess I did."

"You either knew or you didn't, Mr. Pollard."

"Yes. I knew."

"And you did it, anyway."

"Well...I was just going along with my partner and the bartender. They laughed at me when I offered to pay for the drinks."

Feinberg stroked his chin as if struggling to understand. "So you basically caved into peer pressure?"

"I guess you could say that."

"And did your partner lose his job as well?"

"No, sir."

"Why not?"

"I don't know. He'd been on the force longer than I had. Maybe he knew a way to get out of the jam we were in. Or someone who could help him."

Feinberg paced before the juror's box, stopped, and placed his hand on the railing. "Did you tell your story to anyone else at the time? I mean besides the inquiry board?"

"Yes, sir. I told the desk sergeant."

"And who was that?"

"I don't remember. I didn't recall seeing him before."

"Do you see him now—in this courtroom?"

Pollard looked around the courtroom. "No, sir. I don't."

"Do you see your partner?"

"No, sir. I understand he retired recently and moved to Arizona."

"Then there's no one to corroborate your story that you saw Sergeant Watt's pistol sticking halfway out of his holster, put it back in the holster, and secured the strap?"

"No, sir. I guess not."

"You took no notes."

"No, sir."

"Didn't you know, Mr. Pollard, that what you did—or say you did—was tampering with evidence?"

Pollard looked surprised. "I didn't think of it that way."

Feinberg frowned. "No, I suppose you wouldn't have. What about the EMT crew who arrived on the scene shortly after you did? Did any of them see you do this?"

"I don't think so."

Feinberg drummed his fingers on the railing of the juror's box. "No witnesses to what you say you did with the pistol, and no notes or phone calls or communication of any kind about this to friends or associates. Are you married, Mr. Pollard?"

"Yes, sir."

"And did you tell your wife?"

"No, sir."

Feinberg finally left the juror's box and walked over to the witness stand. "Then can you tell us, Mr. Pollard, why you have suddenly come up with this story about the position of Sergeant Watt's pistol more than five years after the event?" He glanced at Kelso. "Did Mr. Kelso promise you anything if you came in here today and testified to that effect?"

"Objection!" Kelso rose to his feet.

"Overruled," the judge said. "You may answer the question, Mr. Pollard."

Pollard looked to Kelso and back again. "He didn't promise me anything."

"But he hinted that he might be able to get you your old job back," Feinberg said. "Is that it?"

"Objection!" Kelso said.

"Sustained."

Feinberg walked back to his table. "No further questions."

"Mr. Kelso?" the judge said.

Kelso stood up and walked slowly over to the witness stand. "Mr. Pollard—why did you do what you said you did that day? Why did you replace Sergeant Watt's revolver back in its holster and secure the strap?"

Pollard massaged his knuckles as if he had injured them in some way. "I thought it might look bad for Sergeant Watt."

"Look bad? Why?"

"Well...he had been accused a few weeks earlier of shooting a Black Puma in the back. It was in all the papers."

"Why would that concern you?"

"Sergeant Watt...well, he was kind of my mentor. He took me under his wing, you might say."

"And how did he do that?"

Pollard smiled. "He took me and my wife out to dinner the first week I was on the force. And he helped me get a plum assignment— for a rookie—patrolling North Beach."

"North Beach? Why was that a 'plum' assignment?"

"Because there's not much crime and there's always something going on."

"Something going on? Like what?"

"Oh, like street musicians and mimes and outdoor poetry read-ings, things like that. Especially in Washington Square."

"Don't most rookies want to get into the thick of things? Like arresting hardened criminals, murderers, drug lords, getting in a shoot out?"

A sheepish grin came to Pollard's lips. "Not me. Oh, I don't mind mixing it up a little with the hardcore types. But I joined the force to protect people. You know, to keep the peace and help people get along. That's why I liked watching all the stuff going on in North Beach. Everybody seemed happy there."

"And you didn't want to see Sergeant Watt's name dragged through the dirt."

"Yeah. I guess you could say that. I felt like I owed him something."

"No further questions, Your Honor." Kelso went back to the defendant's table and sat down.

Erskine grinned at him, his hands still folded in front of him. 'I think you caught Feinberg with his pants down. It'll be a piece of cake now."

"Don't be so sure," Kelso said.

CHAPTER 48

Emma Blériot sat alone in the bleachers at Potrero Elementary watching her pupils' soccer practice. Or rather, watching Travis coaching her pupils at soccer. For this was the reason she came out to watch.

She wondered if Travis would ever stop seeing her as a child. Back when she was a freshman at Palo Alto High, she and her friends would attend the Stanford soccer games whenever they could. They all liked football, but the helmets and facemasks nearly covered the players' faces and you couldn't tell what they looked like. With soccer it was different. No helmets, no shoulder pads, no facemasks. And the boys were cuter.

Travis was the cutest of all. At first he was clean-shaven, then he grew a beard. He was exceedingly handsome either way. At least to Emma. And when he came into her father's flower shop to buy flowers for whatever Stanford coed he was dating at the time, he was so charming and polite. Her father adored him. But not as much as she did.

Of course she was jealous of all the girls he dated, though he never brought one into the shop. Occasionally, she would spot a sleek, sophisticated-looking girl in a wool skirt and knee socks sitting on the sidelines rooting for him and jumping up and cheering madly whenever he made a goal. She always envied that girl, but wanted to strangle her at the same time.

And now he was a priest! How strange, and yet delightful! She had always thought that Travis was a sort of playboy and that he would never marry, or if he did, he would surely be a philanderer. Well, he still was not married, but he apparently had a much more serious side to him than she saw at the time.

Suddenly he stopped running and blew his whistle. All the boys gathered around him. He said something she couldn't hear, and the boys began dispersing and heading for the locker room in small groups, chattering about who did what during the practice.

"A penny for your thoughts."

"What? Oh, Travis—I didn't see you coming. I was watching Keiko and Juan—they've become best friends."

Travis sat down next to her. He was sweating and a musky odor filled her nostrils. "That's a fringe benefit of sports. They were deadly enemies at the beginning of the season, and now they walk off the field with their arms around each other. It's nice to see."

"It certainly is," she said. "And it's all due to your charm and tact."

Travis laughed. "I don't think those boys find me particularly charming. It's the sport itself that generates camaraderie and a sense of fair play."

"I suppose. How's the homeless project going?"

Travis' jovial mood evaporated. "Not so well, I'm afraid. It's been hard to find benefactors. I know a woman in Europe who might contribute, but it will take more than one person to get the foundation up and running."

"And in the meantime?"

"In the meantime the homeless in the Tenderloin will continue to live in the streets. We can only do so much for them without a facility to house them and mental health professionals to counsel them."

"Why can't the Y take them in?"

"Not enough rooms for one thing. And the homeless have special needs. They would drive the regular patrons away with their erratic behavior and the Y wouldn't be able to pay its bills."

"So what's the solution?"

"Money, as usual."

They sat in silence for several moments, each lost in thought. Emma, however, was no longer thinking of the homeless, but of Travis and his personal life.

"Travis..."

"Hmm?"

"Do you ever intend to marry?"

"Marry?" Travis seemed jolted out of his reverie. "I suppose so. But it doesn't seem to be in the cards at any time in the near future."

"Why not?"

Travis smiled and put his arm around her. "Good old Emma. Always concerned about her Uncle Travis."

Emma frowned. "You're not my uncle."

"All right. It's your father who used to call me that when we were in the shop at the same time. But I always felt somewhat protective of you. Still do."

Emma brightened. "You do?"

"Sure. Can't help it. But I realize you're a grown woman now and I promise I'll never mention 'Uncle' Travis again."

"Good. Just Travis and Emma." She leaned her head into Travis' shoulder and closed her eyes. But after a moment or two, Travis withdrew his arm and placed his forearms on his thighs. Then he began to whistle.

"What are you whistling about?" she said.

"Oh, I don't know. I guess a tune just popped into my head."

"What tune is that? I don't recognize it."

"A Beatles tune. 'Eleanor Rigby.'" He started singing, but got no further than the name before he started humming.

Now she began:

> Eleanor Rigby picks up the rice in the church where
> the wedding has been...
> Lives in a dream...
> Waits at the window, wearing the face that she keeps in
> a jar by the door...
> Who is it for?
> All the lonely people...where do they all belong?

Travis laughed. "Don't recognize it? You've got a pretty good memory for tunes you don't recognize. I never heard you sing before."

She blushed. "I sang in the choir when I was little. And I never forget the lyrics to a song I like."

"Well, you've got a beautiful voice.'

"Thank you. The rest of the song is rather sad, though. I like the first part."

They sat again in silence for several moments.

"How's the teaching going?" he said.

"Okay, I guess. I love working with the children. The parents, though, can be difficult sometimes."

"I'll bet. How about Ben?"

"He's doing great. The kids all love him. It's funny sometimes, to hear him in the hallway with his jive talk to the kids, and then in the teacher's lounge it's the King's English."

Travis chuckled. "He's a master of dialect. You should hear him talk to his wife."

"His wife?"

"She's Vietnamese. And no mean linguist herself. She's taught Ben a good bit of Vietnamese and a little Chinese, too."

"I'm afraid I only speak French. And English, of course."

"Well, your dad's French. You spoke it at home?"

"Until I was twelve or thirteen. Then I wanted to be one hundred percent American."

"Don't we all?" Travis stood. "I'd better be going, Emma. I've got three appointments this afternoon. Good to chat with you."

Emma also stood. She was a tall young woman, and nearly met Travis' eyes at his own level. "Travis..."

"What is it, Emma?"

"I don't know how to say this, but it's lonely in the city. I've never lived by myself before and—"

"Aren't you dating anyone? A beautiful, intelligent, well-educated girl like you?"

"Well...I've gone out with one of the teachers here a couple of times, but...I don't know. He seems so dull. All we talk about is lesson plans and teacher/student ratios and—"

"What about the opera?"

"What?"

"The opera. Father Lattimore's got a dozen tickets. Would you like to go?"

Emma clapped her hands together. "Oh, Travis—I'd love to!"

"We'll have dinner first. Any preferences?"

"Oh, anywhere. Whatever you like."

"Ben and Thuy have gotten me into Vietnamese food. That okay?"

"Sure."

"I'll need your phone number. And your address."

"Oh..." She fumbled in the pockets of her coat. "I don't have anything to write on."

"Just call me at Grace Cathedral and leave it with the receptionist.

I've got to go now, Emma. I'm already late." He gave her a kiss on the cheek and trotted down the bleacher steps.

She stood stunned for a moment, watching him jog towards the locker room. "Oh, Travis—when is it?"

"Friday night. The opera's at eight. I'll pick you up at six."

"Okay." She continued to stand there for several minutes, gazing out over the soccer field. She couldn't believe it! She was actually going to have a date with Travis!

But she suddenly—and literally—had a sinking feeling as she sat down on the bleacher seat. What if he only felt sorry for her? She wished she hadn't told him she was lonely. He was a priest, always trying to help people. Maybe he just saw her as another wayward soul who needed guidance and sympathy.

She stood up again. So what if he did feel sorry for her? He had asked her out. It was a start. She would show him she wasn't the pitiful waif lost in the city that he thought she was. She was a woman now and she would make sure he knew it.

She skipped down the bleacher steps like a school girl and began singing:

> Eleanor Rigby picks up the rice in the church where
> 	the wedding has been...
> Lives in a dream...

But she wouldn't end up as an old maid like Eleanor Rigby...She would be...Mrs. Travis Carter!

CHAPTER 49

One by one members of the jury stood as Feinberg polled them.

"Guilty," a white middle-aged man said, and sat down.

"Guilty," an Hispanic woman in her late thirties said. She sat down.

"Guilty," another white middle-aged man said.

"Not guilty," said an elderly black man.

"Guilty," said a Chinese-American man who looked to be in his late twenties.

And so it went until the last juror sat down.

The final tally was nine guilty votes and three not guilty. The judge summoned the two attorneys to the bench and conferred with them as spectators and members of the media looked on in silence.

After several minutes of consultation, Kelso and Feinberg returned to their tables.

"What's the deal?" Erskine said.

"Hung jury," Kelso said. "The prosecution has offered a plea-bargain: you plead guilty to attempted kidnapping and they won't retry the case."

"What's the rap for attempted kidnapping?"

"One to three years, depending on the judge's assessment of your character and the likelihood of recidivism."

Erskine rubbed his chin. "What are the chances of Feinberg getting a conviction in another trial?"

"Fifty-fifty. Maybe better. He'll learn from his mistakes."

"And if he wins?"

"Life imprisonment. Minimum."

Erskine looked down at the table at nothing in particular. "I wish we could've gotten that priest, what's his name—"

"Father Lattimore."

"Yeah. Him. I wish he had agreed to testify as to my character."

"He didn't."

"No...any chance I can serve, say, one year in jail and the rest on probation?"

"Maybe. After all, you returned to this country voluntarily and turned yourself in."

Erskine looked up at Kelso, who stared back impassively. "Okay."

Kelso stood and addressed the bench. "My client would like to change his plea, Your Honor."

The judge looked first to Kelso, then to Feinberg, who also stood. "You may approach the bench, gentlemen."

The deal was done. Sentencing would take place in two weeks.

* * *

Friday night arrived and Emma was at a loss as to how to dress. The opera, of course, was a very formal affair, but then Travis said they would have dinner at a Vietnamese restaurant. Wasn't that rather casual? She would feel silly in an evening dress at a restaurant filled with patrons dressed in jeans and docksiders. But then maybe it was a more elegant restaurant than she thought. Would Travis be dressed in his priest's garb?

She finally decided to compromise. A navy blue pant suit with a chiffon blouse, silk scarf, and low heels.

When Travis arrived at her apartment in Diamond Heights, she was surprised to see he was wearing a red turtleneck beneath a leather sport coat. So unpriest-like!

"I almost got lost in the fog," he said. "You look stunning in that outfit."

"Thank you. It's a little creepy, sometimes."

"There's nothing creepy about the way you look."

She laughed. "I meant the fog. When I walk up here from Diamond Heights Boulevard, I sometimes get lost, too."

Travis looked around the apartment. "Nice place."

"Mama helped me decorate it. She's very French, you know."

"She is. Has good taste, too. You ready?"

"Ready."

Travis went to the door and opened it for her.

"Old World manners," she said with a smile. "Just like my dad."

"We had manners in Michigan, too. They tend to get lost once you cross the Rockies, though."

Travis also opened the door of the van for her and they took the scenic route down Portola Drive, though there wasn't much to see until the fog lifted at Market Street.

The Vietnamese restaurant in the Embarcadero was packed, but they were seated at a table by the window with a view of Treasure Island and Berkeley beyond. They each ordered a glass of wine and chatted for a few minutes about the scenery, Potrero Elementary, and the revitalized neighborhood of Diamond Heights.

"There's Ben and Thuy." Travis said suddenly, looking towards the entrance. "I hope you don't mind me inviting them to join us." He caught their attention and waved them over.

"Oh," Emma said. "Of course not." She did in fact mind, and once again had the deflated feeling that Travis still regarded her as a child.

As they were being served, however, she warmed to their presence, especially to Thuy, whom she had never met. She knew that Ben was married to a Vietnamese woman, and she knew that that woman had been kidnapped in her father's delivery truck. She also knew that Kenny Morris' mother had delivered her firstborn child in the abandoned warehouse on the waterfront during a standoff with the police.

"You are Travis' new girlfriend," Thuy said to her.

"Well..." she said, glancing at Travis, who merely smiled.

"Thuy doesn't like to beat around the bush," Ben said.

"Yes, Thuy," Travis said. "Emma is my new girlfriend, though I've known her and her family for a very long time."

"How nice," Thuy said. "I think we should drink to your happy future together."

"Now Thuy," Ben said. "You're getting a little ahead of yourself here. Marriage may not be in their plans."

Thuy studied Emma for a moment, then Travis. ""I think so. They make a beautiful couple."

Emma glanced at Travis and blushed. Travis laughed.

They all drank to a happy future and continued with their meal. A couple of more glasses of wine emboldened Emma, who was now getting used to Thuy's frankness, to ask her about the kidnapping.

"Did they mistreat you?" she said.

"No, no," Thuy said. "Except for the beginning, when they pushed me into the truck and put the—you know—chemical over my mouth. I got some bruises from that."

"What about when you were in the factory?"

"No problem. They were like perfect gentlemen."

By this time Travis and Ben had stopped talking between themselves and were listening to Thuy.

Emma glanced at Travis and turned back to Thuy. "Kenny Morris was a friend of mine in high school. He was a gentle soul then. I don't know what got into him."

"The Pumas," Ben said. "They got into me, too." He took a sip of his wine. "For a while, anyway."

Emma looked at Ben. "But you saw them for what they were. Gangsters. You testified against them."

Ben sighed. "Yeah, I testified against them. And I still don't know if I did the right thing."

"Well, of course you did," she said. "They can't be allowed to go around kidnapping and murdering people whatever their grievances."

Everyone looked at Ben, who was now sitting away from the table at an angle and twisting the stem of his wine glass on the white tablecloth. "Grievances. They got more than grievances. They got three hundred years of injustice to set right."

"By killing anyone who opposes their methods?"

Ben stared at her for a moment. "No. Not by killing. I've seen enough of that. It just leads to more killing."

There was a silence for several moments until Thuy spoke: "No more talk of killing. This is happy occasion."

"You're right, Thuy," Travis said. "All that's behind us now. The future looks bright. Let's drink to that." He raised his glass, as did the others.

"To the future!"

"Why don't you two join us for the opera?" Travis said.

"The Opera?" Ben said. "We were going to a movie."

"I've got a stack of tickets nobody's using. Come with us."

"An opera," Ben said. "Gee, I've never been to an opera."

Thuy laughed. "In Saigon, we go all the time. Before you two get there. Rossini, Bizet, *Madama Butterfly*—who did that one?"

"Puccini," Travis said. "Tonight it's *La Bohéme*."

"I know that one, too." Thuy tugged on Ben's sleeve. "We go."

Ben smiled. "The Dragon Lady has spoken. I guess we're going."

After paying the bill—split three ways by Travis, Ben, and Emma, who insisted on paying her share—they got into their vehicles and headed for the Opera House on Van Ness Avenue.

Like Ben, Emma had never been to an opera before. Now walking into the grand entrance hall and seeing a number of society women dressed in elegant evening gowns and sparking necklaces, she felt underdressed. She mentioned this to Travis.

"You look fine," Travis said. "Besides, you have a great advantage over them—you're young and beautiful and they're neither."

She slapped him on the arm. "That's not nice—you're supposed to be a priest, remember?"

Travis chuckled. "Even priests are entitled to their opinions—especially when it comes to beauty."

"True beauty is ageless," she said.

Travis gazed up at the barrel-vaulted, coffered ceiling nearly two stories above them. "That's a point."

Ben was also gazing at the ceiling, while Thuy and Emma were gazing at the other women and their outfits.

An usher directed them to their seats, which were in a balcony near the stage.

It turned out the opera was being televised and there were powerful lights set up for this purpose around the stage and in some of the balconies. The glare often overwhelmed the stage lights so that the scenes of Paris behind the singers was a blur. Nevertheless, the singing was superb, even thrilling, and though the tenor and his co-star were long past the age of young starving artists, the final arias nearly brought the house down.

"The big guy reminds me of Fats Domino," Ben said as they descended the stairs to the lobby. "Only he can hold those high notes longer."

"Who's Fats Domino?" Thuy said.

"Rhythm and Blues dude."

"Look," Travis said. "There's Kelso with Vera."

Emma didn't know who Kelso and Vera were, but she saw that the striking blond with the man Travis indicated was wearing a long sable coat. "Oh, my goodness! That coat must be worth a fortune."

"Must have brought it from Russia," Travis said, as they approached the couple. "Sables are as common there as beavers in Michigan. How are you, Ted? Hi, Vera."

After introducing Emma and Thuy, neither of whom had met Vera, Travis asked about Erskine. "I saw that he got a plea deal—where is he now?"

"At my house," Kelso said.

"At *your* house? But Ted, how—"

"Death threats—probably from some cops unhappy with the deal. And they're Pumas unhappy with the fact that he's renounced them as well. I convinced the judge to let him stay with us until sentencing."

Travis stared at Kelso for a moment, then glanced at Vera, who looked uncomfortable with this conversation. Even Ben seemed to avoid Kelso's eyes. "Are you sure it's safe?"

"Sure," Kelso said. "We've got a cop camped out on the sidewalk. A Daly City cop. He gets relieved by his partner every six hours."

"But—" Travis said. "They're outside."

Kelso smiled, in a condescending way, Emma thought. "Erskine's a changed man. Spends most of his time reading the Bible. The rest of the time he watches Lakers' games on TV."

Travis, with his usual tact, changed the subject to the relief of all but Kelso, who seemed to be assured that Erskine was no threat to either himself or Vera.

Emma took the opportunity to compliment Vera on her sable coat, and Vera's eyes came alive again. She told a humorous story of how she obtained the coat in Russia while it was still the Soviet Union, and smuggled it out through diplomatic channels. Low-ranking embassy officials, she said, weren't allowed to display symbols of bourgeois capitalist wealth.

When Travis took her home, she invited him in for a glass of wine. Travis accepted, but seemed troubled.

"What's wrong?" she said as they sat down on the sofa together. "You've hardly said a word since we left the Opera House."

"I'm concerned about Ted and Vera," Travis said. "Especially Vera."

"Why? They have a policeman—"

"That's good. But Erskine is a convicted rapist."

"Oh..." Emma brought her hand to her mouth. "I didn't know that."

"It's true. It's been a long time and maybe he's reformed himself as Ted says. I don't even think it was mentioned at the trial."

"The papers say he's a born-again Christian. Sort of like you."

Travis looked at her and smiled. "I suppose so. People change. I've changed. You've changed."

"Me? How?"

Travis took a sip of his wine and set the glass down again. "You've blossomed into a beautiful woman, and not only that. You've become well-educated, caring, and socially...well, I don't want to sound like a walking cliché, but you seem to have a genuine desire to help those less fortunate than yourself."

She lowered her eyes and stared at nothing in particular on the coffee table. "You're giving me more credit than I deserve. I don't know how long I'll want to teach in the Mission. Or even whether I'm needed there."

"Not needed? Of course you're needed. I can see it in the kids' faces and they way they talk about you. And Ben says the same thing."

She didn't know how to tell Travis that the kids at Potrero Elementary were the farthest thing from her mind at the moment. "A woman is more complicated than that."

Travis chuckled. "I guess I should know that by now."

"Travis..." She turned to him and met his gaze, which was one of sympathy rather than passion. "Oh, Travis!"

Travis, though sometimes slow to discern a woman's state of mind, was not a complete blockhead. He leaned over slowly, closed his eyes, and kissed her.

She responded by throwing her arms around his neck and pressing her lips hard against his.

"Whoa!" he said, briefly disengaging himself. "We men of the cloth are not expected to abandon ourselves to unrestrained passion."

"You're not a man of the cloth tonight," she said. "You're wearing a turtleneck. And I've restrained my passion for too long."

They kissed again, Emma with as much enthusiasm as before, and Travis with the same reluctance.

"Emma," he said, "I need to be absolutely candid with you."

"Aren't you always?"

"I've tried to be. But I've postponed telling you something you need to know.'

"Which is?"

"There's another woman in my life."

Emma wasn't sure whether he was joking or not. Was he about to say 'my mother' and then laugh it off? "What woman?"

"You met her recently at the school."

"Marcella Morgan?"

"The same."

"But I thought you and she were—Marcella Morgan? Travis, she's a big star now."

"I know it seems strange, but—"

It occurred to Emma that Travis was inventing the relationship in order to put her off. "I've never seen anything in the media about the two of you being together."

"The media are resourceful and persistent, but they know nothing of my relationship to Marcella."

"Travis—that was years ago. Are you still dating secretly?"

"It's not a secret, but it's not common knowledge, either. She flew into San Francisco recently to accept an award and, of course, contacted me. I asked her to marry me."

Emma felt as if she had been punched in the stomach. "And did she accept?"

"No. But she hasn't completely ruled it out."

"So...so you're waiting for her to eventually say yes?"

Travis reached for his glass of wine. "I suppose I am."

Emma leaned back in the sofa and gazed at the ceiling for a moment. Then she sat up again and looked Travis in the eye. "I've always thought of you as being so down to earth. Can't you see this is a...a kind of fantasy? Marcella Morgan! My goodness, Travis, she lives in a completely different world than you do. I see her photo in the tabloids at the supermarket almost every day. She has a different man on her arm each time. Stars like herself. Travis, it could never work!"

Travis avoided her gaze and rose to his feet. "You're probably right.

She is a star, and I'm merely a priest. But she's the same girl to me that I met on the streets of San Francisco nine or ten years ago when she was a mime performing for tips."

Emma rose, grasped him by the shoulders, and forced him to look at her. "Travis—I love you and she doesn't."

"But—"

"No! She doesn't. I don't even know her and I can see the kind of person she is better than you. She'll never marry you. She may not marry at all. And even if she does, it won't last long, and she'll marry someone else. But it will never be you."

Travis' eyes suddenly became watery with tears.

Emma threw her arms around him. "Oh, Travis! I'm sorry to be so blunt. But it's the truth. And I *do* love you. With all my heart."

By this time, she was crying as well. They both stood in that embrace, motionless, for perhaps a minute or so.

Then Travis slowly disengaged himself. He gave her a light kiss on the lips. "I'd better go, Emma. I've had a wonderful time with you tonight and I appreciate your being so...so forthright. But I need time to think things over. I'll keep in touch."

Then he headed for the door.

"Travis!" She followed him and he turned at the sound of his name. "I'm sorry. I'm sorry if I hurt you. It's the last thing I want to do. But you will call, won't you? Don't say, 'I'll keep in touch.' I know what that means."

Travis, whose tears had dried up, smiled at her. "It's a bad phrase. I *will* call you, Emma. Tomorrow and the next day. I promise." He gave her one last kiss. "Good night."

Emma watched as he closed the door behind him and stood staring as if she could see through it. Then she went to the sofa, lay down on it, and propped her head up with a pillow. Tears returned to her eyes but she made no sound as she allowed them to flow freely down her cheeks.

CHAPTER 50

Travis did indeed call Emma the next day, and the day after. In fact, it became a daily ritual and Emma seemed to replace Father Lattimore as his confidant.

Father Lattimore, however, was still to play an important role in Travis' life. One day he called Travis into his office for what he described as a serious matter.

Father Lattimore stood behind his desk and greeted him cordially, as usual. Then he invited him to sit down and handed him a letter.

"This is from a French colleague of mine that I met at a conference in Paris a few years ago," he said. "His name is Eugène Dupin. Read it."

Travis looked at Father Lattimore with some bewilderment and then began reading. It was in English:

> "My dear friend,
>
> It has been too many years since we met at the Ecclesiastical Conference at the American Cathedral in Paris. We did have a most agreeable tête-à-tête at dinner, did we not?
>
> I regret, however, that this much belated communication should also contain some troubling information. I have followed with interest the trial of Mr. Erskine as reported in the Parisian periodicals. It seems to me that the 'hung jury,' as you Americans say, was a result of an imperfect knowledge of Mr. Erskine's character.
>
> He was a guest of one of our socialist ministers after he fled Algeria, an event reported to me to have been due to Mr. Erskine's operating a criminal enterprise— drugs, of course—while a guest of that government.
>
> Our minister here, who shall remain unnamed, discovered that one afternoon while he was attending his official duties, Mr. Erskine raped his wife. In his own home. This fact has been corroborated by several witnesses, including members of the minister's domestic staff.

The minister, rather than suffering the embarrassment and humiliation of a public scandal, confronted Mr. Erskine and arranged to have him expelled from France without reporting the incident to the authorities.

I do not know what you can—or should—do with this information, but I understand that you are a man of some influence in San Francisco. If you can exert this influence to ensure that Mr. Erskine does not escape an appropriate punishment for one or more of his nefarious deeds—Lord knows (forgive the expression) that the list is long—it would go a considerable way to setting my conscience at ease. I simply cannot remain silent.

Again, forgive me for such a delayed correspondence, and for one so full of unpleasant news.

I hope that our next meeting in Paris will be a happy and fruitful one.

Affectionately yours,
Eugène Dupin"

Travis handed the letter back to Father Lattimore. "What should we do?"

"I think it would be a good idea for you to give Mr. Kelso a call." He handed Travis the telephone.

Travis dialed the number. Three, four, five rings. No answer. He put the receiver on the hook and handed the phone back to Lattimore. "It's a bit unusual for no one to answer. But maybe both Kelso and Vera are out and Erskine doesn't want to answer for fear of revealing his whereabouts."

Father Lattimore put the phone back on the desk. "Maybe. I think we should see for ourselves." He pushed a button on the intercom. "Mrs. Hamilton, I need for you to make a copy of some correspondence. Would you mind stepping into my office?"

Mrs. Hamilton appeared seconds later, took the letter, and returned with the copy and the original. Father Lattimore put the original in a desk drawer.

They took Travis' van and arrived at the front of Kelso's house about ten minutes later. Traffic was light. Against the opposite curb a black sedan was parked with no markings. This was the Daly City cop that Kelso had mentioned. He noted their presence as they got out of the van, then jotted something down on a notepad.

Travis was the first to arrive at the front door and pressed the bell. After a few moments, a blurry figure appeared in the translucent glass window of the door and the door slowly opened to reveal the figure was that of Erskine.

"Father Lattimore!" Erskine said. "And Father Carter. Won't you gentlemen come in?"

Travis hesitated, glanced at Lattimore, who nodded, and stepped into the house.

"Is Mr. Kelso home?" "Lattimore said.

"He's downtown at his office," Erskine said. "He's been covered up with new clients since the trial. Won't you have a seat? You know, Father Lattimore, I was just thinking about you. I have some questions about the Trinity. Maybe you could help me out."

"I'll do what I can," Lattimore said. "Where is Mrs. Kelso?"

"Oh, she's not feeling well. A rather severe headache. I think she has migraines."

"Can we see her?" Lattimore said.

Erskine seemed taken aback. "See her? I don't think she wants to see anyone right now. Why don't you gentlemen sit down? I'll make some coffee since Vera doesn't feel up to it." He then went into the kitchen to make the coffee.

Travis and Father Lattimore again exchanged glances and sat down in chairs opposite the coffee table. On the table there was a white leather Bible embossed in gold letters. Near the bottom were the initials 'L.E.'

Erskine returned from the kitchen with three cups of coffee and a couple of dainty ceramic bowls on a tray. He set the tray down on the table. "Help yourself, gentlemen. I like mine black, but there's plenty of sugar and milk."

Lattimore stood up abruptly. "We must see Mrs. Kelso."

"I *told* you, Father—"

"This is serious business, Erskine. Where is her bedroom?"

Erskine seemed stunned for a moment, then pointed to the ceiling. "Upstairs. First room on the right. But I don't think she's in any mood to talk."

"We'll see. You stay here with Mr. Erskine, Travis." Lattimore then went into the foyer and started up the stairs, but stopped about halfway up. "On second thought, I'll stay here with Mr. Erskine and you see about Mrs. Kelso." He came back down the stairs to the parlor.

Travis was nonplused for a moment, then realizing why Father Lattimore changed course, ascended the stairs.

"What's this all about, Father?" Erskine said.

"I received a letter from a colleague in Paris this morning. He says that you left Paris under less than favorable circumstances."

"Oh, that," Erskine said, as if the reported incident were a trifle. "No wonder you're worried. Well, I can tell you that whatever allegations Minister Faucher has made against me are false. Yes, I did have an affair with his wife, but she was more than willing. They had been sleeping in separate bedrooms for years."

"Even if that's true," Lattimore said, "don't you think having an affair with the wife of your host is a gross abuse of his hospitality?"

Erskine shrugged. "I can't help it if women are attracted to me, Father. But I have to say that since I've become a Christian—"

A rapid thumping sound was heard as Travis trotted down the stairs and reentered the parlor. "She's crying. And she has bruises on both forearms."

"She likes to work in the garden out back," Erskine said. "Probably banged them against a rake handle in the tool shed or something. There's no light in there."

"Travis," Lattimore said, "ask that detective out front to step in here, would you?"

Erskine exchanged glances with Travis, and again shrugged, "You're making a mountain out of a mole hill, Father. I've done nothing wrong."

Travis went downstairs to the street and returned with the Daly City policeman who had been parked at the curb.

"What can I do for you, Father?" he said.

"It appears that Mr. Erskine here," Lattimore said, "has raped Mrs.

Kelso. Travis, if you'll escort officer—"

"Pryor," the policeman said. He was a young man, athletic-looking and not yet thirty. "James Pryor."

"Escort Officer Pryor upstairs so that he can interview Mrs. Kelso."

Travis led the way and they entered Vera's bedroom.

While the 'interview' was being conducted, Father Lattimore stood staring at Erskine as if he were a deadly snake about to strike at any moment.

"You've got this all wrong, Father," Erskine said, his palms out as if in supplication. "You're going to end up looking very foolish."

At this point the front door opened and Ted Kelso stepped in. He was dressed in a pinstriped suit and carrying a briefcase. He stared first at Erskine, who shrugged his shoulders, then at Lattimore. "What's going on here?"

"To put it bluntly, Mr. Kelso," Lattimore said, "your wife has been assaulted. Travis and Officer Pryor are upstairs with her now."

Kelso stared at Lattimore for a moment in disbelief, then at Erskine, who simply turned away. Then he dropped his briefcase on the floor and ran up the stairs.

He found Travis and Officer Pryor standing at the foot of the bed when he entered the room. They turned to look at him. Vera was on the bed fully clothed in a brightly-colored gingham dress that she often wore around the house and in the garden. She said that it reminded her of her rural origins in Russia.

Kelso brushed by Travis and sat on the bed next to her.

She opened her eyes and threw her arms around him. "Oh, Ted! I'm so sorry!"

"Sorry? Don't be sorry, Vera. You've done nothing wrong. Tell me what happened."

Vera looked around at Travis and Officer Pryor. "Nothing. Nothing happened."

Kelso turned to the two men. "Would you mind, gentlemen?"

Travis nodded and he and Pryor left the room.

"Now tell me, Vera," Kelso said, "what did Erskine do to you/"

"Oh, Ted—" She began sobbing again.

"Vera—this is important. What did he do?"

Vera maintained her tight embrace around Kelso's shoulders. "He said he'd kill me if I said anything."

"He won't be killing anybody. He's going to jail. Did he rape you?"

Vera loosened her embrace and wiped the tears from her eyes. She nodded in the affirmative.

Kelso brought her to his shoulder again. "All right. You've got to press charges. And you've got to let a doctor examine you. You won't have to go to the Hall of Justice. I can arrange for an exam at UC Hospital. Are these the clothes you were wearing?"

She nodded.

"You've got bruises on your arms." He stood up and called the men back inside. "Officer Pryor, I want you to arrest Mr. Erskine downstairs and take him to the Hall of Justice. I'll phone Judge Hulsey and let him know the situation."

"What's the charge, Mr. Kelso?"

"Sexual assault. Travis and I will be taking Vera to the University of California Hospital on Parnassus for a medical exam. If you would, call a female officer to attend her there."

"Yes, sir." Pryor started for the door.

"And Pryor—"

"Yes, sir?"

"Get him out of my sight as quickly as you can. I'll wait here for five minutes, no longer."

"Yes, sir."

Pryor left the room and descended the stairs.

"Travis, " Kelso said, "can she lie down in your van?"

"Sure. I'll just—"

"I can sit up, Ted," Vera said. "I'm all right. I just don't want to see him."

"You won't. Not until he appears in court, anyway." Kelso looked at Travis. "See if he's gone, will you?"

Travis descended the stairs just in time to see Pryor escorting Erskine to the front door with his hands cuffed behind his back. Father Lattimore stood in the middle of the parlor watching.

Suddenly, Erskine stopped and looked over his shoulder. "My Bible. I need my Bible."

Lattimore looked at the elegant white Bible with its gold lettering resting on the coffee table. He went over, picked it up and delivered it into the outstretched hand of Pryor. "I recommend that you go back and start at the beginning, Erskine. First Corinthians."

Erskine stared at Lattimore for a moment before Pryor pushed him forward through the door.

CHAPTER 51

While Lonnie Erskine languished in the Daly City jail awaiting the results of Vera's medical exam, Travis continued to fulfill his duties both to the parishioners of Grace Cathedral and Potrero Elementary School.

One afternoon at soccer practice Emma, as usual, watched from the bleachers and waited for Travis to come and sit beside her.

"Do you like French cooking?" she said.

"Of course. What do you have in mind?"

"I thought you might like to have dinner at my apartment. I took a cooking class at Foothill Community College last summer."

"And your mother is a terrific cook."

Emma laughed. "I'm not up to her standards yet. But I've gotten pretty good at it. Are you willing to take a chance?"

"Sure. When?"

"How about Saturday night—say sevenish?"

Travis rubbed his chin. "I've got two weddings and a funeral Saturday. How about eightish?"

"Eightish sounds perfect. It'll give me more time to shop and get ready."

"Eightish it is."

Saturday night arrived and Travis, dog-tired, took what was intended to be a short nap and woke up at 7:45pm. He called Emma, apologized for his tardiness, showered, shaved, dressed and headed for her apartment.

By the time he arrived it was eight-thirty. "Sorry."

"Don't be. I needed more time that I thought. Especially since I burned the escargot."

Travis laughed and sat down on the sofa. "I was never wild about snails, anyway."

"Oh, but I went to the store and got some more. They came out perfectly."

"In that case, I'll give them a try. Smells good, whatever it is. Can I help?"

"Well...you could toss the salad. The duck won't be ready for another hour."

"An hour?"

"I forgot you had to de-bone it."

Travis rose and took off his jacket. "Well, point me to the kitchen. Have you got a spinner?"

"A spinner? Oh, no—you need to do it by hand. Come on, I'll show you."

Travis entered the kitchen and saw what looked like a chef's paradise but for the small size of the room. An industrial gas oven, large stainless steel refrigerator, a forest of cooking tools hanging from iron hooks suspended above a center island, and an array of professional-looking cutlery parked in a wooden block.

"You'll need an apron," she said.

Once adorned with the apron, Travis set about tossing the salad, which, according to Emma's instructions, consisted of cutting up various ingredients with a special pair of scissors and a small knife. Emma tended to several pots on the burners and periodically opened the oven to baste the duck with an orange sauce she had made from scratch.

Once the duck was ready, she turned down the dining room lights and lit two candles set in a pair of silver candlesticks on the table. Travis took on the responsibility of uncorking an expensive Bordeaux Emma had purchased and the preparations were—almost— complete.

"I forgot the music." She jumped up from her chair and put on an LP of Mozart's violin concertos. She sat down again.

Travis raised his glass and smiled at her across the table. "Bon appétit!"

They clicked their glasses together and Travis received a torrent of French in return for his feeble effort at the language. "What did you say?"

"I said, 'May you enjoy good health and a long life.'"

"Oh,"

The dinner was delicious except for the snails, as far as Travis was concerned, which were made more palatable by a rich béarnaise sauce.

By the time they were finished with dinner and had cleaned up, it was nearly eleven p.m.

"Terrific meal," Travis said. "I think you've even surpassed your mother."

"Oh, you haven't tried her poulet à la Bretonne yet."

"What's that?"

"Chicken—from Brittany, where she grew up."

"Oh, well, in the meantime I think I'll have another glass of red wine."

"Would you like to, uh, watch television or something?"

Travis looked at his watch. "Wow—already eleven. Sure. Johnny Carson's on."

Emma turned on the TV and they sat together on the sofa as the nineteen-inch screen flickered to life.

Travis put his arm around her and she snuggled against his shoulder as Johnny launched into his monologue. After warming up his audience with a few jokes he took his seat, bantered with Ed McMahon for a few minutes, and introduced his first guest: Marcella Morgan.

She entered the set dressed in a chic form-fitting dress, something akin to a sari, bowed to the audience as they applauded and whistled, and sat down.

Travis was transfixed by her image on the screen and absently put his glass down on the coffee table.

Emma was mortified. She glanced at Travis each time Marcella made a witty remark or laughed at Johnny's.

"I understand you started out as a street mime in San Francisco," Johnny said.

"It was the only way I could pay the rent at the time," Marcella said.

Both Johnny and the audience laughed.

"And your tuition, too, I suppose," Johnny said. "Weren't you in college then?"

"That's right. San Francisco State. I was a theater major."

"And so you started acting in plays?"

Marcella looked upward as if recalling those days. "I did. In fact, the first play I was in was in San Francisco."

"And what play was that?"

"The very play that my next movie is adapted from."

"You mean *Alexander and the Bactrian Princess*?"

"It had a different title at the time. It was called *Alexander in Babylon*: *The Last Days of a Conqueror*."

Johnny turned his trademark baleful stare to the camera. "Where the heck is Bactria? Shouldn't they go back to the original title?"

The audience laughed, as did Marcella and Ed.

"I liked the original title, too," she said. "But the producers wanted to emphasize the romantic angle."

Johnny stared at her for a moment and again turned to the camera. "Bactria? It sounds like some place you'd want to avoid if you value your health."

This elicited more laughter from the audience.

"I think it's in Afghanistan," Marcella said.

"And was it shot on location?"

"It was shot in Southern California," she said. "About twenty miles from Burbank."

"I wondered where all those arrows in my front yard came from," Johnny said with a deadpan expression. "Fortunately, the lawn guy called in sick that day."

Ed roared with laughter at this remark and the audience responded with an even louder roar. Marcella suddenly seemed sheepish, as if she were being made the butt of Johnny's jokes.

But then Johnny asked her if she would perform one of her mime routines. Marcella readily agreed, and went back stage as the set was darkened. Moments later, she appeared in a spotlight wearing her leotards, candy-striped shirt and whiteface makeup.

As she went through her routine, Emma watched not her, but Travis, who was thoroughly engrossed in Marcella's performance.

At the end of the show, Emma got up and switched off the set. "She is marvelous, isn't she?"

Travis continued to stare at the darkened screen. "Yes. She's very talented."

There was an awkward silence as Emma tried to suppress the tears welling up in her eyes.

Travis rose from the sofa and yawned. "I'd better get back to my apartment before I'm too sleepy to drive, Emma. It was a wonderful meal."

"I'm so glad you enjoyed it." She rose and wiped away a tear.

"What's wrong?"

"Nothing. Nothing at all. I'm tired, too, Travis. You don't mind letting yourself out, do you?"

Travis put his arms around her. "You were right, you know. Marcella and I live in different worlds now."

"But the way you look at her—it was like I wasn't even in the room."

"I didn't mean to ignore you. It was just a surprise to see her on Johnny Carson. It was difficult not to watch."

Emma said nothing for a few moments. "Would you like to stay here, tonight? I know you're tired and—"

"Emma—don't rush this. I don't want to deceive you. Yes, Marcella is still on my mind, and it will take some time before I can move on. I hope you understand."

Emma cleared away what she hoped was the last tear and met his gaze. "I'm not sure I do. Will you be coaching the kids next week?"

"I will. We have a game with Mission Elementary. I'll see you Tuesday." He gave her a kiss on the cheek and started to leave, but she pulled him back and kissed him passionately on the lips.

Travis pulled away. "I'll see you Tuesday." He went to the door and let himself out without looking back.

CHAPTER 52

Vera Mandlikova rarely ventured out of the house while Lonnie Erskine awaited trial on rape charges at the Hall of Justice. He had been transferred there from Daly City on orders of Judge Hulsey, who had delayed sentencing for the attempted kidnapping charge. But the most recent charge was far more serious. He could get anywhere from twenty years to life if convicted.

Vera spent most of her days in the little garden behind the house while Ted was at work. Ted had hired a maid to take care of the cleaning and some of the cooking, though Vera still liked to prepare the traditional meals of her homeland, and took pride in this.

Her greatest source of pride, however, was the garden, especially her orchids. The San Francisco climate seemed to agree with them, and every variety imaginable thrived there. But there were other species as well, including roses, daffodils, periwinkles, nasturtiums, tulips, and African lilies. There were fruit trees like Japanese persimmon, pear, orange, and fig. She had recently acquired a willow, which she intended to plant adjacent to a Japanese bridge over a pond yet to built. She would need a professional landscaper to do this, but neither she nor Ted were ready to have a strange man there with her while Ted was at work.

Black men were particularly disturbing to her whenever she encountered one on the street or in the grocery store, which is why she rarely went out. Not that there were many black men in this part of San Francisco, but there was always the chance encounter.

She knew that the fact that a man with African features had nothing to do with whether he was a criminal or a saint, but the association with Erskine was still there. She had nightmares in which a black man, usually but not always looking like Erskine, attacked her, clawed at her like a wild animal, and threatened her with a weapon. She would try to cry for help, but the words would not come out. Finally, with great effort, she would awaken and sit up in bed, sweating and moaning like a sick calf.

It got so that she and Ted had to sleep in separate bedrooms. For when she had one of these nightmares—which were nearly every night—it was Ted who could not get back to sleep, not her.

She was happy in the garden, but when darkness fell and she retreated to the house, an ineffable sadness nearly overwhelmed her. It made little difference that the maid, a Chinese woman named Li, was there to keep her company. Li spoke English in a kind of patois that she had difficulty understanding. They could communicate about cooking well enough, but there was no possibility of Li becoming a confidante.

Vera, in fact, had few female friends. Most of the women she knew at the Soviet Embassy had returned to Russia, anticipating Gorbachev's *perestroika*. She attended a meeting of the San Francisco Russian-American Society, but found the members to be stodgy and nostalgic for a Russia they never knew. She played no sports. She had no hobbies other than reading and gardening.

Ted usually got home about six o'clock and Li stayed until he arrived, or sometimes later if she was preparing the meal that night.

At dinner they spoke of anything but Erskine.

"How's the garden going?" Ted said as they were being served a chicken and rice dish by Li.

"The orchids are beautiful," Vera said. "You should come out and look at them in the morning before you leave for work."

"I don't have time. But I'll make a point of it on Saturday."

They ate in silence for several minutes.

"Perhaps we could go on a picnic Saturday," Vera said.

Kelso looked up. "That's a great idea. You need to get out. How about Mt. Tamalpais? It should be beautiful this time of year."

"Yes. That would be nice."

"I'll pick up a bottle of wine on the way home Friday. I could also stop at the grocery store and—"

"Li will do the shopping. I'll tell her what to get."

They continued eating.

"Ted..."

"Yes?"

"I've missed my period."

Kelso put his fork down. "You're pregnant?"

"I don't know. Sometimes it's a false alarm."

Kelso continued eating for a few moments and again put his utensils down. "It could be mine."

"Yes. Possibly."

He pushed his plate away. "If not, you'll have to get an abortion."

"Of course. It is a routine procedure these days. Very safe."

"Thank goodness."

Li came and took their plates away and Kelso rose from his chair. "I've got some work to do, Vera. I'll be in the study for the next couple of hours. Do you need anything?"

"No. I'll be fine. I think I'll do some reading."

"I'll come and knock on your door before I turn in."

"That would be nice."

Kelso dropped his napkin on the table next to his plate and retired to the study.

Vera remained seated, staring at the centerpiece of the table, which was a sterling silver samovar her mother had sent her from Russia as a wedding gift. The bottom was stamped with the imperial crest of the Russian royal family, but then many pieces of silver had such marks that had never seen the inside of the Tsar's household. Nevertheless, tears came to her eyes as she recalled images of her grandfather's farm near Smolensk, where she visited every summer as a child. Her grandfather had been a footman for the Romanovs as a young man and fiercely defended their summer palace until arrested and imprisoned by the Bolsheviks. Ultimately, he was released after declaring his allegiance to the Communist Party and sent to the countryside to join a collective. Somehow he managed to return to the Romanovs' estate and recover the samovar. Or at least, that was the family story.

This reminiscence led to more tears until Li came back into the dining room and she wiped them away with a napkin.

"What's wrong, Missy?" Li said.

"Nothing, Li. Just some fond memories. I shouldn't be crying about happy times, should I?"

Li picked up her plate. "I cry, too, sometimes—about China. When I was a little girl. But it a nice cry—you like desert? I have some lemon tarts in the oven. Very good."

"No thank you, Li. I'm sure they're delicious, though. Save them for me for later."

"Yes, Missy."

Vera retired to her bedroom where she sat at her desk and wrote a letter to her mother in Moscow. Her mother was a minor bureaucrat in the Ministry of Culture. Her father, a pilot with Aeroflot, died in an unexplained crash in the Ural Mountains years earlier. She wrote in the Cyrillic script that she had learned as a child:

Dear Mama,

I have many things to tell you since my last letter so many months ago. I apologize for my dereliction and offer no excuses. I will write more regularly in the future.

Since my marriage to Ted, much has happened. There has been a shake-up at the embassy and I am no longer working there. Many of my co-workers have returned to Moscow, as you must be aware. Ted has a very good law practice with a major San Francisco law firm. He seems to have more business than he can handle. We are very comfortable in a nice neighborhood called Pacific Heights.

How are Pyotr and Ekaterina? And their families? I have not seen Dmitri and Alexander since they were small children. They must be ready for University by now.

Mama, I must also tell you about something not so pleasant. Not long ago, I was attacked by a very cruel man. He was one of Ted's clients. Ted and I were foolish enough to let him stay in our house. Oh, so foolish! But now I am all right and the man is in jail awaiting trial. Please do not worry about this. I must emphasize that I was not seriously injured, only a few bruises.

My only worry is that Ted seems to be drifting away from me. Is this not normal in such circumstances? I suspect it is, as men do not like their women to be considered 'damaged goods.' But oh, Mama, I am not damaged!

I am grateful that you are so sympathetic and un-

derstanding a mother. You always have been.

When this bad man has been put away in prison for good, Ted and I will come and visit you in Moscow. Travel will be much easier now that Mr. Gorbachev is implementing his 'glasnost' and 'perestroika.'

I love you, Mama.

Your Vera

She read the letter over again and, satisfied with it, folded it and sealed it in an envelope. Then she undressed for bed.

She sat against several pillows for the next two hours reading her favorite novel, *Anna Karenina*. She had read it perhaps six or seven times since childhood, but each time she found something new, or something she had missed. Anna, to her, was the most noble—and saddest—heroine of all literature. Somehow Anna's sadness and grim fate gave her courage and hope.

About ten o'clock there was a knock on her door.

"Ted?"

"Are you awake?"

"Of course. Come in."

The door opened and Ted, who had removed his jacket and loosened his tie, stepped in and came to her side.

"What are you reading?"

"*Anna Karenina.*"

He sighed. "Wouldn't you prefer something cheerier? Say, Gogol or Chekhov?"

"Anna is like my best friend. My confidante."

Kelso smiled and gave her a kiss. "Can't I be your confidant?"

"You *are* my confidant. But a male confidant. A woman needs a feminine confidante as well."

"Ah. Then there are some things a man cannot understand."

"I wouldn't say that exactly. Let's just say that women understand things differently."

He seemed nonplused for a moment, then made a show of yawning. "I guess I'll turn in." As he stood and started for the door, Vera called to him.

"Ted?"

"Yes, Vera?"

"Couldn't you sleep here tonight? With me?"

"I...well, I'm very tired, Vera. And I've got to get up early for a pretrial hearing. Maybe tomorrow night."

"Yes. Tomorrow night might be better."

He yawned again. "Well, good night, Vera. I'll see you in the morning."

"Good night, Ted."

He left and closed the door softly behind him.

She stared at the closed door for several moments and then went back to her novel.

CHAPTER 53

Vera awoke Saturday morning feeling refreshed and eager to join Ted in their picnic adventure on Mt. Tamalpais. Her nightmares had subsided and she had slept well the two previous nights.

She brushed her hair and put on an embroidered silk caftan before venturing out into the garden to tend to her orchids. They never needed much water in San Francisco's moist climate, but it had become a ritual to fill the watering can and check on each plant to see whether the soil had become too dry overnight. In spite of the ever-present mist, a steady breeze rolled in from the Pacific and could dry everything out, especially once the sun was up.

She even induced Ted to come out and look at the progress of the garden after breakfast.

"They're lovely," he said, as she pointed out the different varieties.

"Those are pink dendrobiums," she said, with pride. "The pink ones are Phalaenopsis and the deep purple ones are Miltoniopsis— some people call them pansy orchids."

Kelso smiled. "I like the plain old white ones."

"Those are of the Phalaenopsis variety, too. Phalaenopsis Aphrodite, to be exact."

Kelso grinned and gave her a kiss on the cheek. "You've become a real authority. And your Greek is nearly as good as your English."

She laughed for the first time since the 'incident.' I only know a few names of flowers. But I did study Greek for two years at the gymnasium."

"And to think I only speak English. We Americans are spoiled in expecting everybody else to speak our language."

"*I* am an American, Ted."

"Of course you are. I sometimes forget that you're a naturalized citizen now. We'd better hurry if we're going to beat the crowds. And wear some sturdy shoes—we'll be hiking over rough terrain."

Li had prepared a picnic basket replete with fried chicken, yams, egg rolls, piroshki, brie, crackers and smoked ham. Ted contributed the bottle of Rhone wine he had picked up at a wine shop the night before.

By the time they got to the south entrance of the Golden Gate, the fog had lifted and the bridge glowed a burnt orange in the morning sunlight.

Vera gazed out over the bay and thought she had never seen such a beautiful sight. "You know, I've never been on the bridge before. It's quite spectacular."

"Really? I guess it's my fault. I've been so busy, I hadn't thought to show you the sights."

"I was always busy, too, at the embassy. And they didn't want us to travel outside of the city.

"Soviet paranoia. Things will be different now."

"I hope so."

They crossed the bridge and continued on 101 past Sausalito until they got to the turnoff to Mr. Tam. The first stop was the entrance to the Muir Woods, where Ted parked the car and they hiked through the redwoods up to Bohemian Grove. They sat on a bench and gazed up at the majestic trees.

"The beauty of this area is unimaginable," she said. "There's nothing like in Russia."

"Oh, I don't know," Ted said. "Russia's a very big place. But you're probably right. There's nothing like these trees anywhere else on earth."

They sat in silence for some moments, Ted with his hands on the edge of the bench, their bodies not touching.

"Ted."

"Yes, Vera?"

"We haven't talked of...the incident since that night."

Kelso leaned back against the back of the bench and put his hands behind his head. He looked up to the tops of the trees. "Would you like to talk about it?"

"I think so."

"All right. Feel free."

"That's just the problem. I don't feel free. I feel like a wounded bird in a cage."

He sat up and put his arm around her. "I'm sorry, Vera. But I don't know how to help you. That's one reason I suggested we get out of the city and explore the area. I thought it might help you to heal."

"Yes. That was very thoughtful of you. I think it is helping, but..."

"But what?"

"It's more than simply taking in the fresh air and drinking in all this natural beauty. It's...it's us."

"Us?"

"You don't seem to want to touch me."

"I'm touching you now."

"Yes. Only now."

Kelso expelled a breath of air, not as a sigh, but as an expression of frustration. He removed his arm from her shoulder. "I'm trying, Vera. But it works both ways. You seem reluctant to touch *me*."

She turned to him. "I? I not touch you?" She turned away again and stared at the trees. "Yes...I suppose you're right. I was afraid to at first. I didn't know how you would react. But then I did reach out...and I looked into your eyes and saw...indifference."

"Indifference? Vera, I could never be indifferent to you. Here—hold my hand."

Vera looked cautiously out of the corner of her eye at him, then down at his outstretched hand. She reached for it slowly until the two met and Ted grasped hers in a gentle grip. They sat for several minutes like that, neither looking at the other.

"Why don't we walk back to the car," he said. "We can drive up to the top of the mountain and maybe find a picnic table with a view."

"Yes. All right." She turned to him and forced a smile.

He smiled back and they rose from the bench.

They drove up the Panoramic Highway, winding around the mountain, until they reached the East Peak, at more than 2500 feet above sea level. There were a number of picnic tables available since it was still rather early for lunch. They chose one that overlooked the East Bay, though it seemed to be a considerable distance away.

"Actually," Kelso said, "I think the view on the Pacific side is better. And they've got some hang glider sites there, too. We could watch those idiots jump off the cliff and see if they kill themselves."

"That's not funny, Ted. What if one of them did?"

"You're right. I'd feel awful if it happened. But it's not likely. I think this Chateauneuf-du-Pape will go well with the smoked ham."

"And don't forget the piroshki."

"Of course not. Your specialty. Well, let's get started."

While they were unpacking the basket and Vera was spreading a tablecloth over the redwood table, a couple of young hikers appeared at the top of a trail and surveyed the picnic area. The woman was a very attractive brunette with high cheekbones and a deep tan from prolonged exposure to the sun. She wore cutoff jeans and a sweaty T-shirt that clung to the nipples of her melon-sized breasts. Her boyfriend was a good-looking kid wearing cargo shorts and a T-shirt that pictured a pair of ducks in midair, one mounted to the other from the rear with the caption, 'Fly United' beneath.

"Mind if we share the table with you?" the girl said. She was already removing her backpack before receiving an answer.

"Not at all," Kelso said.

Vera noticed that his eyes were focused on the girl's breasts as he said this.

"I'm Bob," the young man said, extending his hand. "And this is Chelsea. You hike up here from Muir Woods?"

"I'm Ted and this is Vera. No, I'm afraid not. We drove."

Bob took off his backpack and dumped it on the ground. "Oh, man! You don't know what you're missing. We came up the—what's the name of that trail, honey?"

"Fern Creek," Chelsea said.

"Yeah, that's it. I mean, it's spectacular. I got some steam beer if you want some."

"Thanks," Kelso said. "We'll stick with the wine. You're welcome to have some, though."

Bob and Chelsea went about preparing their end of the table as Vera and Ted watched. Their backpacks seemed to have a bottomless capacity for food, beverages, utensils, and—frisbees. As if they hadn't had enough exercise hiking up the mountain, they went to a grassy area near the summit and tossed a frisbee back and forth, often going perilously close to the edge of the cliff adjacent to the picnic area.

Ted watched Chelsea's every move as she ran after the frisbee, leaped up to catch it, and spun it back to Bob. And Vera watched Ted.

After fifteen minutes or so of this, Bob and Chelsea came back to the table and began eating their sandwiches, pasta salad and hummus. They ate rapidly, exchanged inside jokes and paid little attention to their table mates. After washing everything down with the steam beer, they went back to the grassy area where they'd been playing with the frisbee and laid out a blanket. And even though there were several couples about, some with children, Chelsea removed her T-shirt and laid on her back to soak up the sun. Bob did the same.

"I think we'd better leave," Vera said. She noted that Ted's eyes had never left Chelsea since he began watching her play with the frisbee. "You'd think she would have some modesty in front of the children."

Kelso merely smiled, still staring at Chelsea's breasts as they absorbed the sun's rays. "Oh, I don't know. What's wrong with going *au naturel?*' Life as Nature intended. I think this younger generation has the right idea."

"I think that's a very naive point of view," Vera said. "She's inviting men to take advantage of her."

"She doesn't strike me as the type to allow that to happen if she doesn't want it to." Ted had briefly taken his eyes off of Chelsea as he said this. He was now looking at Vera, who flushed red.

"Do you think *I* allowed that—incident—to happen to me?" she said.

"No, of course not. Vera, you're—"

"You might as well enjoy one last look, Ted. I'm going back to the car." She abruptly rose and left the table without packing up the basket or removing the tablecloth.

"Vera—" Kelso glanced over at Bob and Chelsea as he stood. They were beginning to make love, kissing, fondling one another, and removing their shorts. "Good Lord." He started packing up the basket, tossing the plates and utensils into it, and folded the tablecloth. By this time Bob and Chelsea were having intercourse and several other couples, especially the ones with children, were moving away.

He went back to the car and put the picnic basket and tablecloth in the trunk. When he got into the driver's seat, Vera was staring straight ahead with her arms folded over her chest. "I think you're right, Vera. Those kids have stepped over the line." He didn't mention that 'those kids' were now having sexual intercourse.

Vera said nothing as he pulled out of the parking lot and headed down Ridgecrest Boulevard towards the ocean.

"I think you'll really enjoy watching these hang gliders," he said. "It's as close as man can come to actually flying."

Vera remained silent.

After a few minutes they came to another parking area off of Ridgecrest. Kelso parked the car and looked at her, still staring straight ahead. "I'm sorry, Vera. I didn't mean to imply that you in anyway encouraged Erskine to come on to you. I don't believe that for a second."

Vera continued to stare ahead in silence.

"Can you forgive me?"

Vera remained motionless for a few seconds and then a faint smile came to her lips. At last she looked at him. "I forgive you."

Kelso smiled and took her hand in his. "Come on—let's see what the hang gliders are doing. It's just a short walk."

They got out of the car and walked the quarter of a mile or so to the first hang glider site. There was a ridge there that overlooked Stinson Beach and the vast Pacific beyond.

Two men and a woman were standing at the edge buckling on the harnesses that would suspend them from the gliders. Kelso went over and started talking to one of the men.

Vera drank in the beauty of the scene, her eyes focused first on the scrub brush and rocks at the foot of the cliff and then the beach and finally the ocean.

"How do you keep from stalling out?" Kelso asked the man, who was wearing an orange helmet and sunglasses. He looked to be about forty.

The man laughed. "Stalling? What's that?"

"I don't know much about flying," Kelso said, "but I read somewhere that a stall is when an airplane, or glider, loses lift. Because it's going too slow."

"It's not because the craft is going too slow," the man said, "but because the angle of attack is too high for the airspeed. Like this." He tilted the glider's wings upward, allowed them to flutter in the breeze for a moment, and then tilted them sharply downward. "That's how you recover. Dive and gain airspeed. Hardly anybody in hang gliding buys the farm due to a stall. Watch that guy."

Kelso turned and watched the other man standing on the crest of the ridge. After testing his controls, he suddenly leapt off the cliff. For a moment, he dropped out of sight.

"Christ!" Kelso said. "Is he all right?"

"Airborne. See?"

Sure enough the glider appeared again and began climbing on an updraft.

"Still," Kelso said. "It's a little scary."

"After the first time the butterflies go away. Hey! You better tell your lady there not to get too close to the edge—"

Kelso looked over at Vera, who was indeed standing very close to the edge, only about twenty yards from where the first glider had taken off. "Vera! Don't stand so close." He started walking toward her. "Vera—it's dangerous. Besides, you'll get in the—"

Suddenly she dropped from sight.

Kelso rushed to the edge of the cliff, thinking that she had slipped and fallen, perhaps only a few feet from the ridge. But when he got to the edge he saw that she had fallen at least a hundred feet. She looked like a rag doll, crumpled over a large rock.

"Vera!"

Several people rushed over to the edge where she had been standing, including the hang glider, who unbuckled his harness and tried to restrain Kelso from hopping over the edge.

 "Don't go down there!" The man said. "There're a lot of loose rocks."

But Kelso kept making his way down the steep slope, hanging on to a branch here, a shrub there, until he reached Vera's lifeless body.

CHAPTER 54

Travis stood on the sidewalk on Green Street looking up at the façade of Holy Trinity Cathedral. It was a compact structure, barely a third the size of Grace Cathedral, but it had an imposing presence nevertheless. The architecture might be called Byzantine, with an irregular assortment of domes, cupolas, and balustrades, while the overall effect was one of a monastery tucked away on some remote mountaintop.

"I suppose we'd better go in," he said to Emma, who was standing at his side, dressed appropriately in black, as were most of the other women.

"Will the service be in Russian?" she said.

"We'll find out."

They climbed the steep stairs to the entry where they were met by a priest dressed in bright green and gold vestments with a matching crown-like mitre. He greeted them in unaccented English.

"Welcome," he said, and indicated the open door.

Once in the nave, they encountered Ben and Thuy, who seemed relieved to see them.

"Kind of weird, huh?" Ben said.

"Compared to what?" Travis said.

"That's a point. A Buddhist temple is even spookier."

"Temples are supposed to be spooky," Thuy said. "To make an impression."

"Yeah, they do that," Ben said.

The four of them were escorted by an usher to one of the middle rows. As they took their seats and knelt down to pray, Travis spotted Kelso sitting in the front row near the aisle, his head bowed. On the altar not five feet away was a bronze urn which Travis assumed were the ashes of Vera.

Kelso was dressed in a charcoal grey suit and mauve tie. He looked thinner than usual. Beside him sat a middle-aged blond woman, somewhat stout, who Travis had never seen before.

The 'spookiness' that Ben had spoken of evaporated when the priest stepped up to the pulpit and the lights were raised. The shadows disappeared to reveal an almost garish array of colors: blue, green, red, and especially gold. Handpainted icons adorned a large wooden panel behind the altar.

The priest who had greeted them at the door spoke first in Russian, then translated it into English. Much was said about Vera's idealism and compassion, especially for orphans in Russia for whom she had established a fund to educate and bring to the United States to live with foster families.

After the service, Travis and the others approached Kelso to offer their condolences.

"Thank you," Kelso said. "Thank you for your sympathy. This is Olga Mandlikova, Vera's mother."

"Very kind of you," Olga said. "Very kind. Vera was my—how do you say it—my rock and roll star."

This comment was met by puzzled looks.

"Is not right?" she said. "My shooting star?"

"She means Vera was the accomplished one in the family," Kelso said with a faint smile. "Kind of like a rock star."

"Yes, yes—that's right." Olga then wiped a tear away. "My English is not so good. Not so many opportunities to speak it in Moscow. Especially the idiots."

"She means 'idioms,'" Ted said.

"Yes, of course. The idioms." Olga seemed to compose herself. "Vera was sweet girl. Always helping people." Then she began to cry again and Ted escorted her to the front of the church.

"That son of a bitch murdered her," Ben said.

"What?" Travis said.

"Erskine. He murdered Vera just as sure as he murdered Dan Watt. Not that I'll miss Dan Watt, but I'll miss Vera. Like her mother said, she was a sweet woman."

No one disputed Ben's characterization of Vera, and the group moved to the front door as the organist began playing a fugue by Shostakovich.

"Do we go to the cemetery now?" Ben said.

"There won't be a burial," Travis said. "The city of San Francisco no longer allows it. She'll be interred at the Columbarium."

"What the heck is a columbarium?"

"Like a crematorium. They put the remains in a little niche with a plaque beneath it. It's near Stanyan Street in the Richmond District. Not far."

"Do we have to go?" Ben said. "I've had enough spookiness for a while."

Travis smiled. "No, you don't have to go. But I think Emma and I will."

"It's hard enough to get him to go to the Temple," Thuy said. "Kicking and screaming like a little boy."

Ben muttered something unintelligible.

Thuy laughed and put her arm in his. "We see you for dinner soon. At our house."

"Looking forward to it," Travis said.

By this time Travis and Emma were standing on the sidewalk, watching the crowd disperse.

"You don't have to go with me to the Columbarium if you don't want to," he said.

Emma put her arm into his. "I want to go wherever you go."

"Emma—this is the nineteenth funeral I've either attended or officiated at this year. Are you sure you want this kind of life?"

She smiled broadly. "I'm sure."

Travis stared at her for a moment. "I've never met anyone so sure of what she wants."

She laughed. "It runs in the family. Dad was sure he wanted to leave France and come to America and he never looked back. Mom was sure she wanted to be with him and she never looked back. And her father owned a castle in Brittany."

"A castle? Really?"

"Well, not exactly a castle. A villa, you might call it. But her dad had lots of money and she never asked him for a sous."

"You frighten me sometimes, Emma."

They walked to the van parked around the corner on Union Street and headed for the Columbarium.

The Columbarium was an even more imposing edifice than Holy Trinity. It was more or less a rotunda with neoclassical entrances on two sides and a large copper dome.

They stepped inside and saw the priest, Kelso, and Mrs. Manlikova standing near the door to one of the rooms that radiated from the center. Some sort of official was with them.

Travis and Emma approached them, but remained silent as the priest said a few words in Russian. Then the official took the bronze urn and entered the room with it. They all followed him into the room, which contained a stained glass window depicting three angels in flight. The official placed the urn in a small niche, which already had a plaque beneath it with Vera's name, date of birth, and date of death on it. Then the official turned around and bowed his head while the priest said a few more words.

Kelso then escorted Mrs. Mandlikova from the building, only nodding at Travis and Emma as he did so.

"What a beautiful place to end your days," Emma said.

"Yes," Travis said, "but it was a bit premature for Vera. She was only thirty-four."

"What will happen now to that man—Erskine?"

"Don't know. She was the only witness. We'll have to wait for the lab results. But that won't tell us whether he raped her."

"Well of course he raped her! How could there be any doubt about that?"

"I don't have any doubts, and Kelso doesn't, but a jury may. We'll have to wait and see."

Emma shook her head as they approached the van. "What an awful man."

"He claims to be a born-again Christian. Recites long passages from the Bible and speaks in a soft, soothing voice. No doubt some jurors will find him to be convincing."

"I can't believe they won't convict him."

Travis opened the door of the van for her and gave her a kiss on the cheek. "Thanks for coming with me today, Emma. You have a way of brightening up even the saddest occasions."

She kissed him back—on the lips. "I can never be sad when I'm with you."

"Yes...well, where shall we have lunch?"

"Anywhere you like."

"How about the soup kitchen on Ellis Street?"

"Perfect."

"You're scaring me again, Emma."

She winked at him.
He closed the door and went to the driver's side and got in.
They were off to the soup kitchen.

CHAPTER 55

Travis' doubts about the conviction of Lonnie Erskine in the rape case were not unfounded. A jury of six men and six women of diverse racial and ethnic backgrounds rendered a verdict of acquittal. To be sure, the lab report established that sexual intercourse had taken place, but the jury was not convinced that the sperm samples were Erskine's, or that if they were, that the encounter was nonconsensual, and relied almost wholly on witness testimony. Father Lattimore's testimony (the judge refused to admit the letter he had received from M. Dupin as evidence) was dismissed as pure speculation on his part, and Lattimore's rather gruff and abrasive manner contrasted sharply with Erskine's gentle and persuasive, even eloquent, account of his religious conversion.

Judge Hulsey, however, ordered Erskine to serve three years in prison on the attempted kidnapping charge at San Quentin.

Kelso, though angry and devastated by Vera's death, was not any more surprised at the verdict than Travis was. He even fantasized about ways to kill Erskine, including hiring a couple of underworld hit men. But he was too well versed in the law and its operations to believe he could get away with it. All suspicion would be directed towards him. Besides, though he was an atheist, his own moral code would not permit him to murder a man, however despicable, in cold blood.

Two months after the acquittal, finding himself unable to concentrate on the cases that came across his desk, Kelso resigned from Dunn, McCracken and Glickstein and accepted an invitation from the International Relations Department at San Francisco State to rejoin the faculty.

Travis and Emma were married at Grace Cathedral, with Father Lattimore officiating. They bought a house in the Richmond District just north of Golden Gate Park. One year later, Emma had a child, a boy they named Emile, and one year after that, she produced a girl they named Nicole.

The same year that Nicole was born, Alessandro Sanchez died of AIDS. He died penniless, but left a will that directed Travis to officiate at his funeral and have his ashes spread over the waters of San

Francisco Bay. The service was performed at Grace Cathedral and was attended by his mother Gloria, a brother, two sisters, and a number of actors.

One of these actors was Marcella Morgan.

Travis became aware of Marcella's presence as soon as she entered the cathedral. It was hard not to notice her, as she was accompanied by several other well-known actors and a number of journalists, though most of the latter remained outside, hoping to get a shot of her emerging from the great bronze doors. He stumbled briefly during the eulogy, but recovered quickly and announced that Alessandro's ashes would be spread out over the bay and that those who wished to attend this ceremony should board the bus waiting outside, which would take them to the Hyde Street Pier.

As Travis approached the entrance, the first of the actors he encountered was Andrea Koslewski. Tears were running down her cheeks and she threw her arms around him.

"Oh, Travis! That was so beautiful!" she said.

"How are you, Andrea? By the way, Alessandro's family is very grateful to you for all you've done for him."

"I wish I had done more. And sooner. You know, they're coming up with new drugs to cure AIDS everyday."

"It may be a long time before they have a cure. Still, some lives may be prolonged, at least."

"She's right, Travis. You did a wonderful job." It was Marcella, who was wearing a black dress and sunglasses, even though it was dark inside the cathedral. She stepped forward and gave him a kiss on the cheek.

"I wish I had known you were coming, Marcella. I could have made some arrangements for you."

Marcella suppressed a smile. "I already have more 'arrangers' than I know what to do with. I didn't want the focus to be on me." She paused for a moment. "It's so good to see you, Travis."

"Likewise." He looked to her companion, an actor Travis recognized but couldn't quite place.

"Oh," Marcella said. "This is Greg Lamonte. You may have seen him in *Doctors' Lives*."

"Oh, yes," Travis extended his hand. "That's a daytime show, isn't it?"

Greg, a tall slim man with sideburns to his jowls and matinée idol looks, shook his hand. "A soap opera. But it pays the rent while I'm looking for something more substantial." He glanced at Marcella. "Marcella's considering a script now that might be right for both of us."

Travis noticed that Marcella looked doubtful. "Well, will you accompany us to the pier?"

"We have a driver outside," Marcella said. "We'll meet you there. Unless you'd like to come with us."

Travis glanced around the small crowd of onlookers, most of whom were friends and family of Alessandro's. "I'd better go on the bus with the others. We'll see you there in a few minutes."

Once settled on the bus, Travis gazed out the window to see Marcella and Greg standing at the door of a long black limousine while photographers snapped their pictures and journalists clamored for mostly, it seemed, Marcella's attention. A few fans managed to break through this cordon and obtained her autograph as their reward.

As the bus turned up Taylor Street and headed for the pier, Travis tried to make sense of his feelings upon seeing Marcella after so many years. Years? It seemed only months. She hadn't changed a bit, though the sunglasses partially obscured her features. She had acquired a certain elegance about her, a poise, that she didn't have when they were students, but it seemed to enhance her natural beauty.

He thought of Emma, at home with the children. Emma was a good wife and a good mother. She was also very good-looking, albeit in a matronly sort of way. She had gained a few pounds since they were married, but she was still attractive. And she had a phenomenal amount of patience and forbearance.

At the pier, Marcella was again surrounded by fans and paparazzi. Nearly everyone else was on the boat before she could break away.

Finally the boat—a sixty-foot sightseeing cruiser chartered by Andrea—cast away from the pier and headed towards Angel Island. Alessandro had stipulated that his ashes be dispersed 'in or near the vicinity of Angel Island' partly because he liked the name and partly because of its 'majestic isolation in the midst of insanity.'

Travis sat near the stern so that he could stand and distribute Alessandro's ashes after the benediction and while the boat was still moving. About halfway between Alcatraz and Angel Island the boat slowed to trawling speed and Travis stood uneasily in his gold and white vestments, holding forth the urn that contained the ashes. He felt the tension in his leg muscles as he tried to maintain his balance in the three-foot waves that slapped against the hull of the boat. At last the benediction done, he lifted the lid of the urn and tilted it sternward towards Angel Island. The ashes tumbled out in a shower of white particles that floated gently in the breeze, settled on the surface of the water, and disappeared.

He sat down again on a bench, relieved. He had thought he might tumble over the stern, or at best, look silly trying to keep his balance while spilling the ashes into the boat.

Marcella came and sat down beside him. "The athlete in you served you well," she said. "We were all watching you maintain your balance instead of listening to the benediction."

Travis chuckled. "Then I didn't do my job. The idea is to inspire the living, as well as the deceased, with hope for the future."

"Travis...do you really believe that? That Alessandro—or anybody else—is going to heaven?"

He smiled. "What a thing to say to a priest. It's our business to put salve on the wounds of the afflicted."

She put her hand on his thigh. "Yes, you're very good at that. I suppose you've found your calling.' She removed her hand and looked towards the bow.

"And you, Marcella? Have you found your calling?"

She seemed to consider this for a moment. "I'm not sure. Just when I think I've found a good part, my best scenes seem to end up on the cutting room floor. Or if it's a play, I soar like an eagle one night, and fall to the earth like a wounded sparrow the next."

"I think I know how you feel."

She looked at him and put her hand on his thigh again. "Yes, I think you do."

Travis suddenly felt uncomfortable beneath her gaze. His thigh muscle twitched. But he didn't want her to remove her hand. He gazed up towards the bow, where Greg Lamonte was talking to the captain. "How are you and Greg getting along? He seems to be a nice guy."

"He's an angel. But like so many of my male friends, he's gay."

"Gay? Then why do you—"

"The studio likes us to be seen together. They see us as a sort of Clark Gable-Carol Lombard vehicle that will make them even richer than they already are."

"So you're not seeing anyone. That is, seriously?"

She sighed. "No. Not seriously."

Travis said nothing and Marcella continued to stare at the bow of the boat as it crashed against the waves and threw a salt spray over them.

Just before they reached the pier she turned to him. "I'm staying at the Fairmont. Will you have dinner with me?"

"Well...Marcella, I—"

"For old times' sake. You'll be home by ten."

"I'll have to call Emma."

"Emma?"

"My wife."

"Oh, yes. Well, then call her. Tell her you're having dinner with a friend of Alessandro's. For old-times' sake."

CHAPTER 56

When Travis got back to the apartment he still kept at Grace Cathedral, he removed his vestments and black shirt with its reversed white collar, and stood before the dresser mirror. He had gained little weight over the years, primarily due to his soccer practices and an occasional game with other faculty members. Obviously, Marcella still found him to be attractive.

And she was even more attractive to him than she had ever been. He even remained seated in the boat for several minutes as the others all rose to disembark because he had an erection due to Marcella's close proximity. Not to mention the fact that she kept putting her hand on his thigh.

This was not a good idea. He should have made some excuse not to join her for dinner. Well, he did offer an excuse and it was a good one. He was married with a wife and two children at home.

But then what was the harm in having dinner with an old friend? He went to his desk and picked up the phone. "Hi, Emma. Yes, it went well. But I'm afraid I won't be home for dinner tonight. Several of Alessandro's friends and family members are getting together at the Fairmont and they want me to join them. Yes—Marcella, too. Well, certainly you can join us. But what about the children? They'll be bored and sleepy by the time we eat. Haven't you fed them by now?"

Emma replied that the children had already eaten but perhaps they could have dessert. Dessert at the Fairmont! It would be a memorable experience for them.

Travis squelched this idea by saying that the Fairmont's main dining room frowned upon small children being served after seven p.m. He didn't know whether this was true or not, but it seemed plausible. And Emma, with a sigh, seemed to accept it. He promised to be home by ten p.m.

He put on the burgundy turtleneck that he had worn a few years ago when he picked Marcella up at the airport. He still wore it occasionally, but more often wore one of the many Polo shirts that Emma gave him every year because she thought they made him look more athletic. In any case, he had never liked ties.

He walked the block and a half to Mason Street and arrived at the front entrance of the Fairmont as a row of limousines lined up and disgorged their elegantly dressed passengers one-by-one. He wondered if he shouldn't have worn a tie after all.

The façade was impressive. It looked like a neoclassical palace that might belong to an English duke. Towering Corinthian columns at the entry with another even taller tier above that. Row after row of ornately framed windows, some crowned with pediments supported by smaller columns. The entire edifice was reminiscent of the Parthenon adapted for the leisurely purposes of the rich.

A doorman with shoulder epaulettes like those of an eighteenth century general directed him to the Venetian Room, once considered the most elegant dining and dancing establishment in San Francisco, and reputed to be where Tony Bennett first sang *I Left My Heart in San Francisco.*

He approached the maitre d' with some trepidation on account of his tieless turtleneck, and asked him if he could direct him to Ms. Morgan's table.

The maitre d' looked him up and down with the air of a drill sergeant inspecting a raw recruit, seemed satisfied, and said:

"You must be Mr. Carter. Miss Morgan said you favored turtlenecks. They're quite acceptable at the Fairmont."

"That's a relief. Is she here yet?"

The maitre d' glanced over Travis' shoulder in a surreptitious manner, leaned forward, and said in a voice barely above a whisper:

"She would prefer to dine in her own room tonight. The Fairmont Suite on the twenty-third floor of the Tower. I'll have a bell boy escort you." He picked up a walkie-talkie, pushed a button, and said something into it. In less than thirty seconds a bellhop, looking like the kid in the old Phillip Morris cigarette ads, only dressed in gray instead of red, appeared and led him to the elevator.

At the twenty-third floor, the doors opened and the bellhop led him down a long corridor to a door with a brass plaque that read 'Fairmont Suite.' He pressed the bell, which remained silent from the hallway, and winked at Travis. "You're a lucky guy."

"Sure you don't want to stick around for her autograph?" Travis said.

"Already got it. Well, I'd better make myself scarce." He did not move.

"Oh," Travis said. He pulled out his wallet and handed him a five dollar bill.

The bellhop looked at it disdainfully.

Travis pulled out another five. The bellhop smiled as he took it and put both bills into his vest pocket. "Good luck, pal." And he walked briskly back to the elevator.

As Travis watched him, the door to the suite opened. Marcella appeared, dressed in a red silk cocktail dress with spaghetti straps and a bodice that pushed her breasts up and emphasized the cleavage.

"I was right," she said.

"About what?"

"The burgundy turtleneck."

"I think they would have turned me away if I hadn't worn it."

She laughed and opened the door wider. "Come in, Travis. Make yourself comfortable."

Travis stepped inside and saw that that wouldn't be hard to do. There was a large living room with a 180 degree view, from Twin Peaks to the East Bay. His feet sank a quarter of an inch into a plush maroon carpet with a blue and white acanthus-leaf border. There were several armchairs upholstered in fabrics of different colors and patterns and accented with overstuffed cushions, along with a pair of back-to-back sofas in the middle of the room. Off to one side, beneath one of the windows with a view of Sausalito, was a hand-carved Chippendale dining table. At another window opposite a sitting area was a brass telescope resting on a tripod.

"A long way from your old digs in the Haight," Travis said.

Marcella laughed. "Actually, I liked that place. It was just a little hard to get any privacy."

"I would think you have even less privacy these days. How did you get rid of the paparazzi?"

"The management is very skilled in that department. Maitre d's, house detectives. They can spot a photojournalist a mile away."

"I guess cameras are a dead giveaway. What about helicopters?"

"I can always close the curtains. Would you like a glass of champagne?"

Travis noticed an ice bucket on the coffee table in front of the sofa. The neck of a champagne bottle protruded from the ice and two glasses rested next to the bucket. "Sure. But I think I'll take a look at the view through the telescope first. Do you mind?"

"Be my guest. While you're doing that, I'll open the champagne. And there're some hors d'oeuvres on the table as well."

Travis went to the window and peered through the telescope. He adjusted the lens until the Golden Gate came into focus and then swept the device slowly across the panorama before him. He was so absorbed in this activity that he was startled when Marcella was suddenly next to him, holding two glasses of the champagne.

"Do you see anything you hadn't seen before?" she said.

He took his eyes away from the telescope and somehow they went straight to her décolletage. "No. I've seen it all. But not from this vantage point." He blushed slightly at his unintended double-entendre and took one of the glasses from her.

"Do you realize that we met just down the street?" she said.

"Down the street? Actually around the corner. California and Hyde. I think I can see it from here." He swung the telescope around until it pointed up California Street.

"Actually," she said, "it was California and Larkin."

Travis looked at her. "Are you sure?"

"I'm sure. That corner was my turf." She peered into the telescope and adjusted the angle. "There. Now you can see it."

Travis looked. "Ah! You're right. There it is." When he was satisfied with this view he turned to her. "Well, I suppose we should drink to something."

Marcella smiled and raised her glass. "What did you have in mind?"

Unsure whether she was alluding to sexual matters, Travis blushed again. "How about... 'to days of mime and roses.'"

She laughed. "That's a terrible pun. How about... 'to the Rose and Thorn?'"

"The Rose and Thorn?"

"Don't you remember? That was the name of the pub theater where we *really* met."

"Oh, of course." He raised his glass to hers. "To the Rose and

Thorn. I wonder if it's still there?"

"It's still there. I paid a visit to Ian, the owner, this morning. He was already three sheets to the wind."

They both laughed and drank from their glasses.

Travis looked around the room. "Is this it? I mean, are you expecting anyone else?"

"I told you, this is for old times' sake. You don't invite a crowd when you want to reminisce."

"No, I guess not. So what shall we reminisce about first?"

Marcella smiled. "We've already started. Why don't we sit on the sofa?"

"I'm afraid I'll sink out of sight."

"Don't worry—I'll save you."

They moved to the sofa and Travis pulled the champagne bottle from the bucket and filled their glasses. He was beginning to get nervous. What were Marcella's intentions? Surely she was interested in romance, but for just one night? Did she want to revive the relationship and become his mistress? Or even to persuade him to divorce Emma and marry her?

"What do you want, Marcella?"

She seemed taken aback by this question. "Why nothing especially. Just to enjoy being with you for a while. Should I want more than that?"

Travis tapped his fingers on the coffee table and looked around the room again. "No, I suppose not. You seem to have everything most people could want."

"The material things come with the territory. It's the intangible things that are harder to come by."

"Intangible things?"

"Surely you know what I'm talking about—friendship, fulfillment in one's career, love..."

"There's no doubt you have plenty of friends, and though you question your own talent, the rest of the world doesn't. That leaves love. I offered you mine once, and you rejected it. You even suggested I transfer my passion for you to someone else. And I did."

"To Emma."

"Yes, to Emma."

"It seems to have worked out."

Travis swallowed the rest of his champagne and poured some more into his glass. "Emma's the cornerstone of my life, Marcella. The mother of my children."

"I knew she would be good for you."

Travis looked at her for the first time since this more serious conversation started. "You did, didn't you? You were the matchmaker."

"I like to see people happy."

Travis looked into her eyes and felt as if he were being drawn into a dizzying vortex, like the rabbit hole in Alice in Wonderland. He put his glass down on the table, knocking it over, and kissed her.

She responded with a gentle kiss at first, then more eagerly, and leaned back against the cushions, pulling him down towards her.

The doorbell rang.

She opened her eyes and smiled. "It's our dinner."

Travis, disheveled, sat up and brushed his hair back. "Great timing. I'll let him in." He got up, tucked his shirt in, and went to the door.

When he opened it, he got a brief glimpse of a man in a parka and jogging suit before he was blinded with a brilliant flash. Then he heard a series of rapid thumps against the heavily padded carpet. When his vision returned, the man was gone.

"He must have bribed the bellhop." Marcella was at his side. "Are you all right?"

"Yeah. I couldn't see for a few seconds. I suppose my mug will be in all the papers tomorrow."

"Just the tabloids. Come back inside." She closed the door and led him back to the sofa by the hand as if he were a child. "I'm so sorry, Travis. They're such a nuisance. But nobody believes their fabricated stories."

"I have a feeling Emma might."

"Just explain to her what happened."

"And what almost happened?"

She withdrew her hand from his and sat back against a pillow. "It's not that complicated, Travis."

"I'm afraid it's going to get very complicated, Marcella. I'd better go." He started to rise from the sofa, but she restrained him.

"I've ordered dinner. Chateau Briand, a wonderful Bordeaux, and Napoleon chocolate layer cake for dessert. It'll all go to waste if you leave."

"I'm sorry for that. But I'd better get home and explain things to Emma before she sees the tabloids."

"That won't be till morning." She put her arms around his neck and kissed him. "Stay, Travis. You don't know how much I've missed you."

Travis felt her lips against his and his will to resist evaporated.

The doorbell rang again. Travis started. "He's back?"

Marcella smiled, her arms still around his neck. "This time it's dinner."

Travis got home about nine-forty-five. Emma met him at the door. She gave him a kiss.

"How did it go?" She was dressed in jeans and a sweatshirt that said 'Potrero Elementary Soccer.'

"The dinner was fine. But something unexpected happened. Are the kids in bed?"

"Sound asleep. What happened?"

"How about some coffee?"

She stared at him for a moment. "All right."

While Emma was in the kitchen making the coffee, Travis took off his jacket and sat in the leather armchair that she had given him for his birthday. Beside it, on an end table, rested a pipe that Emile had given him for the same event. Of course he didn't smoke, but he put it in his mouth whenever Emile was in the room to assure him that the gift was appreciated.

When Emma arrived with the coffee, she sat down on the sofa opposite him and folded her hands in her lap. "You were saying something happened."

"Marcella wanted to avoid being pestered by the paparazzi, so she decided that we would have dinner in her room." He blew across the surface of his coffee and took a sip.

"Just the two of you?"

"Just the two of us."

Emma frowned. "And?"

"It didn't work. The bell rang, I went to the door, and a photographer snapped my picture."

"Uh, oh."

"Uh, oh, is right. It will be in all the papers tomorrow. Or at least the tabloids."

Emma looked down at her hands for a moment. "Did you make love to her?"

Travis felt a tightness in his throat. He took another sip of the coffee. "I kissed her—or she kissed me. I'm not sure who was first. But that was all."

"Are you sure?"

"I'm sure."

Tears came to Emma's eyes. "I was afraid of this."

"The photographer?"

"No. You and Marcella. 'Just old friends,' you said.

"I'm sorry, Emma. I didn't think it would go even that far."

"No?"

Travis sighed. "All right. I might as well come completely clean. I was hoping that we might have one last night together, but—"

"In bed?"

He stood up and started pacing around the room. "You're not making this any easier, Emma."

"It's not supposed to be easy. Were you hoping to go to bed with her?"

He sat down again. "Yes. There. It's all out. You've uncovered more of my secrets than I intended for you to know."

"It's never been a secret, Travis. I saw how mesmerized you were that night she appeared on Johnny Carson. But I didn't think you'd ever see her again. She was too famous, I thought. She had forgotten you. But she hasn't forgotten you. And she seems determined to keep you as...as some sort of plaything whenever she's in San Francisco."

"That's not the way it is, Emma."

"Then how is it?"

He took another sip of his coffee. "The way it is, is that it's over."

"How can you be sure?"

"Because I told her so. The problem now is these tabloids. I might lose my job."

Emma wiped a tear from her eye. "What would you do?"

"I don't know. Father Lattimore is a bishop now. He might transfer me to another parish—somewhere in Northern California, like Eureka, or Chico. Or maybe even more remote than that. On the other hand, he might have me defrocked."

"But you didn't do anything."

"It may not matter. It's the appearance of impropriety that counts. Especially for a priest."

Emma rose from the sofa, came around the coffee table and knelt before him on the carpet. She took his hand and looked into his eyes. "You've told me the truth, Travis? All of it?"

"All of it."

"Then I will go wherever you go. I've always told you that and as long as you're honest with me, I will keep my word."

"I love you, Emma."

"I love—"

"Daddy!" It was Emile, who had just emerged from the bedroom. He ran to Travis and climbed up on his lap. "Why aren't you smoking your pipe?"

"Well, I'll need a light, buddy."

Emile peered into the bowl of the pipe. "You need some tobacco, too. I forgot to buy you some."

"Mommy, Emile woke me up." Now it was Nicole, rubbing her eyes with her tiny fists. "What's going on?"

Emma rose, took Nicole by the hand, and led her back to the bedroom. "Daddy's very tired, children. Come on, back to bed."

Travis lifted Emile up and put him down on the floor. "Better do as Mommy says, sport. It's late."

Emile followed his sister into the bedroom and Travis could hear Nicole admonishing her mother:

"You didn't sing that song when you tucked me in. The one about Jackie."

"Frère Jacques," Emma said. "Come on, now, and help me:

          Frère Jacques, Frère Jacques,
          Dormez-vous? Dormez-vous?

Sonnez les matines, Sonnez les matines,
Ding, Daing, Dong..."

The children joined in and when it was finished, Emma closed the door behind her. She returned to Travis' office and found him leaning back in his chair and staring at one of a dozen photographs on wall. This one was of their wedding in Palo Alto. It showed the traditional cutting of the cake, with the groom guiding the hand of the bride as if she couldn't do it without his assistance. The husband was presumed to be the stronger, the wiser.

"Regrets?" she said.

He turned in his chair and looked at her. The light behind her from the living room formed a sort of halo around her head, making the blond hairs sparkle and creating shadows that partially obscured her face. "None. None whatsoever."

She stepped into the room. "Are you going to follow Emile's advice and actually start smoking that pipe?"

"I'll get the tobacco. But that doesn't mean I have to smoke it."

"Someday he's going to figure it out and he'll realize that you deceived him."

Travis smiled. "Can't we have even a little deception in this house? At least of the innocent kind?"

She came and sat in his lap. "I have a little deception of my own to confess to."

"What?"

"I've been gaining weight."

Travis laughed. "If I were a proper husband, I wouldn't tell you that I've noticed, but I'm not, and I have."

She gave him a kiss. "But you don't know why."

Travis' eyes opened wide. "You're pregnant again?"

"You're so observant, dear."

Travis chuckled. "I need a little hint now and then."

"Of course you do. What's a wife for?"

"Many things, Emma. Thank you."

"You're welcome. Are you so terribly tired?"

"Not that tired."

"Then come to bed." She rose and went to the door, but turned around when she sensed that he hadn't moved. "Well?"

Travis got up from his chair and removed his shoes so as not to awaken the children.

CHAPTER 57

The next morning Travis called on Father—now Bishop—Lattimore.

"Sit down, Travis. I've been expecting you."

"Then you've seen the papers." Travis sat down.

Lattimore remained behind his desk. "The papers? No, not yet. I saw it on the morning news."

"Television?"

"I'm afraid so."

Travis didn't expect the photo to get such broad play. "I'm willing to submit my resignation, Father. I don't wish to cause you or the diocese anymore embarrassment."

"That may not be necessary, Travis. But this photograph of you with Miss Morgan, however innocent, limits our options."

"I understand."

Lattimore stared at him for a moment. "I've had a special interest in you and your career for some time, Travis."

"I'm afraid I've let you down."

"I wouldn't say that. Your behavior up until now has been impeccable, and you've performed your duties beyond my expectations. Furthermore, you're well-liked both among the parishioners and the staff here at Grace Cathedral. I hate to lose you."

"I've put you in a difficult position."

"Difficult, yes. Impossible, no." Lattimore swung around in his chair and rose to his feet. He went to the bookshelf behind the desk, ran his fingers along the bindings of several books, and finding what he was looking for, pulled the volume out. He thumbed through the pages for a few moments, clapped the covers shut, and came around the desk He handed the volume to Travis.

Travis, puzzled, took the book and read the title:

Prison Ministries in California:
Challenge of Faith

He thumbed through the pages. "Prisons?"

"San Quentin has an opening. Are you interested?"

Travis closed the volume and again looked at the title. "I suppose it's fitting."

"Now don't take it as a punishment. As the title of this book suggests, it's a challenge. I don't want you—or any priest under my tutelage to take it on unless he—or she—is determined to make an impact there."

Travis again stared at the title. "It *is* a challenge. And I suppose it will be a test of my faith as well."

"Then you'll do it?"

"I'll have to consult my wife."

"Of course. It will no doubt be difficult for her—and the children—as well. This is not a decision to be taken lightly. But I need to know before noon. There'll be a press conference."

"I understand." Travis stood and handed the volume back to Lattimore, but he pushed it away.

"Keep it. It may help you to make your decision. Pay particular attention to chapter four."

Travis put the book under his arm and extended his other hand. "I'll do that. Thank you, Father Lattimore."

Lattimore shook his hand. "I have a great deal of confidence in you, Travis. But you must decide to do what's best for you and your family. May God be with you."

"Thank you, Father."

Travis drove to Potrero Elementary and waited for Emma to get out of her first morning class.

"Would we have to move to San Rafael?" she said, as they stood in the hallway outside the classroom. She cautioned two boys not to run.

"No. It's not that long a commute. Maybe thirty minutes."

"It could be dangerous."

"Not very likely. Even hardened criminals respect men of the cloth. The last chaplain murdered in a California prison was in 1880 something."

"Do you really want to do it?"

"The more I think about it, yes. These men have hit rock bottom. They need spiritual guidance more than the denizens of Nob Hill, or even the homeless in the Tenderloin."

"Then do it." She kissed him. "I've got another class."

Travis drove back to Grace Cathedral and informed Father Lattimore of his decision.

Lattimore beamed and clapped him on the shoulder. "I was never in doubt. You don't need to stick around for the press conference. I'll just tell them that you've taken a leave of absence. Which you will—starting now."

Travis then went to his office and began cleaning out his desk.

CHAPTER 58

The approach to San Quentin was a long, gentle grade that offered an expansive view of the northern part of San Francisco Bay, and the back side of Tiburon. Sightseeing watercraft cruised in these more placid waters only a stone's throw from the guard towers that kept watch over more than four thousand of the most dangerous criminals in America.

The guard at the gate jotted down his license plate number, noted his clerical collar with a smile, and waved him through to the parking area in front of the main building, which looked like a medieval fortress and reminded Travis of his military boarding school in Michigan.

A guard at the front door asked him to enter his name, address, and purpose of visit in a huge registry book, and directed him to the next guard, who led him to the warden's office.

He expected the warden to be built like a linebacker, with bushy eyebrows and a more or less permanent scowl on his face. Instead, he turned out to be a rather slim, professorial man, with a receding hair line to the crown of his head, wire-rim glasses, and an almost gentle demeanor. Travis noted that he had two or three diplomas on the wall, including a master's degree in psychology from San Francisco State.

He extended his hand. "Jim Cheney. I've heard a great deal about you."

"I hope you don't believe everything you read."

Cheney laughed and indicated a chair. "Father Lattimore set me straight about all that. Some of the inmates, however, may have seen the news reports. You may get some ribbing for it."

Travis took his seat. "I suppose I'll get more ribbing just for being a priest."

Cheney sat down behind his desk. "You'd be surprised how seriously the men take clergymen. Some of the worst cases will open themselves up to a priest before they will to, say, a psychologist like myself."

After some reminiscences on their mutual experiences at San Francisco State, the warden took Travis on a tour of the prison.

There were few surprises here. The walls were a battleship gray with no pictures or decorations of any kind, the cell blocks were arranged in tiers like stacked cages, some with six men confined to an eight by ten-foot space; metal beds with thin mattresses bolted to the floor, a sink against one wall and a toilet on the other. Many of the inmates, in orange jump suits, stared at him menacingly with their arms extended through the bars and their hands dangling from their wrists as if they were puppets whose puppeteers had hung them up for the night. There were no cat calls, however, which Warden Cheney said was common for most visitors, whether male or female.

The most disturbing feature, however, was the gas chamber. Though it had not been used since 1967, Cheney explained, it was kept in tact due to a number of appeals in the court system. The chamber looked like something out of a 1930's science fiction movie, or perhaps a diving bell from *20,000 Leagues Under the Sea*. Painted light green inside and out, a round door with a nautical-looking wheel for an airtight seal, it would be almost comical if not for its grim purpose.

Travis wondered whether he would be asked to preside over an execution if the courts should deny the latest appeals. Would it be ethical? Would it simply be a matter of giving solace to a wretched creature, or would it be contributing to a legal murder?

The last stop was the chapel. This was really just an assembly hall, with folding metal chairs rather than pews. Cheney said that some upholstered chairs had been ordered. The walls, though plain, were painted white. There was a low platform where the altar and choir should be, and a simple cross on the wall behind that. To either side were rather crude paintings, one of Jesus and the other of some saint or another, possibly one of the apostles, kneeling and facing the portrait of Jesus.

"As you can see," Cheney said, "the chapel is pretty Spartan at the moment, but with the new chairs and a couple of paintings now being composed by one of our inmates, it will be a little more inviting."

"What about an altar?" Travis said.

"Oh, we have one. It's locked in that closet on the left, next to the lectern, which will serve as your pulpit. We put the altar away when we use the hall for other things, like craft and shop classes. We're a bit challenged for space here."

Travis was tempted to say that the entire prison was a challenge to civilized notions of humane treatment of the incarcerated, but he remained silent while Cheney escorted him to a small office down the hall from his own. It wasn't much larger than one of the cells they had inspected, with an old-fashioned rolltop desk against one wall, a kind of armoire—or cupboard—against another, and two or three uncomfortable-looking, nicked and scarred chairs.

"I've ordered some new chairs for your office, too," Cheney said, almost apologetically. "Getting funds for these things is like pulling teeth."

"I can imagine," Travis said. He looked around the office. There was a framed photograph of the Golden Gate on one wall, and just below it, a photo of Grace Cathedral at twilight with the sun setting just beyond Russian Hill.

Cheney seemed to notice his fixation on the lower photo. "Oh, our former chaplain was also a graduate, you might say, of Grace Cathedral, like yourself."

"What happened to him?"

Cheney seemed hesitant. "He resigned and went to Mexico where he runs an orphanage. I understand he's doing quite well there."

"A bit less stressful, too, I would think."

Cheney smiled. "This is a job for a young man, Travis. Andy was pushing sixty. Twenty-two years here was more than any previous chaplain could handle. I don't imagine you'll surpass that record, but I'm confident that you'll find the job to be a rewarding one."

"How long have you been here?"

"Three years."

"No sign of burnout?"

Cheney laughed and with a surprising heartiness, slapped him on the back. "Not yet. I think we'll be leaving together."

Travis smiled. "Thanks, Jim. I'm sure that—"

He was interrupted by the wail of a siren. Both men looked up to the ceiling as if an explanation would manifest itself there.

"A little emergency." Cheney's jovial manner of a moment before evaporated. "I'd better see to it. Make yourself comfortable, Travis. You can move in as soon as you like. Let me know if you need anything." He hurried out the door.

Travis listened for a few moments to the siren. Within thirty seconds of Cheney's departure, the sound stopped. He sat down in the desk chair, which creaked under the weight of his body. He would have to remember to bring a seat cushion from home.

Home. He stared at the photo of the Golden Gate. It was like a magnet to so many people. People like Marcella, Alessandro, Andrea, Ben...and himself. And though they were still young, they were truly children then. Children at the Gate, with so many ambitions and expectations, ideals and hopes. Well, it hadn't turned out all bad, had it? Alessandro was gone, but look at Ben and Marcella and even Andrea...

Home. He supposed that, for a priest, it was wherever he hung his hat.

CHAPTER 59

Travis spent the first week in his new job visiting several inmates who had expressed an interest in seeing him for counseling. Most came to his office, which was now more comfortably furbished with new chairs and a number of photographs and paintings. The most prominent of these photos was one of Emma and the children. It sat on his desk opposite a row of books, including his Bible, Kierkegaard's *Either/Or, Mere Christianity* by C.S. Lewis, and Niebuhr's *Moral Man and Immoral Society*.

One of the inmates who visited him was Lonnie Erskine.

He had nearly forgotten that Erskine had been sent to San Quentin. The rape trial, once the media's thirst for the sensational had been quenched by Vera's suicide, was soon relegated to the back pages of the newspapers and not covered by television at all. Erskine's sentence of three years in prison was regarded as a slap on the wrist by some and too severe by others.

Travis noted that Erskine had lost weight. Once fit and athletic-looking, he now appeared to be almost frail. He hunched over slightly and wore steel-rimmed glasses. And he carried his gold-embossed white Bible with him everywhere he went.

His orange prison jump suit reminded Travis, oddly enough, of members of the Hare Krishna cult.

"I see that you've had your own troubles with women, Father." Erskine grinned as he said this.

Travis had grown accustomed to such comments in the short time he had been at San Quentin. "Marcella Morgan is an old friend of mine, Lonnie. The newspapers misrepresented our relationship." As soon as he said this, he wondered at its truthfulness.

Erskine didn't stop grinning. "I know how you feel. They misrepresented my relationship with Vera Mandlikova, too."

"I don't know that the two incidents are equivalent. But I agree that the press doesn't always get things right. Now, Lonnie, what can I do for you today?"

Erskine's eyes went to the books on Travis' desk. "I just wanted to talk, Father. I mean, that's why you're here, isn't it?"

"Of course that's why I'm here. I want to be available to all of the inmates. Including Lonnie Erskine. What's on your mind?"

"A lot of things. But mostly the book I'm writing."

"A new one? I suppose it's been some time since you published *Soul on Fire*."

"Yeah. Ten years. But it's still selling well."

"I see it in all the book stores."

Erskine sighed and looked thoughtful for the first time during the interview. "I've changed since then, Father. And I want to lay it all out. Everything."

"Everything?"

"Yeah. It's a kind of autobiography. And a confession at the same time."

Travis wasn't sure what Erskine was telling him this for. He claimed to have become a 'born-again Christian,' but then he raped Vera Kelso (née Mandlikova) and sent her to her death. Or at least nearly everyone he knew believed he did. "How can I help, Lonnie?"

Erskine glanced at the books on Travis' desk again. "You're an educated man, Father. I dropped out of school in the ninth grade. I thought you might read the manuscript and, you know, correct the errors."

"I didn't see any errors in your first book, Lonnie. In fact, I thought it was beautifully written, even though I didn't agree with everything in it."

Erskine smiled. "I don't agree with everything in it, either. At least not now. And as for the spelling and grammar, my editors cleaned that up for me."

"Then I suppose they'll do it for you again."

"I don't know. It's been a long time and things have changed. They may not even be interested. That's why I'd like you to take a look at it."

Travis looked into Erskine's eyes and tried to see what was behind them. But he saw only the opaque façade that Erskine had carefully built up over the years from the time he was a teenage street hustler in Oakland to a Marxist revolutionary and now a Bible-toting Christian. "I'd be happy to, Lonnie. Just let me know when you've finished it."

"Thanks. I will."

Travis expected him to rise, but he remained seated and stared down at the floor for a few moments. Then he looked up. "There's one more thing."

"What's that?"

"I'd like you to pray for my soul."

Travis was taken by surprise. He wondered whether this was another one of Erskine's cons. "Of course I'll pray for your soul. But do you expect your soul to depart from your body anytime soon?"

"It's possible."

Travis remained silent for a moment. "You're still a young man, Lonnie. I don't think—"

"This is San Quentin, Father. I've got a lot of enemies."

"I see." Travis rebuked himself for his naiveté. Of course Erskine had enemies. And since he had renounced the Pumas... "I will pray for you, Lonnie."

Erskine stared at him for a moment, then rose from his chair. "Thank you, Father." He extended his hand and Travis rose to extend his. "You've been a great comfort to me." He walked to the door where there was a guard waiting to escort him back to his cell. He paused and turned around. "God bless you, Father."

"And may God be with you, Lonnie."

* * *

Three days later Erskine ventured out into the prison yard for the first time since his most recent incarceration. Most of his free time until now had been either in his cell or in the prison library working on his book.

It took a few moments for his eyes to adjust to the bright sunlight. A few inmates stood near the entry to the yard staring at him. He nodded. They nodded back.

He naturally gravitated to the basketball court where there were about a dozen or so inmates, all in their blue smocks with 'CDCR' emblazoned on the back: 'California Department of Corrections and Rehabilitation.' They were choosing up sides.

He had been a better-than-average basketball player in high school before he dropped out. He even had a UC Berkeley scout come to a few games and tell him he could get a scholarship if he continued to play well into his senior year. But things happened and there was no senior year.

"Hey, Bro—you done come out of your cave." It was an inmate named Perry, a big guy, no more than twenty-one or twenty-two, who nevertheless seemed to command the respect of the others. "You shoot hoops?"

"Sure," Erskine said. "It's been a while."

Perry sized him up as he came closer. "You about what? Six-two?"

"Give or take an inch."

Perry smiled. "Point guard. Can you dig it?"

"I can dig it."

Perry suddenly fired the basketball at Erskine, nearly knocking the breath out of him. "Show us your shit."

Erskine palmed the ball and began dribbling towards the center of the court. He stopped for a moment, bounced the ball, and then ran for the basket, weaving between two or three inmates who were just standing around. He made the lay-up.

"That's too easy, man," Perry said. "I want to know if you can shoot."

Erskine picked the ball up again and trotted out to the three-point line. He put a fake on one of the inmates, encountered another who put his hand up to block the shot, jumped and fired at the basket. It was a swish.

"Good shootin,' Bro!" Perry said. "You on my team." He turned to another inmate, a short man, who looked annoyed. "Okay, Mighty Mouse—your pick."

Once the teams were picked—with two alternates each—the game began with a jump ball at the center of the court.

Mighty Mouse proved that he was worthy of his nickname. He was lightning-quick, eluded defenders easily, and had an amazing ability to leap that allowed him to shoot over the heads of all but the tallest opponents. In just fifteen minutes, it was Warriors 34, Trojans 28. Perry's Trojans were down six points.

The tide began to turn, however, after Erskine made a backhanded lay-up followed by a three-pointer. He was sweating heavily now, and breathing harder than the rest. He wondered if he could keep up for a full sixty minutes. Two consecutive fouls by the Warriors gave him a welcome respite and he felt he had a second wind.

After Perry, the tallest player on either team, blocked a shot by Mighty Mouse, he passed the ball to Erskine, who took his time dribbling down the court. Another pass back to Perry, and Perry to Ginger, an African-American with red hair. Back to Perry, who made a looping throw to Tiny, another point guard. Tiny started to shoot from the corner, but was prevented from doing so by Mighty Mouse, who made one of his famous leaps. Tiny passed the ball to Erskine, who rushed in for the lay-up.

At the last second, in the air, he saw a familiar face beneath the backboard.

He made the lay-up, but when he came down it was if he had fallen onto an iron spike. He cried out in pain, clutched his breast and fell to the court with blood spurting out between his fingers. The spectators dispersed. Perry, Mighty Mouse, and the other players stood gaping at the now writhing, convulsive body, unsure of whether to stay or go.

A whistle blew, then a siren wailed. Three guards rushed to the court. One of them examined Erskine, who was no longer moving.

"He ain't gonna make it," the guard said. He stood up and looked at Perry, then the others. "All right, who saw it?"

Perry remained expressionless. "Saw what?"

The guard scowled at Perry. "Back to your cells."

The inmates slowly began to disperse.

Erskine lay on the court in a fetal position, the circle of blood around him slowly expanding like a red tide.

CHAPTER 60

January is the rainy season in San Francisco, and the wind off of the Pacific can turn the Richmond District into a monsoon-drenched tropical village.

In fact, these storms that roll off the Pacific reminded Travis of South Vietnam, only without the lush vegetation and the thatched huts that tended to be swept away, leaving behind piles of debris and sometimes bodies.

With the wind and the rain howling outside, Travis' inner sanctum seemed as safe and dry as any mountain redoubt. After writing several checks for the monthly bills and sealing them in the generously-provided envelopes, he turned to the large box that Warden Cheney had given him after Erskine's funeral. He was quite sure of what it contained, but he had put off opening it for fear that it would incur new responsibilities that he was reluctant to take on. Erskine seemed to have had no family, no wife, and no acknowledged children. What did he expect of him?

He lifted the lid off of the box and was not surprised to see a letter. He was surprised, however, at what the letter said:

Dear Father Carter,

As you are my only friend in this cruel and unjust world, I want you to have the rights to the enclosed manuscript. It is my last—and only—confession. Every word is true, and has been carefully reviewed by myself for accuracy. You will see that it is a litany of crimes and passions of a very imperfect man. If anything, I have not been punished enough.

But I hope that this true account of my life will serve in some way to expiate my sins. Only God will judge.

I have included the contact information of my publisher in New York. He can have no objection: a letter has been sent to him by registered mail and my will—a copy lies herein—has been recorded at the Marin County Courthouse.

Bless you, Father.

Lawrence Sidney Erskine, Jr.

Travis set the letter aside and saw the will. One page, notarized by the warden's secretary, and signed by two witnesses:

I, Lawrence Sidney Erskine, Jr., designate Father Travis Carter, Chaplain of San Quentin Penitentiary and resident of San Francisco, CA, as the executor of my literary estate. I further direct him to disburse all of the assets that remain in my Swiss bank account, USB, Geneva, Switzerland, No. 88B10079-16, to the Episcopal Diocese of Northern California.

All royalties from my books, both published and unpublished, I bequeath to Father Carter and his heirs.

I have no personal property or collectibles, other than my Bible, which I also bequeath to Father Carter.

Lawrence Sidney Erskine, Jr.

Travis set the will aside. Beneath that was Erskine's white Bible, and beneath that was the manuscript, entitled:

Confessions of a Great Sinner
The Autobiography of
Lawrence S. Erskine, Jr.:
Rapist, Murderer, Black Militant, and
Born-Again Christian

It was not a lengthy manuscript—approximately 275 pages. Handwritten in blue ink, with a clear, almost artistic script. Travis would have to have it typed up, perhaps by one of the secretaries at San Quentin. On the other hand, maybe his publisher was used to getting Erskine's manuscripts in this raw form.

He thumbed through the pages. There was no division into chapters, only a few demarcations with titles like, "Childhood," "Hustling," "The Pumas," and "The Killing of Sergeant Dan Watt." This last title piqued Travis' interest and he lingered over it for several minutes:

I had planned the execution of Dan Watt from the

beginning. For that's what it was in my mind: an execu-
tion. I, and my fellow Pumas, had concluded that the
white man's justice was no justice at all, and therefore we
would create and administer our own system of justice.

I told Emmett Smalls of the plan and he willingly agreed.
I did not feel that it was necessary to get the approval of
the Committee. I knew they would applaud it once the
deed was accomplished. And applaud it they did.

I did not tell Ben Franklin, our driver and a fresh re-
cruit at the time. I felt that he was naive, even though he
was a Vietnam vet, and not sufficiently committed to the
Cause. Turned out I was right about that.

Travis turned several more pages until he came to a section entitled, "Rape for Fun and Sport."

In my early years I discovered that women, good-looking
women, were attracted to me. Not only physically, but
personally. That is, I had a gentle but confident manner
and a keen sense of wit. Thus, they let their guard down.
But I was impatient with their coquettish ways: 'yes,'
'no,' 'maybe,' 'let's not rush into things.' I wanted to rush
into things. At first I simply used my physical strength to
overwhelm them. Later, it became amusing to me to
threaten them with death if they did not submit to my
demands. This seemed to give them an excuse to perform
the most degrading acts that I could think of. Early on,
at least, not one of them reported these incidents to the
authorities. Black women, particularly, were reluctant
to involve the police. Later on, when I turned my attentions
to white women, this reluctance was not present. It was
the testimony of three white women that first sent me to
San Quentin.

Many years later, after I was released and had returned
to the U. S. voluntarily as a fugitive from justice (i.e.; for
killing Dan Watt), I became the house guest of my attor-
ney, Theodore Kelso. He had a beautiful wife named Vera.

*Vera reminded me somewhat of Julie Christie in the movie
Dr. Zhivago. Only, if anything, more full-figured. Though
I had become a born-again Christian by that time, Vera
was too tempting to resist. Everything about her—her
throaty Russian accent, her movements in performing
the most mundane tasks, the blue-eyed glint in her eyes
when she told one of her off-color jokes about peasant life
in Russia.*

*One day, while Ted was at work, I was helping her in
the kitchen to prepare one of her favorite dishes, piroshki,
when I couldn't help myself. I said something to make her
laugh, and I felt that that was my opportunity. I kissed her
on the mouth. She seemed startled, but then smiled and
kissed me back.*

*I had little doubt that had I been persistent in the usual
way, she would have submitted willingly. But my old
habits suddenly overcame my better judgment. I grabbed
her by the throat and forced her onto the kitchen table.
She screamed and I responded by sweeping all the plates
from the table with my hand. I used the other hand to
lift her skirt and rip off her panties. She began to fight like
a tiger. I picked up a knife that had remained on the table
and held it to her throat. She suddenly became quiet and
still. I unbuckled my pants and quickly discarded them to
the floor. She put up no further resistance...*

Travis closed the manuscript and put the lid back onto the box.
He stared at the books in the bookcase without seeing any particular title. What was he to do? However much money was in Erskine's
Swiss bank account, he had a legal and fiduciary responsibility to
transfer it to the Diocese of Northern California. Ironic, that one
of Erskine's most vociferous critics, Bishop Lattimore, would be in
charge of disbursing the funds.

But what about the royalties from Erskine's books? They could
amount to a significant annual income over the next few years, even
decades. Could he and Emma allow themselves to benefit from the
reprehensible conduct of such a man, born-again Christian or not?

He heard a knock on the door followed by the door opening.

"Are you so totally absorbed in your work that you can't join your family for dinner?"

Travis turned around in his swivel chair and smiled. Emma was radiant, as usual, and smiling while at the same time admonishing him. "Of course not. I was just about to close up my little cubicle for the night."

"What's in the box? The children think it's something to eat."

"In a way it is. Lonnie Erskine has left us some money."

Emma's smile evaporated. "Money? From his books?"

"Exactly. I'm to receive the royalties until the copyrights run out."

Emma sat in a chair just inside the door. "Can you accept it? I mean ethically?"

Travis leaned back in his chair, clasped his hands behind his head and sighed. "I don't know. What do you think?"

"It's blood money."

"That's what I was thinking."

"Then you'll have to give it to his family. They should—"

"He had no family. At least no known family, though I wouldn't be surprised if some heirs, legitimate or otherwise, pop up once the terms of the will are made public"

"What about the church?"

"He's made another provision for that."

Emma seemed to search her mind for an answer. "What about the homeless mission? You say you've had trouble getting funding for that."

Travis dropped his hands and sat up. "That's an idea. A very good one." He took Emma's hands in his and looked into her eyes. "It could mean giving up tens, even hundreds of thousands of dollars, Emma. We could use the money. The kids are going to need more room than we have for them now, especially with another on the way. And then there're music lessons, bicycles, sporting equipment, not to mention college tuition—"

"Mommy!" It was Nicole at the door. "Emile's eating the desert and there won't be any left for me."

"Goodness!" Emma stood and picked Nicole up in her arms. "We'll have to put a stop to that—it'll spoil his dinner as well as yours."

She turned to Travis. "You'd better come discipline your son, Travis. He'll eat us out of house and home before he's old enough to graduate from middle school, much less college."

"Tell him there'll be no television tonight if he doesn't lay off the sweets. I'll be there in a minute."

Emma frowned. "He'd rather eat chocolate fudge than watch *Mayberry, R.F.D.* And he enjoys reading nearly as much as you do."

"I'm coming."

Emma left with Nicole and Travis stared again at the boxed manuscript. He couldn't help wondering how the publication of the book would affect Kelso. 'She would have submitted willingly,' Erskine wrote. But then would she have?

He turned out the light in the tiny room, closed the door, and went out into the living room, where he found Emile looking a little guilty and wiping chocolate from the corners of his mouth. Nicole was watching the news as if it were a Saturday morning cartoon.

He picked up Emile. "Soccer players don't eat dessert first, sport. It makes you weak. You don't want to be weak and left off the team, do you?"

Emile wiped the last remnants of chocolate from his cheeks and shook his head.

"*Variety*, the Bible of show business," the newscaster said, "reported today that Marcella Morgan and Greg Lamonte, her co-star in the upcoming movie *Alexander and the Bactrian Princess*, have been secretly married in Puerta Vallarta, Mexico."

A studio still of Marcella and Greg dressed in exotic Persian costumes appeared on the screen. Then the commentator said:

"It's been rumored for years that Greg is gay, but this apparently puts all those rumors to rest. The couple are reputed to be heading for Gstaad for a skiing honeymoon. In other news today—"

Travis reached over to the set and turned it off.

"I want to be an actress like Marcella," Nicole said.

"You can be anything you want, sweetheart." Travis said. "Anything at all."

Nicole beamed.

"Dinner!" Emma emerged from the kitchen and laid a platter of roast chicken down on the dining room table. "Poulet à la Bretonne!"

"Again?" Emile said. "Why can't we have cheeseburgers?"

"Because cheeseburgers don't go with chocolate cake, sport." Travis pulled up a chair and sat down.

Nicole climbed up into her chair. "I'm going to be an actress like Marcella Morgan."

Emma looked at Travis.

"She and Greg Lamonte just got married," he said. "It was on the news."

Emma sat down. "It can't last."

"You're overlooking the possibility that she may actually be in love with him. Shall I say the blessing?" He reached out to Nicole and Emile and grasped their hands.

"I want to say it," Emile said.

"Okay, sport. You have the floor."

"May God bless Mommy and Daddy and Nicole and..."

"Don't forget yourself."

"And Emile, and..."

"And Grandma and Grandpa Blèriot."

"And Grandma and Grandpa Blèriot..."

"Anybody else?"

"And all the homeless people in the Tenderloin...and all the prisoners at San Quentin, even the ones who murdered women and children."

Travis abruptly opened his eyes as if awakened from a nightmare.

Emile, feeling the intensity of his father's gaze, looked up.

"Are you sure you want to forgive those...the last ones you mentioned?"

"I...yes, Dad. You said even the worst men deserved to be forgiven."

"So I did...so I did."

"Travis?" Emma said. "What's wrong?"

"Nothing, Emma. Nothing at all. You may continue, son."

Emile looked at his father in some bewilderment and bowed his head again. "And...God bless Grandma and Grandpa Carter in heaven. Amen."

"Amen," Travis said.

"Amen," Emma said.

Nicole, whose eyes had never closed, looked around the table. "Can we eat now?"